W9-AEG-496

PRAISE FOR PATRICIA RAYBON

"An engrossing, thrilling 1920s murder mystery. Patricia Raybon's novel races across its Denver landscape at an exhilarating pace with an unforgettable protagonist, Professor Annalee Spain, at the wheel. The story of Annalee's murder mystery is captivating, the history of the western city's racial divide enlightening. This intrepid sleuth would certainly give Sherlock Holmes a run for his money."

SOPHFRONIA SCOTT, author of *Unforgivable Love*

"In Professor Annalee Spain, Patricia Raybon has created a real, rounded, and very human character. . . . Not only a good mystery, but a realistic insight into the African American experience in the 1920s."

RHYS BOWEN, *New York Times* bestselling author of the Molly Murphy and Royal Spyness mysteries

"Readers will be hooked from the first line of Patricia Raybon's captivating debut novel, *All That Is Secret*. This well-respected nonfiction author proves her worth with fiction as she delivers rich characters and a page-turning mystery set in the beautiful wilds of Colorado."

JULIE CANTRELL, *New York Times* and *USA Today* bestselling author of *Perennials*

"A winner. Patricia Raybon's *All That Is Secret* is a fast-paced, intriguing mystery that grabs and holds the reader from the opening."

MANUEL RAMOS, author of *Angels in the Wind*

"It's the rare journalist who can succeed at also crafting compelling fiction. But that's what Raybon has done here with *All That Is Secret*, an engaging, evocative period piece as timely as tomorrow's news. Brava, Patricia, for weaving a tale as instructive as it is captivating."

JERRY B. JENKINS, *New York Times* bestselling author

"Patricia Raybon is a masterful storyteller. She is a standard-bearer for honesty as she takes her readers on a journey with an amateur sleuth who has the potential to change our perspectives and help us solve the mystery of how to come together and heal. I highly recommend it!"

DR. BRENDA SALTER McNEIL, author of *Becoming Brave: Finding the Courage to Pursue Racial Justice Now*

ALL THAT IS SECRET

AN ANNALEE SPAIN MYSTERY

ALL THAT IS SECRET

PATRICIA RAYBON

Tyndale House Publishers
Carol Stream, Illinois

Visit Tyndale online at tyndale.com.

Visit Patricia Raybon's website at patriciaraybon.com.

Tyndale and Tyndale's quill logo are registered trademarks of Tyndale House Ministries.

All That Is Secret

Cover designed by Lindsey Bergsma

Edited by Sarah Mason Rische

Published in association with the literary agency of WordServe Literary Group, www.wordserveliterary.com.

Unless otherwise indicated, all Scripture quotations are taken or paraphrased from the *Holy Bible*, King James Version.

Luke 8:17 is taken from the *Holy Bible*, New Living Translation, copyright © 1996, 2004, 2015 by Tyndale House Foundation. Used by permission of Tyndale House Publishers, Carol Stream, Illinois 60188. All rights reserved.

All That Is Secret is a work of fiction. Where real people, events, establishments, organizations, or locales appear, they are used fictitiously. All other elements of the novel are drawn from the author's imagination.

For information about special discounts for bulk purchases, please contact Tyndale House Publishers at csresponse@tyndale.com, or call 1-855-277-9400.

Library of Congress Cataloging-in-Publication Data

A catalog record for this book is available from the Library of Congress.

ISBN 978-1-4964-5837-7 (HC)
ISBN 978-1-4964-5838-4 (SC)

Printed in the United States of America

27	26	25	24	23	22	21
7	6	5	4	3	2	1

Thank you, Aunt Bette, for believing.

"For all that is secret will eventually be brought into the open, and everything that is concealed will be brought to light and made known to all."

LUKE 8:17

PROLOGUE

The little baby was four hours old. Still unwashed. Barely crying. But Joe Spain's old ears recognized the sound. A human infant. Somebody's mistake left in the Colorado cold to die.

He twisted his mouth, pulled the reins on his cutting horse, Barrel, and turned into the freezing wind. Barrel's ears stood straight up, trembling. The horse heard it too. On the cold, open plains, the wide early morning silence rendered every sound bigger, as if magnified.

The cry was half a mile away. But Spain still heard it clear as a bell.

"C'mon, girl," he said to Barrel. "We best go see."

He let the big horse pick her way through the frozen scrub and prairie grass. A light snow the night before had dusted the ground, leaving a far and white horizon under the blinding blue sky.

The horse was fresh and eager, but already both of them were breathing hard, their breath turning to white vapor in the sharp, bracing frost.

Spain, a part-time cowboy, stood up in his stirrups and

1

scanned the prairie with narrowed eyes, peering in all directions. His lean body, still skinny after sixty-odd years, steeled itself against the cold. As a Negro man, he knew some considered him out of place in such environs. But he had known no place better or longer than these High Plains, and the pure respect he felt for the rough landscape bordered on its own kind of adoration, if not sheer awe.

Scanning the terrain, he stood in the freezing wind, the brim of his worn wool Stetson pulled low and humbled in the shining, cold glare.

Then he saw the tracks. Footprints in light snow. He looked beyond the traces and saw the county road. Right away, he figured what had happened. Before daybreak, somebody drove their vehicle down the road until it turned to dirt. Then they hopped the low, barbed-wire fence that bordered the road, trekked a cold mile into Lazy K pastureland, and looked for a dip in the flat landscape.

There in the open, in a draw in the middle of the range, they left the child. No attempt to bury it. Coyotes would eat the evidence. Or a family of foxes.

As for the snowy footprints, they would melt in the dry air and blazing sun—just as they were doing right now. By noon, the cold prints would all be gone.

Spain nosed the horse to follow the tracks toward the sound. If the child was going to make it, he'd have to find it now.

Sure enough, the cry was growing fainter. Barely a whimper now. But finally he saw the bundle, wrapped in a torn piece of dirty tarp.

The horse saw the dark bulge and pulled up, dug her hooves into the cold ground.

2

"It's okay, girl," Spain said. He patted the animal's neck, slid out of his saddle, and dropped the reins. Barrel stood alert, agitated but waiting.

Sighing, Spain crunched across the frozen grass and looked down at the tarp. He pushed the hat back on his head and knelt in the snow. Pulling back the tarp, he felt his gloved hands go cold.

It can't be. Not again.

The tiny child was wrapped in a man's white dress shirt and nothing else. Blood on its slick black hair had started to ice. The baby was shivering, lips almost blue. A low moan, no longer a cry, emerged from its tiny, perfect mouth.

"*Lord Jesus*, pretty little baby," Spain said.

He reached down, picked up the child, flicked the bloody ice off its head, letting the tarp fall off. "Good grief, what a hateful way to enter this ol' world."

He opened his old shearling jacket, pressed the baby onto his chest, breathed hot breath on its face, took off his gloves with his teeth, and rubbed his large hands on the baby's ice-cold back. Coaxing it. Scolding it. "C'mon, little bit. Ol' Joe's got you."

For half a second, he considered how easy it would be to leave the child and turn back. Nobody would ever know. These were bad, bad times. He didn't need the bother. Besides, he was leaving by train tonight to visit his only daughter, his Annalee. In fact, after too many years, they finally were making some kind of peace. His own sweet "little bit" girl, as he called her—grown now and working hard and smart at barely twenty-three. Why start trouble now with somebody else's child?

He sighed and cradled the infant, letting the rank newborn

smell fill his nostrils. He buttoned up his jacket as far as he could and turned toward the anxious horse. But at the last minute, he turned back for the tarp. The boss might want to see it. Or the police. Or *somebody*. He wasn't sure. But Spain bent down to bunch up the tarp in his arms.

Then, just as quick, he shook it out again, looking for— what? A hidden note, a tarnished locket, some last-minute trinket tucked in by the baby's mother, trying to make a wrong thing right? Hoping to leave a piece of herself with the child that others said must die?

But there was nothing, so Spain balled up the tarp again. Holding the baby against him with one arm, he strapped the tarp on his saddle with the other.

He mounted the horse, grabbed the reins, and clicked his tongue. With a fast trot, Barrel carried him and the baby across the open prairie to the ranch house.

It was a large and impressive adobe, set on the highest point on the 2,800-acre spread. The owner, Lent Montgomery, was busy inside. Spain figured as much. A sleek black car was parked in the gravel yard next to the sprawling house. The entire ranch and acreage were for sale. Everybody in Denver knew that. Fancy cars with bidders and bankers had been coming and going for weeks.

But Spain knew his place. He didn't like interrupting.

Still, he tied up the horse and walked across the gravel to the big front door. Pulled the bell. Knocked twice. Not too hard.

After a while, a young Mexican girl barely opened the door. The cook's daughter.

Spain pushed back his hat. "Need to see the boss. Hurry, little bit, and go get him."

The girl looked him over, her gaze stopping at the bulge in his jacket. She shook her head. Started to close the door.

Spain stuck his grimy boot in it. "This can't wait."

The girl considered this. Looked over her shoulder. Looked back at Spain. Saw he wasn't backing down.

"*Sí, señor,*" she whispered. "Okay."

She moved to close the door, but Spain pushed his worn boot in farther. "I'll wait inside."

The girl frowned for a second but yielded.

Spain stepped into a wide foyer and looked to his right down a hallway. The carved door at the end was closed, voices rising on the other side.

The girl wrung her hands. Fretting and sighing, she rushed down another hallway. In a few minutes, she came back, not with the boss but with a woman. Her mother the cook, Rosita Montez. The woman looked annoyed. She wiped her hands on her apron.

"What now, Joe?" she whispered. "Mr. Montgomery's in a meeting."

Spain shifted the cold baby inside his jacket. "I know, Rosie, but I really need to see him."

"Well, you can't! He's in a big meeting!"

"But I found something. Look here . . ."

Spain yanked open his worn jacket. The baby's bloody head emerged.

The girl moaned, jumped back. "*Mamá, Dios mío.*"

But the woman took one look and understood immediately. She shouted to the child in Spanish and the girl ran off.

Together, Rosita and Spain pulled off his coat. He held on to the baby as they knelt on the slate floor of the foyer. Rosita bunched Spain's jacket into a bundle and reached for the baby. She laid it in the leather nest.

But they both knew. It was too late.

The baby's limp, dead body sank into the folds of the coat.

Spain sighed. He closed the baby's eyes. "I'm so sorry, little bit. I'm so god-awful sorry."

Rosita shook her head and started to weep, loudly blessing the child in Spanish, caressing its little hands, kissing its bloody forehead, not worrying about silencing her sobs. The daughter, returning with blankets and a metal basin, dropped them in a clanging heap, water sloshing all directions. She, too, started to sob.

Spain reached out to comfort.

A door slammed open. "For the love of . . . !"

A tall, silvery man stormed down the hall into the foyer.

Spain looked up at his angry boss, Lent Montgomery, and clambered to his feet. He pulled off his hat, pointed to the bundle. "A little baby, boss."

The boss looked down at the bunched-up jacket, the dead infant, the bloody white shirt, the mess on his foyer floor. He cursed. "Where'd you find it?"

"South end, boss. In a shallow draw."

Montgomery squeezed his forehead, cursing again. He spoke in Spanish to Rosita. The cook nodded, wiped her eyes with her skirt, and left for the back of the house.

"Wait here, Joe, and then—"

"So this is how you turn me down, Lent?" A city gentleman in a well-cut black suit and city shoes walked with importance through the hallway door and into the foyer. He looked down at the floor. His face went white.

"Sorry about this," Montgomery tried to explain. "Joe here found a baby. All this blood . . . a dang mess."

The city man looked at Joe Spain. Looked back at the baby.

"Well, curious . . . a colored baby." Thus, the man spoke what they all had observed but hadn't mentioned. He gestured to Spain, turned to Montgomery. "You don't mind me asking, Montgomery: is this cowboy ours?"

Montgomery frowned. "*Ours?* With all respect, Senator, you haven't bought the ranch yet."

"Of course. I'm trying to get an understanding. So I'm asking—is this cowboy part of the ranch?"

Lent Montgomery squared his back, peered at the man. "What difference does it make who he is? He works for me and he found a baby on my property. I'll take care of it from here."

But the city man wouldn't back down. "A colored boy finds a colored baby. Dead. And that doesn't seem strange to you? I know this is still your property, Montgomery. But the Douglas County sheriff is going to find this very strange."

Montgomery pulled to his full height. "What's strange is you standing in my house questioning how I handle my business! And you want to buy a ranch? You don't know a rat's tail about what it means to own a ranch. Or keep loyal ranch hands. In fact, you can get your—"

"You threatening me, Montgomery?"

Lent Montgomery stepped over the baby. "Get out of my house, Grimes. And get that big, ugly car off my property!"

The city man turned up his collar and pushed through the open doorway. He looked over his shoulder. "I'll be back to finish the contracts."

Montgomery slammed the big front door. But all in the

house could hear the car spin on gravel and ice, then squeal onto the ranch road leading back to Denver.

Spain looked to his boss, knowing what he must be thinking. It *was* curious that Joe Spain, a colored cowboy, had found on his property a little colored baby. Dead.

But Lent Montgomery didn't mention it.

In fact, that morning was the last Joe Spain would ever see of his boss. Or Rosita. Or the city man. Or anybody else.

Because by morning the next day, Joe Spain, too, was dead.

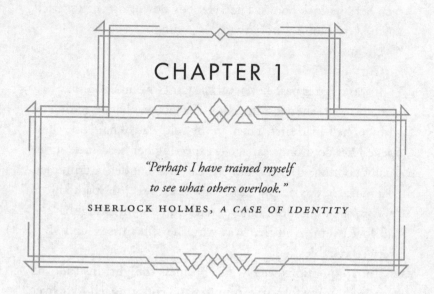

CHAPTER 1

*"Perhaps I have trained myself
to see what others overlook."*

SHERLOCK HOLMES, *A CASE OF IDENTITY*

CHICAGO, NOVEMBER 1923

Sunday night and she was late beyond redemption. Professor Annalee Spain grabbed her bulging satchel off her desk, stuffed in her notes, checked the streetcar schedule, brushed lint off her good black suit—actually her only suit—and dared turn back to . . . what, to *pray*? As if prayer, of all things, would get her what she needed, let alone what she wanted.

But no time to bother over that. She'd do better to answer the knock rattling the devil out of her splintered, freezing, rent-by-the-week rooming house door.

Tap-tap-tap-tap.

"Hold on, little bit," she called out. One of "her kids." They pestered her all hours, begging for pencil stubs, scraps of paper, even her Sherlock books. The Tyler boy downstairs had scarfed down every Holmes story twice. "Coming!"

No answer.

Curious.

It was quarter past eleven on the last November Sunday in a merciless year. She'd lost her rainy-day job, was barely getting by with her half-paid first. Then, in the cold way of hard life, she'd opened her door one year ago—expecting her hard-luck father finally coming to visit—but instead was handed a crumpled telegram. He was dead. "Regrettably." Or was Joe Spain killed?

Lord, that question. It never released her—insisting that she had loved him. And that was why she still missed him? But every regrettable day?

Tough questions weren't her business tonight. Instead, she despaired for the forty-five minutes and counting left to deliver her latest paper—*God, let them approve it*—to a British publisher's Chicago office by midnight. Hard deadline. But her stipend for it, despite the trouble, would be waiting in a narrow envelope at the publisher's first-floor desk.

Tap-tap-tap-tap.

But first, that *infernal knocking.*

She tossed down her satchel, jostling india ink, riled to see thick dribbles soak into her piles of papers, her notebooks and newspapers, her table, the satchel. She groaned, knowing she could scoff at her mishap if she weren't so desperate. Instead, she threw a ragged towel across the inky trail and trudged to her cold door. Then she heard the warbling voice.

"Professor Spain?" Her name, but muffled.

"Who's there?"

No answer.

"State your business!"

"Western Union!"

She tensed. This late on a Sunday night, in a brawny Chicago snowstorm, not even Western Union would dare to deliver—even if she'd wanted the insult of another telegram.

Why no good news? she pondered. A thank-you note. An early Christmas card. She eyed the door. Even a love letter? She glanced in her cracked mirror, winked at herself but shook her head, jostling her wild black curls. What a foolish idea. She'd never known "love" or received such a letter. She couldn't even imagine what one would say.

Instead, she took in a hard breath, faced the door, pressed her young shoulder into the crumbling frame, unlatched all but one cheap lock, then opened with caution her warped door.

A thin sliver of watery light edged into the pitch-black hallway.

What stood on the other side looked drowned or half-dead. Or maybe both.

A shrunken figure—half a foot shorter than her and wrapped in too many moth-eaten coats, plus knee-high work boots, thick leather gloves, a worn plaid scarf, a soiled knit cap pulled low—stood before her.

"Professor Spain?" The muffled voice again.

She peered at the coat pile. "What on earth?" she whispered.

As if in response, a grimy hand unwrapped and unwrapped and unwrapped and *unwrapped* the scarf and finally a small face emerged.

A boy.

A white boy.

Annalee stepped back. *Lord, not tonight. Clock still ticking?*

*But maybe he isn't white? Or surely he is white. But should that
even matter?*

Because the boy was sniffling and shivering, his chapped
cheeks raw, his red lips peeling. His nose dripping and running,
his eyebrows iced, his gray eyes blinking and alert. His skin
grimy and unwashed.

Then the unexpected. The boy grinned.

Rotten front teeth and all.

"Telegram for Professor Spain!" He covered his bad teeth
with his scarf. From inside his layers, he retrieved a thin yellow
envelope—cold as ice—and thrust it at her.

Her full name, Professor Annalee Jane Spain, was typed on
the front.

"You're just a child," she said, half-scolding. "In a blizzard."

"Message came at ten," the boy rushed to explain. "But the
storm slowed me down."

She fingered the envelope, not trusting it. Surely not wanting it. But she held on to it, thinking, waiting, ignoring whatever she was trying not to feel.

The boy stood and waited, stamping his oversize boots,
watching caked ice fall onto her warped wooden floor. Then,
just as quick, he stood stone-still, showing regrets for his mess.
Annalee looked down at his feet. The boots would be his
father's. A dead father, for certain.

She narrowed her eyes, looking harder at the boy, knowing, suddenly, exactly who he was: He was like her. Some kind
of orphan. Caught up with a tangle of ordeals and questions.
Probably his sick mother's lifeline. Father long dead in some
Chicago bar brawl. So the boy peddled his matches. Delivered
his telegrams. Scraping together pennies and nickels to help his

young mother put food on their table—on the rare day she felt like cooking it.

Annalee slipped the telegram into her fraying sleeve, deciding it could wait. She sighed silently, not thinking of the theological analysis she'd spent one grueling month wrestling over for the British journal, aware that for some reason the highbrow paper no longer seemed so distinctive—or so urgent, if it ever mattered at all. "The Theology of Teaching"? But what if your hungry student just needed a gracious piece of kind bread?

She looked the boy directly in his alert, gray eyes. "Had any supper tonight?"

The boy blinked, peeked past her shoulder into her room—searching her desk, hoping to see some dinner, which, of course, she didn't have. He shrugged under his pile of coats.

She tried again. "I've got roast meat and some crackers."

The boy licked his lips, but he kept his dignity. "I can't go in rooms." He looked past her shoulder again. "And I got another delivery."

"Won't take long," she said, turning her back on the pestering clock. "Come stand by the fire. I won't report you." She gestured him inside. "The people who write those rules never worked all night, slogging through three feet of snow to deliver a message."

"Thankin' you, miss." The boy shuffled into the room as she stoked her cold embers. He pulled off his late father's gloves, warming his small, chapped hands at the bare fire. Looking around, he would see her riotous desk, her cluttered floor, her piles of books, her stacks of journals. Towers of newspapers. Writing pens and bottles of india ink. Her life, if she had one, occurred in this place, right there at her rickety desk.

She pushed back one of her wild curls, knowing he wanted to ask, *"You? The professor?"*

But his father, it seemed, had taught him manners. So she answered for him.

"I teach downtown," she said, "at the Bible college."

The boy's gray eyes showed he was listening. Thinking. *The Colored Professor? The one in the newspapers?* Looking even younger in person, amber face aglow, bright eyes sparkling?

"Downtown?" He nodded.

"Theology," she told him, eyeing him directly, testing him. He seemed uncertain. "New Testament," she added as if he understood. "Well, prayer." She said that not wondering if he'd read those newspapers or their raves about her "delightful" research—the hidden "prayer codes" in "original" places such as the detective stories she devoured. *"What an original, clever mind,"* one paper declared.

"Despite her race."

The boy was frowning, weighing, pondering. She could see his mind working, swirling, considering. "Like in religion," he finally said.

She nodded, smiled, knowing her lopsided dimple emerged. "Probably close enough."

An astute boy, she concluded. Observant and discreet. His father would be proud. Then she guessed: the boy's late father was a preacher. Yes, of course. This was a dead preacher's boy—and from the poor looks of the child, a Methodist preacher, at that.

So Annalee wrapped her cold-meat-and-crackers meal in waxed paper. Wrapped it again in newspaper. Tied it with a string. From her bulky teacher's satchel, she pushed past her papers to dig out a dime. Looked harder at the boy, then decided on two. Then, because it was proper, she gave him all three—all the little money she had left, until that stipend. She counted the tip into his shaking hand, her own hand shaking at giving away her all.

"One for the Father. One for the Son. One—"

"For the Holy Spirit," the boy whispered.

"And may it be so," she whispered in return, adding another quick smile.

The boy nodded under his dirty scarf. Then he smiled back, covering his teeth again.

"Blessin' you, Professor," he said, clumping toward the door, pocketing the dimes. He looked back at her cold room, letting his gaze stop at something. The big Stetson—hanging on a nail on the cracked-up plaster wall. But he didn't ask. So she didn't explain. He started out the door.

"Don't forget your food." She handed him the bundle. As he took it, stowing it in his coats, she added, "Merry Christmas."

The boy laughed. He would know it wasn't Christmas. Not for him. Not for her. But as he clump-clumped in his father's boots to the stairs, he turned at the landing and gave a small wave. "Merry Christmas."

She waved back, certain she'd never deliver her paper on time. If ever. Why, indeed, would she?

Instead, she stoked her small stove, turning to her iced-over window—scraping away a patch to watch the boy disappear into the black November night. But for some reason, it felt like it could be more. Maybe even Christmas.

Until she opened the telegram.

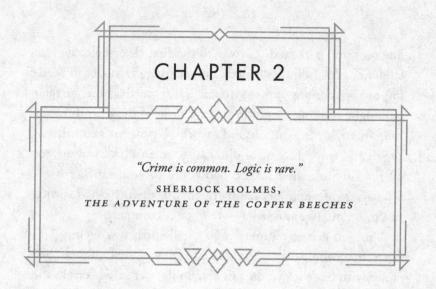

CHAPTER 2

"Crime is common. Logic is rare."

SHERLOCK HOLMES,
THE ADVENTURE OF THE COPPER BEECHES

THE PARLOR DOOR DOWNSTAIRS whined open. After three long nights expired, Annalee still let the envelope sit in her sleeve, refusing to read it again, giving it the business when it fretted her. *"I am not afraid."*

Hearing the words whispered aloud in her cold leased room, she knew they were a lie. But she fibbed to herself most days. To not feel her stomach beg, to pretend she wasn't dirt-poor, to tamp down her greatest fear—that in life, she was alone, regrettably all on her own. So she was unloved? Whatever on earth love even meant.

Still, after a year of hearing nothing—not one word—about her father's curious murder, if that's what it was, she felt terrified to wonder who was contacting her now.

She just wished to God she didn't care.

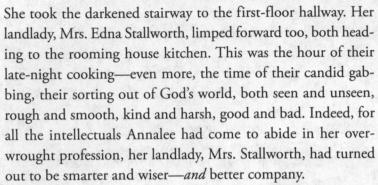

She took the darkened stairway to the first-floor hallway. Her landlady, Mrs. Edna Stallworth, limped forward too, both heading to the rooming house kitchen. This was the hour of their late-night cooking—even more, the time of their candid gabbing, their sorting out of God's world, both seen and unseen, rough and smooth, kind and harsh, good and bad. Indeed, for all the intellectuals Annalee had come to abide in her overwrought profession, her landlady, Mrs. Stallworth, had turned out to be smarter and wiser—*and* better company.

"So you gonna tell me?" Mrs. Stallworth was saying. "It's been three whole days." She cocked a brow. "Well, nights." She stood with her back to the kitchen door—yet acted certain the young professor, and not some other tenant, had just entered her domain.

Annalee smiled to herself, ignoring the question. "Watch your head." She stepped around her landlady's wide frame, reached to pull down a soup pot from a jumbled rack.

"The neck bones," Mrs. Stallworth said, announcing her meal.

Annalee twisted her mouth. Not her favorite. But she wouldn't complain. "Your last meat?" She knew well Mrs. Stallworth's end-of-month struggle to feed her boarders.

"House'll be hungry come morning." She huffed around her chaotic kitchen, off-balance in her late husband's too-big slippers and frayed apron over too many nightclothes. Her peppery hair, pushed under a dark cotton cap, framed her hardworking, caramel-colored face.

Annalee, still wearing a faded dress and her worn-over,

secondhand, only pair of shoes, grabbed a handle on the pot. Together, they wrestled it to the big iron stove.

"You can help me, Professor," Mrs. Stallworth said, eyeing Annalee over her spectacles and adding with a mumble, "Since you're still up."

Annalee acted matter-of-fact, standing taller, straightening her shapeless black dress, feigning her teacher best. "Slumber, my lady, is 'the poor man's wealth, the prisoner's release.'" She sighed. "And isn't the poet ever right."

"Can't say that I know." The landlady pointed to the cellar door. "Potatoes, Professor."

"And onions?" Annalee lifted the latch and headed down.

"Onions. A carrot. Whatever you find down there, Annalee."

Then for the next two hours, they made soup. Annalee chopped. Her landlady braised. Annalee stirred. Her landlady simmered. Annalee tasted. Her landlady seasoned.

The kitchen was warm and steaming. Windows fogged over. Big pot bubbling. The aging iron stove exhaled its heat, slow-roasting the room, defying the arctic cold outside.

"My young student," Annalee said.

"Which one?"

"The one with the paper 'The Theology of Cooking.'"

"Lord, have mercy," Mrs. Stallworth said. "Whatever was that about?"

"About the girl's uncle—you remember. The line cook at the state penitentiary."

"Mercy, Lord."

"I gave her an honest A," Annalee said. "Mailed her paper to a publisher—who loved her theory that cooking for imprisoned felons will mirror, as she wrote, Christ's gift of himself. 'My body broken for you—'"

Mrs. Stallworth gave Annalee a look. "Pour me some buttermilk. I'm fixin' to mirror up some corn bread."

Annalee poured buttermilk, gave her a grin. Then got serious. "My dean overrode my grade."

"Meaning what?"

"He struck down my A. Gave the student an F. Said her paper was heresy. Expelled her from school. Warned me I'd be next."

"Can you please speak English?"

"The student blasphemed God, dishonoring the Lord. So says my dean."

Mrs. Stallworth huffed. "That man never made a pan of corn bread in his life." She pulled back a chair for Annalee, joining her at the table. Then she grabbed at Annalee's fraying shirtsleeve, pushing it up, and yanked out the telegram.

"You gonna tell me?" she asked.

Annalee grabbed back the telegram, taking her time to open it, to read it—her eyes wishing they didn't have to see it. "Funny thing about telegrams. This one's saying I did the right thing."

"Meaning what?" Mrs. Stallworth grabbed at the telegram again, but Annalee held it tight.

"I'm going to Denver," she said. "To solve a crime."

"Crime? What crime?"

"The crime in Denver. I'm going home."

Mrs. Stallworth eyed Annalee over her spectacles. "You're leaving your job? And your paycheck?"

"I resigned my position yesterday."

"*What?*"

"I'm grading my last papers now. Classes are over. I won't be back after Christmas."

Mrs. Stallworth slipped off her eyeglasses, rubbed them hard with a dish towel, set them back firmly on her nose. "If this is about Joe Spain—"

"It's about his murder," Annalee said, thinking of her drunken, life-worn, frustrating, disappointing, dead father. "But somehow I suspect it's about much more."

"You suspect? You're not the police, Annalee. You can't solve your daddy's murder, even if it was murder. Lord, I can't believe I'm saying that word in my house!"

"*If?* Well, there's one sure way to find out." Annalee's breath caught, but not to cry. What she felt for her father wasn't simple grief. It was righteous anger. For too many reasons, Joe Spain— Ol' Joe, as everyone called him—was the last man anyone would defend or worry over.

Yet for no clear reason, someone threw him off a moving train, tossing him out on the tracks like an afterthought. Some farm kids out by the Kansas-Colorado line found him the next day, barely recognizable—save for a nickel belt buckle he always wore, a recent letter from Annalee, and his beloved Stetson hat, found crumpled nearby.

"He didn't deserve it." Annalee folded the telegram. "So I'm going home to find the truth."

"The truth will eat you alive!"

"Probably, unless I'm tough—and don't back down." Annalee looked determined. "Because a simple colored man isn't murdered like that unless he stumbled onto something. Something unusual. Something dangerous. Something . . . damaging."

"Lord, have mercy."

"Or something secret?" She shook her head. "Whatever it was, I'm going home to Denver to find out."

Mrs. Stallworth frowned. "But what do you know about solving a killing? You're not your Sherlock. Besides, the police said it was an accident."

"The police? In Denver?" Annalee gave her a hard look, thinking about her city's graft. Sunny town. Bad people. "Sunshine and Scoundrels"—the unofficial town motto summed it up right. "They ruled it a *regrettable* accident. Then they dropped it. Daddy wasn't, well—"

"'Important' enough."

"To investigate. So he 'fell' off that train."

"Or . . ." Mrs. Stallworth pursed her lips. "Maybe your daddy got into a fistfight—"

"Not Daddy." Annalee set her jaw. "He had his troubles. No doubt about that. But my gut—"

"Your gut? You're letting your gut say something was crooked. You wouldn't know a real crook if he walked through that door."

Annalee thought for a moment. "Or she?"

"*Lord*, Annalee, you read too many detective stories." Mrs. Stallworth sighed. "Besides, aren't you afraid?"

Annalee considered that. "If I'm honest, I'm terrified. But not of the killers. I'm afraid that my daddy was murdered, for some fool wrong reason, and people who could be doing something about it don't even care."

"But vengeance is mine and *I* will repay, thus saith the Lord?"

"No, I don't want vengeance," Annalee said. "For this, I'm

looking for justice. Do you know the genesis of that word, Dr. Watson?"

Mrs. Stallworth gave her a look. "I'm waiting."

"It comes from the Latin—*justitia*—meaning how the law is administered. But for Joe Spain? The law wasn't administered at all."

Mrs. Stallworth took that in, sat quiet, shifted in her chair. She rubbed another spot off her eyeglasses.

"Well, that's a big enough idea," she finally said.

"And what's that supposed to mean?"

"It means when it comes to unraveling life's big mysteries, you don't aim at the big parts of the problem. You work on the *small*." She whispered the word.

"But this is murder."

"Oh, I know, baby. And nothing in this life is worse than taking another man's life. But to unlock a big mystery like that you don't grab a hammer and beat down the door. You work on the hinges."

"Hinges. The small things—"

"Don't mock me, girl!"

"—on which big things swing." Annalee weighed it, feeling Mrs. Stallworth was right but not wanting to admit it. She sighed. "Sometimes I don't know why I bother talking to you."

"Why?" Mrs. Stallworth squared her shoulders. "Because small is the gate and narrow the road that leadeth to life—and only a few shall find it. Thus saith the Lord! In case you forgot!"

"Forgot? The Sermon on the Mount? I *teach* New Testament!" Annalee sighed. "Well, I did." She played with a crumb. "Besides, the gate is 'straight'—"

"Same difference."

"Really, Inspector? Is that why you're quoting the Bible every other chance you get tonight?"

"No, I'm speaking God's truth because you're going home to solve God's problems. But you still haven't figured out your own."

Annalee ignored that, folding her arms tight. "As I said, I'm going to Denver to find the truth."

"Truth taketh no prisoners," Mrs. Stallworth whispered.

"That's not what Saint Augustine says," Annalee whispered back. "Not to mention Sir Arthur Conan Doyle."

Mrs. Stallworth grabbed the telegram, reading it. "'Attention Professor Spain: The house is burning—'" Mrs. Stallworth dropped the telegram like it was on fire. "Oh, Annalee. Look what you started."

She picked it up again, hands shaking. But Annalee took it from her. If she was going to solve an actual murder, she had to read it again for herself.

"'The house is burning.'" She took a moment. "'But I have the key.'"

"Key? What is this? Who sent this?"

Annalee read the signature, felt her heart jump. "It's from my father's pastor. The Reverend Blake."

"That old preacher? Why is he writing *you*? It doesn't make any sense."

Annalee pondered that a minute. "It's not supposed to."

"What?"

"He's not writing to me. He's *summoning* me. It's a call."

"Oh, mercy alive."

"He's discovered something. Something about Daddy's

murder. Something too sensitive, too dangerous, to write in a telegram, but something important enough to call me back to Denver—to help me solve the crime. He even wired ticket money for the train. Although the timing is curious."

"Too curious to feel right, if you ask me. Right as you quit your job. Your *good* job. And when's the last time you been in a church anyway?"

Annalee pressed her mouth. This was off-limits. Mrs. Stallworth knew how weary Annalee was of being confounded by God, so confused after her father's death she'd forgotten how to do the one thing she once did best. Just pray.

She looked away.

Mrs. Stallworth straightened her eyeglasses, tried to brighten her up. "Besides, who's going to take you serious in those down-in-the-mouth teacher dresses you always wearing? Well, your *two* dresses?" She shook her head. "And both of them plain, long, raggedy, and to tell the truth, downright ugly!"

"They're *mourning* dresses."

"Mourning doesn't mean ugly."

Annalee gave her a look.

"What I mean is, baby, a young woman like you—pretty little thing with a fine, young figure like yours—needs a little lace. At least round the collar!"

"So I can flirt while I mourn?"

"You've never flirted a day in your life," Mrs. Stallworth said. "Although at age twenty-four *and counting*, it wouldn't hurt you to try."

"Is that a dare?" Annalee pushed the telegram back in her sleeve. "Well, I accept. Except I'm looking for a murderer, not a man." *As if I know what looking for a man even means.*

"Well, at least you got your stipend," Mrs. Stallworth said. "Is it enough?"

Annalee didn't answer.

"Mercy, they didn't pay you!"

"It's 'in the mail.' My paper was late, I admit. I put off sending it. But when the stipend comes, you'll send it to me. Of course you will."

"Oh, Annalee!" Mrs. Stallworth hugged herself, rocking back and forth. "White folks can be so dangerous!"

Annalee thought for a moment. "Black folks, too." She pursed her lips. "Actually, all folks."

Mrs. Stallworth considered that. "Lord, the world's turned upside down!"

"Or right side up," Annalee said.

"And I promised your daddy I'd look after you."

"Oh, you kept that promise. In *six* years, you've never let me out of your sight." Annalee tried frowning but smiled.

"Don't give me that dimple!" Mrs. Stallworth scolded. "But if you gotta use it, *use it*!"

Annalee grinned at her, moved to Mrs. Stallworth's side of the table. She knelt, hugging her landlady's neck, leaning into its softness.

Mrs. Stallworth hugged her back. Then digging into her apron pocket, the landlady pulled out two tightly folded one-dollar bills, shoving them into Annalee's sleeve. Insisting.

"No, you'll need it—"

"Hush. I'll send your books on later," Mrs. Stallworth said into Annalee's ear. She pushed away a wild curl.

Annalee leaned back. "And my three-legged desk?"

"And your other ugly dress." Mrs. Stallworth sat up. "Goodness, and your kids?"

"Let them have whatever's left. Pencils, scrap paper, newspapers, ink. Theirs for the taking. And the Tyler boy—his choice of a Sherlock. No, make it two."

"I'll take care of it."

She understands now, Annalee assured herself, hugging her landlady again. But to be certain, she held her tighter, leaning into her strength, holding on to hope, listening to the steaming kitchen, resigned to whatever God himself was calling Annalee Spain to do.

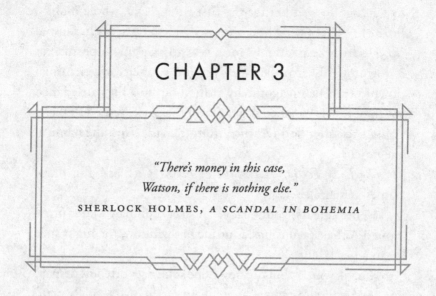

CHAPTER 3

"There's money in this case,
Watson, if there is nothing else."
SHERLOCK HOLMES, *A SCANDAL IN BOHEMIA*

ONE HURRIED WEEK LATER, Annalee boarded the Chicago Limited for Denver. Claimed a seat in the only half-empty car, gripping her pocketbook with Mrs. Stallworth's two dollar bills buried so deep inside that, if she needed them, she'd have to pry them out.

Thus, as the train rocked and clacked, rocked and clacked, she stared at two days and nights of gray flatlands and frozen hills, purple dawns and blazing sunsets. But with each mile she was reviewing what she knew so far about the murder, anxious but excited to be thinking on it.

I'm solving a murder. But with what?

Just scraps. A bit here. A thread there. Like the fact that a year before her daddy was killed, he'd traveled all the way to Chicago to visit her for the first time. "One whole month, little bit!" That's what he'd promised. Then he actually showed up. He'd worked odd jobs for a year to save up—doorman at a downtown Denver hotel, driver and runner for a rich man downtown. Then he got itchy, drifted out to a big cattle ranch south of town. Punched cows. Loved the place, settled in there, going back after he'd returned from the visit. And the name of the ranch?

The Lazy T? Bar S? Double L? Flying C? Blast! Too many names and alphabets.

"Refreshments, young lady?" A sleek Pullman waiter interrupted Annalee's musings. Outside her window, the night sped by in a black blur.

"Thank you, sir, but not now." She smiled, courteous, despairing to spend any money, grateful so far for Mrs. Stallworth's packed snacks and sodas.

But the Pullman waiter lingered. His smile formed a casual half-moon.

The Lazy K. Yes, that was it. Her daddy adored it. Couple thousand acres of open range. Cattle by the hundreds. The ranch hands ran cows for endless, unmarked miles, following the grass and the rains. A sky without ceilings. And the *quiet.* Stillness and empty quiet like city folks would never know or understand. *"You could hear a tumbleweed scratching the ground a mile away,"* her daddy said, winking. But he was only half-kidding. In fact, he loved the natural, raw solitude of the place.

Yet there was trouble at the ranch late that summer. Something about water?

But here was the waiter again.

"Orange juice! Fresh from California! A mighty fine refreshment. Just right for after dinner."

"Thank you, but . . . not tonight." She smiled. *Why won't he just go away?*

"Just a small glass?" The waiter leaned in. "Let me bring you something from the lounge car. On the house."

Annalee shifted in her seat. The waiter had been attentive the entire trip. Nice at first. But now? Annoying. And odd. As if he wanted a reason to hold her attention.

She searched his face. Late forties, maybe fifty or somewhere still near it, yet with that debonair bearing. Spotless white jacket, smooth ebony skin, sharp jet eyes.

Observant eyes, darting in every direction.

She couldn't imagine the things he'd seen on trains. Didn't want to think about what he'd seen. Except she needed to know, didn't she?

She sat up. "Well, maybe you're right." A small juice might yield her a clue.

"Now that's the ticket. What will it be, miss?" Still smiling, far too eager.

"One small orange juice, please."

"Nothing to wash it down with? Ham sandwich? Salted peanuts?"

"Just the juice, thank you." *And now what?* Annalee aimed her gaze at him, testing his next move.

The waiter stood nodding for a second, but finally he turned for the lounge car, stopping to chat up other passengers, courting more drink orders, his feet steady in the swaying car.

Annalee watched him, studying his sure gait. He knew the train and the tracks—and the moving of the train on the tracks—like the back of his steady hand. So he knew by the time on his watch when the car would shift left. Or shift right. Or take a wide lean.

An inside man. Annalee silently weighed the thought. This man knew when the train crossed over a bridge. Or a trestle. Or a valley. Or a hill. Or a rocky ravine. Like the ravine where her father's broken body took its last unjust breath.

Annalee shut her eyes, breathed deep.

A train employee.

Of course. So obvious. Because a train worker would know people—the good, the bad, and everything in between. She just never imagined it, that a train worker—a porter or a waiter, possibly, not unlike the debonair waiter bringing her the overpriced glass of orange juice—could have something to do with the murder of a part-time, broken-down cowboy from Denver.

Or why.

But indeed, why not? This was a different world. Not academic and proper like a quiet, private, self-important college. Not that a college couldn't be a dangerous world in its own way. But this was the real world. And in this world, was there anything that *somebody* wouldn't do?

Annalee looked up. The door to the car opened. A blast of train noise. Acrid fuel smell. The waiter stepped through the door, balancing a silver tray of drinks in one hand, letting the door close behind him. Noise fell to its normal level. The train rocked and clacked. Rocked and clacked.

The waiter stopped to serve a cold tomato juice, the glass sweating. With his free hand, he offered a spotless napkin, positioned the drink in the passenger's hand. Made correct change and small talk. Then he stood by, discreet and gracious. Long enough to receive a tip.

Then on to his next passenger.

No drinks spilled. No change dropped. No clumsy mishap. A portrait of composure.

Watching him, Annalee decided: she would ask him about her father. Surely he would have heard. He might've worked that very night. He might've pushed—

The waiter looked down the long aisle. Caught Annalee's eye.

She held his gaze. He looked away.

She considered what to say. *I'm Annalee Spain. Do you remember the colored cowboy? The accident?*

Then finally the waiter stood at her side. The napkin. The drink.

"Joe Spain!"

The name shot from her lips.

"What?" The waiter's cool hands suddenly shook. The orange juice tipped.

"One year ago. November 26?"

The silver tray took to the air. The glass of juice, sloshing, spilling, spraying across the front of her secondhand, ill-fitting black travel coat.

"Oh, my apologies, miss." The waiter dabbed at her coat with a white napkin.

But in the same instant, Annalee stood, steadied her gaze at the waiter. "Guess you'll have to help me get this cleaned up." She moved toward the aisle.

The waiter grabbed her arm. *Hard.* "I'll get my valet case, miss. If you'll follow me—"

"No." Annalee pulled back. "You can follow me." She cleared her seat, yanked out of the coat, watched her satchel, pocketbook—holding Mrs. Stallworth's precious two dollars—all of it fall to the floor. But no time to catch everything. She needed to get this waiter in a quiet place to talk.

"No, I insist." He gritted his teeth, reached for her again. With a forceful push, he tried to steer Annalee toward the rear of the train.

Annalee planted her ugly secondhand shoes on the dark-red carpet, determined not to move unless by her own power, thinking suddenly of small things, hearing Mrs. Stallworth's warning.

"No," she said, keeping her voice down. "You can come with me. We need to talk, don't we?"

A few passengers were looking at them now.

"If you insist." His whisper was a hiss. He smiled at other passengers, intent on not making a scene.

"The lounge car?" Annalee's voice sounded firm but quiet.

His eyes darted. "The lounge car is fine. You know the way?"

"Yes." She didn't—didn't know anything—but she suspected, and that was worth something.

She walked tall to the end of the car.

The waiter followed. "Just a small problem . . . just cleaning a spill." He passed each row of seats. "So sorry, sir. Excuse us, miss. Yes, my apologies, ma'am."

Annalee kept walking straight, determined not to waver or look confused.

At the end of the car, she could see into the vestibule—the no-man's-land connecting her car to the next. It was unlit and ink dark.

The waiter leaned past her, pushed open the door, the train noise blasting in her ears. Thick smoke filled her nostrils.

Annalee gagged for a moment, coughing. "I have some questions—"

But the waiter pushed her into a corner, jerking her body around to face him. His eyes were black flints.

She stood her ground. He raised his arm.

Annalee saw it go up but refused to scream, thinking of her daddy. "What do you want from me?" she yelled.

The waiter gripped her by the shoulders. "Miss Spain!"

He knew who she was.

"I said what do you want?"

"Please! You have to come on with me . . . *now.*"

He was trying to help? Or was that a threat?

"Come with you? Where?"

"Please! It's dangerous. Let's move. *Now!*"

"Not until you explain."

He looked hard at Annalee. "I know about your father. Just go quiet. Like everything's natural."

"But—"

With a push, he opened the next car door, let Annalee enter another passenger car. A few passengers glanced up at them, then went back to their reading, talking, dozing.

"George!" A red-faced man gestured to the waiter.

Annalee tensed.

"Yes, sir!" the waiter said. "Coming, sir!"

The waiter moved them both forward. They reached the man's row. The waiter whispered, "Another cold drink, sir?"

The man grinned, gave Annalee a once-over. "Just a *tiny* lemonade." Hard, boozy voice. He winked at the waiter, handed him a wad of folded money, winked at Annalee. She turned away. The man laughed, pulled out another folded piece of money for the waiter.

"*Thank you*, sir." The waiter half bowed. "Right away, sir."

The waiter whispered to Annalee, "Please hurry." She was already ahead of him—to more cars, more vestibules. The train seemed endless, a perfect vehicle for killing people—a noisy, endless, clackety distraction. Nobody would ever notice. But finally they reached the lounge car, its neat little sign on the door. The waiter pushed.

Voices rang out.

"George!"

"George!"

"Back here, boy!"

Well-cut men with well-dressed ladies called out to the waiter from both sides of the car, ignoring Annalee.

"Coming. Right away, sir."

Annalee kept her eyes straight ahead. *Just keep moving.* But a hand reached out, grabbed her hard by the arm.

Annalee flinched.

"Well, looka *here*. What's *this*, George?"

Annalee held her breath, her heart pounding. Should she shake him off? *Darn right I will.* She geared up, ready. But the waiter beat her to it.

"Excuse me, sir?" The waiter bowed.

The man had grabbed Annalee's other arm, trying to turn her to him. He dropped his hands to grab hers. Her heart galloped. She clenched her fists. Hold his hands? *Not on my life.*

"A *sophisticated* little gal. All dressed in black." The man laughed. "Traveling to see your honey, *honey?*" He looked her over.

But the waiter pushed between them. "Just a young lady's gal, sir. The young lady needs something from the luggage car. Right now, sir."

The luggage car. Good idea? Bad idea? Annalee tried to think.

The well-cut man winked and sat down. "Must be quite a lady."

"Yes, sir," the waiter said.

"Well, give the lady my regards."

"Yes, sir."

His hands let go. Annalee stiffened her back and walked with dignity, she hoped, through the loud car. The well-cut man whispered something to his friends, fancy men and women. A burst of laughter erupted.

Annalee let herself feel it, forcing herself to understand that *this* was what it meant for *her* to get involved in solving a crime. People would laugh. Push at her. Refuse her help. Sniff down their noses. Not see her for *her*—not that much different than her college life. Or life in general.

Yet if she was aiming for the truth—about her daddy, the murder, maybe even about herself, about being alone in the world when she knew she shouldn't be alone at all—she'd have to stand up to danger and to ridicule and take charge. But when? Good grief, *now.*

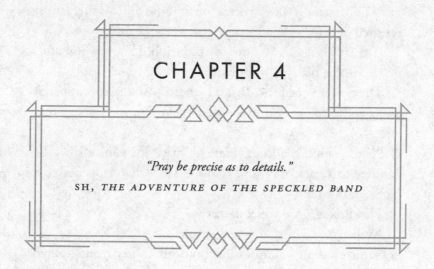

CHAPTER 4

"Pray be precise as to details."

SH, *THE ADVENTURE OF THE SPECKLED BAND*

ANNALEE SWUNG AROUND, the waiter on her heels. She pushed open a last heavy door. The waiter jangled keys, unlocked a final heavy barrier. A posted sign read, *Train Employees Only.*

The luggage car.

It was unheated, cold, stuffy, no windows. A freight car with luggage. Annalee drew in a long breath, wondering the obvious: *How did I, the up-and-coming colored theologian of a downtown Chicago Bible college, end up here?* The train didn't answer. She looked around. Two dusty light bulbs, one on each end, offered the only light. She could make out towers of luggage and valises, heavy trunks, big cartons and canvas bags of US mail.

She turned to the waiter. "I'm Annalee Spain. That's my name. But you already know it. Now tell me yours."

"William. William Barnett."

"I understand, Mr. Barnett. You and the other waiters must get tired of being called George."

Barnett shrugged. "Comes with the job. I know who I am."

"I'll find a place to sit down."

The waiter wiped the dust off a narrow suitcase, propped it on its end. "You can sit here, Miss Spain. I'm sorry about that juice—"

"Never mind the juice. Here's a place for you to sit." She gestured to a stack of valises. "Now tell me what happened that night on this train—"

He blinked. "Are you a detective?"

"What?"

"You're asking me questions and all. When you shouted Joe Spain's name, I figured you were somebody. Or maybe his daughter. *The Colored Professor.* Read about you in the papers."

Annalee nodded.

"But if you were his daughter, I figured you were in danger. Besides, ever since the night—and I'm sorry what happened to your daddy, miss, I really am. But ever since your daddy died, this route's been running over with police. Well, they look like police. Except they look like they're up to no good. Same kind of men on the train tonight was on the night your daddy was . . . killed."

"Police in the lounge car?"

"In every car. Looking suspicious." He gave her a look. "*Are you a detective?*"

She shifted on the suitcase. "I'm . . . looking into everything." Her best answer, to him and to her. For now, anyway. She squared her back. "You were trying to protect me back there?"

"I didn't mean to push you so hard."

She nodded, showing thanks. Unless he was lying. Just a good actor? She couldn't tell. "And now can you do something for me? My satchel and my coat—"

"I'll take care of it."

"Then we'll arrive in Denver . . . what time?"

He looked at his pocket watch. "Nine. Exactly an hour from now."

"Fine, well, when you leave, I want you to lock me in here."

"Lock you *in*?"

"Yes. To lock them *out*." She paused. "Whoever *they* are. Isn't that why we wrestled each other back here? For safety?"

"I wasn't going to lock you in—maybe ask you to slide a big trunk in front of the door. But if you say so, I'll lock you up in here. I don't like it."

"I'll be fine." But she didn't feel it. "When we get to Denver, if you can, I'll need you or a porter to help with my satchel and find my coat and purse."

He nodded.

"Once I'm in the station, I'll go straight to the person who's picking me up—a Methodist pastor. I know I can trust him. But for now I have to believe I can trust you."

The waiter stood to his full height, straightened his white jacket. "Miss Spain, what happened to your daddy was the worst thing's happened on my route since I started. If I can help you get to the bottom of it, it'll be a great honor to me." He looked down. "Maybe I could've stopped it."

"Maybe you could've." She couldn't offer him more. "Thanks for taking care of my things, Mr. Barnett. I'm sorry I don't have a tip." She stood and shook his hand.

With a last look, he turned and pulled open the heavy door,

train noise blasting. With a heave, he shut the door behind him. After a moment, he jangled his keys in the lock. He was gone.

Annalee watched the door, shaking off the feeling of being not locked in but locked *up*. Thinking she had to use the next hour to, well, think. Like a detective. But Mrs. Stallworth was right. She wasn't her Sherlock. He'd study footprints, compare handwriting, measure fingerprints, decode cryptic messages—letting faithful Watson declare his "moody" detecting brilliance. But she was alone without one clue.

She listened to the train. *Talk to me, please.* But she heard nothing. Just what she already knew. *It's 8 p.m. Yep, Friday night. In one hour, the train arrives in Denver.* So solving crime was about knowing the time? But she didn't even own a watch.

She sighed but, time-wise, saw a glimmer. First thing in the morning, she'd get downtown—to the rich man who hired her daddy for odd jobs. Maybe he'd shed some light. Then out to the Lazy K Ranch, talk to the owner.

And those men would tell her what? Same thing they told the police? Nothing. But she wasn't returning home not to try.

Besides, Reverend Blake could drive her. Although her father said they'd had trouble at that ranch. But—

Crash.

Annalee jumped.

A suitcase. Something in the back of the car fell. A loud tumble.

She froze. *What now?*

The pale light shone on stacks of luggage. Nothing moved except the train. Rocking and clacking. Her heart skipped an odd beat. She narrowed her eyes.

"Who's there?" Her puny voice.

No answer. Out of nowhere, a shadow inched into a shape against one wall. Under the rail noise, she strained to hear.

Instincts kicked in. She stood taller, looking for some defense, something heavy and sharp. She reached down for the suitcase under her. It was heavy enough, fitted on each corner with a metal reinforcement. It wouldn't kill anybody, not that she would even try. But it could stop somebody long enough for her to scream. *If only William Barnett could hear me.*

The shadow inched bigger.

"Who's there?" Her cautious voice.

"Who's there?" Finally loud. She hoisted the suitcase, grunting, steeled her feet on the floor against the motion of the train. *Daddy.* She thought of her father. At six feet two and 180 lean but muscular pounds, he didn't stop a killer on a train. At her size—five foot four, maybe, and 110 pounds, sort of—who could she stop? Instead, she thought of Mrs. Stallworth and her fuming about small things. *You don't break down a door; you work on the hinges.*

Of course, now wasn't the time to wrestle with that. Yet the thought helped her to relax. To bring down her arms. She set the suitcase back in place, pulled up to her height, and crossed her arms. "If you weren't such a *coward*, you'd step forward *now.*"

The train rocked. The shadow didn't move. She spoke louder. "Come out, *coward.* Now!"

A lumpy dark figure crawled from behind a jumble of luggage and into the pale light. A scarf hid the face. In the dark car, she squinted to focus. She didn't want to believe it. She didn't have enough patience, time, or *theology* to believe it.

He let his soiled scarf fall.

The boy. The white boy. The Western Union child.

She yanked the scarf off his shoulders. "*You?* What are you doing here?"

He shrugged forward. "Professor! *Please* don't send me back!" He pulled off his dirty hat. Underneath, his hair was a grimy mess.

She looked him over, thought about small things. So she chose her words while he searched her face, gray eyes blinking. Waiting. Praying?

"You're going home," she finally said.

"But I don't have a home!"

"Neither do I!" she shot back.

"But, listen . . . Professor!"

"*No*, you listen." She didn't want to sound harsh, but it was exactly how she felt. "I'm involved with something very important right now. And I need to know why you are here."

She was breathing hard, trying to hold in anger, frustration, disbelief.

The boy dove in, trying to explain. "I'm going to Denver. Like you." He covered his teeth for a moment. "I mean, I figured I could go with you. The rooming house lady told me that's where you were going, so I followed you on the streetcar."

"Me? Where I'm going?" She looked at him, suddenly remembering he knew exactly who she was. But she kept shaking her head, confounded at his gall, knowing she shouldn't be angry or frustrated, but she was furious.

"What about your mother? We're two days gone! She must be worried to death."

The boy blinked. "I don't have a mother. Well, not anymore.

She's . . . well. She's dead. Six years ago. Right before Easter. On Maundy Thursday. During Holy Week."

Annalee moaned, disbelieving. The boy was his own liturgical almanac. A theological orphan. *Lord, have mercy.* "But why Denver?"

"That's where my father lives."

"Your father? But I thought he was dead."

"No, he's missing. I mean, he went to Colorado when I was a baby, to work in the mines. To make more money for us."

"Wait. He's not a preacher?"

The boy looked at her oddly. "Well, gee, he was a preacher, but we never had enough money. So he went out to Denver to work the mines. But he never came back. Or maybe he came, but we kept moving. Seemed like every month we moved to another house, town, room. I think he came back but couldn't find us." He covered his teeth again. "Then Mother died. But people helped me sometimes. Like that night you gave me food. I went back a few days later to tell you thank you, but the lady said you just left for Denver. So I thought I'd find you and go too."

Annalee rubbed her forehead, thinking of . . . God? Of the arrogance it took to believe she could study God or comprehend who God is in a world that rarely makes a lick of sense, because it's so God-forsaken and desperate and crazy. So here she stood, with a child who'd followed her onto a train, when she wasn't sure herself where in the world she was going or what she was doing. All she knew, in fact, was she didn't know one sure thing about *anything* anymore.

"Come over here," she said. She pulled the boy to a stack of suitcases and sat him down. Even with the coats, he weighed next to nothing. Soaking wet.

She sighed. "How old are you?"

"Fifteen," he mumbled.

She narrowed her eyes at him.

"Fourteen?" he whispered. But he looked away.

"Look at me." She stared him down, dead in the eye. "I have patience for only one thing tonight and that's the truth. Can you say *that* liturgical word?"

He nodded. Mumbled the word.

"So I'm asking you again. How old are you?"

The boy twisted his face. "Already eleven."

"What?"

"But I'm almost twelve. In four weeks. My birthday is January 6 and it's a Sunday!"

She looked him over. He was dirty, smelly, and a liar. And his teeth were rotten. She had to get this boy to an orphanage— and a dentist.

He read her eyes. "But I'm grown up! I been taking care of myself. Look!" He reached in his right boot and pulled a rusting hunting knife from a slim leather sheath. An old bowie, wooden handle. She recognized the blade. Her daddy had one, not much cleaner. She sighed. The filthy knife shook in his gloved hand.

"Young man—" She realized she didn't even know his name. "First, tell me who you are. Let's start with your name."

"My name? My name is—"

The luggage car shuddered for an odd moment. The lights flickered and died. The car went black as pitch.

"Professor?" Panicky voice.

"I'm here," she said, assuring, needing to sound and feel strong even though her hands shook. "It's okay."

She could hear the boy's breathing. The car swayed.

She heard the boy swallow.

"You all right?" she asked, trying to calm him.

"I . . . think so."

But the next noise was a deafening rumble, something large moving in the car.

"What's going—?"

Out of nowhere, a bulk force landed on Annalee's chest, throwing her hard onto her back. On the way down, her head slammed into a pile of luggage. A flash of white light flared right behind her eyes. Her head went numb. Then ringing pain. *"Aaaagh!"* she groaned, trying to think, to see.

"Professor!"

She struggled to get up, tried to speak. "I'm—" But something pushed her down hard against the cold floor. She struggled to resist, flailing her legs, kicking at luggage, knocking over valises. She heard a heavy piece slam to the floor.

"Professor Spain!" the boy screamed.

"I'm—" she tried to answer, but somebody's hands were around her throat. She could feel them squeezing, squeezing hard—a man's strength. She tried to catch a breath, but the deliberate hands tightened. Her mind searched for escape, thinking with every squeeze: *I can't breathe!*

And I'm angry about it. She struggled to turn, to break the grip. Wondering, *Who?* But no time to analyze. *Just break this grip.* She grasped at the awful hands, found flesh, dug in fingernails.

"Aaaaagh!" A man's deep voice. He cursed, released her throat.

She shouted, "Help . . . me!"

The man slammed her head back down, grabbed for her throat.

Oh no you don't. Ignoring the blinding pain in her head, she flailed in the dark, scratching at hands, at arms, at the unseen face. Anything to make him *stop choking her now.*

"Help me!"

"Aaagh—"

The form above Annalee seized, slumped, gagged. He exhaled a wet smell. Stale beer, burned onions, dreadful food from some dreadful place. His body twitched violently. Then it didn't move. She pushed his awful weight away, struggled to sit up, pain slicing through her head, the skin of her throat on fire. She touched the back of her head. "Owwww!"

"Professor?"

"Boy—"

"I'm here."

"Can you . . . find the lights?"

"I think so!"

The boy made scrambling noises, stumbled and fell down, crawled across the cold floor, pawed at walls for a light switch. "I found it." He clicked a switch. A wall lamp flickered.

They froze. A tall, thin man in a dark suit was lying still as a stone, facedown amid a tumble of suitcases, his back pierced by a huge bowie knife. The boy's knife. The knife's wooden handle stood straight up in the man's back.

The boy scrambled to Annalee, clung to her, trying to stifle a wretched sob. "Professor!"

"It's okay." She tried to convince the boy, tried to convince herself. But she was thinking their awful truth.

This child just killed this man. And this man tried to kill me. Her hands trembled, her whole body shaking, recognizing that solving murder wasn't a game, some Sherlock story she read after supper. It was a life-and-death struggle. So she let the boy cling, searching the scene beyond his heaving shoulders.

An oversize steamer trunk lay upended—wide-open and empty—right next to the light switch. The man's hiding place. Clever.

The boy's breath was racing now, as fast as hers. She held him tighter.

"It's okay." She said it over and over, trying to convince herself, trying to convince the boy. The train whistle screamed. It cut the air. The whistle screamed again. But nothing was okay, and it was too late to turn back or change what just happened. Especially now. Chicago was another place in another world in another universe. This, Dr. Watson, was Denver.

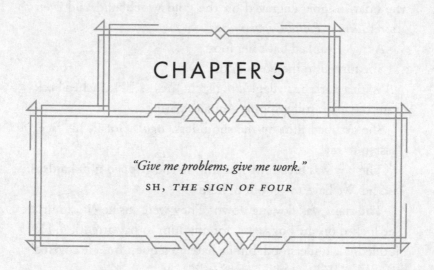

CHAPTER 5

"Give me problems, give me work."

SH, *THE SIGN OF FOUR*

EDDIE BROWN JR. The boy's name.

"Your real name?" Annalee searched his eyes.

The boy nodded. He was still clinging to her coat, gripping her arm like a vise. But she couldn't push him away. Or, as she figured, *I can't* not *hold him.*

Because the child's face said *shock*—and disbelief at being a young boy caught in the middle of a horrible and *very* grown-up situation. Indeed, she wanted, at that moment, to allow all the time in the world to assure him, comfort him, hold him. To act like the grown-up in this ordeal. But no time to linger. They had to figure their next steps, try not to look at the dead man on the floor.

But the man's hand was almost touching Annalee's foot, his wristwatch ticking. The Bulova clockface said nine sharp, but the bold insignia engraved on the gold watchband said even more: *Denver Police Department.*

Annalee yanked back her foot.

She turned to the boy. "Eddie!"

With a start, he struggled to listen. "Yes . . ." He inched back from the man, still gripping Annalee's arm.

She grabbed him by the shoulders, *tight.* Got in his face. "Listen to me!"

The boy was breathing fast still, so she gripped him harder. "Eddie! We have to get out of here."

The train was slowing down. They were inside city limits. She locked on the boy's eyes, forcing him to pay attention. He nodded. He understood, but he had a big question. He covered his teeth. "Will . . . will I go to jail?"

"For saving my *life*? They'll give you a medal. But this guy probably has friends, bad friends. We've got to get out of here, Eddie, now."

Annalee ran to the door, pulled on the heavy lever. Still locked. She searched the car. No windows, no vents in the ceiling. Searching the half-dark, she looked to the back of the car, finally seeing, at the farthest end, a heavy wooden door, surely locked.

But she scrambled through the piles of luggage to test it. Eddie followed on her heels, knocking past suitcases, trunks—determined to move as far as possible from the dead man on the cold floor.

"Hurry. Back here." Annalee grabbed at the big door lever. Yes, locked. Of course.

She turned to Eddie. "Listen to me. We've got to figure out how to open this door."

He dropped his scarf, swallowing hard, nodding. He dug

down in his boot, pulled out a small tool. A lockpick. His hand shook, offering it to her.

An orphan's offering.

He started to weep. But she could read his eyes. Loneliness? Shame? The life of an orphan. What he'd done to survive had taught him life's worst choices.

She drew him to her, assuring him it was okay. "Put it away, Eddie. I'm the one these idiots are after." But in the same instant, she saw the terror in his eyes, understanding that "these idiots"—whoever they were—would be after him, too.

That did it. She yanked up a suitcase, slammed it against the lock, her head throbbing. But she slammed it harder, harder, harder. She bit on her lip. *Harder.*

Split.

The lock apparatus broke in two, the lever hanging loose from the wooden door. But the door still wouldn't budge—and the train had slowed to a steady crawl. They'd reached the train yard. She looked around in the shadows. Something in the corner. A rusty fire extinguisher, good for nothing but its heft.

Somebody pounded on the other door, jangling the lock.

"Someone's coming." *Not* William Barnett. He would've called out her name. Or would he?

Her stomach twisted. The waiter hadn't returned to the luggage car. Had he run into the "idiots"? Or was he one of them?

She wrestled with the extinguisher. "Help me, Eddie!" The boy scrambled over to grip it tight. She gripped the top. Together, they pounded it into the door, harder with each blow. Harder. *Harder.* But no give in the door. So she whacked it harder, worrying. *Please don't let this extinguisher explode.* But finally they heard a colossal crack. The wood split again, both of them kicking at it now. The whole lock dropped to the floor. Annalee kicked it aside. Together they pushed the sliding door open, grunting to make clearance. The two stepped over the rubble, looking out.

A blast of icy air hit her face.

"We're near the roundhouse." Annalee looked down, knowing the obvious. *We have to jump.* She took one long, deep, resolving breath, trying to stop her own shaking. "Can you do this, Eddie?"

She watched him nod, saw his fear.

Oddly, she thought of her daddy, daring her to jump from the big leaning maple tree in their ramshackle backyard. On steaming summer days, the green leaves lured her up. She'd climb to the tip-top but couldn't get down. Then came her laughing daddy: *"Jump, little bit! Right into my arms! I won't let you fall!"*

Oh, she'd longed to trust him. But with her daddy, she never could be sure.

She looked down at the ground. It looked ice-cold, rock-hard, gravel sharp. Not moving unworldly fast. But fast enough to break a leg, sprain an ankle, twist a foot. Or get pulled onto the rails—or worse, if another train ran alongside?

And Eddie with all his scarves and jackets. *And me—* Annalee thought—*without even a coat. Or decent shoes. Or my blasted purse.* The pounding on the door, at the same time, was growing louder. Somebody was determined to break through.

She gripped Eddie's hand. The crisp air was ice dry. A perfect Denver winter night. Moonlight on the rails. *Home.* Her eyes tingled, welling up. But Denver wasn't her home anymore. Without her daddy, it couldn't be home. She'd never really had much of a home anyway, except at the end. Then his last year, he'd tried so hard to make amends, to make everything better. But now he was gone and everything had changed forever. Now she was in a once-familiar town, with a newly strange child. A white child. An orphan like her. But she faced work to do: Find a murderer. Or murderers. Discover what they didn't want her to know. *And stop crying.*

She took in a hard breath.

Wiped at her eyes.

She checked the black ground sliding by below, the gravelly surface lit only by moonlight on snow. In the distance, the train station was all aglow, gleaming like a fancy jewel box—with Reverend Blake outside waiting. She'd alerted him. Nine sharp. But was his home a safe place? *Mercy*, she hoped so. Or at the least, she figured he'd know a Denver cop—a good cop—somebody who'd understand her ordeal and help.

She took a deep breath. The banging on the locked door was louder, harder, angrier.

"With me, Eddie?" She looked down, steadied herself in the open doorway, gestured outside, looked back at Eddie.

But he wasn't looking at her.

His head was down.

Praying.

Eyes shut tight, mouth barely moving, covering his bad teeth, beseeching heaven for all he was worth.

Annalee groaned silently, pressing her mouth tight—thinking over the year since she'd really called on God, not knowing anymore if she even knew how or wanted to or could. After all this time—after still being so blasted confounded with God—what in the world would she say in a plain prayer?

Please, Lord. Help us.

She looked at Eddie. Thought of Mrs. Stallworth.

And while you're at it, save us from breaking our fool necks.

"Amen!" Eddie yelled. His eyes snapped open.

"Okay. On three," she yelled back. They counted together. They jumped as one.

The air slammed into their faces, the ground rushing up to meet them, an iced sledgehammer, pounding without mercy. *Ooomph!* Annalee bounced and rolled. Eddie did too—rolling beside her, groaning. *"Awwwww!"*

Annalee gasped, grabbing for the cold ground rushing past under her, yanking back her fingers from a frozen sticker bush, trying to grasp *anything* solid to make her body stop rolling, to make her mind stop thinking about this awful night. The train. The boy. The dead Denver cop.

With a final roll, she lay sprawled on her back, gasping at freezing air. And *hurting*. Appalled at *everything*. The pain in her head. Her body. Her hand. The freezing cold. And the impossibility of their situation. She tried to sit up, grateful to hear Eddie's groans. He was alive at least.

"Eddie!"

She felt her arms, legs, body. No broken bones?

"Eddie!"

In the moonlight, she saw him crawl to all fours, struggling to catch breath. He groaned, blinking hard at her.

She reached for him. "Are you okay? Can you *walk*?"

His voice was an odd whisper. "I . . . I never jumped out of a train before."

She fell back, laughing. "That's two of us." She laughed again—at the two of them, at everything. "But you can walk, right?"

Eddie struggled to stand, still bending over. "I think so."

Annalee scrambled to her feet, too, her head zinging. Her body screaming in protest. Only her head felt worse. But there was no time to fuss or worry or assure herself she was okay. Annalee peered into the dark, across the rail yard. She could hear shouts, see flashlights, feel fear—yes, the fear of realizing she wasn't smart or tough or big enough to fight off a cadre of nighttime killers. The dead cop had friends? Who followed them off the train?

"Under here! *Now*," she whispered at Eddie, scrambling under an empty freight train. He scrambled behind her. But the voices and flashlights got closer, pressing on them, hunting them.

So we're playing cat and mouse, Annalee thought. *Well, I can play that game.*

She scrambled under to the other side, ripping the front of her long, black skirt on something sharp.

"Stay close," she whispered to Eddie, both of them scrambling under another train. Her stockings ripping, his scarf trailing. They zagged out and under another freight car, heading not *away* from the flashlights but parallel to them. Finally three tracks over, they cut a perpendicular turn, heading away from the noises now, closer to another freight train on the track in front of them. Annalee motioned to Eddie and crawled under. He crawled after her.

Both gasped for air; both lay flat on their backs under a train. *And this is insane*, Annalee thought. *But I can outsmart some goons with flashlights.*

She blinked. She had no idea whatsoever who she could outsmart, was appalled she'd ever thought of it.

She gave Eddie a shaky, half-confident grin. "Still with me?"

"Okay."

Brave boy. Nobody could ever tell her he wasn't one brave child. She reached for his hand in the dark, trying to assure. His breathing was racing. Hers, too. Her heart pounded.

Then a flashlight slit the dark. A man shouted, "Over here!" The flashlight snapped closer.

Annalee grabbed Eddie's arm, ready to bolt. He lifted up on his elbows, but the car jerked. The train was moving.

"Hurry, Eddie!" she whispered. *"C'mon."* She waited for a break in the wheels, scrambled out, pulling skirt, knees, feet behind herself fast. She turned back to grab Eddie's hand. "Watch the wheels!" But he wasn't moving!

"What's wrong? *C'mon!"*

"My . . . my coat!"

"What?"

"My *coat*. It's stuck!" Eddie wriggled his arm. Something snagged at the sleeve.

"Eddie, *leave it*. Take it off." But he was still wriggling his arm, determined to free the sleeve. *And this isn't happening*, Annalee thought. *His coat?*

"Eddie!"

"It's *my coat!"*

"Eddie, now!" She tried to reflect, to hear the panic in his voice, to slow her breathing so she could hear what he was trying to say. His coat. His *father's* coat. Everything he wore, he was trying to explain, belonged to his missing father—even if the shouting and lights flashed closer.

"Okay," she whispered. "What's holding your coat?"

"It's my *sleeve*," Eddie groaned. "A big nail or something!" He covered his teeth with his free hand.

Annalee watched him, not believing. "*Eddie.* Rip it. *And stop worrying about your teeth.* I mean, the coat's going to tear. But we can fix it. *Do you understand me?*" She searched his eyes.

"Yes," he said, his voice small. Finally.

"Then rip it *now. Pull.*"

Eddie grimaced and yanked. His arm jerked up. The cloth tore. He reached across the rails, grasped the ground in front of him with both hands.

"Watch the wheels!"

He yanked back his hands. The next set of wheels rumbled past. More shouts cut closer. Annalee begged him. *Now!* She watched him scramble in some crazy, slow-as-Grandma's-molasses crawl, taking him *forever.* Finally Annalee reached down, dragged him up by the shoulders.

Then they ran. Hightailing it.

Breathing hard, Annalee freezing in her thin black skirt and thin cotton blouse, her cheap black jacket—every thread of her "new" secondhand outfit, a hard-earned farewell gift from Mrs. Stallworth, now filthy, ripped, or torn. Her wild curls shook, angry and muddy. Eddie ran panicked behind, still gripping his scarf, his coat, his grimy hat, his torn coat sleeve flapping in the frigid breeze.

Annalee pulled up, stopped, gasped for breath. Looked around. No voices behind them. No bright lights. She peered into the blackness, instantly knew her bearings. The mountains were west. They were at the southwest end of the train yard. If they stayed south, she thought, and circled back around, through upper downtown, they'd avoid the terminal and anybody searching for them around the rail yard.

"Maybe we should hide here," Eddie shouted at her.

"No. This way. Run!" She turned straight south, away from the rails. The ground was cold and dry—no new snow. Therefore, no traces in snow. After half a mile or so, she turned them east into lower downtown. Knowing they looked wild. And odd. And suspicious. But she forced herself to slow to a walk. She looked over her shoulder, allowed herself to let out a measured breath.

No lights. No shouting. Nobody following.

Oh, thank you, God.

Her eyes welled.

But that's not a real prayer.

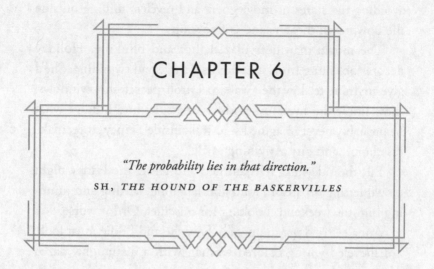

CHAPTER 6

"The probability lies in that direction."

SH, *THE HOUND OF THE BASKERVILLES*

ANNALEE LEANED INTO THE FREEZING AIR, clearing her mind, knowing this wasn't the time to chew over *that* worry, or anything else, about her prayers. Instead, she'd better find their waiting helper, the Reverend Blake. And God bless that old man, her father's pastor.

He'd be waiting in the station—pacing and searching—wondering where in heaven's name she was. Or he'd figure it out, go back to the church parsonage to wait. She'd just have to trust he'd detect a kink in her plans.

Besides, she didn't have a choice. They had to move *away* from the terminal—farther up Sixteenth Street, the main drag, and deeper into the business district, away from flashlights and shouting and murdering goons. She led Eddie close to the buildings, hurrying the two of them past restaurant windows, avoiding the stares of moviegoers and revelers milling outside the downtown theaters and coffee shops.

The movie marquees blazed, hot and blinking. Holiday decorations hung from streetlights, festive and twinkling. She'd give anything to slow their walk to a stroll, peer in shopwindows, show Eddie the swell toys and whatnots, let him indulge what he probably never imagined—to walk inside a fancy store, make his choice, and buy. Anything at all.

But the sidewalks felt jammed and tense, the Friday night crowd letting off steam, loud and laughing, flirting and jumping into the weekend. Looking for mischief. Or for worse.

Annalee tried *not* to imagine how she and Eddie must look: a disheveled young colored woman with a distraught, dazed white boy clinging to her arm.

She cut over to a side street.

"*Hey.* Gal!"

She turned to Eddie. "You getting hungry?" Trying to sound matter-of-fact, ignoring trouble, wishing Eddie would keep moving.

"You know that man?"

"Roast beef? You like that? Mashed potatoes?"

Trouble turned to his friends, weaving, half-drunk. "Hey! I said *you*. Right, fellas?"

"And gravy," Annalee said, pressing Eddie ahead.

"Hey! You dumb—!" The man cursed, his friends calling him back. But the man grabbed a handful of grimy snow off the curb, balled it up, let it fly.

Slush hit the sidewalk, glancing off Annalee. The loud man started to laugh. He grabbed more snow, threw another gritty ice ball.

"Hey, cut it out!" Eddie yelled.

"Hey, cut it out!" Mocking Eddie. "Cut it out!"

Annalee put her arm around Eddie's shoulder, pushing him to walk faster. "Ever been to Denver?" she asked.

He tried to grin. "I guess not."

"Then let's get moving." She looked at the street sign. They were on Curtis Street, three miles south, or maybe two as the crow flies, from Mount Moriah AME. "We're going to my church." She paused. "Well, my daddy's church." She sighed. "Well, to church."

She pressed ahead. "We'll hide behind the sanctuary until Reverend Blake comes back. The parsonage is next door. He'll let us stay."

Eddie nodded again, still panting. Maybe the altitude? He could keep up, but he looked exhausted. *We both are,* she said to herself. *And freezing.* She could ask Eddie about borrowing one of his coats but didn't want to get *that* going again. Instead, she quickened her pace, Eddie dragging. His scarf hung limp around his neck. Her head throbbed. Her right hand stung.

And a dead policeman lay on the train.

Annalee pulled them into an alley to catch their breath. The cold night air was punishing, and the city seemed so different. When she left for school six years ago, these same streets were jammed with horses and buggies. Now a motorcar almost cut them off. The driver honked. Annalee pulled back, yanking Eddie with her. The driver shouted, cursed.

But Annalee kept moving them through the press of Friday night revelers, plotting their route in her mind. Just a few blocks to Welton Street, then a sharp turn north would point them to the church. Dead into Five Points, the streets of her childhood. She took a deep breath, not wanting to think about those years now.

Then she heard it.

Boots on pavement.

She turned. Eddie turned. Every head on the crowded street turned to look for the sound of steady marching. The sound grew closer.

"Look," a red-haired young woman leaving a café yelled to friends. She pointed at the corner.

The heavy traffic seemed to part. Behind it, a line of marchers—four marchers per row, as far as the eye could see—all wearing white robes over their street clothes, pounded the pavement. Pointed white hoods, with a long flap in front, covered their heads and faces, only little round openings showing their eyes.

"Take off your stupid masks!" the young woman sneered, turning away. "They look ridiculous."

But one of her girlfriends, a tall blonde, got wide-eyed and pulled her friend back. "Don't leave yet. I want to look!"

"Yeah!" Eddie said. "I want to look. Who're those guys? Why're they wearing robes?" He pulled on Annalee's arm, wanting her to stop.

She pulled right back. "Oh no you don't."

The Klan? Silly fearmongering men. She couldn't be bothered, wouldn't let herself worry one millisecond over their stupid terror and mayhem—certain that, without their hate, even they understood that they added up to nothing. All that threatening and stomping around. Annalee refused to feel it. Not tonight. Besides, her head hurt.

"Down this way, Eddie."

"*No.* I mean, please. Wait! I wonder how many?"

"Doesn't matter," she said, not looking back, not counting the rows of white-hooded men playing dress-up—looking like toy soldiers. Hundreds of them? Maybe a thousand? She refused to count or even to care enough tonight to give in to fear, not after what she and Eddie had already been through. The march was just a dog and pony circus show, nothing but a nighttime annoyance. All in the name of Jesus? Even her dean agreed it was half-baked theology. But their bogus crusade wouldn't be her next paper. She wouldn't waste her time.

Still, on both sides of the street, customers spilled out of coffee shops and restaurants, craning necks to see. Somebody threw a rock. A café window shattered, spraying the sidewalk.

"This way, Eddie!" Annalee grabbed his arm, pulling him back from the shards.

The red-haired young woman turned and saw them. Her eyes went wide. "You better get out of here, honey!"

Annalee glanced at the woman, felt somebody else shove her. She yanked Eddie's sleeve and pushed them away from the crowd, not looking behind, shoving past angry faces, ignoring curses, not liking the tightness in her stomach.

"Where're we going?" Eddie yelled, stumbling behind her.

She didn't answer, just kept moving. Fast, straight, hard. Not for herself. But for the boy. And maybe for her daddy? And for all that she seemed to be up against in her hunt for a murderer in her strange hometown. But for now, she scrambled fast—her cheap shoes squirting slush—aiming herself down Welton. *We are moving,* she told herself, *away from the ruckus, away from the anger, away from the intentions of marching hooded men.*

Then a screech. A big navy-blue sedan raced around the

corner. The driver slammed on the brakes, stared at her through the open side window. Stared harder. Frowned at Eddie. Finally . . . "Annalee?"

A young man. Dark suit. Clerical collar.

Handsome face. *Handsome?*

Nope, *handsome* wasn't the word she'd just thought. She'd never once used such a word. Not once. Not ever. She squinted.

But *very* handsome face?

"Reverend . . . *Blake?*"

It couldn't be. Except it was.

Reverend Blake—but thirty years younger. Well, forty years younger—with a strong, umber-colored, downright handsome face. So that *was* the right word, even on a night like this.

He saw her confusion and grinned. "I'm the *nephew!*" Deep, warm voice.

Her stomach flipped. *My stomach?*

"Nephew?" she mumbled.

"Yes! And . . . *get in!*"

"But there's two of us."

"Two's great." He grinned at her again, holding her gaze.

She blinked, trying not to stare, and piled into the car, pulling in Eddie—all three of them jammed on the front seat of the sleek car.

Annalee looked up at the young reverend. Grateful? Confused? Just swept off the street by a knight in shining armor?

But Reverend Blake was two steps ahead, already explaining.

"I've been searching all over town for you." He grabbed the steering wheel, spun the car—wheels screeching—and sped north, flying down Welton, the lights of downtown fading behind them, the car a smooth bullet.

"Holy cow!" Eddie said. The speed and squealing tires seemed to revive him.

"You like?" Reverend Blake said to Eddie. "Wait'll you see what we do on an open road." He gave Eddie a big grin.

Eddie grinned back, his teeth showing, but forgetting to worry about them now.

Reverend Blake winked at Annalee, making her stomach flip again. *What in the world?* She grinned back, letting her dimple flash—but not meaning to flash. So he held her gaze a bit too long again, smiling at her.

Annalee didn't trust herself to think about what *any* of this meant. Still, to be honest, she was grateful for it. Reverend Blake would know the Klan marched, guess she'd hit delays or some trouble. But why worry about that now? His look said she was perfectly safe, right now, with him, and that's what mattered. Thus, she sat up in a prim, feminine way—*if that's what this is called*—trying with all that was holy to look, what, professional? Despite her wild curls going ten different directions, her clothes grimy and torn. Her head zinged. Her feet were ice. But she couldn't help but notice Reverend Blake's strong young arm pressed next to hers or smell the clean scent of his aftershave—*aftershave?*—or whatever that gorgeous scent wafting around her was.

She took in a deep, long, confusing breath. *I'm in shock.* On that train, she'd experienced the worst trouble of her natural-born life. She and Eddie were blessed to be in the land of the living. Then God, in his mercy, had sent her to this—and she wouldn't notice who'd picked her up? Because never in her life had she found herself sitting so close to an actual man. Except for her father. But that didn't count *at all*. Not like this.

She took in another long breath, forcing her gaze to the road, determined to draw in her complicated thoughts and think of something else, *anything else*—such as familiar passing streets and the feeling of being home, if she could still call her town that.

After the next block, the young Reverend Blake slowed the car and eased it into Five Points proper, onto a narrow street with small houses, rows of Victorian roofs, a few shotgun shacks, front yards crusted with remnants of snow, nobody on the sidewalks. Lights shone inside shade-drawn windows.

Annalee turned in her seat, looking behind them.

Reverend Blake laughed. "You can relax. Nobody followed us here."

"Did I look worried?"

"Yep. But I drive too fast." He grinned again, teasing, and gunned the motor a minute, holding her eyes.

She blinked again, feeling tipsy still about her rescuer. *And that's enough of that.*

A porch light came on. "My neighbors." He pointed out the window. "And there's home."

Annalee craned for a look. She let out a long sigh as she took in her childhood church, Mount Moriah AME. The church *did* look like home. So she missed it all? The people, the preaching, the singing, the Sunday hugs and Monday morning faith? Lasting all week long? And now she'd solve a murder here? She sat up straighter, not sure what to fully feel. Longing? Sadness? Confusion? Guilt? All of it seemed mixed up in the robust, earnest brick building and in her dismay that she hadn't been inside a church for so long. She could try to go back. But the stained-glass windows were dark, the church locked up tight.

This was her childhood refuge—and her daddy's sanctuary. Well, sometimes it was. But not enough.

For her, it was her harbor—until her daddy died. No, was killed. *Isn't that right, God?* She was too weary, dirty, and cold to think, to know exactly what the church would be to her now. But if the church held "the key," she would find it.

"And here's my castle," the pastor was saying to Eddie.

Eddie sighed, eyes wide. Annalee could see what he was thinking. *A real house.*

Reverend Blake pulled the car onto a small gravel driveway next to a modest Victorian-style cottage. The parsonage, Annalee thought. Yes, *old* Reverend Blake's house.

It sat on a small lot north of the church—close to the street—leaving a tiny front yard, fenced in wrought iron. A light shone in a window. The *old* Reverend Blake waiting inside?

The young reverend took a deep breath. "Well, where's my manners? Let me get you two inside."

Eddie tumbled out. Annalee slipped across the seat and followed, determined to look dignified despite her ripped skirt flapping, her cheap shoes squishing slush. She tried to walk confident, to feel in control when she knew for a fact she wasn't. But she followed Reverend Blake and Eddie, all of them crunching in the gravel onto a side path, then onto the front porch.

On the way, Reverend Blake checked the street, both directions. Silence all round. He unlocked the door, maneuvered them all inside to a small front hallway. Closed the door. Pulled down the shade on the window. Annalee turned around to look where she'd landed. Eddie did, too. A plain, modest, spotless, cozy—welcoming, yes—home awaited them. With electric lights and real heat, good smells beckoning from the kitchen.

Annalee let out a thankful breath. *Thank you, Jesus, from whom all blessings flow.*

Eddie pulled off his filthy cap. "Blessin' you, sir."

"Amen, son," Reverend Blake said. He patted Eddie on the shoulder. With the same welcoming smile, he reached for Annalee's hand—an awkward handshake. "Let's make this official—I'm Reverend Jack Robert Blake."

"Ow!" she winced. The sticker bush.

He dropped her hand. "You're hurt."

"It's nothing. I'm fine." She gave him a smile, but she felt so self-conscious. And she knew why.

Reverend Blake was a flat-out charmer but in a good and proper way, or so it seemed. Not proud and cocky. But broad-shouldered and friendly and square-jawed and—*yes, Mrs. Stallworth*—good-looking as all get-out. Yet he seemed not the least bit taken with being so broad-shouldered, friendly, square-jawed, and good-looking. So his earnest black eyes sparkled, his easy grin charmed. Thus, the fact of him was unexpected and appealing but also *distracting*.

She didn't come home to Denver to get distracted or charmed, and certainly not by a man, let alone a young, available man. If that's what he was. Besides, what would he see in her anyway? Annalee could hear Mrs. Stallworth. *"You should've worn some lace!"*

But lace won't help me now, Annalee thought. *Besides, I'm solving a murder.*

She looked down at her feet.

Her cheap black shoes were covered with black slush and muddy grit—all of it dripping on a spotless needlepoint rug. *"Mercy."* She stepped quickly off the needlepoint, gestured to

Eddie. His boots had left a trail of black filth from the porch to the threshold to the rug.

She gave Eddie a look, trying to gesture to his feet. He stepped off the rug to a wood floor, looking for a place to settle. But finally he just stood there, melting black slush.

A big hallway mirror could've told Annalee the rest of the story, but Annalee refused to glance, figuring she already knew exactly how she looked: like a wild woman. She touched her face.

Mud and dried slush lay caked across her forehead. Her curls stood in half a dozen directions. Her black skirt was gritty and wet, torn at the hem, ripped at the knee, embedded with dried grass, leaves, stickers—dried orange juice splashed down the front. One sleeve of her thin blouse was torn at the shoulder. But if those things weren't bad enough, she noticed that she smelled, and not like Mrs. Stallworth's lemon-scented pure castile soap bar she'd borrowed two days ago. Now she smelled unwashed, unkempt, and *unprofessorial*. And that wasn't even a word.

She glanced at Eddie, aware that he looked and smelled not just as bad but *worse*.

She decided to explain. "We—"

But Reverend Blake was pointing them to the kitchen. "You two want dinner? The biscuits won't take long."

At the word *biscuits*, Eddie seemed to swoon. "Thank you, sir," he sighed.

Then the pastor touched Annalee's elbow lightly.

Respectful.

But also protective?

Annalee closed her eyes, feeling them well up. *Again?*

Was that gratitude? Relief? Surprise to be touched with real regard? Or shock at how amazing and deserving that actual regard could feel? Her life, her teaching rarely provided that, and her private pep talks only lifted her so far.

Or was she embarrassed that maybe Mrs. Stallworth actually could be right—that the small things in life always matter most. In the simple, small hours of life. In work, play, prayer. In first meeting an actual man? Or, in fact, in everything.

She refused to sort the barrage of feelings now. Instead, she attempted to pat down her hair, wipe the mud off her face, but her sticker-sore hand hurt too much.

She gave Reverend Blake a modest glance, half-laughing in spite of herself. "Is there a washroom?"

"It's all ready for you," Reverend Blake said, pointing to some stairs. Then he reached down, started to touch her arm again, but pulled his hand back. "I guess we'll have a lot to talk over," he finally said. His sparkling eyes suddenly looked serious.

"Well . . . just a few things." She gave him a wry but grateful smile. "But if it's okay . . . ?" She pointed toward the stairs.

"Of course!" He winked at Eddie. "Hear that, buddy? Supper's a-calling. Let's eat."

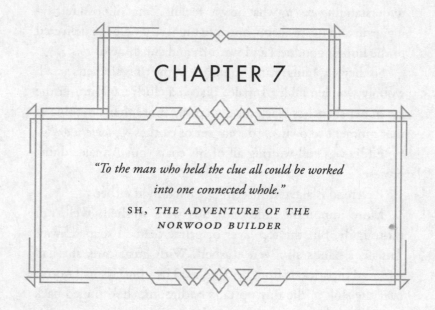

CHAPTER 7

*"To the man who held the clue all could be worked
into one connected whole."*

SH, *THE ADVENTURE OF THE
NORWOOD BUILDER*

THE MEAL WAS PLAIN, HOT, AND HONEST. Chicken and dumplings in a stew. Buttermilk biscuits and butter. Canned peaches. Hot coffee. "Home-cooked food," Reverend Blake said, "thanks to the boardinghouse lady next door. She cooks for me. Cleans, too." He sounded almost apologetic. Embarrassed? Annalee couldn't tell. But she felt grateful beyond words for food and shelter.

Still, she blinked. What about old Reverend Blake? Dead? Buried? Alive and thriving? Moved away? Nope, she'd ask about him later. For now, *let me just enjoy this.*

And Eddie? He sat on one side of a small table, his eyes almost wet with gratitude—waiting for Reverend Blake to dish up the bowls. Annalee smiled at Eddie across the table, understanding *exactly* what he was feeling. That out of a terrifying, evil, and unspeakably horrible night, they'd been delivered to the honest goodness and warmth and sunshine of *this*.

So they sat, hungry and humbled, at the tiny kitchen's small, wobbly wooden table. Annalee placed a cloth napkin over the lap of her shapeless black skirt, wanting more than anything at that moment to own *one* decent set of clothes—*please, Lord?*

Eddie was still wearing all of his coats, but Annalee didn't protest.

Reverend Blake didn't seem bothered by it either.

More important, Eddie's hands were washed. Well, not thoroughly. But the top layer of grime seemed soaped away. Annalee's hands also were washed. With great care, she had removed the stickers from her fingers. Then in the small mirror over the sink in the tiny upstairs bathroom, she'd pulled back her wild curls into a kind of topknot. Splashed hot, running water on her face. Allowed a wry smile at herself in the mirror. Thinking what Mrs. Stallworth would say to her now. *"Girl, pinch your cheeks! And twirl yourself some spit curls!"*

But for now, it seemed enough to feel cleaned off and grateful to eat. In that way, Annalee sat straighter in her seat at the little table. She closed her eyes, her mind not sharp but relaxed, listening to the sounds of the little house. The rhythms of a handsome young preacher preparing to share his dinner. She knew this moment of peace for her and for Eddie couldn't last, not in the middle of trying to figure out her own father's murder. But she was determined not to worry about that right now.

Maybe that's why neither she nor Eddie seemed worried by the other obvious thing:

Reverend Blake had a slight limp.

Just a hint, but a limp nevertheless.

Annalee noticed it right away. She was sure Eddie did, too. Because as they rushed from the car, following Reverend Blake into the house, the pastor favored one knee as they took the path to the house, then into the house—and now *around* the kitchen. So his faint limp was obvious.

But ironic. It made him look stronger, tough . . . solid? Thus Eddie didn't hesitate when he opened his mouth to ask:

"You injured in the war, sir?"

Annalee glanced up, not sure how Reverend Blake would react. But he didn't skip a beat. He kept dishing chicken and dumplings into the bowls, his broad, strong back to the table.

"Yep. Shrapnel. But could've been much worse." He turned to Eddie. "I was with the 369th. One biscuit or two?"

"The Harlem Hellfighters?" Annalee asked.

"Two biscuits sounds great." Eddie looked at Annalee, but she didn't protest. "Two sounds great, sir. Thank you, sir."

Annalee nodded at Eddie's manners. But Eddie couldn't stop. He had another question for Reverend Blake about that gait.

"That's something, sir. France. I read about the 369th."

Reverend Blake stayed silent for a moment. "You followed the war, son?"

"No, I was a little kid."

"Good thing," Reverend Blake said, smiling.

Eddie went on. "But I had a paper route last summer. I'd look over the leftover papers—still telling stories about the war and battles and stuff." He frowned. "Seems like war is awfully hard."

"It's no picnic, son," Reverend Blake said. "But believe it or not, some things may be harder."

"What kind of things?"

Reverend Blake moved to the table, carrying a bowl piled high with meat and corn. Two biscuits sitting on top. "This enough to get you started?"

Eddie reached up for the steaming hot dish, his eyes wide. "Holy cow. I mean, thank you, sir."

"Now, how about we say grace?"

"Oh! Sure, let's—" Annalee started to agree.

But Reverend Blake had laid his hands on their shoulders. Annalee held her breath, closing her eyes, surprised at her reaction to the strong warmth of him. She held still, not wanting to pull away, yet aware of *not* pulling away. But Reverend Blake didn't seem to notice. He blessed the food. Acknowledged the hands that prepared it. Blessed God for providing it. He prayed naturally, simply. Even in a kitchen, still wearing his dark suit and a preacher's collar, he looked comfortable in his own skin, with himself.

He turned to Annalee. "Your bowl's on the way, Professor."

She thanked him, wanting to know how he prayed so easily— not to show good manners, but because he meant it. "Don't wait for me—" she started to say to Eddie.

But Eddie was already spoon-deep into his meal. Elbows flying. Eyes closed. Chewing and gulping and swallowing all at once. Annalee thought about asking him to slow down, to use his obvious good manners, but not on this night. Some meals, she knew, are meant to be devoured headfirst. Eddie was doing just that, his war questions put on hold. His manners, too.

That left Annalee to ponder the appeal of Reverend Blake— well, she assumed some women might find him appealing. She was determined not to bother that he was, in fact, drop-dead appealing—and possibly a war hero too. But probably he was more? And now this hero, who was more, was serving her chicken-dumpling stew?

"Can I ask—what did you do in the war?" She spooned into her bowl.

Reverend Blake was silent for a moment, turned back to the stove. "How's your stew?"

She took a bite, aware her war question was off-limits for some reason. So she dropped it, spooned up her food, enjoying every bite. "Does your neighbor lady cook this good all the time?"

"Have some more. Let me top you off."

She accepted, looking around gratefully at his modest but pleasing kitchen. A Sears calendar on the wall showed today's date circled. December 7. Her name—*Annalee Spain*—was written in the square under it.

Annalee gazed at her name, not sure what to think, but liking Reverend Blake's plain but solid handwriting spelling who she was.

Eddie, slurping heartily, had emptied his bowl, so accepted more.

She kept looking at the calendar, hanging nicely over a shelf holding a small radio. She then closed her eyes a minute, feeling her fatigue. But she opened them as Reverend Blake pulled up a wooden stool to the small table and sat down, right between her and Eddie.

She lifted her fork, ready to finish eating, but he felt *so close*. Their shoulders almost touched, his knee briefly touching hers when he stretched his legs out under the table. She took another deep breath, let it out slowly, quietly. But he didn't seem to notice. Instead, he was already spoon-deep in his stew.

"Hm . . . that's really good." He swiped the sides of his bowl with a biscuit. But he noticed Annalee watching him, so he got up to get a napkin for himself, grinning as he passed another one to Eddie and one to her.

If he was embarrassed to be eating with such gusto before a female stranger, it didn't show. He gave her a sly grin, smacking a bit. So she grinned back, wanting so bad to smack a little herself, but hearing Mrs. Stallworth loud and clear. *"Girl, don't you dare."* She did wipe the side of half her bowl with a piece of biscuit, smiling to herself, thinking about the college faculty in Chicago and what they'd say to her about *that*. She stuffed the piece of biscuit in her mouth, chewed, and swallowed sort of ladylike. Her good meal over.

He smiled. "Food okay?"

She nodded.

"One test down," he said. "I didn't know what to expect from 'the Colored Professor.' I thought you'd make me debate the finer points of systematic theology."

She laughed. "Not likely. I'm just . . . just me. My daddy was a cowboy. Part-time at that. So we aren't fancy." She looked down. "Well, it's just me now. Sounds funny to say that, but it's just me. And I'm not fancy."

He searched her face. "You look like Colorado."

She blinked. Nobody had ever told her anything like that or mentioned her looks one way or the other—except Mrs. Stallworth. Well, businessmen on Chicago streetcars made untoward remarks to her. Mrs. Stallworth explained why. *"You look like a ripe peach, ready for picking. Just ignore them."* But here she couldn't ignore Reverend Blake, not sitting right in his house, at his kitchen table, gobbling down his food and grateful for every bite.

She shifted in her chair. "I'm not too sure how I look. I guess I've been gone from home too long."

He held her gaze again, smiled at her. "Well, I'm glad you're back."

She looked away. *Why is he saying these things?* She longed to reply in a clever way. *C'mon, Colored Professor.* But she came up empty, so she said an ordinary thing—"You're welcome"—which made no sense.

Maybe she really was in shock. Her head still zinged. Her hand felt better but looked angry. Besides, for all her bravado tonight, she felt sure of only one thing: she looked like a raving disaster. But he didn't seem to think so? Feeling off-kilter, she changed the subject.

"Reverend Blake, may I ask you a totally frivolous question?"

"Sure . . . frivolous," he said, still chewing. "Here's to more of it."

"When you were a little boy growing up, did you ever hear the fairy tale . . . the one about the three bears who ate all the porridge?"

Eddie looked up. "Excuse me, Professor, it wasn't the bears who ate the porridge . . ."

Annalee frowned. He was right. "I forgot that. Of course it wasn't the bears. It was the little girl."

Reverend Blake nodded. "Right, frivolous Goldilocks."

"Yes, the frivolous little girl," Annalee said. "She broke into the bears' house—"

"Excuse me, Professor, she didn't break in. They left the door unlocked."

She looked at Eddie again, thought about what he said, considered that she was just trying to use a lighthearted fairy tale to get to the punch line—"and she ate it *all* up"—to say how much she enjoyed Reverend Blake's delicious dinner.

Instead, she believed, Eddie had just given her a clue. The first piece in the puzzle of solving a murder. Perhaps.

Eddie yawned, covering his mouth, his teeth—his eyes growing heavy. But Annalee suddenly felt wide-awake.

She straightened in her chair. "I know you're tired, Eddie, but please say that again."

Eddie rubbed his eyes. "They left the door unlocked. The bears. That's how Goldilocks got inside."

As Eddie yawned again, Annalee turned to Reverend Blake. "I have something to tell you. About what happened tonight. About why I didn't meet you in the terminal. And why Eddie is with me."

"I was waiting for that." Reverend Blake pushed back his bowl. "But let me get those pesky stickers out of your hand."

"My hand's fine. I can clear the dishes if you can show Eddie where to bed down." She paused. "I mean, if that's okay. I'm not assuming we can stay here tonight." She was trying to stay on track, show decent manners, to not get ahead of herself and certainly not him. "But after that, Reverend Blake, we have to talk. If you have time . . ."

He searched her eyes. "Sure, but would you call me Jack—?"

She felt herself blush.

"That's what . . . friends call me."

"Then *Jack* it is. But if I agree, you know what that means?"

"Yes, but why don't you tell me."

"You have to call me Annalee."

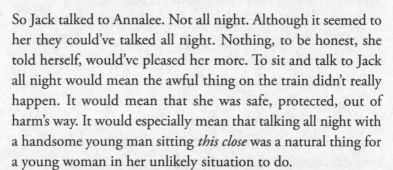

So Jack talked to Annalee. Not all night. Although it seemed to her they could've talked all night. Nothing, to be honest, she told herself, would've pleased her more. To sit and talk to Jack all night would mean the awful thing on the train didn't really happen. It would mean that she was safe, protected, out of harm's way. It would especially mean that talking all night with a handsome young man sitting *this close* was a natural thing for a young woman in her unlikely situation to do.

But sitting across from Jack Blake couldn't mean any of that. Not yet. Instead, for now, Eddie was finally asleep upstairs after a too-quick hot bath, bedded down in a spare bedroom, overcoats and all. He'd asked Annalee to sit with him until he fell asleep. Of course, she told him yes. It seemed the least she could do. In fact, when she reached across the covers and held Eddie's hand, he gripped it tight, still holding on after he fell asleep.

Still, it seemed odd. Before tonight, she'd only seen Eddie once. Now she owed him her life. Even more amazing, he'd been willing to save it.

Now, with the house silent, she'd pushed all that aside. Jack waited at the kitchen table with two cups of steaming black coffee, never mind it was almost midnight. He sat down opposite her, his jacket now off, white shirtsleeves turned up at the forearms. Giving her a look, he pushed her cup across the table.

She glanced back, accepted the cup. The coffee was bitter and black. He didn't take cream. So she wouldn't either. Not tonight. Not a good night for indulgence or distractions or creamy coffee. Jack seemed to understand.

"Guess I'm eager to hear. Where do you want to start?"

"I guess with the other Reverend Blake," she said. "What happened to him? I'm hoping he didn't pass away."

"My uncle? No, he's too ornery to die, and I don't blame him. If I live well and long, I pray I'm too ornery to die before my time too. I hope you'll allow me to say that."

"You're allowed. And his wife?"

"My aunt Jessie? The two of them moved back to New York—that's where our family lives. When I came out to help them move and preached a few times, the bishop asked me to consider coming back here. To take over at the church."

"Out to the wild, wild West."

"Considering one or two of the chief members weren't too happy about an East Coast stranger like me taking over, it's been more than wild. But after France and, well, the war—and getting ordained two years ago—I said why not? I was up for a new adventure."

"But how'd you know your choice was right?"

"I didn't. You make a choice by faith." He laughed. "Hey, you've got me preaching."

She laughed too but didn't tell him she hadn't gone to hear a single sermon preached in the past year. But she promised herself to go to hear him. She gave him a smile.

"I'd love to see New York."

"No place like it. But I prayed for *new* territory."

"You had a plan?"

"Nope, I pounded heaven. Begged like crazy to find a place with clear air and a fresh start. Something not, you know . . . frivolous. Some place open. Brave people. Like those folks in France."

"Where'd you serve? Can I ask?"

"In mud . . ." He squinted. "Up to my neck in trenches, watching folks die, on the front line. We recaptured Séchault, held another town called Challerange, the railroad junction there too."

She listened, intrigued by the sound of the French names. "It sounds . . . far away."

"But people are people. And they needed help. They didn't care who we were." He shook his head. "War—didn't mean to talk about all of this."

"I shouldn't have asked."

"Most people here don't know all that happened." He shifted his chair. "Can we talk about something else?"

"I understand." But she didn't. Not really. Who can know of another's life? Or even understand every corner of one's own? She pointed to his cup. "More coffee?"

He didn't reply, squinted a second.

"It wasn't fighting those Germans. That wasn't the hard part. It was battling our own Army—their propaganda against us, printed in 'official' French—saying *soldat noir*, Black soldiers are dangerous. *Villains*. Rough customers. Stay away from us. But the French people didn't buy it."

Good for them, she thought. "They sound smart—"

"And clever. We loved their art, their food, their style. They loved our jazz, our marching, our joy. We sang, whistled, and played our songs through every mile of that war. Then we fought together—"

"Then you had fellowship."

"A lot of it!" He laughed. "So we fought like crazy for those people. And for the people back home. Those German soldiers didn't understand it. They printed their own propaganda trying to get us to join them. But like the French said, we were hell-fighters. Too stubborn to back down."

She tilted her head, studying him. "Are you a hero, Jack?" *A wrong question?* She wasn't sure.

"Never thought about it." He got up, poured them more coffee. "God decides things in the end."

"God . . . decides." She twisted her mouth. "Will God *ever* decide for us?" She shook her head. "Don't answer that question."

"Okay, Habakkuk."

"What?" She laughed, letting him call her the complaining Bible prophet. *"How long, O Lord!"* But now she pushed away her cup, looked at him soberly.

"Jack, why'd you call me back to Denver?"

"To help you . . . to help all of us. Five Points. Our messed-up city. When I came to Denver and heard about your father, a church member, and nobody working to solve his murder—"

"Not an accident," Annalee said.

"Hardly. The third one this year."

"What?"

"Third in this neighborhood, anyway. First in my church. Three innocent men gone."

Annalee frowned, thinking.

"Killed in the same way? Like my daddy?"

"I don't think so." Jack drank from his cup. "But there is something else. You've heard of this, well, Invisible Empire."

"We saw them tonight. A big march through downtown."

"That's why I sent you the telegram. I'd seen good people threatened and disappear . . . and die. Houses bombed or burned up."

"'The house is burning.'" She quoted the telegram he'd sent her.

"'But I have the key.' Your daddy always said that when I greeted him at church. 'How's it going, Brother Spain?' 'The house is burning, Pastor, but I got the key.' Then I received this."

He reached into his back pocket, pulled out a polished brass key, placed it on the table between the two of them. Annalee picked it up, turned it over. Rubbed her fingers over its filigree bow—admiring its smooth, gold-colored edges.

"What does this open? It looks old."

"The mortuary found it. It was in your dad's shirt pocket."

"What . . . ?" The key dropped from Annalee's hand, fell to the table, spun around. It came to a rest pointing at the calendar. "My father had *this*?"

"You don't recognize it, do you? I'm not surprised. It didn't fit the door to the place where he was living."

Annalee's eyes teared up again, seeing her daddy's river shack in her mind.

"Or the trunk under his bed."

She wiped at her eyes. Jack reacted.

"I'm sorry. I should've waited to tell you. The mortuary mailed it a few weeks back. They'd never sent it to you. Some oversight. I was shocked to get it."

"I'm okay," she said. But in fact, she hated hearing about her daddy in the past tense. She picked up the key again, took a deep breath, slowly exhaled. She asked a hard question:

"So you believe the key is connected to . . . to the KKK? And the Klan to my father's murder?"

"Actually, no. That's the thing. I think whoever did it wants it to *look* like the Klan was involved. You know, the Klan as the natural suspects."

"Clever."

"Same with the other killings. Especially if the newspapers are right, because thousands show up at their regular meetings—and not just your ordinary rabble-rousers but the mayor. The police chief. Cops. City councilmen. District judges. A couple of US senators—"

"The governor," she added. She'd seen that even in Chicago papers.

"*And* preachers! Some of the most influential in town. Plus, a horde of local business owners."

For a moment they both were silent, thinking on the prominent and the powerful.

"I'd sure like to know what they're so afraid of," Annalee said. "Change?"

Jack frowned. "They're afraid of being afraid. Losing control of a world they never controlled in the first place."

"But what does this have to do with my daddy and his murder? Where's the connection?"

Jack crossed his arms, looking serious. "That's what I'd like to help you figure out."

"So you sent me a telegram?"

"And you answered. I wasn't sure what you'd think, but here you are. And I'm glad."

She considered this. Jack was a soldier, a food bearer, a preacher, a pastor. A medal-winning hero. And now he would help her unravel her father's murder.

"But why? Why do you care?"

"Because murder is wrong. For everybody involved. Does it have to be any more complicated than that?"

She thought of the toy soldiers marching. "No, and I see what you mean. It's that simple."

"Yep—and that complicated. So will you let me help you?"

"Only if you know the whole story." She took a long, deep breath.

"What else is there to know?"

She gripped the key in her hand. Let herself exhale. "On the train tonight, Eddie killed a Denver police officer."

"What?"

"He was trying to save my life!"

Jack jumped from his chair. "Not that boy! A Denver cop?"

"Yes, but—"

"I thought he was just an orphan, some kid from the train you were trying to help. And now you're telling me that hungry, ragtag boy—sleeping upstairs in *this* house—killed a Denver policeman?"

Annalee sat straight in her chair, looking up at him, trying not to panic at his reaction. "I wish I could say no. But that's exactly what I'm saying." She searched his eyes. "I regret you're involved now. But it happened, and I can't change that it happened."

"So now—"

"Now I tell you the whole story."

Jack nodded. He sat down again, pulling his chair back to the table but not away from her.

It seemed to her, in fact, that he pushed it closer.

CHAPTER 8

"Precisely."

SH, *THE ADVENTURE OF*
THE REIGATE SQUIRE

So SHE TOLD HIM all that happened.

"You jumped off a *moving train?*"

"It wasn't going *that* fast." Annalee shifted in her chair. "I stirred up this trouble. But tomorrow I want us to see somebody, get some answers." She shifted again. "If you'll go, that is. You know the district attorney? Well, the former district attorney? Sidney Castle. Daddy did odd jobs for him sometimes."

"You have a plan?"

"Not much." She gripped her father's key. "But I have a hunch. And maybe Mr. Castle can help us."

"Castle . . . Sidney Castle. I know him. If anybody can help—"

He stopped. A noise.

"Somebody's in your backyard," Annalee whispered. Her heart skipped. She gripped the key tighter. "They're killers, Jack."

He shoved back his chair to stand. "Not tonight." He flipped the light switch next to the back door. Instantly light flooded the yard. Jack yanked open the door, stood at his full height, held his muscular arm across the door.

"Hey!" He bolted to the side porch, down to the small yard.

Annalee followed. "You saw somebody?"

"By the fence." He moved to the alley, walked the border of the yard. "They're already gone. Maybe just kids." But he didn't sound convinced. He grabbed her good hand. "Let me get you back inside."

She felt his strong touch and her poor stomach did a double flip. She nodded, avoiding his eyes. She'd never felt so young, ill-prepared, and frivolous in her entire life. Jack was only a year or two older at most, but compared to him and what he'd been through in France—in a real war—she felt utterly out of her depth. Yep, frivolous. A downright novice. Naive and rattled and a novice, especially about real life. *Are you a detective? No,* she thought. *You're a silly young woman who should've stayed in Chicago arguing over corn bread with Mrs. Stallworth. You don't even know how to hold a man's hand.* Still she didn't pull away, feeling herself sighing at every step.

Back inside, Jack secured the door, shutting it firmly. He clicked the dead bolt, then turned to her. "I know what you're going to say."

"I'm sorry—" she started.

"This isn't your fault. *I* invited you to this."

"I've brought trouble to your house."

"Trouble was already here."

"But a dead policeman?"

"Your daddy was killed a whole year before that. Aren't you ready to find out who did it? And why?"

Annalee pressed her mouth. She *was* inexperienced, ill-prepared, more frivolous than she cared to admit. But for her daddy and Eddie and herself, and now for Jack, she had to make a choice. So she stood tall and made it.

"I've been ready since I jumped off that train."

They talked a while longer. Jack listening closely. Asking smart questions. Giving good answers.

Then to sleep. Or the details of sleep, both agreeing, her shyly, on who slept where. Eddie was still in the spare room. Jack would sleep on the sofa in the first-floor parlor. Then Annalee accepted Jack's hospitality and agreed to sleep in his big bed upstairs. Yes, in Jack's bedroom. Well, it was his uncle and aunt's former room. But now it was his room. And his bed.

And Mrs. Stallworth would flip twice double time if she knew.

So Annalee tiptoed lightly in the space, not wanting to disturb anybody or anything, especially her own thoughts. She knew she was stretching the bounds of propriety by daring even to look at Jack's bed, let alone lie down in it and sleep. But without her purse, her luggage, her coat, her satchel, Mrs. Stallworth's hard-earned two dollars, where else was she going to spend the night?

Still she kept asking: *Is this wrong?* She asked knowing she wasn't just talking to herself. She was talking to God. Impossible.

She was angry at God. *Or I've tried to be angry.* But now? *Lord, I'm praying?*

After a whole year of not praying, now here she was, sitting down on the side of a man's bed, holding her breath, thinking God must be laughing to beat the band, sighing and saying, *"You ready to pray? Well, Professor, how about starting right here. Just pray away."*

She let her eyes take in the room, ran a trembling hand across the soft, clean, quilted spread, letting her heart get steady—daring to take in the whole of where she'd landed. Thus she realized she wasn't only seeing Jack's tallboy and dresser, his Army boots in the corner, his starched white shirts hanging on the back of his bedroom door, his well-thumbed Bible on the nightstand, his window seat crammed with Army magazines and books and the week's newspapers, his leather-seated rocking chair, as much as she was looking at how God makes us. Piece by deliberate piece.

And, Lord, I like what I see.

Then it happened again. *Thank you for bringing me here to this house, to this room, to this man's room, to his bed.* But that couldn't possibly be a prayer.

Even if it was, she was too exhausted to try to weigh it— too worn-out to pick up Jack's Bible, thumb through it to the apostle's pleading call: *"Continue in prayer."* But do you know what *devote means, Mrs. Stallworth?*

Annalee smiled to herself, hearing her landlady's voice.

"I'm waiting."

Well, in the Greek—

"Lord, have mercy."

So Edna Stallworth indulged me, Annalee thought, *letting me run my mouth, professing about Greek this and Latin that, lecturing her. So prayer is where God meets us—if we stay strong in it. On purpose.*

Mrs. Stallworth would clean off her eyeglasses, give her a look. *"Well, if you don't mind my mentioning it, I already told you that."*

Annalee smiled, already missing their talks, but knowing that after her daddy died, she'd neglected such things. Just walked away from it all, God included. Therefore, she hadn't been really living—because she hadn't been praying or walking and talking—with God?

She rolled her eyes. *Blasted theology.*

She laced her daddy's key onto a piece of ribbon she found on Jack's aunt's dresser and placed it on Jack's chair. Then she tiptoed across the hall to his modest, plain bathroom, ran the bath, filling the claw-foot tub close to the top.

With a sigh, she slipped out of her clothes, piled her hair higher on her head, then stepped into the tub, letting herself sink down forever and a day into the deep, endless healing goodness of warm clean water. Then there it was again.

I'm so grateful.

She sank deeper.

I almost died tonight. And I was terrified. And angry. And freezing cold. But you were merciful. A little child—who I don't even know—saved my life. And now he needs me, God, and I don't have one clue what to do about that.

But I don't have to think about that now. I just have to lay here and soak it all away. Soak away aches. Grime. Worry. Fear.

Well, maybe not all the fear. Not yet.

But I can soak away the shame.

Yes, thank you, God? That I don't feel shame about crawling tonight into a handsome man's bed for sleep. Because I need the rest. Eddie, too—in the spare room now, sleeping his little eyes out. And Jack needs sweet rest too. Grant him your strength and good peace.

For we, your children all, I thank you. And I'm not kidding.

Yes, bless us all.

One by one.

The living and the dead.

Amen.

Back in the bedroom, she found a nightdress Jack had laid out on the rocking chair. His aunt Jessie's. It was cotton, plain, modest. A high collar. She held it up, considering its size. Not too big. Not too small. Just right.

A fairy-tale nightdress.

And they left the door unlocked. That's how Goldilocks got inside.

Because the key unlocks something that *isn't* locked?

Too much to ponder. Instead, she turned off the lamp on the nightstand. For one slight moment, she was naked. Bare, vulnerable, goose bumps threatening. Then she slipped on the nightdress. It smelled lightly of lavender—clean and simple and flowery, the scent of nighttime and sleep. She climbed into the bed, snuggled under the covers, letting herself breathe, listening to the quiet, inhaling the scent of flowers and clean air and bedding dried in High Plains sunshine. Thus, she thought of her daddy.

And of Eddie.
Then of Jack.
She asked God please to bless Mrs. Stallworth.
Then darkness.
Eyes heavy.
Then sleep.

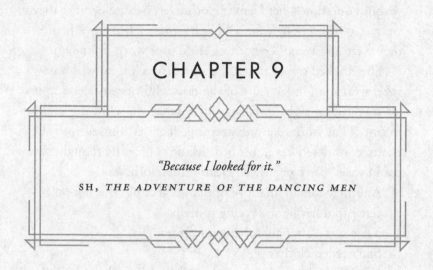

CHAPTER 9

"Because I looked for it."

SH, *THE ADVENTURE OF THE DANCING MEN*

AN HOUR AFTER DAWN, Annalee snapped open her eyes to blinding sunshine. She stretched an endless minute, then crawled out of bed to gaze out of Jack's bedroom window.

Mercy alive.

She smiled at a sky she could understand. Clear and dry, cold and blue. If she never stepped foot in gloomy, freezing, sleeting, hard-luck Chicago again, she wouldn't miss it. *Well, I think that's right.* She took in deep, deep breaths. Grateful for it all, but also breathing in a surprise.

On the window seat, Jack had laid out a small pile of clothing—two stylish dresses, a navy-blue suit, a couple of other choices, each bearing a hand-sewn label inside the collar: *First Lady Jessie Blake.* His New York City aunt was a fashion plate, without question—her Denver clothes left behind because they weren't stylish enough for a big-city move? But for Annalee, they were a heaven, like nothing she'd ever worn or known.

She reached out to touch the suit, struggling to weigh how she'd wear it or, in fact, any of the downright pretty items. She let out a long sigh, understanding what the clothing really meant. That while she was sleeping, Jack let himself into the room, considered her in his bed. Made choices he thought she could wear. *Good grief.* Even clean underclothes.

Another woman might've fumed, objecting. But her practical sense told her he was trying to help.

They were, after all, solving a murder.

She needed clothes.

Out of the neat pile, she selected the slim navy-blue suit. Its silky blouse matching the fine silk lining of the suit. Black lace around the high collar. After freshening up in the bathroom, Annalee slipped on the prim suit and sighed. Humbly. The feel of it was exquisite. The fine hand of the cloth, the good fit, expert tailoring, shorter skirt. *But not too short, Mrs. Stallworth.*

She grabbed the beribboned key, slipped it around her neck, sliding it under the lovely jacket. She wriggled into Aunt Jessie's black, high-heeled, T-strap pumps, adding on a slim black coat and black leather gloves. Fairy-tale clothes. Not frivolous. She stole a glance in the mirror on her way downstairs. But she stopped in her tracks and gasped.

Good gracious. Her reflection seemed a dream. She felt her eyes well up. *Goodness, look at me.* She looked *professional.* Finally. Even more, she felt—what? Looked after. By Eddie? Mrs. Stallworth? God? Now, indeed, by Jack? He'd conjured up fine clothing he'd taken care to select precisely for her—yes, well-made and excellent clothing. So Jack was saying she was well-made and excellent too? Her sore hand felt better, so she let herself rub the nub of the coat, marveling at what she, Annalee Spain, was actually wearing on her amazed twenty-four-year-old body.

Thus, her next thought: *I am alive.* She'd never once written about the theology of *that.* A tear fell then—because in some beautiful and wonderful way, being alive meant more than everything. She'd come to Denver to solve a crime. But now she stood at a fancy mirror, looking like a young woman who could solve it, as if she belonged—to the world. Even to God? Belonged, perhaps, even to Jack? But she shook her head. *Don't get ahead of yourself, Professor.*

Downstairs, she took the last step into Jack's kitchen, eager to see him, searching for words to thank him, but ran instead smack into Jack's frowning, seething Saturday morning visitor. A bubble burst.

"It's Brother Prince," Jack said to her.

She recognized him immediately. Slater Prince, chief trustee of Mount Moriah AME Church and prominent Five Points restaurateur. Unofficially, as everybody knew, Prince was the mayor's man in Denver—the mayor's *colored* man, that is. He delivered votes. Bridled hotheads. Kept the peace. In turn, the mayor delivered favors to Prince and his beloved neighborhood. So Prince was well-positioned, pious, and *purposefully* political. Upper-crust *and* uppity. He looked the part in his expensive, fur-trimmed chesterfield, his barbered silvery haircut, his van-dyke beard clipped close to his jutting jaw.

Self-made and self-important, Prince wouldn't give the time of day to a plain, rumpled man like Annalee's grizzled daddy.

She gave Prince a curt nod. "Sir, it's been a while. I'm Annalee Spain—Joe Spain's daughter." She offered her feeling-better hand.

He didn't take it. Nor, however, did he seem surprised to see her. He looked her over, frowned at her fancy borrowed clothes, turned up his nose at her having come down from an upstairs bedroom.

He turned to Jack. "It's Saturday morning, early, and one of your neighbors complained—said a young woman spent the night in the house with you. Alone with you, that is, in the parsonage of Mount Moriah AME *Church*."

"Professor Spain got in from Chicago last night. She needed lodging," Jack said. He took a step closer to Annalee.

"Got in on the Chicago Limited?" Prince asked, as if he didn't know.

"Got in at nine. Lovely trip." She didn't blink. "At any rate, Reverend Blake and I have a business meeting across town." She moved closer then to Jack, felt Jack slip closer still to her. They stood practically arm in arm now, showing a determined unity.

Prince took a quick breath. "I'm a busy man, Blake, and this is a complex town. Personally, I don't care *what* you're doing and with whom. But not in this house. Because you don't own this house. The church built it. The church owns it. The trustees run it, and what happens here doesn't just affect you. It affects all of us in Five Points and—"

Prince stopped midsentence. They all turned. A rumble on the stairs, then in the hallway.

"Eddie?" Annalee's breath caught. She tried to talk to his eyes. *Go back upstairs. Please.*

But Eddie was yawning and rubbing his eyes, wearing his coats, dragging barefoot into the kitchen, mumbling, "Did I miss breakfast?"

Slater Prince stiffened. His thick face reddened. "What in the devil is this?"

Annalee put her arm around Eddie's shoulders. "*This?* A boy who needed a place to sleep last night. An orphan. And since a little Christian charity is always a good thing, I'm proud to introduce Eddie Brown."

Prince's eyes showed . . . disbelief? Shock?

"Eddie Brown—"

Eddie, looking confused, decided to add, "I'm Eddie Brown *Junior*." He offered his half-washed hand.

Slater Prince pushed past Eddie, whirled at the doorway, pointing at Jack. His hand shook. "I'll be back here tonight, Reverend. I expect to find this house—and this household—in proper order." He turned up his expensive collar. "And God help you if it's not."

"Help? 'My help cometh—'" Jack started to say.

But Prince slammed out of the house, the back door rocking on its hinges.

Jack ignored the insult. "Breakfast is ready, son." He pointed to the table.

"Does that man know my dad?"

"*That* man?" Jack frowned. "That man knows more than he *shouldn't*—"

"And not enough of what he should."

"Amen," Jack said under his breath, helping set up a quick

breakfast—cold biscuits, peach jam, scalding coffee. Annalee grabbed napkins.

Then Jack lifted an easy send-off prayer. "Grant us your composure, Lord." After a pause, he finished it simply: "And help us today to tell the truth. Find it, too."

"Amen." Annalee's voice was a whisper.

With that, they'd head across town to the home of Sidney Castle, the city's former district attorney. Annalee had asked Jack to drive them there. She wanted to meet this powerful man her daddy had done odd jobs for.

"You'll like Castle." He grabbed his keys. "He tries to do right."

"Well, that's one person in this town."

Outside, the neighborhood was still sleeping, barely stirring. At the end of the block, a man walked a small dog. Jack cranked the car's throaty engine. A curtain pulled back from a window. The complaining neighbor? The local gossip?

Annalee hoped not. But *somebody* was getting an eyeful—a young, unfamiliar, bright-eyed, shapely woman wearing First Lady Jessie's fine clothes and a scruffy white boy in a bunch of coats, both climbing into the new preacher's car after sashaying out of his house on a Saturday morning. Enough to keep tongues wagging for weeks.

Annalee scooted over next to Jack.

"How'd you sleep?" He held her gaze.

"Thank you." She smiled at him, knowing that wasn't really an answer. But he seemed to understand. Prince's visit was unnerving. At barely 9 a.m. on a winter Saturday, after sleeping in Jack's house, in his bed, wearing his hand-selected clothes, she felt a bit scandalous, even if she'd slept as sound and pure as a baby. Saying more would ruin it.

But Eddie was full of talk. He ran his almost-clean hand over the car's dash. "What's this, sir, a Buick?"

"Yep. My uncle's touring car—1923. Brand-new this year."

Eddie looked harder at the dash. "Fancy car." His voice dropped. He gave Annalee an awkward look.

"For a Methodist preacher, you mean?" Jack said. He laughed. They all did.

Jack pressed on the throttle, winking at Annalee. The car shot off down Welton.

No question, she thought, Jack was a good driver.

"You like to drive," she shouted over the wind noise.

"What about you?" he shouted back.

She laughed. "I've never driven a car in my life."

"Well, we'll put that on your list—solve a murder, learn to drive." He looked her way, smiled at her again, his eyes sparkling. She felt her stomach flutter as she smiled back.

"I'll make a note," she said.

Sidney Castle's house was a hefty, three-story brick manse in a swank part of town, not far from the classy new Chessman Park. "A fair-minded guy," Jack told Annalee. "Smart, too."

Annalee knew him only from secondhand news and gossip from Denver. Out of office only six months. Still in hot water for cracking down on crooked cops, bad judges, organized crime, the Klan. He barely survived a nasty recall fight. But he was sticking to his guns, like the war hero he was supposed to be. In fact, everybody still called him Colonel and still called him the DA, even his enemies.

"He may not have time to see us." Jack steered the car onto the half-circle drive in front of Castle's house and parked.

"He's my first stop anyway," Annalee said. "Daddy did odd jobs for him sometimes."

"I can wait," Jack said. "Until you talk to him."

Annalee thought a moment. "No, let's all go, please. Eddie too."

A wisp-thin Negro maid in a starched gray-and-white uniform answered the bell. Irritated frown. Barely opening the door.

"No! Deliveries in the back." She scowled. Then she saw Jack. "Oh! Reverend Blake." Suddenly congenial, she gave a pat to her tight marcel wave, a tiny diamond ring sparkling on her ring finger, right hand. She opened the door a bit wider. "You have to give a girl warning, Pastor. You're out early." She looked over his shoulder, her dark eyes taking in Eddie, staring down Annalee.

Jack struggled for a name. "Yes, Sister . . . Sister *Bernita*?" He looked at Annalee. Looked awkward. "You remember Professor Spain—" He stepped aside, starting to acknowledge Annalee. But the maid seemed to know who Annalee was. Just as Annalee knew who she was. They were two young Black women, exactly the same age—members of the same church, both raised in the same neighborhood. And both possibly with an eye for the new pastor? The handsome new pastor?

A voice interrupted them.

"*Bernita.* You're in the way. What is it now?"

A small-boned woman with immense blue eyes and a long white housecoat pushed past Bernita, filled the doorway. She squinted in the sunshine glare. "You're late. You said delivery by seven thirty." She looked at a slim gold wristwatch. "It's after nine. Bring the flowers around back."

Composed, Annalee didn't react but stepped closer. "I'm not the flower man, Mrs. Castle. I'm with Reverend Blake, here to see the Colonel on business."

"Reverend Blake?" She squinted at Jack, pulled her house-coat tighter.

"Yes, ma'am," Annalee said. "From Five Points. Mount Moriah AME."

"You came to my church with your husband for our vet-erans' lunch," Jack said. "He gave the keynote address."

"Oh, the Negro church. Well, yes." She turned to her maid, still ignoring Annalee. "Please go on, Bernita." She pretended not to see Bernita glare, looked past Jack's shoulder at Eddie and Annalee, frowning. "Now, Reverend, you say you have business with the Colonel . . . this morning? Goodness, it's cold."

Annalee stepped forward. "We should've telephoned ahead, Mrs. Castle—"

"I can see you're busy," Jack said. "Ten minutes. Fifteen if he can spare it."

"No bother," the woman cut both off, annoyed. "But I've been waiting all morning for the blasted florist for my mother's birthday party tonight, and my Christmas parties start next week, and now the locksmith is late—"

"The locksmith?" Annalee broke in but didn't regret her words.

Mrs. Castle narrowed her eyes. "Excuse me."

"I beg your pardon." Annalee extended her hand. "I'm . . . an acquaintance of Reverend Blake's. I should've introduced myself." She gestured to Eddie. "This is my young friend Eddie Brown."

The woman looked past Annalee's hand, gaping at Eddie— and at Eddie's coats.

Jack cut in. "You mentioned a locksmith, Mrs. Castle, and my friend here has—"

"Nothing really." Annalee hoped Jack could read her eyes. Because she didn't like how this was going. Nor was she sure yet about this woman. Friend? Foe?

But she also didn't like waiting outside on the cold porch— with her hat in hand, so to speak—trying to explain herself. But *not* liking the waiting felt like its own problem, too.

Annalee took a breath, shook off the feeling, played down the talk about the key. "It's just a problem with a . . . lock," she said.

"Well," Mrs. Castle said, still looking at Eddie. "I'm missing a key myself, the one that fits my . . . Well, I'm rambling. I suppose you can come on in and wait. I'm going in circles this morning."

The woman pulled the big front door wide-open to a white marble floor. She looked down at Eddie's boots.

Eddie covered his teeth. "I can take my boots off, ma'am." He leaned down to untie them.

"Just come in. All of you. Please. So I can close this door." She gestured them into a small sitting room to the right of the foyer. "Wait here. This'll keep you out of harm's way."

She flashed half a smile, but no joy in it. Her eyes were cold.

Flat. Distant. "Goodness, where *is* that florist? I've got to help Bernita for tonight. The Colonel will be back shortly. I'll tell him you're here. Have a seat."

She looked back at them. "Did you hear me? I said *sit*."

Annalee straightened her back. "I hear fine," she said.

"Thank you," Jack added.

CHAPTER 10

"There is nothing like first hand evidence."

SH, *A STUDY IN SCARLET*

So Annalee stood to wait for Sidney Castle. Stood to get her bearings, to get composed, to feel less like this was a place she shouldn't be.

Jack stood, too, Eddie right with him. All of them on their feet, walking about the delicate room, up to the window, then the door, opposite the bookshelf, facing the big Biedermeier secretary. Annalee knew the name from her dean. His favorite furniture style.

Mrs. Castle's Biedermeier, meantime, was loaded, top to bottom, with a collection of windup toys.

"Music boxes, I think," Annalee said to Eddie. She walked to the desk, stood next to him, peered in the locked, glass-fronted case. The toys were all sizes, some ornamental and gilt, some plain and wooden. A few, apparently needing repairs, sat in a small box on the floor. Others sat in places of honor——front and center on the glass shelves.

For a minute, Annalee stared at the lock, guessing what size key might open it.

Eddie eyed a tiny airplane. "If we wind it up . . . ," he said, reaching for the case.

"It's locked." Annalee was sure they had enough to worry about without breaking one of Mrs. Sidney Castle's expensive music-box toys.

Jack came up behind her, peered into the glass cabinet. "Interesting. Look at this one." He put his hand on her shoulder. She didn't move, not letting herself think about his touch. So respectful. Familiar but affirming. Why couldn't he be a scoundrel?

But he'd already moved his hand. He pointed to a doll on a high shelf. Set in a vignette, the fancy-dress doll wore a tall magician's hat, a magic wand in her tiny left hand. The doll stood behind a table bearing tiny playing cards.

"Look at the sign over her head. It says—"

"Card Trick."

"Colonel! Good morning." Jack crossed the marble floor, extending his hand to the distinguished, well-dressed older man.

"You've got a good eye, Sergeant." Castle glanced at Annalee. "Card Trick is the rarest toy of the bunch. That little doll cost me a small fortune." He shook Jack's hand. Nodded at Annalee.

She nodded back, watching.

"Does she move, sir?" Eddie piped in, determined to see a toy in action. "Like the airplane?"

Sidney Castle laughed, gave a long look at Eddie. "For an

alert young man like you, yes. She moves." He walked to the cabinet. "The airplane, too." He dug a key chain out of his waistcoat.

"Please, Mr. Castle." Annalee said, giving Eddie a look. "We're here with a few questions. Don't want to bother you—"

"Do I look bothered?"

Annalee thought he did. He also looked worried. But he selected a small gold key on his chain. It was smaller than the one found on her daddy, Annalee noticed.

Castle unlocked the cabinet. Stood on his tiptoes. "Mrs. Castle's been collecting these since our honeymoon, for our future grandchildren . . . which, of course, we still don't have. Sergeant Blake, reach up to that top shelf. Grab me that over-priced doll. The airplane, too. Let's show this boy how they go."

"Thank you, sir!" Eddie grinned. He watched Jack bring down the windup doll and the airplane, bend down and set the toys on the marble floor.

"Which one first, young man?" Castle asked.

"The airplane, please, sir?" Eddie dropped to his knees at Jack's feet. So did Sidney Castle. Annalee did, too.

Castle reached for the painted airplane. His hands shook a little, Annalee noticed. But he wound up the plane, set it back down. As little gold-colored propellers began to turn, a musical tune played.

She realized she knew the song.

"'I'm al-ways chas-ing rain-bows—'" Jack started to sing it. Not horribly, but a solid baritone. She smiled at him. He grinned, charming.

"'Watch-ing clouds drift-ing by—'" Eddie broke into song too. *Beautiful voice.* A clear choirboy's soprano.

"Eddie," Annalee said. All of them were looking at Eddie now.

"Goodness, young man!" Castle said.

"Million-dollar voice," Jack added. "Where'd you get those pipes?"

Eddie covered his mouth. "From my father," he said through his scarf.

"Your father . . . ?" Castle said, frowning.

At that, Annalee stood. "Mr. Castle, we need to tell you something." She gestured to Eddie. "Jack and I. It involves Eddie."

Sidney Castle nodded. Pushed up off his knees. "Yes, I believe that you do, Professor."

"So you know who she is," Jack said. He didn't look surprised.

"For better or worse, Sergeant Blake, there's precious little in this town that I *don't* know about."

"Somebody told you what happened?" Annalee asked.

Castle hiked an eyebrow. "I know you took a train from Chicago. Then disappeared en route. But why don't you fill me in on all of it."

Annalee cleared her throat. "Somebody tried to kill me. First, my father," she added.

"The cowboy." He looked at Annalee. "Not enough evidence to prosecute, I understand."

"Yes," she said. "But somebody tried to kill me last night."

"I see. Murder attempts seem to be going around these parts. But thank the good Lord, you're still alive."

"Because of Eddie," Annalee said.

"The boy?" Castle looked surprised.

She told him about their train escapade. He reacted like Jack.

"You jumped off a *moving train*?"

"It wasn't going that fast," Jack said, giving Annalee a look.

"Besides," she added, "with a dead Denver policeman in our wake, our options for escape were slim."

"A dead policeman. That's curious," Castle said. "Because no policemen have been reported dead or missing in Denver or anywhere else on the Front Range. I'd know about it if there were."

"But he was wearing a policeman's watch. I saw the engraving myself," Annalee said. *"Denver Police Department."*

Eddie listened, watching Annalee closely, finally looked up at Castle. "Will they take me to jail, sir?"

"Without a body, son—and without a missing person—we don't have a crime. But even with a body, it wouldn't be easy to make a case against you." As he spoke, Castle looked distracted. He looked at Jack. At Annalee. At the airplane. Looked at Card Trick.

He picked up Card Trick. "Watch this," he said. He turned the key on the table in front of the doll. The music started. "The Blue Danube" waltz. The little doll's left hand moved its wand over a tiny velvet box. The right hand lifted the box cover, revealing two tiny playing cards. Then another pass with the wand. This time, when the doll lifted the box cover, the playing cards were gone.

"Wow." Eddie was intrigued. "How'd she do that?"

Then another pass of the wand. The playing cards reappeared. Another pass of the wand. The playing cards were gone again.

The waltz music continued for a while. Finally the song slowed to a halt. The sleight of hand ended.

Annalee looked at Mr. Castle. "My daddy did odd jobs for you last year, didn't he, sir?"

"A few."

"Did he ever ask you for help? Or let on he was in trouble?"

"Was he hiding something, you mean?" Castle asked.

"I'm not sure what I mean. I know things aren't always as they seem."

"And dead men wearing DPD watches aren't always Denver policemen."

"But why try to kill *me*, Mr. Castle? Not to mention kill my father?"

"When you find that out, you'll know who *and* why. But for now, you have a more immediate worry, Professor."

"How to stay alive," Jack said.

"By staying out of sight," Castle added.

Annalee thought a moment. "Or I could do the simple thing," she said, "and hide in plain view."

"What are you saying?" Jack looked worried.

"Nothing complicated. I mean taking the kind of job that renders a colored woman completely invisible—more or less."

Jack looked hard at Annalee. "You can't be serious."

"If it means getting close to a murderer, I've never been *more* serious."

Castle looked at them. "I don't follow. What are you talking about, Professor Spain?"

"She's talking about working as a housemaid. You know, *in service*. As a domestic."

"You, Professor? Probably been done before. But still clever."

"Not so clever, actually," Annalee said. "What I *don't* know never ceases to amaze me."

"Your humility is a virtue," Castle said.

"For what, sir?" Eddie asked.

Castle looked at Annalee. "For an undercover job."

"A *live-in* job," Annalee said. "Besides, it's decent work. I need a place to stay. I need a job. And I need a way to hide."

"While you find the killer," Eddie chimed in. "Like a detective!"

She winked at him. "Yes, why not?"

"Then you're hired," Castle said.

"*What?*"

"Cool!" Eddie said.

"Hold up!" Jack frowned.

"Mr. Castle, I wasn't suggesting that you take me on *here*," Annalee said.

"Not me. My wife, Elizabeth. She's up to her neck with her big Christmas parties. Plus a birthday party tonight for her mother. Keeps begging me to bring on more help. Says Bernita can't handle everything."

"Bernita?" Annalee said.

"Yes, you know Bernita? Her mother worked for my wife's family for years. Elizabeth keeps her on. No good reason why. But, well, that's not important." Castle shifted on the fancy sofa. "What matters, Professor, is that between now and Christmas Eve—working undercover as my wife's new maid—you'll encounter pretty much everybody in Denver—well, everybody with a secret motive to kill anybody."

"In *this* house?" Annalee looked skeptical.

"Denver's a curious town." Castle picked up one of the music boxes. "The best and the worst, the good and the evil, all seem to move in the same circles."

"But you're talking about high-class folks," Jack said. "Well, so-called high-class folks."

Castle nodded, his face sober. "They're the ones with the biggest secrets."

"And the most to lose," Annalee said.

Castle set down the toy. "I mentioned that once to your dad. He was a good listener—like many handymen—letting me talk while he worked." He sighed. "Goodness, your father's murder was regrettable. Throwing an old cowboy off a moving train? To hide some dirty secret?"

Annalee nodded but tried to think.

Jack cut in. "Especially since secrets always have a way of coming out. As a pastor, I know that better than most."

Annalee searched Jack's face, then turned to Castle. "You think somebody will talk, don't you?"

"If they don't choke first, while eating the Christmas pudding."

Annalee raised a brow, tried to guess Castle's motivation. His offer was generous but curious. Why, she thought, was he so keen to expect a murderer right in his house? And how could that possibly be tied to her?

She didn't know . . . *But I'm going to find out.*

"My answer is yes."

"Yes, you'll come aboard?"

"The sooner the better."

"Start tonight—the birthday party. Your trial run."

"Yeah," said Eddie, reaching for the airplane. "What could happen at a birthday party!"

Annalee looked at Jack. "Eddie has a point. What could

be dangerous about scrubbing floors and serving meals? What colored woman doesn't know how to do *that*?"

"A precious few."

But her stomach turned a bit. She looked at Sidney Castle, watching his eyes, searching for some small and hidden reason to go with this plan. Then, as he turned, she saw it—an almost-imperceptible flash of *fear*.

Castle was afraid. About something he was hiding? Or suspected? And he was willing to use her as bait?

But she nodded at him.

"Then that settles it." Castle stood up. "I'll tell Elizabeth. You can move in today."

"But what about me?" Eddie frowned.

"He's trying to find his father, sir," Jack said. "Eddie Brown Senior."

"Eddie *Brown* . . . ?"

"This morning I called the new orphanage—"

"*No!*" Eddie bounded from the floor, gripped Annalee's arm. Just as the window over the fancy sofa shattered, glass flying. Annalee jumped. They all did.

Castle grabbed his head. Staggered. "*What?*"

"A gunshot!" Eddie yelled. He turned to the window.

"Watch the glass!" Annalee pulled Eddie back. She turned to Castle. "Good gracious! You're bleeding! Let me help."

An angry slash under the district attorney's left eye dripped a red line to his chin. Jack dug in his pockets for a handkerchief.

Castle pushed away help.

Until they heard the scream.

"*Elizabeth!*" Sidney Castle yelled his wife's name. She screamed again.

Castle ignored his eye, pushing past everybody, rushing out of the small room into the foyer. Annalee, Jack, and Eddie followed in a crush after him. Castle shoved through double swinging doors into a butler's pantry, past another small hall-way, and finally into a soaring, tall kitchen.

At a wide sink, Bernita stood scraping skins off of raw potatoes.

Castle hollered, *"Bernita!"*

She jumped but kept scraping. "Yes, sir?"

"Where's Mrs. Castle?"

"On the back porch . . . I guess. You're bleeding, sir." But Bernita was looking at Annalee, at Jack.

Annalee tried to read her eyes. Something was registering. Anger? Sadness? Shame? Annalee wasn't sure. *But I'm going to find out.*

Castle was steaming. "You *guess*? Didn't you hear her calling for help?"

Bernita looked back at Annalee—still trying to figure her out?—then started to speak.

But Castle didn't wait for an answer. He pushed past a long wooden table, knocking over potatoes, and pulled open a heavy wooden back door. Frigid air poured into the kitchen.

But the winter cold wasn't as chilling as the confounding sight on Sidney Castle's screened back porch.

Crouching beside a stack of summer lawn chairs, Elizabeth Castle moaned and rocked at the sight of a foot-long bowie knife—Eddie's rusty, bloodied blade—standing straight up in the Castles' pine picnic table.

"Professor." Eddie clasped her arm, trembling.

"Good Lord," Annalee whispered.

"God, have mercy," Jack said, reaching for Annalee, for Eddie.

"Yes. Well, I'd call it a not-so-subtle warning," Castle said. He peered closer at the knife, shook his head. He cursed. Apologized for cursing. Straightening, he reached for his wife, helping her to her feet. She grabbed his arms, moaning.

"Oh, Sidney! I am so *tired* of this!" She eyed him hard, shaking her head. "And just look at your eye!" She reached for his face but instead rubbed her own, streaked now with tears.

Castle steadied her but seemed preoccupied. "Some nasty joke. I'll figure it out," he said, thinking out loud, turning from his wife, leaving her wobbling.

So Annalee stepped forward, helped Elizabeth Castle sit down in a lawn chair. The woman glanced at Annalee for half a second as if trying to remember where she'd seen her.

Annalee moved back, giving her space, then turned back to Castle. "Is this about the Klan?"

"Who else?" Mrs. Castle sneered.

Castle reached for his wife's hand, rubbed it absentmindedly.

"The Colorado Klan are stupid and noisy, Elizabeth," Castle said. "But so far, they aren't killers—as far as I know."

Eddie stepped forward. His voice shaking. "But that's *my* knife, sir," he said, pointing to the bowie.

Castle reacted.

Jack, too. Both looked at Annalee.

"He's right," she said. "The one from the—" But she stopped. Because as she said it, a tiny piece of the murder puzzle tried to dislodge, struggled to fall into place.

Annalee looked at Castle, seeing his dark despair, his obvious worry over something, his seeming intention to be on the right side of the law in all matters, to get now to the bottom of not one murder—but two? Her dad's and the man on the train? Then something came to Annalee.

"Do you know the Lazy K Ranch?"

He looked at Annalee oddly. "Yes, of course."

"I've got to get out there."

"That's Lent Montgomery's place," Castle said, glancing at his wife, mentioning another name Annalee had heard from her father. But as he said it, he looked uncomfortable. Elizabeth Castle did too, glancing down a moment. Sidney Castle shifted his weight.

Annalee watched this but kept her focus. "My daddy's last job was there. Somehow, I don't know, I'm sure there's some connection. And this knife . . . the gunshot. Those were warnings to me. I feel certain."

Castle frowned but held his tongue.

Annalee turned to Jack. "I hate to ask, but can you drive me out there—to the Lazy K?"

"A real ranch!" Eddie whispered. "Wow, can I go?"

Jack looked at his watch. "I have to finish my sermon for tomorrow. And I've got some repairs to check on in the sanctuary. What about your new job? Aren't you working for Colonel Castle now?"

Elizabeth Castle looked up. "Working for *Sidney*?" She eyed Annalee hard.

Castle jumped to explain. "Actually, Miss Annalee here will be working for you, sweetheart."

"Working for *me*?" She frowned. "*Miss* Annalee? That's your name?"

"Yes, Annalee Spain—" Castle turned to introduce her, but Annalee interrupted.

"I know this is awkward, ma'am," she said. "But your husband told Reverend Blake here you needed extra help with the house—so we agreed I'd start this afternoon. For your party tonight."

Elizabeth Castle gave Annalee a slow once-over. "I don't know what's going on here. But be here at 3 p.m. sharp. Bernita has extra uniforms." She looked Annalee over one more time, then pushed past her husband to enter the house, slamming the door.

"Welcome to the Castle household," Castle said. He didn't smile. He pulled a frayed tarp from a stack of lawn chairs and threw it over the bloody knife, wiped his hands on his well-tailored pants.

"My head is telling me to stop your little crime-fighting plan, Miss—*Annalee*. But I'm going with my gut, Professor. I just pray I don't regret letting an amateur use my house to find a killer. So I'll see you back here at three." He turned to enter the house but swung back. "And please figure out what to do about the boy!"

Jack checked his watch again. "I can get us back here by—"

"*Us?*" Eddie edged closer to Annalee. "So I really can go with you? To the ranch?"

"Right, and we better get moving."

"*Thanks*, Professor."

"Then something else," she said to Jack.

"I think I already know."

"That's right. You have to teach me to drive."

CHAPTER 11

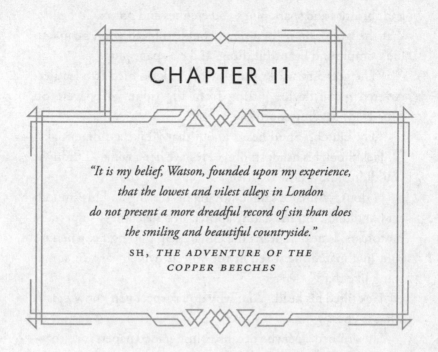

*"It is my belief, Watson, founded upon my experience,
that the lowest and vilest alleys in London
do not present a more dreadful record of sin than does
the smiling and beautiful countryside."*

SH, *THE ADVENTURE OF THE
COPPER BEECHES*

THE HOUR-LONG RIDE to the Lazy K Ranch was bumpy, sunny, and cold.

Eddie asked to sit by the door. That put Annalee in the middle, next to Jack, making her feel self-conscious again. Like a girl. Again. But she was aware of liking the feeling anyway. Especially after the sadness of seeing Eddie's bloody knife again. It had killed a man, and murder was just so unspeakable. Why weren't people more dismayed by such horror, more intent to keep each other alive?

She looked at Jack. He was talking about cars. A lovely Saturday morning topic, and she was glad for it—to feel his arm next to hers, to listen to him go on about car parts and tires and throttles and spark plugs and engines and power. To believe that the world, on its best days, could still lead good people to life's simple and beautiful things. Like a spark plug.

"The gearshift works the clutch." Jack pointed to a leather-covered metal device jutting from the floor. They were on Broadway, heading south out of town.

"The clutch." She'd heard about that. "Like a differential?"

Jack shook his head, smiling. He gave her a wink. "I thought you didn't know how to drive."

"I don't," Annalee said, enjoying his teasing and his smooth car handling. "But my daddy appreciated machines—especially motorcars. I mean, doesn't the clutch help the engine, when it's running, match the speed of the wheels, which vary, or something like that?"

Jack tilted his head. "And why do I suspect you know *exactly* what it does?"

She grinned. "Maybe because I just graded papers on a theologian's theory. In fact, I heard his famous lecture about it—on 'The Prayer Theology of the Motorcar.'"

Jack laughed. "And what was *that* about?"

Annalee was silent for a minute, watching a tiny white cloud form—then break up—over the mountains to the west.

"Actually, it was about ambition. And how God's ambition for us is always better than our own. Especially regarding our life with him, starting with our prayers."

"Oh, so we need to gear down our prayer wheels to his engine—or gear them up—or something like that?"

"You sure you weren't at that lecture?" she teased him back.

"No, but I can guess where you sat—right in the front row."

"Best seat in the house—right on the center aisle, if you

must be precise." She fell silent, thinking that the best seat in the house hadn't yielded her a God life that was settled, confident, or steady.

Not like Jack's seemed to be.

He was grinning again now, grabbing the clutch, shifting down hard. He punched the throttle, giving the Buick more gas. The car shot ahead. "Here we go, Eddie!"

Eddie whooped, leaning his head out the window opening.

But Annalee didn't pull Eddie back. Instead, she looked at Jack, thinking how comforting it felt—after the confusion of a hard morning, with its screaming and broken glass and ugly bowie knife—for Eddie and her to be riding along with him. Even in a fast car. Even if she didn't know exactly where they'd end up.

Which made her think of her daddy.

The ache in her heart stayed fresh but always hidden—and she didn't want it to fade. For all its hurt, it reminded her of the joy her daddy had brought her during their happy times. Their good times. Their normal times.

The few times.

But the bad times always loomed larger, and far more frequent, like a dark-gray winter. With lightning and hard rain. Like the time when she was nine, with the lead part in the Easter play at their Five Points church. Her daddy promised her a new dress. *For Easter, baby! Something pretty. With yellow in it. You be beautiful in yellow, baby girl.*

So she walked downtown by herself. Nine years old. Gazed with longing in every store window. She turned the corner of California at Sixteenth Street and stared at a store display—at a dream. Her fantasy dress. In yellow. The most beautiful dress she'd ever seen in her entire life. She ran all the way home. *"Daddy! Daddy! Daddy!"*

Hoping.

Believing.

Crying when, once again, he forgot. She wore the too-small hand-me-down she'd worn all year. Her daddy stumbled into the Easter play at the end, half-drunk, apologizing, carrying a load of fluffy yellow baby chicks in a crate for all the children. He asked her for forgiveness. Such a flawed man at his worst, such a beautiful man at his best. So hard to make any sense of it, unless she focused on the good times. The normal times.

The few times.

She watched Jack drive, looking out at the crisp blue sky, clear and full of hope—like her daddy's last year. His drinking stopped. His demons quieted. He came to Chicago afraid, he said, to ask again for forgiveness. But he knew finally that he needed to ask. *"You're my sweet girl, little bit. You don't have to forgive me. But you're like your mother. I know you will."*

He hugged her tight, like a daddy should. She didn't want to hug him back as if she loved him. But she'd always loved him. At that moment, maybe she never loved him more.

"I'll find your killer, Daddy," she whispered to herself. "I promise I'll find your killer. If it kills *me*."

But for right now, she allowed herself to feel her sorrow, like a normal daughter, even as she let forgiving eyes take in the sunny winter vista. The Front Range mountains gleamed with their icing of snow. With every mile, as they got closer to the ranch, she could see why her daddy loved working in such raw, wide-open spaces.

Out here, south of town, the land was scrubbed clean with

a plain and noble beauty. Not a single false thing about it. Nothing to hide. Nobody to please. A redeemed ground. Just like her daddy tried, at the end, to be.

The Lazy K Ranch fit that bill. Its rugged 2,800 acres stretched into an almost-endless horizon, beyond where the eye could see. The spread was weathered but regal, harsh and dry but natural and lovely—the whole of it lit, Annalee thought, like a painting rendered by the flat winter sunlight.

"So beautiful," Jack said.

She nodded, smiling at him. He held her gaze.

"Would you like to live in a place like this someday?"

"It's like a dream."

"Even better if you're wide-awake." He gave her a teasing look.

She swallowed, not sure what he meant. *Are you a detective?* If she could figure out a man, and what teasing meant, maybe she could solve a crime.

They entered the ranch on its northeastern edge. Jack steered the car under a tall, rustic gate fashioned from pine logs. The Lazy K name announced itself in carved letters burned into a wide header.

"They have horses?" Eddie searched the horizon.

"And cows. *Lots* of cows," Annalee said. "Probably more than you can count."

But for miles, they saw neither. Instead, they drove the ranch's rutted, hard road—seeing neither man nor beast. The Buick's stiff leather seat was accommodating, but the ride was hard and rough. A driver's car, Annalee thought, looking at Jack. Enjoying how much he was enjoying this drive. Thinking how much she was enjoying it with him, sitting so close to him. She felt barely older than a wide-eyed coed, with stomach butterflies. He couldn't be perfect. Nobody was. Compared to her father, the only man she'd known up close, Jack seemed steady, reliable, trustworthy. Yet that's a Boy Scout—not a man who sets a young woman's heart on fire. *Lord, have mercy.* Why was she thinking of such things? *Explain it, Mrs. Stallworth.*

She looked over at Jack. He was already looking at her.

"A penny for your thoughts," he said.

"A nickel for yours."

"There's not enough money between the two of us."

She smiled at him, confused but not bothered. "Probably not."

He turned to gaze out at the land, but his mood suddenly changed. "If something happens that's not safe here, stay close to me," he said. "Stay with me, got it?"

"I'll remember." She wasn't sure what he expected, but she repeated his warning to Eddie.

Then they crested a hill, an expansive pasture and two big barns coming into view. Black cows in large groups were feeding from huge bales of hay—their breath turning the air around them white with vapor. By the horse barn, alert horses huddled in the sun in small circles, tails together—their faces pointing out.

"There," Eddie yelled. His face went dreamy as his eyes took in the animals and the surroundings. Cowboys in long coats and big hats were busy with the livestock, adding a sentimentality to the rural winter scene. "My dad would love this."

"My dad would too," Annalee said, soaking in the scenery but wondering at the same time if such a pastoral setting could hold the secret to his murder.

A chill ran suddenly down her back at the thought of Jack's

warning. But she had to get her focus. She sat up straight, feeling her attention sharpen. "That looks like the main house."

"You want to start there?" Jack pointed to a large adobe-and-log manor, set on the highest point of the area.

"Right." But she still felt a chill.

Jack steered the car along the rutted road, taking them closer to the big adobe lodge.

A sleek black sedan was parked in the gravel yard next to the sprawling house. It looked important. The latest in a parade of bidders coming for an entire year to haggle with the owner? Except he wouldn't budge, according to Denver papers she'd read on the train, on his steep price.

"Bad timing." Jack gestured to the sleek car.

"I'm not so sure. In fact, maybe our timing is good."

Jack gunned the motor, then killed the engine, removing the keys. They piled out of the car and headed toward the front of the house—a long porch, covered at the eaves with pine garlands. Ready for Christmas?

"Somebody's opening the door," Eddie said.

It was a young Mexican girl. Barely older than Eddie. Pretty little face. Two long braids spilled over her shoulders, each tied with a blue ribbon bow. Sweet as a picture.

Except she wasn't smiling. As she crossed the threshold, striding toward them, her dark eyes looked . . . worried? Or sad? Or yes—*angry*? Indeed, she was shaking her head *no*, waving her arms—but not to welcome them. Instead, Annalee could see in her beautiful eyes exactly what the child was determined to say.

"Go away."

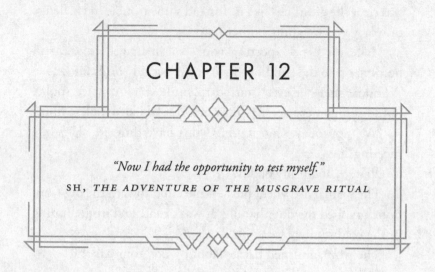

CHAPTER 12

"Now I had the opportunity to test myself."

SH, *THE ADVENTURE OF THE MUSGRAVE RITUAL*

"SOMETHING'S WRONG," Eddie said.

"Watch what you say here, Eddie." Annalee turned to Jack. "Do you know this child?"

"No, but I'd say she's a cowboy's child." He frowned. "Or maybe the cook's daughter?"

But they didn't have to guess. In that same moment, the door swung wider and a soft-faced woman in a long dress and apron, with braids like her daughter's, rushed from the house.

"Mija!" she called to the girl. *"Vente pronto!"* She grabbed the girl's shoulders, turned her away, hugged her tightly, kissed her forehead, assured her in their mother-to-daughter Spanish. *"Está bien, mija. Sí, sí, sí.* It's okay."

The woman squinted at the visitors, tried to smile—but it

was clear she didn't feel like it. Instead some trouble or challenge or worry was weighing on her hard.

"Is Señor Lent expecting you?" she managed to ask, still holding on to the child but focusing especially on Eddie.

Eddie met her eyes, started to smile. But Annalee spoke. "Mr. Montgomery doesn't know me. But I'd like to talk to him."

"*No*, not today, señorita. He won't have time. . . . He's in a meeting."

"It's . . . about my daddy."

The woman frowned, pushed the child toward the big front door, grabbed the door handle. It was ornate and iron, glinting in the cold sunlight.

The woman turned back. "About who? Your *papá*?"

"He was a cowboy!" Eddie said. "A *real* one."

Annalee pulled Eddie close, smiled at the woman. "He punched cows, wrangled horses."

The woman faced Annalee directly. "Your *papá* worked here? For Señor Lent?"

"Yes, ma'am. In fact, maybe you knew him?"

"Worked here?" she asked again. Her voice trembled. Fell to a whisper. "About a year ago, señorita?"

Annalee felt her stomach tighten, aware the tension in the woman's somber eyes was reflected in her own.

"Joe Spain. He worked here until last November . . . November 26," Annalee said, feeling afraid to breathe.

The woman searched her face and eyes. But finally she nodded. "*Sí*, I knew this cowboy, señorita—for many years."

"Tall and rugged and skinny," Annalee said.

"And very kind," the woman said. "Yes, I knew him. I knew Joe." She finally smiled. "Such a kind man. *One for the Father.*

One for the Son . . ." She made the sign of the cross, as if ready to reminisce, and offered a shy laugh.

Annalee smiled, but her voice caught. Jack grabbed for her hand.

"Take it easy," he whispered. "You okay?"

Eddie followed suit, his hand on Annalee's elbow.

"No," Annalee said, being truthful. Would she ever understand the whole truth of what she felt about her daddy? "But she remembers."

The woman reached out, touched Annalee's face for a moment. "Yes. I remember. I'm Rosita Montez and I remember. Yes, I remember him well. I can never forget Joe Spain."

"Did he get in trouble?" Annalee searched Rosita Montez's dark eyes.

"I better go inside." Rosita turned.

"Can you tell me what happened?" Annalee reached for her. *"Please."*

"It wouldn't help if I did," the woman said. "But I tell you this. He was a *good* man."

But Lent Montgomery didn't look sentimental when he burst through the doorway. "What in the *devil*, Rosita!" he growled, his voice thick and rugged like his leathery, sunburned face. Yet his prominence was evident. His jeans and khaki shirt well-worn but well-made. His silvery hair was thinning on the sides but groomed and barbered. He looked prosperous, like a man who owned 2,800 acres of prime land, ranch animals, and every perk that went with it, even if he desperately needed to sell it.

Rosita Montez, in turn, looked like a woman who knew what her boss needed—but maybe she'd stopped caring. She spoke to Montgomery in a flat voice. "You have a visitor, señor," she said, voice closed, but taking a moment to smile at Annalee.

Lent Montgomery saw the smile, glanced at Annalee. "I don't believe . . ." He sneered, stomped off the porch. "Whose car is that on my yard?" He didn't wait for an answer. "The three of you, whoever you are—" he waved his hand—"turn right around and leave. This is *private* property. Leave *now*. And, Rosita! No more interruptions!"

He swung back, but Annalee stepped in his path. "No, sir, we interrupted *her*." She planted her feet in his way, crossed her arms, met his direct look, did her best not to back down.

He narrowed his eyes. *"What?"* He whirled on Rosita. "If you don't get these people off my property *now* . . ."

"But, Señor Lent, they're here to see you," she said.

Montgomery's rough face went red. His nostrils flared wide. His next words cut the air like a scythe. "I've put up with that child and her sniffling and your moping all year. But this time you've taken me too far. Get rid of these people now!"

Rosita shook her head at him, defiant. But before Montgomery could react again, a shadow flashed across the threshold.

Everyone froze. The young man standing in the doorway commanded it. It was his look—dark, sleek, sensual, handsome, dangerous. Because he looked so young? Younger, for sure, than Annalee. Yet his well-tailored charcoal-gray "business" clothing fit him like he was grown-up royalty. Or trying like heck to look like it. A lit cigarette in a tortoiseshell holder hung off his babyish lip. He was daring and danger in one perturbing mix—both sinister and singular in his own arresting but disturbing way.

Maybe it was his face, so coldly familiar, Annalee thought. Or maybe it was his words.

"More trouble with the Mexicans?" he said to Montgomery, laughing at Rosita as if she weren't there. Then he narrowed his eyes, looking at the visitors. He spat on the ground, inhaled his cigarette, frowned behind the smoke. "And what's *this?*"

"*Nothing.* Nothing at all," Montgomery said, dismissive. "In fact, you can go on back inside. We'll finish with those blasted contracts." He turned on Rosita again. "As soon as she takes care of her *friends* and their *problem.*"

The young man narrowed his eyes again. "Problem? Look, Lent, if I'm going to do my first big business deal with you—"

"Trust me, these people don't concern you," Montgomery said.

At that, Annalee could feel Eddie shift his weight. She grabbed for his hand, just as Jack grabbed for his shoulder. But Eddie primed his mouth and dove in.

"Excuse me, but how do *you* know what concerns us?" Not quick enough, he tried to add *"sir."*

Montgomery glared at Eddie, then erupted. *"You,"* he said, turning on Annalee. "Ten seconds! Get your no-count little group of scavengers out of my yard. You two *and* the boy!"

The sleek young man watched the exchange, his youthful eyes going back to Eddie, to Jack, to Annalee. He pulled on his cigarette, peering through smoke, staying silent but still looking, studying, considering. Not missing a detail. "What a clever kid, Montgomery. Now who'd you say this is?"

Eddie pulled up to his height, prepared with pride to announce his full name.

"We didn't say," Annalee said. "Because this doesn't involve him. It's about me, Mr. Montgomery, and my father. He used to work for you."

Montgomery's eyes narrowed. "Work for me? If this is about money—"

"Hardly," Annalee said. "It's about murder."

Montgomery shifted his thick body, but the young man let his mouth form into a dark, wry smile.

"A murder, Montgomery?" he asked.

"I have no idea whatsoever what she's talking about," Montgomery began.

"Yes, Señor Lent! But you do!" Rosita interrupted. "You remember *Joe*. The best old cowboy you ever had. You said so yourself. And this is his daughter."

"What daughter?" Montgomery asked.

It was time to tell him, so Annalee did the telling.

"*This* daughter," she said, pointing to herself, her hand at her heart. Her voice broke for a moment. But she recovered, sounding resolved. "I am the daughter." She said it again. "*I* am the daughter of the murdered cowboy, Joe Spain!"

The well-cut young man sighed. A long sigh. A heavy sigh. A sigh that lasted as long as it took him to pull back the vent of his fine waistcoat—to show his hefty pistol.

Not a fancy man's gun. No pearl handle or sleek barrel. Instead, it was muscular and ugly—a .45 for certain. Probably a war gun. A Browning, Annalee thought such guns were called. A gun for enemies. So it wasn't meant to frighten. Or to protect. It was meant to kill.

Jack tensed. Eddie flinched. Rosita pressed her daughter to her body, letting out a loud "No!" But Annalee found herself smiling, looking from the fancy young man to Montgomery—thinking, *Now we're getting somewhere.*

The fancy man toyed with the pistol. Pointing it randomly. Then at her.

Her mouth went dry. The ranch owner snapped at Rosita, "Take the girl in the house!" Then he turned on the young man. "Oh no you don't, Hunter. This isn't your property yet."

Hunter? Annalee caught her breath. She'd heard that name. Or seen it. Or read about it. But where?

"Just one more contract to sign and it will be." The fancy young man—Hunter—took a drag, tossed away his cigarette.

"Unless you burn it down first." Montgomery ground out the cigarette with the sole of his boot. "Just like the rich fool people say you are."

The young man ignored Montgomery. Instead, he spoke to Jack, getting in his face. "You know this gun, don't you?"

Jack didn't blink. "A 1911 Browning. War issue."

"Then you know what it can do."

"Know it well." Jack nodded.

"Yeah," Eddie suddenly yelled. "Probably knows it better than you."

The young man laughed. Turned to Montgomery. "Oh, I like this kid. Dirty as all get-out. But smart as a whip. Aren't you, boy?"

Eddie narrowed his eyes at him. But the young man didn't laugh this time. Instead, he cocked the trigger.

Montgomery reacted. "Not on my property, Hunter."

The young man spat on the ground. "Don't worry yourself, Montgomery. In fact, your guests and I are leaving—going for a long, leisurely ride. Aren't we, Miss Spain?"

He glared at Annalee, looked at Jack. "Give the Colored Professor the key."

Jack looked hard at Annalee, hesitated, but dug it out of his pocket. He pressed it into her palm. She could feel the heat of his hand right through her glove.

The young man sneered at Annalee, gestured her to Jack's car. "Get in."

Annalee hesitated, horrified at what was happening but rejoicing, at the same time, at what it meant. That surely this man knew things. Who she was. Probably who killed her father—and why. Indeed, he might have committed the murder himself.

Because with great purpose, he was pointing the ugly weapon right at her. But not like in a Sherlock story—this was happening too soon. Her villain revealed already?

"I said move."

And such a nasty voice, Annalee thought. A desperate voice. The voice of a spoiled, rich rogue who would make mistakes. She aimed for the passenger side, but he stopped her. "*No. Driver's side!*"

Driver's side?

She flashed a look at Jack. He met her eyes. No reaction. But she could read him. *Just do what he says.*

With intent she walked behind the car, edged to the driver's door, opened it, climbed in, slammed the door. Making the point: *I am in the car.*

The young man turned, glared. "Nice and easy, little professor."

She glared back. Dropped the key in her lap. Put her hands on the steering wheel—as if she knew what to *do* with a steering wheel. Her stance must've been right. The young man turned to Eddie.

"Now *you*," he said, aiming the gun at Eddie's head, making Annalee flinch. *If he hurts that boy* . . . But gratefully Eddie held his tongue, scrambling to the car, climbed in beside Annalee. His breathing was fast, agitated.

So he, too, was horrified.

But she could tell he was excited, too. They were on track to find a killer. And maybe, at the same time, to find Eddie's father? At this ranch, indeed, at this point, nothing would surprise her.

"Stay cool," she whispered to Eddie.

"Got it," he whispered back.

Montgomery snapped at the gunman, "Now what?"

"*Now?* That's easy. The three of us take a little drive up in the hills." The young man spat again, his voice ugly and dark.

Jack reacted, starting to protest.

"Don't even try." Hunter leveled the gun at Jack, walked behind him. With one hand, the man pulled a long silk kerchief from his pocket, jerked Jack's hands behind his back, ordered Montgomery to tie Jack's wrists together with a tight, hard knot.

"I don't like this," Montgomery grumbled but tied the knot.

With a shove, the man Hunter pushed Jack to his knees. Jack stifled a groan.

"*For the love of* . . . ," Montgomery shouted. "Just hurry up with it!"

But Hunter ignored them both. Instead, he strode to the car, climbed in the passenger side, growling at Annalee.

"Start her up, *Miss Spain*."

She looked at the dash of the car, surveying the dials and gadgets, recognizing only a small clock. *Half past one. And Castle said be back by three, which clearly won't happen. But why am I worrying about time now?*

"I said *start her up!*"

"With the *key*," Eddie whispered, prompting her. He nodded to her lap.

Annalee picked up the key. Looked for a slot. Found a likely place. Then with a slow, deliberate breath, she placed the key in the slot. A slow turn. A prayer for the engine to fire.

But nothing.

She let out a deep breath. Ran her eyes over the dash again, *closely*—needing it in the most desperate of ways to tell her what to do.

"*Hey*, you're aggravating me. I said *get going.*"

Eddie nudged her. *What?* She couldn't read him. So taking a chance, Eddie reached for a lever himself, but she saw it too. *The starter switch?* She hadn't paid attention when Jack cranked up the car. Or when he was driving. *Too busy running my mouth*, she thought—and about what? *The Prayer Theology of the Motorcar.*

But wait, what did the lecturer say?

Such a wiry, wild-haired little man. Almost lost behind the big lectern, save for his hair and his spring-loaded little voice. She could hear him chirping now. "*The driver doesn't drive the car; the engine does.* It *does the work! But even the best engine doesn't go without a* starter. *In the church, too many try to ignite their faith without pouring in fuel—without praying—without flipping the switch!*" He pounded the podium.

Annalee flipped the switch. The engine sprang to life.

Just as the whole wide world exploded into a ball of blazing fire.

"*What the . . . ?*" Montgomery's face went white.

Hunter sprang from the car, the door swinging wide behind him.

"The *house!*" he yelled at Montgomery.

Montgomery whirled, faced the big adobe—where a riot of black smoke and orange flames boiled from a ragged split in a corner wall.

"*Fire!*" Montgomery shouted. He was running toward the front door when—*kaboom*—another explosion rocked the house. The ground shook.

"Jack! *Rosita!*" Annalee screamed, struggling to see through the smoke and confusion. But thick black billows raged, flames soaring from a cavernous hole in the side of the house.

"*Ring the bell!*" Montgomery yelled at the young gunman, who hesitated and turned back to the car.

Montgomery erupted. "*Hunter.* Ring the blasted bell!" Montgomery pointed to an old school bell and rope, hanging from an iron hook plastered to the opposite corner of the house.

The young man looked back at the car again. He cursed, ran for the bell, grabbed the rope, started pulling like crazy. Loud peals split the air.

Eddie and Annalee both grabbed at their ears.

"*Annalee!*"

It was Jack, scrambling into the car, yelling at her over the din. His eyes showed pain, anger, panic.

"Let's go!"

"What?"

"Get moving!"

"*What?*"

"He said *drive*!" Eddie reached across Jack, yanked the door closed behind him.

"I know! But—"

"Hit the gas!" Jack yelled.

Annalee looked at the floorboard. At *three* pedals?

"No! Steering wheel—left side!" Jack screamed. "Hit the lever, up! Now!"

Steering wheel? Lord, have mercy! She hit the lever.

"Now, *throttle*!" Jack yelled. "Steering wheel, right!" He yelled at her again, clearly not worrying about sounding nice. "Annalee, listen to me! Drive!"

"*I am!*" she screamed back. But who was she fooling? Sure, she'd heard a theological lecture on the prayer secrets of automobiles. She'd heard her daddy describe the inner workings of motorcars. But she didn't know *one thing* about how to drive a dang car. And a maniac ringing a bell was pointing a gun at their backs, clearly intending to kill them.

The gun fired.

Annalee gripped the steering wheel, slammed her foot on the right pedal. The car shuddered, stopped.

The bullet missed.

Yes.

But the engine coughed hard. Halted and died.

"*No!*"

Jack shook his head. "Listen to me, Annalee. *Neutral!*"

She could hardly hear him. The bell kept ringing, clanging, ringing.

"Put it in *neutral*!" Eddie yelled.

Neutral?

Annalee blinked hard, thinking, *Oh, what a lovely theological dissertation I could write about all of this if only I could get the blasted car moving.*

Eddie grabbed the gearshift stick. *"Neutral!"* he shouted.

"I heard you!"

"Well, start it . . . again!" Jack yelled.

Annalee thought she might laugh. Because this was *crazy.* Still, she flicked the starter switch again. The engine fired. The steering wheel business.

"Left foot to the floor!" Jack screamed. "Clutch pedal!"

Okay, Annalee thought. Left foot down.

"Now, throttle! On the steering wheel! Now let off the clutch . . . left foot . . . *slowly!"*

Left? Right? Steering wheel? She couldn't *think.* But there wasn't *time.* There was only dead silence. Because the bell ringing stopped.

Eddie groaned. "He's coming!"

Just as Montgomery shrieked: *"Hunter,* I'll shoot you myself if you don't keep ringing that bell!" Montgomery was coughing, gagging. Running in and out of the smoke-filled house. Dragging rugs and pictures and furniture out. But where was Rosita?

The bell started again. At the pealing, from out in the far pasture, cowhands were running up the hill toward the house. From another pasture, wranglers on horseback galloped hard, drawn by the noise and chaos and smoke.

"Eddie!" Jack yelled. "Put it in first!"

Eddie jerked the stick.

Jack again. "Annalee! Give it more gas . . . *slowly."*

No clutch? More gas? It didn't make sense. But the car was *moving.* She gave it more gas. The car kept moving. Wheels turning. Engine running. Inching across the gravel yard. Still moving. Forward. The engine *so close* to dying. But she gave it some gas, let off the clutch completely. A little lurching.

Another gunshot. A bullet hit metal, ricocheted off the windshield frame. Without thinking, Annalee punched the throttle.

"Go to *second*, Eddie! Annalee! Clutch in . . . release *slowly* . . . now, *gas*! That's right, *throttle*!"

The car bumped along the gravel yard. Now through the gated fence surrounding the house. Now onto the hard road.

"That's it! Annalee, that's it!"

"Which way?" she yelled, looking left, toward the cowhands—and back toward town.

"Go right!" Jack yelled. "Away from the wranglers!"

Annalee swung the steering wheel. The car's back end fishtailed for a second. Eddie shifted down. She did her foot dance with the pedals.

Then . . . the car was heading straight.

And . . .

Impossible.

Incredible.

Indescribable.

I'm driving.

"Good Lord!" she hollered.

So *this* was the theology of the automobile.

She gripped the steering wheel and marveled at the going and rumbling and swaying and shaking and gliding of Jack Blake's car—that yes, if you engaged the starter, punched the throttle, hit the right pedals, the engine's power would propel you forward, progressively and surely and simply. But not without a starter.

Do that and driving is wonderful and sublime, far more marvelous than what lay behind them—the burning south end of Lent Montgomery's sprawling adobe home, not to mention the nasty end of the man Hunter's ugly gun.

In fact, the only thing better was the sight of what was hiding in a draw at the bottom of the next rise.

"Rosita!" Eddie screamed.

Thank you, Jesus.

"*Señora* to you," Annalee said, thankful to see her.

"Yeah." Eddie laughed. "But there she is! And her little girl, too!" He leaned across Jack, waving out the window, shouting, "Señora! *Señora!* It's us! Get in!"

"Slow her down!" Jack yelled over Eddie's screams. "And, *Eddie*—get my penknife in my vest pocket. Cut this silk rag off my wrists."

So Annalee had to shift down by herself. So she just did it.

From third gear, she dropped to second, her footwork still right. Then from second down to first. More foot dancing and switching. Then finally she brought the car to a smooth enough stop. Engine still running.

"That's it!" Jack said.

She was in neutral.

"Oh, *gracias a Dios!*" Rosita shouted, letting Jack help her scramble into the back seat with her wide-eyed, beautiful child. Then immediately both of them started pointing to a side, obtuse path.

"No, turn! *Here*, señorita!" the girl shouted.

"Yes, right *here*," Rosita said. "It's a shortcut!"

Annalee swung the car onto the rutted, bumpy path. She was shifting like crazy, with Jack calling the cues. For a while, the ground wasn't a road but a bumpy, weed-choked path.

But in no time, they found themselves on a farm road leading them back to town.

With Annalee driving.

"I knew you could do it!" Jack said. But he frowned. "Except—"

"Oh, don't tell me!"

He shook his head but laughed.

"I don't have a driver's license!" Annalee said. "I don't even know how to get one."

"But, señorita, it doesn't matter. Because you saved us. You saved our lives," Rosita said.

"No, that wasn't me," Annalee said, looking over at Jack.

"You are right," Rosita said. "I think that was God."

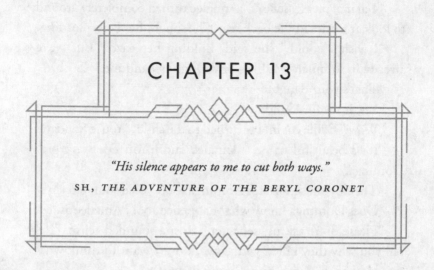

CHAPTER 13

"His silence appears to me to cut both ways."

SH, *THE ADVENTURE OF THE BERYL CORONET*

ON THE MAIN ROAD, Jack drove them back to Denver. Eddie in the middle. Annalee on the window, still shocked—and thrilled—that she had managed to drive a car.

On the way into town, Rosita explained what had happened. That when she saw the man's ugly pistol, she knew only some wild distraction would save them all. Then on the way to the kitchen, she literally stumbled over two big cans of gasoline—purchased by Montgomery the day before to fuel a new tractor he'd bought for the ranch.

It was the girl's idea, they told Annalee, to put one can on the hot cookstove—where it would soon explode—with the second can nearby, just for backup. Then hightail it out of there.

"We should've left that place a year ago—when your father was killed," Rosita said. "Too many evil things at this ranch."

"Tell me, please, señora." Annalee turned completely around to look at Rosita in the back seat. She sought her eyes, pleading.

"I wish I could," she said, holding her gaze. "But we're already in so much trouble—my Dominga and me."

"That's your daughter's name?"

"Yes, it means 'Sunday.'"

"Wow!" Eddie cut in. He turned to the child. "You're Sunday!"

"It's a beautiful name," Annalee said. "You're a brave girl, Dominga."

"Thank you, señorita." Dominga's soft voice sounded shy.

"Does Dominga know what happened too?" Annalee asked.

"Please don't ask us, señorita." Rosita sounded tense. "If I tell you why they killed your *papá*, I don't want to think what would happen to me, but also my daughter."

Annalee understood. Still she argued for information. "There was a key. Found in my father's shirt pocket. What could it unlock? Can you think of anything?"

Rosita blinked. Said no. "I'm really sorry, señorita. But I can't say any more." She reached across the car seat for her daughter, enveloping her into sheltering arms. "I've already done and said enough."

"And we're grateful."

The woman asked Jack to drop them off at a truck farmer's place just outside of town. At the gate, she thanked them profusely. But as Rosita knocked on the window and pushed her Dominga into the ramshackle little house, she didn't turn around to wave.

Now it was a quarter past six. Night already falling. The three of them were late, especially for Sidney Castle's party.

"How much longer?" Annalee asked Jack.

He looked at his watch. "I'm guessing by seven. But first, we'll stop somewhere for gas. I'll make it quick."

Annalee didn't protest. No point. Besides, it had been her grand idea to drive to the big ranch in the first place.

Yet, despite everything that *hadn't* gone right this afternoon, she realized she still felt excited. Because if her hunch was right, the Castles' dinner tonight would shed more light on their little ranch episode. She was certain of it. Something about Sidney Castle's look, when she asked him about the Lazy K, told her he knew or suspected *something*.

Perhaps that Lent Montgomery would be invited to Elizabeth Castle's dinner? Or that fancy gunman Hunter? Now wouldn't *that* be something.

She was eager for the dinner party to start. But first things first.

She turned to Eddie, still sitting between. "So are you ready?" She held her breath.

He looked away. "I really don't want to go to that orphanage, Professor."

"I can't keep you with me."

"I know. But if you think about it, Professor, I'm really not an orphan anymore."

"Oh, Eddie." She knew where he was going with this.

"Because, Professor, I have *you* now," he said. "And the reverend—"

"Well, yes. You do," she said. But they all knew the problem. A fresh-mouthed white boy couldn't live with Black people. Not in Denver. Not now. Not this year. Not ever, until the stupid laws got changed. Even if they tried to get around them, with the way Eddie spouted off without thinking—especially after what happened this afternoon—he'd give them *all* away. Himself included.

Eddie stared out the front windshield, watched the sky grow dark.

"It's a brand-new home for boys, son," Jack finally said.

"Yes, sir." He turned to Jack, looking somber. "But the three of us! We're solving crime, like detectives."

"Except we haven't solved anything yet," Annalee said.

"I know, but what if I don't like the home? What if the teachers are mean? And stingy? And all we get to eat is cold porridge?"

Annalee laughed.

Jack smiled. "Son, if it's that bad, I'll be the first to come rescue you myself. But I hear it's a fine place. Just opened last year. Big sprawling outfit east of town—lots of boys your age. I called and they're expecting you. They've got teachers. And doctors. Even a dentist."

Eddie looked down. "So just boys there?"

"Well . . . yes," Jack said. "All young men, like you. What's wrong with that?"

"Nothing. I don't know. I can't explain it. My mama's passed away. But not my dad. He's just *missing*. So officially I'm not an orphan. But how can I find him if I'm cooped up in a boys' home?"

Annalee thought for a moment. "If you're a real detective, Eddie, you won't let that stop you. Why don't you see what you can find out from the other boys?"

"Find out? About my father?"

"Exactly. Boys know things. And hear things. So why don't

you ask around—but with discretion, Eddie. You know, quietly and carefully."

"Like Sherlock Holmes?"

She smiled. "Well, Sherlock used science and reason to solve mysteries. You can just ask around."

Eddie nodded, understanding.

"Then," Annalee added, "if you find out anything important, write to me—in care of the Castles. Do you remember the address?"

He nodded, repeated the street number and name.

"Okay, so you're ready now?"

He sat up straighter. "I'll be . . . fine. And I'll be asking around—about my father."

"But on the sly," Annalee said. "Just ask around about a man whose name is Eddie Brown Senior."

Eddie nodded. Annalee started to pat his shoulder. But Eddie grabbed for her, hugging, tight, desperate, needing her, not wanting to let go. She hugged back tight, showing him they were together in all of this. Through all his coats, he felt too small and vulnerable to leave behind. But they both knew she didn't have a choice. She hugged tighter, in the same way he was hugging her, making sure he understood she wouldn't forget him, what they'd been through, and what they still were trying to do.

She whispered in his ear, "We're getting close, Eddie. We'll figure everything out. I promise. Hang on. You're brave."

He nodded. "That's right, Professor." He pulled back, looked into her eyes. "I've always been brave."

So Eddie didn't turn to wave. Instead, like a veteran sleuth, he crept up to the fancy front door of Denver's newly opened Cannady Home for Boys—and let himself inside.

As Jack and Annalee drove away, making their way under darkened skies across town to the Castles' place, neither of them found the right words to say in Eddie's absence. So they both were silent. Then after a while, Annalee noticed that Jack seemed lost in deep thought. In particular, he seemed to pull back his mind, his spirit, his *self* a million miles from Annalee's side of the car—as if to step back, for a while, from associating with *her*.

She felt his distance.

For half a second, she turned to ask him about it. Maybe it was her imagination. But he seemed at the same moment to pull himself away even farther, deeper over to his side of the car.

In response, she turned deeper over to *her* side, feeling rejected and hating the feeling. Because she knew it all too well. So she shrugged against her door. With a deep sigh, she yanked her coat tighter around herself. She inched her body closer toward her door's open window, letting the cold night air take her mind off her one worst fear—that, if Jack were honest about it, he would tell her he was fed up with her interruption of his life and with her ridiculous adventure. But especially she feared he was fed up with her.

Unless he understood.

That her little adventure *wasn't* ridiculous. That she was trying, in every way she could possibly figure, to uncover a truth that nasty people were murdering to hide.

Yet she didn't feel smart enough or wise enough—or maybe good enough—to figure out who or why. More than that, she had to stand up to the worst thing of all. Deep down, she was afraid.

Her adversaries were killers.

This wasn't a game. In truth, she didn't know if she was up for it, and she didn't know how to confess that. Not to Jack. Not to herself. Not even yet to God.

She thought hard about this now, about her years of unanswered prayer. Of not knowing how to hear from God. Or really talk to God. Or believe with confidence that God was hearing or listening.

The same problem dogged the bad years with her daddy. Would it dog her years with Jack?

My years? I've known him less than a day.

But by meeting Jack and being with him—and surviving a gunfire attack, of all things, with him—she realized how much she needed the help of someone strong and capable and willing to walk with her to the end of her dangerous, hard road. No matter where it led.

But more than that, she realized that because of Jack, she finally knew that she needed the one thing she'd never admitted. But could she even say it?

I need love?

She stifled a moan. *That's what I've been looking for, God. In life? In you? In prayer? In this world that seems to despise me? Simply to be loved? In fact, to be treasured? But do you ever love us that much? Does anyone?* Of course she knew the answer. *Look at the cross.* Extravagant love means infinite sacrifice.

Was that what Jack already understood? Was it why he was pulling away? He couldn't give her that much? He didn't have it? She couldn't dare to believe it.

Not tonight. And not after today—a day that had started with her slipping into the beautiful clothes Jack had chosen for her to wear, no detail forgotten—down to her toes. What kind of man did that? Only one who believed a woman was worth it. A man who wanted her suited up for war but also for life. A good and real life?

She sighed silently, steeling herself for an awkward goodbye. She glanced over at Jack. But he didn't return the look. Instead, he steered the car onto the Castles' wide street.

Jack geared the motor down, letting the car ease up to the Castles' big manse. Annalee looked straight ahead. Waiting for what to do next. Just bolt from the car? She sighed again. *What now?*

But as Jack pulled into the circle drive, he put the car in neutral. She noticed the gear. And he noticed that she noticed. So she couldn't help herself. She smiled at him. But shy. So a dimple flashed. He opened his mouth, his dark eyes searching hers for what he seemed to need her to know.

"I made a bad call, Annalee. I'm asking you to go back. Back home."

"To *Chicago?*"

"You could've *died* today. Eddie, too. And for what? Some crazy wild-goose chase? I never should've sent you that telegram."

"But we're making progress. *I'm* making progress. Today was a breakthrough." She frowned. "And Chicago's not my home. *This* is home. And things here need to change. I'm willing to fight tooth and nail to make that happen."

"But it's not just your battle," he said. "In a fight, if you fight it alone, people don't always survive. I need you to survive this—"

He didn't finish. Maybe he didn't know how. Or maybe he didn't trust his own words—that he was telling her *go* but knew he didn't mean it.

Instead, he reached across the seat, and with a groan, he pulled her into his arms, holding her close. He smelled of smoke and sweat and longing and the after-essence of an impossible, deadly, dangerous day. So she didn't push him away. Instead, she yielded herself to his scent and his strength and the promise of his unfinished words.

In her yielding, he pulled her closer, leaning away only to gaze into her eyes with the kind of longing—and need?—that made her catch her breath, letting her shed a lone, glistening, surrendering tear. He brushed it away, placing it onto his mouth, tasting all that it might mean.

Then he did what men do in steamy dime novels and moving pictures and the best of treasured fairy tales.

He tipped her face to his, holding her closer, his eyes saying he never wanted to let her go.

Then he kissed her.

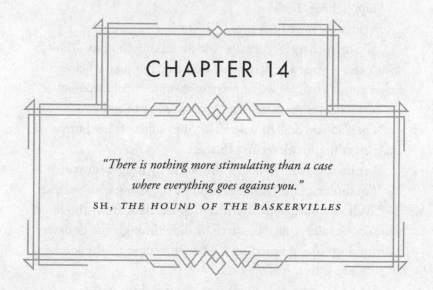

CHAPTER 14

"There is nothing more stimulating than a case
where everything goes against you."

SH, *THE HOUND OF THE BASKERVILLES*

AT THE CASTLES' HOUSE, every light, it seemed, blazed bright as the starry heavens. Every window aglow. Every candle lit. The place shone like a Christmas tree, bright and festive. A holiday postcard. But not at the back door.

Bernita yanked open the door, holding it like she owned it, one hand gripping the handle, daring Annalee to enter *her* realm—*her* kitchen—without showing just the right amount of humility and supplication.

"You're *late!*"

Bernita's dark eyes flashed . . . what? Annoyance—and territorial anger? She was already dressed for dinner. Starched black uniform. Spotless white apron. White lace cap propped to the side of her tight marcel wave—not one hair out of place. What, indeed, could a professor say to sound right?

"Just call me *Annalee*."

Bernita narrowed her eyes. *"What?"*

"You're in charge!" Annalee added, talking too fast. "This is your place—your kitchen, your domain. I'm just a helper. So forget about *professor this* or *professor that*. Just call me *Annalee*."

Bernita's eyes grew tighter. "I know what to call you."

"I'm glad you do," Annalee said. She pulled off her borrowed coat, breathing hard, feeling flushed.

Bernita noticed. "What in the world's wrong with you?"

"I'm running late," Annalee mumbled, fussing with her coat.

"Well . . . hurry up." Bernita stepped back from the door, allowed Annalee a slice of space to slide through the doorway, still fuming. She pointed to a bathroom next to the kitchen. "Get dressed. In *there*."

"Right," Annalee said, not wanting a fight.

"My extra uniform's hanging on the back of the door."

"Your uniform?" Annalee asked. "You okay with that?"

"As if I had a choice." She patted her hair. "And don't break off any buttons!" Bernita added, looking Annalee over. "I just sewed them back on last week. And if there's one thing I hate, it's sewing on buttons!"

Annalee looked back at her, suddenly thinking Bernita sounded a lot like Mrs. Stallworth.

Bernita frowned. "Well . . . *hurry up*! And pull back your hair."

Annalee wasn't listening now. Instead, she slipped into the tiny bathroom, pulled the cord on the light, shut the door, turned around, looked at herself in the mirror, and thought about what would happen next.

But first . . .

Jack kissed me.

She touched her lips, closed her eyes, breathed deep. She could still taste the strong, assured, sweet strength of him. And the strong, assured, sweet strength of his sighing, his longing for *her*, and his tenderness—his brushing away of her tear, tasting her reaction to him. If that's what kissing was like, she was convinced she would like to try it again, thank you very much. But right now? While trying to solve a murder?

Because she also still felt Jack's worry—for her. How did he put it? In battle, people don't always survive. *"I need you to survive this."* Did that mean he'd lost someone in the war—a close friend, a war buddy? A lover? *Good Lord.* With one kiss, she'd fallen headfirst into a world of grown-up possibilities—to her, a strange and foreign land. She opened her eyes, breathed deep, daring to marvel and even smile a little at herself, trying to avoid her own eyes in the mirror, despite her shy disbelief that Jack Blake had found something *kissable* in her. But she had to look at herself and ask, *Why not?* If no one else had found her desirable or kissable, was that her fault? She wasn't sure. But she did know this: Jack's kiss wasn't uncertain. He *wanted* to kiss her, so it didn't feel wrong. Even if it was her very first kiss ever. But was it *his* first?

She let out a long sigh, knowing it couldn't be. Surely he'd kissed a woman before—or more than one? Indeed, more than once? She caught her breath, glanced at her reflection in the mirror, knew from the look in her eyes that she longed to reflect about this one moment in a slow, deliberate, leisurely, beautiful, glorious, delicious way.

But Bernita. Rattling dishes and pots. Sounding more impatient and annoyed with every second because Bernita didn't know what Annalee knew—first, that Jack Blake had kissed *her*. But there was more.

A murderer might be coming for dinner.

Annalee forced herself to concentrate—on her breathing, on Bernita's maid uniform. On, yes, her "undercover" outfit. She looked it over. A black, narrow dress starched to a tough, hard sheen. Perfect, she thought. Well, perfect enough. But she looked closer—at the battalion of black glassy buttons marching down the front, the spotless white apron, stiff white collar, and white lace cap.

These are the honest clothes, Annalee thought, *that will transform me from embattled academic to domestic, from second-guessed intellectual to would-be servant.* Except weren't they all the same doggone honest and decent thing? In theory, maybe.

But in fact, if she'd had a tough time trying to live life as the Colored Professor, Annalee knew that in this uniform, she would simply disappear. Her identity would blur and fade, then—*poof*—disintegrate. No wonder Bernita acted so angry. In these clothes, people didn't even see her.

Yet Annalee was more than willing to wear these clothes, and take on this life, if they helped her unearth her father's murderer.

She turned on the faucets, yanked a towel off a hook on the wall. She soaked it with scalding soapy water, ran it around her face, her arms, her body—knowing it wasn't enough to wash off all the smoke and complexity of the day, but giving it her best try.

Bernita's clothes fit well, meantime. Maybe too well. Or at least well enough to bring on more of Bernita's wrath.

Bernita banged another pot, in fact. So Annalee moved to

finish, buttoning the last black button—breaking it off, while also breaking another button in half. She shoved the button bits in a side pocket, smoothed back her hair, plopped the lace cap on her head, and opened the door.

Bernita whirled. "Took you long enough!" She gave Annalee a once-over, missing the broken button—for now.

"How many for dinner?" Annalee asked, trying to distract.

Bernita frowned, turned back to the stove. "What business is that of yours?"

"It's not my business. I just asked so I could help you get ready."

"Help?" Bernita slammed down a pot. The tiny diamond on her right ring finger flashed. "If you wanted to help, you would've been here at three o'clock this afternoon, when I was plucking feathers off pheasants *all by myself.*"

"Well, it smells fantastic in here," Annalee said, thinking fast. "But then I always heard you were the best cook around. Everybody says so, everybody . . . at church."

At that, Bernita banged down a spoon, sending sauce flying. She walked across the kitchen to take Annalee on, standing nose to nose. "Listen to me, *Annalee.* I don't know what you and Colonel Castle got going on here. But I won't be mocked in this kitchen where I've worked—and my mother before me worked—ever since I was a girl."

"Well said—" Annalee tried to interrupt.

"Maybe I didn't go to some highfalutin college like you, but you can take your phony flattery and put it—"

"You're right," Annalee snapped back, trying to stop this.

Bernita looked at her hard, moved back a step.

So Annalee repeated herself. "You're *right,*" she said, softer.

"But to tell the truth, Bernita, I was trying to get on your good side."

"My good side's been up since 5 a.m. this morning, trying to get ready for Miss Elizabeth's party."

"Right, and then here I come out of the blue, coming to work in your kitchen."

"Yeah, and *four hours* late."

"*And* wearing your fancy-dress uniform."

"*And,*" she said, looking Annalee over, "breaking *my* buttons!"

Annalee tried to stifle a laugh. "You mean you saw that button?"

"Girl, I don't miss much of nothing around here!"

"No—you probably don't," Annalee said. She grew quiet.

Bernita narrowed her eyes, lowered her voice. "So what exactly are you saying, *Annalee?*"

Annalee didn't answer. So Bernita spoke louder.

"I said, why we not supposed to call you *professor?* But not only that, why you dressed up in my clothes, acting like you a maid?"

"I can't tell you yet."

"And that's just the wrong answer."

"Well, it's the only answer because if I tell you, you could get hurt. Or you could get—" Annalee stopped herself.

"Get what?"

"Killed."

Bernita stepped back. "Girl, what in the world you talking about? Killed?"

"Well . . . you read the papers. Nobody's safe these days."

Bernita grabbed a chair, sat down at the big kitchen table,

pushing aside a jumble of polished silver serving spoons. "*Lord,* if I didn't need this job—"

Annalee looked at her, thought of her dismay, reflected that Bernita, like Rosita, was saying she'd stayed too long in a household she longed to flee.

But with Bernita, Annalee was determined to know *why.* Because Bernita didn't seem simply tired. No, something else was dogging her.

Annalee pulled a chair across the floor and sat down to face her. "Have you ever had a problem that was just too big to carry alone?"

Bernita considered that, looking away as if to ignore her. Annalee tried again.

"I know it's crazy for me to ask you this now, but what goes on in this household that's got you worrying so?"

Bernita didn't answer.

"Bernita, please, what *happened* here?"

Bernita's eyes darkened. She took a deep breath. Slow, deliberate, endless. "I told myself I'd *never* tell."

"Was it last November?"

"*Lord,* some secrets weigh so heavy."

"Believe me, I know they do."

"*No.* You *don't* know! Because if I told you—"

"*Bernita!*" The kitchen door swung open. Elizabeth Castle whirled in—all white chiffon and ostrich feathers, high heels and perfumed curls, pearl necklaces and diamond earrings. She looked stunning. Turning on a thin heel, she surveyed the scene, looking at Annalee, taking in her uniform.

"You're late—as I expected—and guests are coming in to table. The fruit compote, Bernita. In two minutes."

Bernita pulled to her feet, held her tongue, fussed with the serving spoons, waiting for Mrs. Castle to leave as she'd come, through the swinging door.

Annalee leaned close to Bernita. "After dinner, where can we talk?" she whispered.

But Bernita pulled away, handed Annalee a serving spoon, ignoring her question. Instead, she walked to the icebox, took out two crystal bowls piled high with fruit, carried one in each hand, placed each on a tray. She added other bowls. Whipped cream. Fruit syrup. The whole setup.

"Dinner's starting," she said to Annalee. "Serve from the left, clear from the right—and *no* drips and drabs." Bernita heaved a tray at Annalee, picked up her own. Headed to the butler's pantry.

Annalee nodded, adjusting her hands to steady the heavy tray. She straightened her back, pushed past Bernita, and started for the dining room door.

"Wait," Bernita hissed. *"Gloves."* She fumbled in a drawer, shoved white gloves at Annalee, pulled on her own pair. Sighed. "Well, here goes nothing. Start serving from the Colonel. I'll start from Miss Elizabeth. Then counterclockwise around."

Bernita set off for the dining room, then swung back. "And don't just slop it in the bowls. Place it in careful—all pretty-like. You got that?"

"I got that."

"And no drips and drabs!"

"Oh, Bernita, no drips and drabs. How many for dinner?"

"What? Girl, please stop asking questions!" Bernita gave Annalee a hard frown. "Now hurry up. Here we go."

Yes, here we go, Annalee thought, looking up. *Show me* something *tonight, Lord.*

With a flourish, Bernita swung through the butler's pantry into the Castles' ornate dining room, Annalee following. The room sat in a burnished glow, lit only by the refracted gleam of the crystal chandelier.

"*Aah.*"

"*Oh.*"

"*Lovely.* A compote! Oh, Elizabeth, you know it's my favorite! Thank you, sweetheart."

"All your favorite Florida fruits, Mother. For your special birthday."

The chic, white-haired woman was dripping in dark-red silk, big sparkly brooch on her left shoulder. She sat enthroned at the head of the table, Elizabeth to her right. Next on that side came an elderly balding man—the woman's husband? He asked Bernita for more wine.

"So I can toast you properly, Naomi," the man said. "My beautiful wife, the unsinkable Mrs. Gibbons."

"Oh, Ernest, I can't bear to hear another word about Molly Brown."

Everybody laughed. The man winked at his wife, lifting his half-empty glass. In turn, she lifted her glass. Apparently, Annalee observed, not even the Denver district attorney observed Prohibition in the privacy of his own home.

Indeed, a beefy young man sitting midtable also asked for wine. Also, a jet-haired flapper woman seated at the end. "Just half a glass."

Bernita nodded, discreet. "Yes, right away." She turned to a sideboard for a decanter, filled the wineglasses.

"Down here too! Another *tiny* little glass of *lemonade* for me too." Then a boozy laugh.

Bernita nodded.

But Annalee froze. She knew the voice. The face. She just couldn't believe it. Except there he was, seated in the last chair on her serving side. The red-faced man from the train.

"George! . . . Just a tiny lemonade!"

She pulled in a breath, blinking in disbelief. The boozy man—at the birthday dinner for Mrs. Castle's *mother*? Oh, how *curious*. Odd and dangerous and too curious to be random.

Bernita flashed Annalee a look, sensing something wrong, warning Annalee with her eyes.

Annalee nodded once, stepping back into the shadows around the table, her little scheme to hide in plain view suddenly seeming naive.

Because next to the man from the train sat a starchy little woman Annalee recognized as president of the Denver school board—the same president who'd refused to award her a commendation when she'd graduated with honors from high school. Then across from that woman sat her beefy husband, a prominent Denver pastor. He'd pinned corsages on the honorees— except for "the colored girl," Annalee—at that same graduation ceremony. Not that it mattered now, or that either would remember her, Annalee thought. But then again, the way her day was going, maybe they would.

Why, indeed, did the jet-haired flapper woman on Bernita's side seem to be staring so hard? Right at Annalee? Had their paths crossed too? Annalee wondered. She sighed silently.

Mrs. Castle flashed her a look. She stifled another sigh. What a dinner party this was turning out to be.

She made a quick count. The table was set for ten. Two

chairs on her serving side were empty. But Mrs. Castle wasn't waiting for latecomers.

She gave Bernita a silent signal. Following Bernita's lead, Annalee hurried to the far end, stood to the left of Sidney Castle—who looked her over quickly. Just as quickly, he looked away.

"Fruit, sir?" Annalee said quietly.

"Not too much," he said. "Thank you," he added.

"Oh, *Sidney*," Elizabeth Castle said. "Have a good portion—especially the apricots."

"If they're not too sweet?" He looked down the table at his wife. Annalee looked, too. Wrong move. Mrs. Castle saw Annalee's look, huffed, narrowed her eyes back. Eyes that spoke volumes. *"I wasn't talking to you."* Or more clearly: *"Stay in your place."*

Annalee looked away, reached over to spoon the fruit and syrup into Castle's little dish, struggling in vain to keep her hands from shaking, to make it *pretty-like*.

But too late. Sidney Castle moved his arm, jostling her hand, sending a long, thin dribble of orange-colored syrup across the spotless white tablecloth.

"Oh." Annalee stifled her voice while Castle reacted.

"Sure, why not. I'll have the apricots," he said, loud, almost too obvious. "Whipped cream, too." With a feigned stretch, he placed his forearm over the mess, covering for Annalee. "What about you, Hank?" Castle turned to the "lemonade" man from the train on his right. "How about some fruit? All your sister's favorites."

"Then I can't refuse. Can I, Lizzie?"

Elizabeth Castle gave him a look.

He laughed. "Oh, how my niece hates that name."

"Then why use it?" Mrs. Castle's mother snapped. She frowned down the table at the man Hank—who was her brother? The lemonade man was Elizabeth Castle's *uncle*?

Mentally, Annalee was putting these people on a chart. She'd ponder it all later tonight. For now, Elizabeth Castle's mother was shouting down the table at her brother.

"I mean, just for once, can't you please behave, Hank."

"Oh, Sis, relax. It's your birthday." The man Hank took a loud sip of wine, lifting his glass back at his sister.

"So let her enjoy it, please," Elizabeth said.

"Long as the food's good. What's for dinner tonight, Bernita?" He looked up at Annalee and scowled. "*Hey*. Hey, you're not Bernita. Where's Bernita?"

Annalee felt her heart jump.

Bernita stepped forward out of the shadows. "Yes, over here, Mr. Hank. Can I help you, please, Mr. Hank?"

"*No*. Not from way over there—and anyway, who is *this*?" He pointed a shaky finger at Annalee.

Annalee froze. Glanced at Elizabeth Castle, seeing Mrs. Castle's eyes dare her to speak.

Sidney Castle cleared his throat.

Annalee's heart pounded harder.

"Just a new girl," Castle said, sounding dismissive.

Annalee sighed silently.

But Hank was persistent. "*What?* She doesn't have a *name*?" He gulped more wine, his drunkenness showing, voice slurry. "I'm just saying I like to know the *name* of the girl putting food onto my plate, thank you very—"

"*Hank!*" It was Mrs. Castle's mother. "Would you *please*."

Castle broke in. "Dinner will be great, no matter who's serving—which reminds me, has anybody eaten recently at the Brown?"

"Just last week!" The school board president seemed proud of it. Others agreed. The new chef at the Brown Palace, the swank downtown hotel, was *simply marvelous*. So *continental*, agreed Mrs. Castle's mother.

The table conversation turned to Denver restaurants in general. Bernita retreated to the butler's pantry. Annalee followed, right on her heels. Bernita set down her bowl. Annalee did the same, took a deep breath, wiped her brow. But they were just getting started.

"Can't relax now," Bernita said, flashing her a look. "We got salads next."

"Two guests are missing on my side."

"What is your problem? Take all five plates. The dressings. In case the late people come in while we're serving." She huffed. "Which, knowing them, is sure to happen."

"Who are the late people?"

But Bernita was off with her tray. Annalee lifted hers, groaned. Too heavy. Bernita made it look so easy. But maid's work was *not* easy, Annalee thought, and not just for the obvious reasons. She grimaced. Lifted the tray again, steadied herself, willing herself to carry it through the pantry, into the glittery dining room.

This time, no mishaps. No interruptions from Lemonade Hank. No narrowed eyes from Mrs. Castle. And no drips or drabs. Only one thing—the jet-haired young woman's stares still followed her every move down the table.

Annalee wanted to glance back, to try to read her eyes. But

knew she didn't dare. Bernita was already back in the kitchen. Annalee hurried herself, finished with her salads, steadied her empty tray. She swung through the door to the butler's pantry.

Then she froze.

Bernita was in the kitchen talking to somebody. A man. A Black man. His cadence, his voice made it clear he was a Negro man in service.

"On the table?" he was asking Bernita.

"No, on the counter," Bernita said. "During the entrée, I'll put on the *umpteen* candles."

They both laughed.

The birthday cake, delivered by the caterer.

"Tell Mr. Prince it looks beautiful."

Annalee listened harder. *Mr. Prince.* Slater Prince? The cake was from his restaurant and catered to the Castles?

Annalee huddled in the darkened pantry between the two doors—one to the dining room, one to the kitchen—and considered this information. She leaned closer to the swinging door to listen.

"And they tell me he's the best in town," the man was saying.

"You a new man? With Prince, I mean? I haven't seen you around," Bernita said.

"Just started today."

"Really? Where you work before?" Bernita getting familiar.

"The trains—Chicago Limited, Southern, Missouri Pacific, B & O. I was a waiter."

Annalee's heart pounded. She laid a hand on the kitchen door, pushed it open an imperceptible fraction to see what she didn't want to believe.

The man in the kitchen was the debonair waiter from her

train—the waiter who led her to the luggage car. The waiter who promised to "take care of" her purse and trunk and luggage. Yes, standing in Elizabeth Castle's kitchen—talking with swagger to Bernita—was the sleek, efficient, accommodating, orange juice–spilling Pullman waiter.

It was William Barnett.

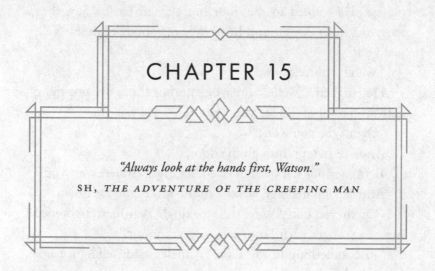

CHAPTER 15

"Always look at the hands first, Watson."

SH, *THE ADVENTURE OF THE CREEPING MAN*

ANNALEE TENSED, trying not to breathe. This wasn't making sense. She needed to think. But no time. Bernita was looking for her.

"Mercy alive, where is that girl!" Bernita was heading for the pantry door.

"Looks like you're real busy tonight." William Barnett started to excuse himself.

"Always busy at this house. But please, stay a while," Bernita said. "I'll make you a plate. I roasted a bird. All the trimmings. You can tell me about your train travel."

But William Barnett was turning to leave, Annalee sighing a silent thanks.

"Maybe another time—when I come back for the cake

plates." He walked to the door but turned back. "Say, they have one quiet day around here? When nobody's home? Well, just you?"

"Watch yourself now."

He laughed. "Well . . . maybe another time. I've got more deliveries tonight. I'll see you around—" He was gone.

"Or maybe you won't."

Annalee swung through the door.

Bernita shook her head, flashed her eyes. "Where were you!"

Annalee ignored her, walked to the table, and sat down.

"Oh no you don't! We're still working!" Bernita straightened her cap. "That's what I'm trying to do anyway."

"Just something in my shoe," Annalee said, telling a bald-faced lie, bending over, catching her breath, trying to compose her thoughts. To *think*. But there wasn't time. Annalee sat up. Stood. "Okay, what's next?"

Bernita pulled up to her height. "Pick up the salad things."

Annalee grabbed a tray, headed back to the dining room.

"And don't drop anything!"

But Bernita didn't have to worry.

Because suddenly Annalee felt alert and focused. Not because she knew why so many curious people—Lemonade Hank from the train, Slater Prince, William Barnett—all had a connection to the Sidney Castle household. Or who else would show up before the night was over. But because she knew she was going to figure it out.

Maybe not tonight, she told herself, but soon.

With or without Elizabeth Castle's approval.

Or Bernita's, for that matter.

These people were involved in *something* that felt connected to her daddy's murder. How'd she know? Intuition? Threads of connection? If she had to wear a maid's uniform every day for the rest of her life, she was going to find out what they were hiding.

She entered the dining room, tray at her shoulder. Eyes steady. She waited in the shadows near Mrs. Castle's corner of the room.

Elizabeth Castle signaled. Annalee moved to her right. No stopping. No lingering. She was a picture of efficiency and sub-servience. Nothing but quiet manners. "Thank you, ma'am." "Thank you, sir." "You're welcome." Barely whispering.

No dribs and drabs.

The tray was heavy, but she ignored that, too. Instead, she willed herself to carry it. No stumbles. No obvious effort. No reason to call attention to herself. Just blend in to the woodwork.

So she didn't listen to the conversation. About the KKK? She didn't skip a beat. Didn't break a sweat when the Castle guests claimed—in her earshot—that the Klan actually was *helping* Denver. As the school board president put it, "Why, just the other day, I was telling the mayor how the separation of races and religions improves the quality of life in Denver . . . and of course, the mayor agrees with me!"

Everybody laughed, except Sidney Castle. He glanced at Annalee.

"Of course he'd agree!" said the woman's husband, winking around the table.

Everybody laughed again.

Annalee ignored them, picked up her salad things, her hand steady, realizing that she felt assured and confident that none of these people would stop her from her goal—finding out exactly who in this household, or in this town, had murdered her father. *And* who was trying to kill her.

But most important, *why*.

Yes, the *why* would unlock every question.

In the kitchen, Bernita was putting the last entrée plate on a serving cart—on wheels. A small blessing. She pointed to the business end of the cart. "You push," she said to Annalee. "I'll serve."

"Yes, fine," Annalee said.

Bernita cut her a look but held her tongue.

The doorbell rang.

"Wouldn't you know it? Late again for his mother's dinner table. Right when we're serving the main plates." Bernita arched a brow. "And ringing the bell! As if he didn't *have a key*."

Annalee thought for a moment, just as Bernita said, "Go get the door."

Annalee looked at her. "I can't."

Bernita put her hands on her hips. "And that is just the wrong answer."

Annalee took a step toward her. "And I don't have time to explain. But that's one doorbell I will *not* be answering."

Bernita gave her a look. She left the cart, swung into a back hallway to go round and answer the front door. But Annalee was listening, ears on alert.

Right away, the dining room noises got louder.

"*Well*. Look who's here!"

"Late *again*. As always."

"Now the party can start."

"Oh, you're such a tease."

"Our future US senator!"

"Down the road, Mother—"

"But handsome as ever. And look at the beautiful girl on your arm. Introduce her, sweetheart."

"But first, give your mother a hug."

"And your grandmother!"

"And go kiss your father!"

Everybody laughing, loud and festive, except Sidney Castle.

"Actually, a handshake will do," Castle said. Annalee heard him push back his chair and stand.

Then Sidney Castle spoke a name that, for all the right reasons, refused to surprise even Annalee.

His deep voice was steady. "Take that seat by your mother. I know she'll want to talk to her boy—her one and only. She's been waiting for you all night. But you know that. You're always her darling son—aren't you, Hunter?"

Annalee grabbed the kitchen table, steadied herself, refused to cave in over what was happening. That the finely dressed young gunman who tried to murder her—only a few hours ago—just sat down to dinner.

But now she—of all people—was the new maid, set to serve him a meal.

She grabbed a chair, scrambled for the seat—telling herself, *No, this isn't happening.* Instead she stood, pushed away the chair. No time to sit down. No time to unravel.

Hunter Castle.

She whispered the name to herself, rolled it around on her tongue, certain she had seen that fanciful name sometime in just the past day. On a flyer? A billboard? In a newspaper? At Jack's house during breakfast? Then she remembered. *Hunter Castle.* She had seen the name that very morning—on one of Elizabeth Castle's expensive music boxes.

One of the music boxes waiting for repair. Missing its key.

"How long you gonna stand there?"

Bernita held open the door to the pantry, one hand on the filled-up serving cart. *"Well?"*

"I'm coming!" Annalee said. Her voice was steady, but her legs were shaking, her heart racing. Because she felt certain one of two things would happen. Either Hunter Castle would notice her immediately, turning his mother's dining room into a war zone, or his conceit and self-centeredness would render her, in his presence, utterly invisible. Fifty-fifty odds. But she had to figure his conceit would win out, and he wouldn't even notice her. She hoped. No, she didn't hope. She prayed. *Jesus in heaven, it's been a while, I confess, since my good praying and all, but please, Lord, make me an invisible blur—even though that's what I always thought I didn't want to be in this world. Invisible. But, Jesus, that is what I need—right now!*

She took a deep breath, headed toward the swinging door. *Amen.*

Bernita frowned. "You okay? You look . . . kind of funny."

"Actually, I'm right as rain," Annalee said. "Let's go." She grabbed the cart handle. "I'll follow your lead."

Bernita shrugged. Pushed open the door.

The atmosphere in the dining room had turned jovial, almost carefree.

"*Splendid.* A sacramental merlot. A church wine, Father?" Hunter Castle examined his glass as Bernita poured. He sat opposite his mother, his back to the pantry door. His date, a glittering blonde, sat to his left, drawing attention. "A bit holy for you, Maggie," he said to the girl. "But it'll do, won't it?"

She laughed. Purred over the wine. Sipped boldly.

Annalee took in the scene, pushed the cart behind Hunter Castle's chair, forcing herself not to walk too close. She held her breath. Then told herself to relax. *He won't notice me. He won't notice me.*

She made her rounds, passing out the entrée plates, on her way back to the pantry door.

"I don't get my supper?"

She froze. All eyes on her. Then eyes on Hunter Castle. Elizabeth Castle frowned. Bernita scowled. Lemonade Hank wrinkled his brow. The blonde stared. Sidney Castle's laser eyes darted from his son to Annalee and back again. Warning her. *"Don't mess this up."*

"Right away, sir," Annalee said, finding her maid's voice, forcing her determined hand to steady. Feeling idiotic that she'd overlooked him. She placed his entrée plate down in front of him in just the right place. Steady hands. No dribs and drabs. Willing him *not* to turn to look directly at her.

His thick black mane was barbered and slicked, his face shaved. He'd recently showered. No smoke smells. Instead, the costly scents of a custom men's fragrance and, no doubt, a barber's private shaving lotion—lemony and expensive-smelling— wafted around him. She breathed deeply and silently, but not gritting her teeth, willing him *not* to look up to *see* her.

"No supper?" the jet-haired woman said, drawing attention to the opposite end of the table. "*You* must've been a bad, bad boy, Hunter."

Big laughs around the table. Except for Sidney Castle, looking somber.

And Annalee, standing frozen *this close* to Hunter Castle, not sure whether to move or stay. *Or bang a tray down on his murderous, conceited, rascally head.*

She stepped back. Hunter never once turned around. To him, she was just a maid. A nothing. Delivering his dinner plate.

"That will be all," Elizabeth Castle said, glaring at Annalee, "for now."

Annalee nodded, turned toward the butler's pantry. She didn't look back to get Sidney Castle's approval.

"Oh, not so fast!" The jet-haired woman was talking again. *"You,"* she said, pointing to Annalee. "I spilled wine on my dress. I'll need your help for a minute."

The young woman stood, grabbed her handbag, left the table, didn't look back, intending for Annalee to follow.

Annalee looked at Elizabeth Castle. But Elizabeth was already motioning Annalee out. "Well, hurry up." She turned to her son. "Now, you were telling us how you two met—you and this beautiful creature."

Annalee's chance to duck away. Hunter Castle never looked her way. She held her breath, cutting through the kitchen. Back to the front hallway. The jet-haired woman was heading up the curving front stairs.

Annalee followed, dying to know *what in the world* she could possibly want. She followed the woman up the carpeted stairs, their footsteps silent, weighing the cut of the other woman's expensive kid leather, T-strap shoes. Acting discreet, Annalee stepped back to wait for the woman to enter first at the powder room door.

But at the door, the woman yanked Annalee by the arm, pulling her inside, locking the door behind them, shocking her with a whispered question.

"Where's the kid?"

"*What?*" Annalee stepped back.

"The little kid I saw you with? Last night? You know—*downtown*? With the white kid?"

"Excuse me, miss," Annalee said. Her maid's voice. "You must be mistaken."

"Look, honey. I never forget a face." Still whispering. "And I saw *you* last night—downtown! On Sixteenth Street. With a white boy. Scruffy-looking kid. Drowning in a pile of old coats."

Annalee searched her eyes. Thinking. Weighing.

"That wasn't me," she said.

"Oh, you remember all right. The Kluxers were marching. I warned you to run. Maggie was with me."

"Maggie?" The blonde downstairs at the table with Hunter? Annalee frowned, confused. "But your hair—" The woman she saw the night before had flaming-red hair.

"A dyed wig." She tossed her black curls. Shrugged. "Friday nights. I like to change it up. But this isn't about me. What about *you*? And that boy? Who *is* he? And what in the world are *you* doing *here*?"

"I can't answer that now. But—"

A hard rap on the door interrupted her. "Is everything okay, Olivia?"

Elizabeth Castle.

Annalee caught her breath.

"I'm fine!" the young woman sang out. "Be down in a second!"

"Your name is Olivia," Annalee whispered.

"Olivia Franklin. Here's my number if you . . . get in a jam." She tore open her handbag, pulled out a scrap of paper and a black eyebrow pencil. She wrote down her phone number on the yellowed paper. "You know . . . if you need some help."

"Why would I need help?"

"Because," Olivia Franklin said, eyes serious, "you're dealing with dangerous people."

"What are they hiding?" Annalee asked.

"More than you want to know."

"I'm not backing down."

The young woman sighed. "Then take this." Her phone number.

"Thank you," Annalee said. "But I'll be fine."

The young woman searched Annalee's eyes. "But maybe you won't."

With a whirl, the woman flung open the door, swirling out of the powder room.

Elizabeth Castle was waiting in the hallway, looking perturbed.

"Everything okay, Olivia?" Mrs. Castle asked again. Her eyes searched Olivia Franklin's flowery dress, then Annalee's face, her eyes, her uniform.

Olivia Franklin was casual, easy. "All fixed," she said, tossing her curls, gesturing for Mrs. Castle to follow. But Elizabeth Castle was staring at the paper scrunched in Annalee's hand.

"What's *this*?"

"Some old trash," Olivia said, laughing. "My purse is a junk pile. Your girl was kind enough to throw it away for me. Which reminds me. That *beautiful* bag you were carrying at the Gloucesters' dinner party last Saturday. Please tell me you purchased that in Denver—"

She burbled down the stairs, talking nonsense about handbags. Elizabeth Castle followed, looking back to check on her new maid.

Annalee returned her gaze, standing at the top of the stairs. Finally Elizabeth whirled and headed back to her dinner party. For a moment, Annalee watched Elizabeth Castle descend the stairs, her right hand gripping the banister—to hide, it seemed, the fact that it was shaking.

So Annalee stuck Olivia's note into the pocket of her uniform, straightened her shoulders, and followed, her right hand gripping the banister—to hide that it *wasn't* shaking—keeping her eye on Elizabeth Castle's stiff back, knowing what she now had to do.

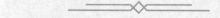

"You gonna do *what*?"

"Create a diversion."

Bernita reared back, hands on hips. "And what in the world is *that*?"

"Please listen, Bernita," Annalee said. "I know everybody in this house is hiding something. And you're afraid."

Bernita looked away, not responding.

Annalee pressed. "I've got something to be afraid of, too. But if I can get to the bottom of it, we'll be free of it—both of us."

"What are you saying now?"

"I'm saying I'm not asking you to tell me what you're hiding. I understand you're afraid. But tonight I need to create a diversion—a disturbance—to get everybody out of the house for a few minutes."

"Okay. But *why*?"

"I—I can't tell you. It's too dangerous."

Bernita sighed deeply, paced the room. "Well, I don't like it." She pointed a finger at Annalee. "You gonna make me lose my *job*."

"That's why I'm not getting you involved. But for now will you just trust me?"

Bernita pulled a chair from the kitchen table and sat down wearily. "*Lord*, this is some kind of mess." She inhaled deeply.

Annalee considered that but smiled. "It's nothing two smart women like us can't handle."

Bernita broke into a thin grin. "Hand me that cake knife."

Annalee grinned back. "I thought you'd never ask."

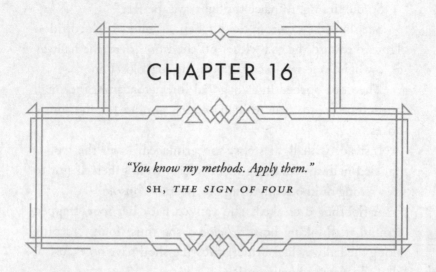

CHAPTER 16

"You know my methods. Apply them."

SH, *THE SIGN OF FOUR*

THE DINNER PARTY was in full swing. Laughter, loud and bois-terous, erupting from the glittering dining room. Wine flowing, open and expansive. Lemonade Hank slurping and slurring, struggling to match Hunter Castle quip for quip but failing. Hunter was the life of the party, every woman gushing over him. The school board president. The blonde. Olivia. Even his grandmother. Hanging on his every word.

"Oh, you're just my *darling!*"

Elizabeth gushed pride. "Well, you just spoil him, Mother. Doesn't she, Sidney? Remember that time, last July, down in the Springs—"

Elizabeth started her long story, her ode to her darling off-spring. Her perfect, precious Hunter.

So the timing, Annalee thought, was perfect.

She slipped away from the kitchen, around a back corridor. Tiptoed toward the coat closet off the front foyer, the hallway in low light, one small sconce near the coat closet door.

The door opened in a diagonal line across from the small music-box room. But Annalee wasn't aiming for the music boxes.

Instead, with light steps, she grimaced down the wood-paneled hallway, straining to be silent, willing herself not to step wrong or knock anything off the long console.

A floorboard creaked. She yanked back her foot, stepped around it, thinking how *ridiculous* she must look, creeping along the hallway like a thief, knowing she'd have no excuse at all if she were suddenly noticed.

Then out of nowhere, a straying thought: *And what would Jack think if he saw me?*

She took in a long breath. *Jack.* She realized she wanted him *here.* Close to her. Helping her. Believing in her. Cheering her on.

Holding her? Kissing her? *Oh, Lord.*

Because her plan, she knew, was downright *crazy.*

But now she was at the coat closet. She straightened her back. The door sat ajar. She wiped her hands on her apron, reached for the door. Perhaps it wouldn't squeak.

"But that's a wild idea, Hunter." The grandmother. Still at it. "I'm captivated. Tell us about the ranch. We heard there was a fire out there this afternoon."

"What?"

"At the Lazy K?"

"Poor Montgomery. He's having a lousy year."

"Lost his shirt in those water deals—investing in canals and ditches and whatnot."

"What in the world? He wasn't half thinking."

More voices from the dining room.

Annalee grabbed the door by the knob, shut her eyes, pushed inward. No squeak. She pushed herself into the long, narrow closet. Half closed the door.

Standing now in near dark, she was surrounded by expensive-smelling coats, wraps, furs, muffs—the closet bursting with overcoat bounty. Hunter's coat would be the last coat hung. Or the man's coat closest to the door. The *white* one? What a dandy he was. The long blond mink next to his would belong to his date, Maggie.

Annalee jiggled his big white chesterfield. Heard keys. She dug in the coat pockets, snagged the key fob, gold and ornate. *Of course.* Big letter *C* insignia on a coin-shaped medal sat aside a gold-toned cross and four rungs for keys. One rung empty.

She clutched the key chain in her hand, ready to open the door.

"Wait, Maggie. I'll get my coat. It's in my pocket."

Hunter Castle.

Annalee froze. She jammed the keys back into his coat pocket, clawed herself through the furs to the back of the dark closet, ducked between the last two coats, let the giant mink envelop her.

She prayed the coats weren't swinging on their hangers. But Hunter Castle flung open the door, setting the coats stirring. He flicked the light switch. Hard light from a low, bare bulb flooded the narrow space. Hunter jostled his coat, talking loud. "Hold your horses. Just take me a second."

But he wasn't checking his coat.

He moved deeper into the closet, scrounging through other pockets. He was searching for something, not able to find it, cursing under his breath. With each coat, he moved closer to Annalee. The big coat tickled her face, her nose—sneeze threatening. She held her breath, willing herself to sink lower into the ridiculous furs, to act invisible, feel invisible, *be* invisible. *What in the world is he looking for?*

Hunter stopped. Annalee froze. Held her breath longer.

Hunter Castle was thinking? Or he saw her?

A trickle of sweat slid down her face, clung to the fur nearest her face. Her chest burned, begging her to breathe. But for some reason, at that moment, she thought of Edna Stallworth—and of small things. She exhaled quietly, relaxing, sitting smaller, forgetting to be afraid, letting her panic fade.

Then through a slice of space, she saw.

Hunter was switching one of his keys onto somebody else's ring. He dropped the keys, cursed again, pawed the floor, missed her feet, found the keys. He jiggled one onto the other ring.

"Good grief! What's taking you so long?"

Hunter whirled casually. The door swung wider.

Maggie. The blonde. Frowning. Pouting. "Hey. I want my cigarette."

"That's all?" Hunter Castle, cool and calm. He patted the chest of his suit jacket. "Got it." He pulled out a silver cigarette holder.

She stuck out her lips, wanting a kiss. But Hunter stuck a cigarette in her mouth.

"We're leaving soon?" she asked, teasing, grabbing the cigarette.

"After the blasted cake," Hunter said. "Half an hour. Tops."

He pushed her back into the hallway, laughing at her. She laughed back. He flicked off the light. Slammed the door.

In the dark, Annalee listened to her heart, exhaled, leaning on a mink. *Half an hour.* She had to scramble to make her plan work. She clawed back through the coats and dug into the pockets of Hunter's silk-lined, white chesterfield. She grabbed his keys, nudged open the closet door. The hallway was deserted.

Annalee slipped from closet to kitchen. Bernita was in the cellar, rummaging for something. Perfect. If Bernita was questioned about what was getting ready to happen, she could say— with truth—she hadn't seen Annalee head outside. Or at least Annalee hoped she would say that.

Annalee dashed out the back door, stopped cold as frigid air cut through her thin maid's dress. But no time to turn back for a fur coat. Wouldn't that be something? To be caught wearing a stolen fur.

Instead, she scrambled off the back porch, hustled through the yard, dashed around the south side of the house, ran smack into a pile of lawn chairs, banged her knee. Groaned too loud. Too long.

An annoyed dog next door howled, loud and indignant. Annalee tensed. She waited for a neighbor to turn on a light, check the yard, but nobody stirred.

She didn't stop. In the dark, she followed her nose down the shadowy path between the two houses, not waiting for the dog to settle. She scrambled to the Castles' front yard—knowing exactly what she was searching for.

Hunter Castle's car.

A black Cadillac? Like the one at the ranch? The key fob would match. She checked the street. Black Cadillacs everywhere. Both sides of the curving, steep street. A Cadillac parade.

But who would own the biggest Caddy? And *white*. And parked in a provocative spot.

She jutted her jaw. *A spoiled, murdering rich kid who can afford more than one car, that's who.*

Hunter Castle's big white Brougham sat positioned at the crest of the steep street, facing down the hill, aimed right at his mother's house. He'd parked in the last good space. Then walked down the hill with his gushing, glittery new girlfriend, Maggie.

Annalee retraced his path, walking up the rise, breathing hard. Hugging herself in the cold, she ran up on the car, jangled the key in the lock on the driver's side, yanked open the door. She heard a twig snap behind her. In the dark, she whirled, eyes blinking.

"Listen! *Professor*."

"*Eddie?* What on earth?"

"I can explain! It's *important!*"

She searched his face. His *clean* face. "*Good Lord*, they scrubbed you half to death, head to toe." But something was wrong. "Where in the world is your coat?" He was wearing some plaid, secondhand mackinaw. Too small. And *ugly*. He still gripped his filthy scarf.

Annalee shook her head, trying to get her bearings, to not worry about his bad-fitting borrowed coat. Yet she felt angry somebody had switched his—even if she couldn't worry about that now. She searched his eyes. "You discovered something."

Finally she hugged him. "Oh, *Eddie*. Your father. You found him. I knew you'd find out some news."

But he burst into sobs, covering his teeth. He pushed his filthy scarf up to his scrubbed-clean face, over his mouth.

A tight feeling gripped her stomach. "Oh, *good gracious*," she whispered, understanding now. Eddie's father was dead?

Sobs racked his body. She hugged him tighter. No good words to console. "I'm *so* sorry."

Understanding the awful pain, she let him sob into her chest, his shoulders heaving, his hurt spilling over. She wiped his tears with the sleeve of her maid's uniform, not worrying, for now, about the dirty swipe.

"He's in a better place," Annalee whispered finally, using a phrase she knew never made it better.

Eddie reared back. "No, he's *not*."

"What?" Annalee frowned, seeing his anger. "Wait a minute. He's alive?"

"*Yeah.*" He spat out the word, gray eyes flashing.

"Eddie. *Tell me.* I'm running out of time!"

Eddie scrunched up his face. "He's *alive*. And he's leading the stupid Klan. Right here in Denver. Their new leader." He kicked the ground. "And I *hate* him."

He yanked off his scarf, tossed it on frozen mud. Stomped all over it. "The stupid, dumb idiot. He brought scrawny *turkeys* to the boys' home for Thanksgiving. And pumpkins, rotten. Betcha he stole it all. But *he left us*."

He kicked mud at the filthy scarf, broke into sobs again, his bad teeth showing. A dog behind a corner house fell to barking, loud and angry.

Annalee whispered, "The boys at the school told you this?"

"When they heard my name, they *laughed* at me. *'Where's your white hood, Eddie Brown Junior? Where's your white hood?'*"

Annalee searched his eyes. Trying to sort this out. To *think.* To forget the yelping dog, going crazy.

"Listen, Eddie." Still whispering. "We're in the middle of something big. I don't know, but you've got to get back to the boys' home."

"No!" Eddie moaned.

"I know. But can you go back? Keep your ear to the ground? Just ignore the teasing. See what you can find out."

"I hate him."

"I know." She yanked open Hunter Castle's car door. "Goodness, I've got to hurry." She let off the brake.

"No, let me," Eddie begged. He pushed toward the car.

"No. Get back."

But Eddie ran behind the Caddy. Laid his shoulder into the trunk, busting to shove, not even knowing why, just wanting to hurt something, to break something. Just as a hulking black automobile turned onto the street. Painted letters on the body.

"Police," Annalee hissed. Eddie dashed back around, sidewalk side, both of them ducking. The police car slowed.

A flashlight clicked on. A needle of light pierced the dark.

Annalee flattened her body on the ground, groaned silently at the *cold.* She yanked Eddie down by his arm, both of them hugging the frozen, rocky, cold dirt.

The cop car jerked to a stop, dog still barking. Just not so loud.

The two cops inside, with their sixth sense, sniffed for something wrong, knowing a barking dog means *something.*

The driver geared to neutral. Annalee heard the gear shift, the engine idling. She held her breath, thinking.

About Mrs. Stallworth.

About staying small.

From under the car, she watched the flashlight sweeping the street. The driver mumbled something to his partner. The dog settled down.

The two cops seemed impatient, ready to leave. The flashlight clicked off, the car crawling down the hill, crunching on snow and gravel. It slowed for a minute at the Castles' house, finally picking up speed. At the bottom of the hill, it swung into the black night. Silence.

Eddie bounded up, scrambled around to the back of the Cadillac.

"No, *wait*," Annalee whispered. "I'm not going to do this. It's wrong."

Eddie's eyes went wide. "No, it's *not* wrong, Professor. Not if it helps us solve a crime."

"Detectives don't solve crime, Eddie," Annalee said.

"What? Yes, they do, Professor."

"Detectives let crimes solve themselves," she told him.

"That's crazy. That's stupid."

"I don't understand everything either," she told him. "But we'll figure all this out. The right way."

She opened the car door. Reset the brake. "I'm going back to the house. When I turn the corner to the backyard, I want to look up here and see you gone."

He shrugged. Nodded. Mumbled okay.

"Good man," she said. She turned and took off, then stopped. She ran back, hugged Eddie.

"I'm sorry about your father, Eddie. But we'll unravel this. I promise. My daddy's killer. Your father. The whole nasty mess." She looked him over. "And *please*—get back your coat."

He nodded, grabbed his scarf off the ground, jerked it around his neck. His scrubbed face was still wet from crying. He looked serious and not so young anymore. "Run, Professor."

But she didn't just run. She flew down the dark street, scrambling past shining Caddies, defying the icy air in her thin clothes, gripping the car keys in her hand. Trying to figure how she'd get them back in Hunter Castle's coat.

She stalked around the side yard, climbed up the back steps into the house.

Just as Eddie pushed.

The crash was spectacular.

And deafening.

The dinner party screeched to a halt.

"What was *that*?" Elizabeth shrieked.

Chairs fell back from the table. The party scrambled to the front door, pushed outdoors. Screams and groans.

"Oh, *Hunter*." The girlfriend. "Your *car*. Your fancy new one."

Then Elizabeth. "Somebody did this."

"Somebody will *pay for it*." Hunter Castle stomped outside, cursing.

Bernita looked across the kitchen at Annalee, turned back to the sink, picked up another plate to wash, not saying a word. Except one.

"Diversion."

Annalee stayed silent, realizing Eddie had disobeyed. Worse, she forgot to lock the blasted car. Or did she? Either way, would she take advantage of the chaos she'd created? She knew it was wrong, hated it was wrong. But she rushed past Bernita, bolted up the winding stairs to the second floor, pushed open bedroom doors, looking for . . . Elizabeth's room? This one? *Too masculine. That's Sidney Castle's.* Annalee set her jaw. At a door across the plush hall, she pushed. Yes, *this* one. Elizabeth's impressive suite.

Annalee eased the door open wider, let light from the hallway reveal frilly bed getups. Big canopy. A riot of ecru lace smothered everything. Bedspread, windows, armoire, nightstands, a rolltop desk. A lace-covered negligee and robe waited on a fancy chair.

What would be hidden here by Hunter's indulgent mother? The adoring Elizabeth. So nervous over Olivia's private talk with Annalee. So closemouthed with her husband.

Annalee licked her lips, eyed the massive floor-to-ceiling cabinet. Dark, heavy, foreboding, looking out of place, with a dozen drawers at least. What in the world was locked in all those drawers?

Annalee yanked the ribbon from around her neck, ran to the bedroom door, listened to the group still gaggling outside. Neighbors joined them from around the street, clogging the pavement. Police cars raced up, lights flashing, officers yelling.

Annalee tried her father's key. Dresser. Nightstand. Bookcase. Armoire. Knew she wasn't getting anywhere. Knew time was running out. They'd be back inside any minute. She started on the dark cabinet, bottom drawer.

Nothing.

Tried the next drawer. And the next. Still nothing.

She'd have to try later.

She scampered out the door, slung the key around her neck, pushed it inside her uniform. She scrambled down the stairs, gulping deep breaths, hit the bottom step.

And ran right into Sidney Castle.

He looked up the stairwell behind her. Looked her up and down.

She smiled barely. "Is everything all right? Sir?"

"No." He narrowed his eyes. "But you already know that."

"Beg your pardon?"

"Miss Spain, your uniform is a sight."

She looked down. Her white apron was streaked with mud and grass.

He whirled away, heading back outside.

"What about the cake?" she called after him.

He spoke evenly, not bothering to turn back in her direction. Instead, he pushed open the front door.

"The party is over. Send it back."

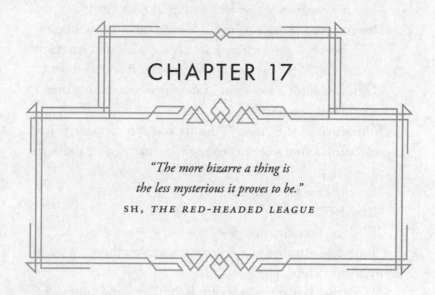

CHAPTER 17

*"The more bizarre a thing is
the less mysterious it proves to be."*

SH, *THE RED-HEADED LEAGUE*

"WHAT HAPPENED?" Bernita asked at last.

Annalee exhaled a guilty breath—after bolting to the coat closet, dropping the keys in Hunter Castle's coat pocket, and dashing back to the kitchen to switch aprons and grab a dish towel. She closed her eyes for a quick moment, slowing down her mind.

The two of them were tackling the dirty dinner dishes. Bernita washing, Annalee drying. A steaming sink of scalding dishwater and suds churned up between them. Annalee gripped the towel.

Bernita handed her a dripping glass. "What you scowling about?" Trying to tease her. "You making progress now? In whatever your little scheme is?"

"Making progress? At what? Getting us both fired?"

"*No.* Are you making progress at learning about rich people?"

"Rich people?" Annalee took in a breath. "Is that what I'm doing, Bernita?" She was starting to feel doubt and to show it.

"Girl, you didn't know that? I can tell you everything there's to know about rich people."

Annalee considered that. "I'm sure you can. Because you're smart, Bernita. You've heard enough in that dining room to know—"

"Exactly how they get rich."

"Exactly?"

"It's four—no, five things—"

"But wait," Annalee said. "What makes you think I want to know about rich people?"

"Well, that's what this is about. Isn't it? You and your *diversions*? You working here and acting like you're a maid, *wearing my uniform*?" Bernita frowned. "Isn't that what you're doing? Studying on rich people?"

"So teach me," Annalee said.

"I don't know half of what you're talking about."

"No, you know *twice* as much. Maybe more. So what about the five things?"

"Now *that* I know," Bernita said. She counted on her fingers. "One, oil. Two, water. Three, ore. Four, land. Five—"

"Murder," Annalee whispered.

Bernita gave her a look. "No, *votes*."

Annalee listened. "Oh, Bernita, you *are* so smart."

"Maybe I just know that's what it takes to move all that business to market. That's how rich people talk—around the dinner table. Always moving something to market."

Annalee put down the glass she was drying. "Like the nursery rhyme."

"To market, to market?"

"That's right. To buy a fat pig."

"To buy a fat pig . . ."

Bernita shrugged again. But Annalee thought of Eddie. He'd know every word of that nursery rhyme, words taught to him by his beloved mama after she was abandoned by his Klan-running father.

Annalee stopped. She felt her nerves jingle. With excitement? She turned to Bernita, spoke carefully.

"Hunter Castle . . . is he running for political office?"

"I guess. Planning to be the next state representative. Not next year. A couple years on when he's 'old enough.' So he says." She shrugged. "Except he's awfully slick. Don't seem much like a representative to me. But what do I know?"

Annalee grabbed a glass, started drying. "You know plenty. Like what's the largest amount of money you've heard somebody talk about at that dining room table?"

"That table?" Bernita laughed, tossed her dishrag in the sink. "I don't even have to think hard to answer that."

"Really?" She leveled her gaze at Bernita. "When was it? Recently? Or last year?"

"Well . . . a year ago. Thanksgiving Day. Everybody clinking glasses. Miss Elizabeth giving everybody seconds. Toasting the senator."

"The senator?"

"The Colorado senator. He's 'grooming' Hunter. The old guy." She laughed. "The *rich* one."

"Grimes." His family owned half of Denver. A possible buyer for the massive Lazy K Ranch.

"Right. Him and Elizabeth and everybody just praising ol' Slater Prince."

"Slater Prince was *here*? From Mount Moriah AME? For Thanksgiving?"

"Sitting right at that table, as natural as you please. And Miss Elizabeth *drunk* before it was all over. Mr. Sidney not happy about *that*, let me tell you! And Hunter late—as usual. But kissing *everybody*. *On the mouth*. Even me." She blushed. Then a deep sigh.

"Kissing . . . How much money, Bernita?"

The door swung hard.

"Aren't you two finished yet?" Elizabeth Castle whirled into the room. She flashed a look at Annalee.

"All finished," Annalee said. Telling a lie, but not easily. "I was helping Bernita wash up."

"Well, you can leave. Our dinner is over. Come back Monday and Mr. Castle will pay you." She started to turn.

"But Mr. Sidney wants her to stay here . . . to keep working."

Bernita's voice was clear, not yet shaking under her own lie. A lie for sure, Annalee recognized—understanding what Bernita would know. That in this household, the Castle wife and husband probably rarely spoke to each other anymore. Maybe not at meals. Not during the long evenings. Or certainly not later. Thus, Elizabeth Castle wasn't likely to ask her husband if Bernita's remark was the truth.

Annalee took a breath. "He said there's an extra room I could use." She picked up the dish towel. Hoping her white lie wasn't any more evident than Bernita's. "Or the basement.

I believe there's room down there." She started drying another wet glass. It was cut crystal. Probably imported. Bernita handed her another one.

Elizabeth narrowed her eyes. At Annalee. At Bernita. At Annalee again. Back to Bernita.

"Is that so? Well, Bernita's room is behind that little bathroom. But it's small. So you can sleep in the attic."

Bernita reacted, muttered something, not hiding it. She turned back to the sink, grabbed another glass.

Annalee tried to look calm. Still drying with the towel. "Thank you. It's such a cold night—"

Elizabeth cut her off. "Bernita will loan you a blanket or something. One of hers." She lifted the skirt of her fancy dress, turning to the swinging door. Then she gestured to Annalee. "Your uniform's a mess. And don't you dare break any goblets. They were a wedding gift." She narrowed her glance at Annalee. "And hold down the noise. You've already made enough racket in here for one night."

Swirling her skirt, she was gone.

Bernita threw down her dishrag. "The attic! Girl, that attic ain't fit for nothing, let alone sleeping!"

"It's nothing. Temporary," Annalee said, thinking. An attic. Good place to hide. Good place to look around, or that's what she tried to tell herself. She grabbed another glass, turned to Bernita. "The money. How much?"

"How much what?"

"Bernita, you know what I mean!"

Bernita turned her back, bent over the sink, plunged her hands into the sloshing water. "*Lord*, I can't even speak of that much money. Not out loud."

"And this is some place to work, isn't it, Bernita?"

Bernita sighed, lifting her hands from the sink. She gripped Annalee's shoulders, wet hands dripping. Putting her mouth to Annalee's ear, she whispered the unspeakable. The unbelievable.

Thus, she didn't look surprised that, in her shock, Annalee let one of Elizabeth Castle's cut crystal wedding glasses fall from her determined hand, not even trying to catch it.

It hit the hard wooden floor like the interruption of an impossible dream. It bounced once. Then it shattered.

Annalee swept the fragments. Bernita gripped the dustpan. Both of them quiet, except for Bernita's muttering under her breath, neither of them saying the obvious.

Instead, Annalee searched her thoughts. Thinking about evil. Not knowing how to get inside its head. But knowing, to solve a murder, she had to topple evil from its underside, to think as it thought, to see what it saw.

"Who else was at that Thanksgiving dinner, Bernita?"

"Oh, girl, why do you want to know?"

"You know why! For my daddy. My *murdered* daddy!"

"Your daddy," Bernita said, sighing. "He was a nice man."

Annalee swung around. "You knew my daddy? Joe Spain?"

"From the church. And right here. He did odd jobs. Never really talked to him. Except once." She looked at Annalee. "And *don't ask me.*"

Annalee searched Bernita's eyes. "Who else, Bernita? Who else was at that dinner? Last Thanksgiving? Last November?"

"Well . . ."

elected, goes to Washington as, say, a senator or representative. Gets on committees."

"And sends money back. In government contracts." Bernita said it with confidence. Clearly she'd heard the exact same words at the Castles' dinner table.

"Contracts worth millions," Annalee said.

"Worth more than that, girl. Get enough Klan members to fear somebody—you know, Catholics, Blacks, Jews . . ."

"Right."

"They'll keep throwing you money,"

"To fight your cause, support a campaign—"

"Buy another badge for your ridiculous costume. Girl, it's a money machine. By the time the dust settles and everybody get they cut—they call them 'kickbacks'—all them folks rolling in *high* cotton."

Annalee nodded, thinking. "So Hunter? He was at the dinner."

"I already mentioned him. He came in late."

"Right. And anybody else?"

"Well, all the wives of course. And girlfriends. Everybody dressed to kill."

"I can imagine," Annalee said.

Bernita frowned. "*Oh.* And that little mayor. Well, his town is little. Some little town. You know—way up in the mountains!"

Annalee took in a deep breath. Little mayor? Little mountain town? In Colorado? With its umpteen towns dotting the twists and tangles of the high country. Big towns. Small towns. Ghost towns. She tried out names. "Frisco. Breckenridge. Buena Vista. Central—"

"No, no, no . . ." Bernita lifted a pot out of the sink.

"Bernita. *Please*."

"*Okay,*" Bernita said. "There was the big rancher man, Lent Montgomery."

"And?"

"The governor."

"The governor of Colorado?"

"Well, what other governor do you think?"

"Of course," Annalee said. Trying to listen. Knowing the governor was a bidder for the big ranch, too. So she tried to follow Bernita's mood, tried to understand. To figure. She was making her mental list. So she said:

"And the man from the Ku Klux Klan? Eddie Brown? He was here, too, wasn't he?"

Bernita narrowed her eyes. "Well, if you know so much already, yes, he *was* here. Visiting Denver. To check it out, I guess." She cocked her head. "But that don't mean a thing."

Annalee frowned at her. "Meaning what?"

"Girl, don't you know nothing?"

"About the Klan?"

"They just a front."

"Bernita, a dangerous front."

"Making a lot of noise. Burning the *cross*." Bernita scoffed. "The Klan's about money, girl."

"And votes?"

"Now you getting it! They pick one man. Get all their people to vote for him."

"Like in a bloc," Annalee said, thinking. "Then they control him." She searched Bernita's face. "No, *he controls them*."

"You smart as me," Bernita said, chuckling.

"Oh, Bernita," Annalee said. "The Klan candidate gets

"Fairplay, Creede, Conifer, Silverthorne—"

"*No.*"

"Silver Plume—"

"You're confusing me, girl," Bernita said.

Annalee sighed. "No, I'm confusing myself. But together we're going to figure it out, Bernita. To market, to market." She thought. "But first to the attic."

Bernita gave her a look. "Girl, just sleep in my room."

"Sounds crazy, but I think I actually prefer the attic," Annalee said. "A place to think."

"You *are* crazy." Bernita sauntered across the kitchen to the attic door. Opened it. A stale, attic smell wafted through the doorway. She flicked a switch. A watery bulb flickered at the top of a narrow landing. "You prefer that?"

"Well, it's quiet."

"Yeah, just you and the spiders. And mice. And whatever else is living up there."

Annalee stood at the first step of the attic stairway. "Is there a lock on this door?" she asked.

Bernita jiggled the doorknob. Opened the door. Slammed it. Set the lock.

"And you're thinking what I'm thinking," Annalee said.

"That's right. You are not sleeping in that nasty attic."

They both laughed. "I'll make a pallet on the floor—in your room," Annalee said. But Bernita gave her a defiant look.

"No, Bernita. I am not taking over your bed. I can sleep right on the floor."

Bernita sashayed toward her tiny bedroom. "Ever heard of *hospitality?*" she said, spouting the word over her shoulder. "It's right out of the Bible."

"I'd almost forgotten." But she grinned.

"So you accept?" Bernita asked.

Annalee nodded, turned off the kitchen light, and followed her, too tired to even argue.

But Bernita snored. Loud. Like a freight train, roaring through the night in her pile of lumpy sheets.

Still, I can tend to my thoughts, Annalee pondered. She washed up in Bernita's bathroom, soaped and rinsed the uniform and apron, hung them up to dry. Then why not? She scrubbed the bathroom—sink, tub, mirror, floor, everything else—so Bernita wouldn't have to worry with it in the morning. She liked the feeling of making order, of setting straight, of coming clean, of *not* studying her winsome face in the shining mirror. Instead, after the cleaning, she washed herself up, crawled into Bernita's narrow bed in her slip, and stared at the ceiling. In the dark. Thinking of Jack. *Yes, Mrs. Stallworth.*

While Bernita snored.

While Annalee pondered. *Lord, I'm some kind of vagabond. Sleeping in different beds. And getting shot at!* She twisted her mouth. *But I don't feel hopelessly lost.* She pulled her covers up. *That's the curious thing. I can't see the end of the road. But I don't feel lost. And for that, I thank you. For letting me be your detective.* She smiled, stared at the dark, turning her mind to her mental lists.

Thinking about people.

The whole curious lot of them. Hunter Castle. Sidney Castle. Lent Montgomery. Slater Prince. Lemonade Hank. Eddie Brown. A US senator. Colorado's governor.

A little mountain mayor.

She thought harder.

Elizabeth Castle.

A great big cloud of witnesses.

Celebrating around a Thanksgiving dinner table. Making merry, yes, because of a huge pile of money.

One hundred million dollars. Fantastical sum. Annalee couldn't say it aloud herself. Nobody would believe a sum like that. *One hundred million dollars.* Too much cash to fathom.

Yet this bunch was rolling with glee? Because just a few days earlier, her darling, fare-thee-well, run-down, beloved, *frustrating* daddy—with some connection to almost every person at that table—had been murdered? And was no longer some kind of threat?

Annalee narrowed her eyes in the dark. Forced her sight to grow accustomed to the night blackness. She considered Bernita's snoring, her unsettled snoring, thinking, as well, for some reason, about the simple advice of Edna Stallworth.

After a while, Annalee switched on the night-light. Pale little lamp. It sat on Bernita's nightstand, giving off an aura of soft warmth in one corner of the tiny room. But Bernita didn't waken. Sighing, the Castles' maid grabbed her lump of sheets and turned over. Surprising, Annalee thought, that in all of this, Bernita seemed the one person most frightened. The others were agitated. But without a doubt, Bernita was frightened. Of what? Annalee frowned in the low light.

Frightened of the same things that frighten everybody?

Of being over our heads in something we don't understand? Opening up doors we shouldn't touch? Being so determined to dig up old secrets that danger lurks at every hand?

Or was Bernita simply afraid? Period. Of small things.

Annalee lay in the bed, not moving, listening to her own breathing. The quiet of it. The simple rightness of it. *Yes. I'm alive. And I thank you, heavenly Father. And I've got the good sense to tell you. So I'll say it again. Thank you, Jesus.*

Too simple?

Annalee pulled the covers higher and lay still. She realized she hadn't prayed big, as the theology professors at her college liked to say. Or as one insisted: *"Why limit God?"*

Yet she thought of her little prophet. "Do you wish to rise?" the curious St. Augustine wrote. "Begin by *descending*. You plan a tower that will pierce the clouds? Lay first the foundation of humility."

So Annalee listened to the midnight quiet. *Bring me down, Lord.* She closed her eyes.

They blinked open. *And forgive me. For wrecking that blasted car. I knew Eddie was going to shove it down the hill. I knew Eddie knew how to let off the brake. So, yes, forgive me my trespass. And thank you, in advance, for tomorrow.*

The promise of a new small day.

And the rest of this night.

A little prayer. Nothing fancy. So Annalee wasn't anxious as her eyes traveled around the room. Checking out the faded wallpaper, stuck like a pincushion with Bernita's fashion magazine clippings. Little articles ripped from Elizabeth Castle's thrown-away copies of a magazine called *Vogue*. Annalee didn't know what it looked like inside. But here in Bernita's room, tacked to the wall, was *Vogue*'s "Guide to Summer Chic in the City."

Annalee smiled, thinking about Bernita, imagining her

looking chic in the summer, her marcel wave set in place. Pretty straw hat propped *just so* on her hopeful head.

Indeed, next to the "Summer Guide" Bernita had pinned the "Guide to College Chic."

Then the "Guide to Bridal Chic."

Then the "Guide to Homestyle Chic."

Annalee sat up, looking down at the pallet and at Bernita. She was probably dreaming about being a chic, summer-fresh, marcel-waved college bride.

With a sigh, Bernita turned over in her covers, sleeping more soundly now, finally getting rest in this tiny place—this room filled with her aspirations and dreams and hopes to be more, have more. Rise higher.

Higher than Annalee herself had ever dreamed. Sure, she'd worked hard to get into college, to graduate, to convince her Bible college to go against every social tradition and give her a teaching job, even if underpaid. But to be a bride? Dreaming of a trousseau and a lovely little house with a white picket fence? Pretty roses a-blooming?

Never had she imagined such dreams. She'd never thumbed through a fancy magazine, drooling over dreamy photos of things to covet—lilac bushes in bloom, wildflowers swaying in dappled sunshine, climbing vines of summer roses. Or a sweet little house to make her own? She swallowed. With a handsome husband coming through the front door. Such pretty dreams.

Annalee looked at Bernita, raised a brow. *But big, pretty dreams like that take resources.*

Where in the world would Bernita find that?

Annalee aimed her gaze at a scramble of photographs, taped by Bernita to a tiny mirror over her small chest of drawers.

Annalee slipped out of bed, bedsprings creaking, to study the photo collage. Bernita slept soundly, allowing Annalee a closer look at her family snapshots.

First, from Bernita's mother. *To "B"—my darling daughter. Love, Mama.*

Annalee let her eyes linger, knowing she'd never own a photo like this. *To "A"—my darling daughter. Love, Mama.* Annalee sighed silently, telling herself not to think of such things but wondering what it felt like to know your mother from your birth, certain she loved you to pieces—calling you darling.

But I don't know that and I never will. She moved on to the next pictures.

A baby-faced boy in his soldier's uniform. *Love you, Cousin!* A schoolgirl photo of *Bernita Jamison, Whittier School, 1909.* A framed photo of the New Tabernacle Usher Board, Mount Moriah AME Church, 1922. *What a year! With love and blessings to Bernita, our faithful vice president!*

Another church photo, this one of the cornerstone laying—right after the fellowship hall and new wing were added a few years back. With *old* Reverend Blake, a crowd of Prince Hall Masons, Slater Prince, holding a small ceremonial shovel—because his money paid the tab—plus other church officers, associate pastors . . .

Annalee's breath caught.

And her daddy.

Standing in the back, off to the side. Holding a real shovel. The only one in the crowd in a cowboy hat.

And half smiling.

Or was that a wink?

Annalee gazed at her daddy's face. She tried to read it. He

was speaking to the camera. To the eventual viewer of this photograph. But what was he was telling them? No, telling *her*?

She touched the photo with her fingers. Traced the rugged cut of her daddy's face. Searched his sad, impenetrable eyes. *Tell me, Daddy!* But her whisper caught in the back of her throat. She spoke her questions in her mind. *What did you know? Overhear? See? Find?*

But her daddy was silent as stone. Half smiling.

She closed her eyes. *Oh, Daddy. I miss you so much.*

The good years. Even the bad? She looked again.

But her daddy's photo wouldn't speak back.

Annalee let her gaze drop.

Not breathing.

Not expecting a photo of Jack.

Unsigned. Actually it was a newspaper clipping from the *Rocky Mountain News.* "Colored Church Receives New Pastor." Jack's name, *Reverend Jack Blake*, was underlined. In red ink.

Gracious, what else? Atop the little bureau, Annalee counted three letters typed on stationery from Negro colleges—one a fancy school in Atlanta for elite Negro girls. To read the letters, as Annalee took the liberty to do, was to complete the portrait she was piecing together of the young woman Bernita Jamison and her *very* big hopes, dreams, and prayers.

All of them needing a pile of money.

Annalee clicked off the light. Bernita shifted in her covers, sighed in her sleep. Annalee crawled back into bed, pulled up the covers, clung to the pillow, breathing in Bernita's rose-scented perfume sachets tucked inside. Knowing exactly what she would demand Bernita tell her—first thing in the morning.

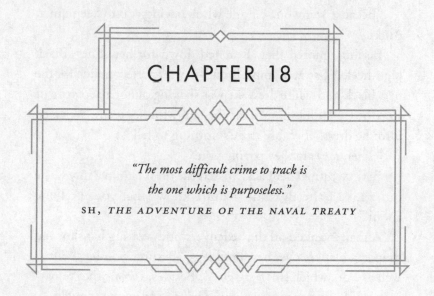

CHAPTER 18

*"The most difficult crime to track is
the one which is purposeless."*

SH, *THE ADVENTURE OF THE NAVAL TREATY*

"So HOW MUCH are they paying you? To keep quiet?"

Bernita turned her face, didn't answer. She was folding the blankets and sheets from her pallet. Outside, it was still dark. Barely morning. But dawn was coming, a slice of light already creeping through the blinds.

"We gotta get the breakfast," Bernita said, ignoring Annalee's question. "Before Miss Elizabeth and Mr. Sidney gets downstairs." She nodded toward the window. "Ol' sun be up before you know it."

"That's called changing the subject, Bernita."

Bernita whirled around. "And you don't know what you're talking about."

"Because you won't tell me who's paying you to keep quiet. And *why*."

Bernita ignored that. Reached down for her shoes. Black high-heeled T-strap pumps. Brand-new. A perfect match for the new black-and-white dress she was shaking out of a department store box. Bernita snipped off the tags with her teeth. Wriggled into the dress. "Because there's nothing to tell."

"Then *why* are they paying you?"

Bernita turned her back. Tossed the dress tags in a tiny waste can. "Like I already said—I don't know what you're talking about."

Annalee yanked off the bedcovers, still wearing her slip, and draped a blanket over her shoulders. "Bernita, you lie about as well as I do, which isn't very good. Besides, I *know* they're paying you. I just don't know why." *Or how much,* she thought.

"What? You been snoopin' around my room—while I was asleep?"

"Me? Snooping?"

Bernita narrowed her eyes. "Well, you right about one thing. You don't lie good as me." She pushed past Annalee. "We gotta get breakfast on. Or we'll be late for church."

Annalee stopped. *"Church?"*

"It is *Sunday*. So hurry up. I don't like walking in after service starts."

Annalee smiled to herself, weighing Bernita's bossy attitude, her all-too-obvious cover-up for all the things she feared and was hiding.

She watched while Bernita made a show of making her way to the kitchen, rattling over the coffee things, putting on bacon, setting out bowls. Her kitchen noise was a convenient distraction for Annalee's persistent question: Who was paying Bernita to keep quiet? One of the Castles for sure—if Bernita's job was on the line. But which one?

Annalee set the question aside for the moment, shifted her attention from Bernita and her intrigues to the prospect of going to church.

Knowing she would see Jack, feeling the thought of him take her breath away, make her stomach do its flips, confuse her thinking, leave her stammering at the sight of him. *Goodness, what in the world will I say to Jack Blake?*

After last night.

And that kiss.

But for now:

"I don't have anything to wear," Annalee said, still standing in her slip in the doorway between the kitchen and the little bathroom. She felt wary of wearing Aunt Jessie's fancy suit to church. Somebody might notice, especially with her wearing Aunt Jessie's ritzy coat, too.

"I figured you'd say that." Bernita set down the oatmeal spoon. "I ironed *two* church dresses for you before you woke up. Pick one." She pointed at two dresses hanging on hangers from the bathroom door.

Annalee stared.

"Now what's wrong?" Bernita asked.

"They're *red*, Bernita." *Poppy* red. "And one's a party dress. I never wore a party dress in my life. Let alone *red*."

"Well," Bernita said, "here's your opportunity." She looked annoyed. "Pick a dress—and hurry. If you going with me, I got to do *something* with your hair."

The walk to church was brisk. Sunny. Crisp.

Denver streets were just waking up, the air brittle with cold. The canopy of trees lining the neighborhood blocks was bare of leaves, allowing sun to press past the branches and heat the sidewalks. Still it was a cold walk.

Bernita complained, but she was jaunty and confident, sporting her new dress and shoes, fur-trimmed chesterfield coat, and a new wool hat cocked to the side. She'd pulled off the tag at the last minute.

Annalee was hatless. On purpose. Bernita had twisted, brushed, swirled, and spit-curled her hair into a real style. More dramatic than Annalee expected or would've designed herself. But to be honest, she sort of liked it. A lot.

I think?

She also liked the dress—Bernita's red dress, but not the party frock. The "regular" one was dramatic enough. In fact, she liked it more than she should. A red silk shift with matching red swing jacket. Brand-new.

And expensive. Too expensive for a maid's salary to buy. But despite the color, it was downright gorgeous. As pretty as Bernita's outfit. *Goodness*, maybe prettier. If she were comparing and on this bright morning she wasn't.

They both smelled like roses, in fact. With Bernita's fancy rose-scented soap bar—her favorite scent for certain—Annalee had sponge bathed herself again, head to toe, rinsing with hot water and a clean white towel, toning down the rose aura to a hint, not a hammer. Bernita had apparently done the same.

So both of them were smiling self-consciously as they fast-walked across town to church, scented like a garden. A clear sky overhead promised a day of wintry beauty, shimmery with sunshine. But it was cold, nevertheless, to the bone.

Annalee's heart was pounding, but not from cold, as she walked up the steps to the big church doors. Nor from wearing a pretty new dress—red. She knew precisely what she was feeling.

Anticipation.

Jack was somewhere inside those doors, putting on his preacher robe, making his mental notes, double-checking his sermon points. And praying.

One of his beautiful prayers was poised even now on his lips, she imagined.

"Heavenly Father, let the words of my mouth, and the meditation of my heart, be acceptable in thy sight, O Lord, my strength, and my redeemer."

God would hear that prayer, Annalee thought. And bless it too. She felt certain of it.

But, she wondered, what about her? Was she acceptable now to God? Walking up the church steps sporting a new do, wearing Bernita's sleek new red dress? Probably paid for with blood money? *Lord*, the same money covering up her own father's murder?

Annalee took in a breath, trying to clear her mind, knowing she was sashaying into church, hair all done, fancy dress swirling around her knees, a bit too short. And the former pastor's wife's expensive shoes on her feet and custom-tailored coat on her back—both fitting *too* perfectly. But her tongue tied shut.

Because what in the world would she say to Jack? And what would he say to her?

Annalee didn't dare imagine a romantic moment between the two of them. His eyes meeting hers, her hand in his. She'd run out of time for frivolous thoughts. And this, after all, was the *church*.

She stepped into the narrow narthex. Pulled off Aunt Jessie's coat, keeping her eyes down but seeing her church home without looking—knowing it from memory as well as she knew her own name. The gleam of the well-polished wood. The carpet swept within an inch of its fraying life. The big glass vase on the small visitors' table, filled with winter evergreens. A journal sitting open for guests to sign.

"Good morning! Like to sign our visitors' book? *Oh*. Mercy, as I live and breathe. If it isn't our little professor. *Miss Spain*. So glad to see you, baby."

"Good morning, Sister Calloway. I'm glad to see—"

The greeter reached out to hug her.

Just as her arm was yanked almost out of its socket.

It was Jack, dragging her into the cry room off the front church hall.

"Did you get my message?" His eyes searched hers. "Are you okay?"

She reared back. "Good morning!" she finally whispered, not wanting to be heard from the church hallway.

Jack stepped back. His pastoral robes gave him a distinguished air. But the top snap was broken. He'd dressed in a rush. "I wanted . . . I'm sorry about last—"

She stopped him. "How are you?"

"Well, first . . . The thing is, you—"

Annalee searched his eyes, waiting.

"You look . . ." He seemed embarrassed.

"What?" *What was he saying?*

"Annalee. You're beautiful."

She could feel herself starting to smile. Should she say thank you? But he startled her.

"No."

She pulled back again. "Jack, *what?*"

"Yes. I mean . . ." He took a deep breath. "I was worried about you."

At that, she felt self-conscious. And shy. But good. A good shy.

"I'm wonderful actually."

"I heard about some big car crash near the Castles'."

"Everything's fine." Then she read his eyes. "But is something wrong? What is it?"

"Your dad, Annalee. Did he have a shovel?"

She tensed. "Shovel?"

"And are you going back there?"

"To the Castles'? Jack, it's fine there. Everything went fine. I'm fine." Well, she was worried about Eddie. Where'd he go after last night? "Well, not totally fine. But what are you talking about? A shovel?"

An usher looked around the door.

"Pastor Blake. Service is starting."

The pipe organ was gearing into the processional music, the ancient hymn "Holy, Holy, Holy." A line of choir members, swishing by in white satin robes, plowed into the opening stanza.

"Our song shall rise to thee!" A too-loud soprano barely hit her note.

Jack winced. "Service is starting. Would you wait right here for me? Right after church?"

"Sure, but I don't understand."

"It's crazy—I know. I'll explain later." He started for the door but stopped, pushed the door closed again. He rushed back, grabbing her into his arms, almost pulling her off her feet.

"Jack!"

He held her close but gently, the aftershave, morning-bath scent of him making her knees weak.

"About last night," he said, "I hope . . . well, I hope you're okay with everything." He moved to touch her face but pulled back his hand.

"Okay?" *Is he kidding? I'm dizzy with okay,* she wanted to reply. But in the next instant, he yanked open the squeaking door. The pipe organ boomed.

In a rush, he was gone.

Annalee took in a long breath. *Lord, what does this mean? About Jack. About me. About us. And what did he ask? A shovel?* It didn't make sense. Then he was worried about kissing her? *Do I look worried about that?*

But no time to think. The door to the cry room squeaked open again. A young woman toted in her fussy baby, gave Annalee a distracted smile. She started unpacking diapers, bottles, rattles, blankets, shushing the baby.

"Sweet li'l baby. Mama's sweet baby. Hungry?" She cooed, fussed, kissed—but the baby still cried.

Annalee moved out of her way, slipped to a chair across the room. She sat there, trying to contain her thoughts. She fussed with a shoe, acting as if a pebble or stone was the trouble. She turned over the shoe, looking at the sole.

The young woman gave her an odd look.

"Stepped in some mud," Annalee said, giving her an assuring smile.

The young woman smiled back. Pretty face, lovely smile. A sad smile? The young mother nodded, showing she understood. Life gets muddy sometimes. But she stayed busy with the baby—the pride and joy of her young life. Cooing, singing, kissing, fussing, giving the baby a look Annalee never would know in life.

The look of a mother's love.

Annalee watched for a moment, envying, if she were honest, but letting the young mother go back to her baby. She sighed silently. *Lord, this world is complicated.* Just two short weeks ago, she was in gloomy Chicago, living a perfectly predictable life, writing her papers, teaching her wide-eyed students, debating Mrs. Stallworth over corn bread, retreating to her Sherlocks, enjoying her make-believe detective—giving not one thought to the irony that Holmes's first adventure, "A Scandal in Bohemia," involved his conflicted heart.

How did Watson start that first story? "To Sherlock Holmes, she is always *the* woman."

Now, here Annalee sat in sunbright Denver in the cry room of Mount Moriah AME Church, understanding Holmes, and maybe her own heart, like never before. Because against her better judgment and despite her intellectual and theological common sense—*oh, God, could it be?*—she was falling in love.

CHAPTER 19

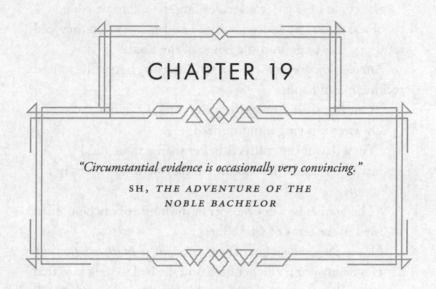

"Circumstantial evidence is occasionally very convincing."

SH, *THE ADVENTURE OF THE*
NOBLE BACHELOR

"GIRL, CHURCH HAS STARTED! You coming or what?"

Bernita again. She was standing in the doorway of the cry room, hands on her hips, looking sharp as a tack in her brand-new dress. And her jaunty hat. Set off with a peacock feather, thank you very much. Bernita smiled at the baby's mama. The young mother nodded.

"Save me a seat," Annalee whispered. "Baby's sleeping. And *here*." She reached for the brim of Bernita's hat, gave it a little yank. "There. Perfect. You look amazing."

Bernita grinned. She whirled away, skirts twirling—peacock feather trembling—heading toward the sanctuary.

A sacred place. Such is a church. Annalee felt welcomed by the walls.

She could hear Jack's voice, leading the call to worship.

"I was glad—oh, indeed, saints, I said *glad*—when they said unto me, 'Let us go into the house of the Lord!'"

Annalee knew every word of the liturgy by heart. She started reciting out of habit.

"'Our feet shall stand within thy gates, O Jerusalem!'"

Or was she saying it out of need?

"'For a day in thy courts is better than a thousand.'"

Just five minutes in Mount Moriah with Jack already felt like a gift.

"'I had rather be a doorkeeper in the house of my God, than to dwell in the tents of wickedness . . .'"

Or was she saying it out of fear? *Gracious, so much to figure out.*

Her daddy was no longer here, and she had to walk into that sanctuary. But as she rushed past the usher—grabbed a church bulletin, nodded a thank-you and a good morning, looked for Bernita, pushed her way past other latecomers to join Bernita on apparently her favorite pew: third row from the front, on the aisle—she was thinking only of one thing.

Daddy's shovel.

And Jack.

But this wasn't the time or place for challenging thoughts. Jack was telling the congregation as much himself.

"Many of you here," he said, looking across the packed sanctuary, "walked through these church doors with burdens and worries—and also desires, hopes, and dreams—in your seeking hearts."

"*Yes*, Lord," a woman up front moaned.

Annalee looked up at Jack, watching him at his work.

Wondering what he was thinking.

"I did as well," Jack said.

"Well, *that's all right*, Pastor," another woman sighed.

The rustling congregation settled in the seats, eager to hear more.

The pews seemed to lean in toward him.

Jack's voice sounded clear and even, centered and knowing, not tainted by doubt, prepared to minister. Annalee looked over at Bernita. She was staring up at Jack, taking in his every word, ready to follow. Annalee smiled to herself, looked back at Jack. Listening.

"But I would invite you now to lay down those burdens and worries on the altar of God's heart—and leave them there."

"Oh *yes*," the sister up front shouted out.

Was it Annalee's imagination, or did Jack's eyes seem then to find hers? She could've hoped for some secret communication between them. But his eyes were serious. He was looking at his congregation.

"Because our gathering this morning, my sisters and brothers, isn't so much about us—and why we've come here—wearing our nice clothes and our fancy hats and our new shoes—"

Bernita squirmed a bit. Annalee sat deathly still.

"Instead," Jack added, "we gather in this place—this holy place—to worship and praise our God. So draw in the wanderings of your minds, turning from your concerns and worries, and let's turn our attentions solely on *him*."

His dark eyes shone, scanning the sanctuary, seeing almost every pew filled. "Would you agree to do that with me now? To invoke his Holy Spirit to bless us as we turn our thoughts on our Lord, our Savior, and our God?"

With that, Jack adjusted his robe, knelt—leaning on his

good knee—bowed his head, and began to recite the formal invocation.

"Almighty God, from whom every good prayer cometh—"

His voice rolled out into the air over the sea of bowed heads. A clear voice. Deep, undoubting, determined.

"And who pourest out on all who desire it, the spirit of grace and supplication—"

Beseeching.

"O heavenly Father, deliver us, when we draw nigh to thee, from coldness of heart and wanderings of mind—"

"Oh *yes*," the sister up front agreed.

Annalee drew in a breath. Exhaled.

Urged herself to turn her thoughts.

From a shovel.

"That with steadfast thoughts and kindled affections, we may *worship* thee—"

And from Jack.

"In spirit and in truth; through Jesus Christ our—"

"Lord," she whispered, wanting to join Jack in concluding his clear, invocatory plea.

But Jack stopped midsentence. The organist, playing softly, stopped mid-measure. Heads jerked up, then turned to follow Jack's hard gaze. At the back of the church, pushing past the ushers and strolling down the center aisle, was the drunken, disheveled presence of the last person any in the sacred sanctuary expected to see entering Mount Moriah AME Church on a bright and brittle Sunday morning.

It was Hunter Castle.

Bernita's eyes got big as plates. She moved to stand, to speak. Or both. "Mr. Hun—!"

Annalee glared at her, yanking her arm. *"Not here,"* she whispered at Bernita, sinking low in the pew. Shielding her face with her bulletin.

"What?" Bernita whispered, eyeing Annalee funny, showing she wasn't sure why Annalee needed to hide. Or why the two of them were whispering. But Bernita took the cue, slunk low in the pew, pulled down the brim of her new hat.

Annalee looked away as Hunter Castle, his white wool coat half-on—reeking of expensive whiskey and tobacco and a night with his fancy woman or more than one—strolled past. He didn't even notice Bernita or Annalee, focusing instead on the pulpit. And on Jack.

Jack stood from his knees, pulled to his full height, his broad shoulders flexing under his pastoral robe.

He stepped forward just as Hunter came to a swaggering stop at the altar, lifted his right leg, and placed his gleaming black boot on the chancel rail.

A collective moan rolled through the crowd. Then just as quick, a stony silence.

Jack reared back to speak, looking at faces in the crowd. "Brothers and sisters. We have a visitor." He looked down from the pulpit, directly at Hunter. "Even if he is late for service!"

A ripple of laughter, light but nervous.

"So you're a comedian *and* a vaudevillian?" Hunter adjusted his boot on the rail.

"For starters," Jack said.

Hunter laughed. "Oh, you making some *theological* point?"

Jack didn't blink. "If you're keeping score."

Hunter stopped laughing. The tense room grew more silent.

"I'm not keeping score. I'm taking roll," Hunter said,

scowling at Jack. "And you know exactly who I intend to find." He swung around, set both feet firm. "Roll call."

He strolled along the front pew, looking at every face. At aging stewards and trustees on one side of the center aisle. At prim stewardesses lined up on the front pew on the opposite side.

"Let's see who's here. *You.* What's your name?" Hunter shouted at the woman on the aisle. She shrank back, turning her face, showing disgust.

Hunter ignored her, strolling to the trustee side of the aisle. "And *you?*" He pointed to a man seated on the front pew. Annalee recognized the man, a hotel janitor on weekdays and probably Saturdays, too. But on Sunday, he took off his floor-sweeping clothes and put on dignity and a worn but well-brushed unmatched suit, serving the Lord with deep regard and confidence, two things he was never granted in his life during the week.

The man stood. He spoke quietly. But the voice pierced the air.

"You don't scare me," he said.

Hunter Castle peered at the man and broke into laughter. He stood in his face, nose to nose. "You're not scared?"

Hunter turned to the next man on the pew—a longtime church steward, grizzled with age, leaning on a cane, but neat as a pin in a blinding-white Sunday shirt and stiff black suit. As the man unfolded himself to stand, Hunter yelled in his face.

"And what say you, old man?" Hunter gestured to the other man. "Think he should be scared?" He shoved at the grizzled man's shoulder.

With that, Jack came off the pulpit, stood before his stewards, his trustees, his ushers. All alert.

But the grizzled man cleared his throat, not to speak but to shout. His aging voice trembling. "What I say is you need to leave here, Mr. Castle," the old man said.

Hunter glared at the man. "Oh, you know my *name*? So you can report me—to the police? Tell 'em you know my *name*?" He sneered.

"Everybody know who *you* is." The aging man barely reached Hunter Castle's shoulders. But in his speaking, he seemed tall. Annalee sat up in her pew. Dropped the bulletin from her face, needing to be that brave.

"You the DA's son," the old man said. "Came here as a boy—years ago—with the youth group from your church. The one across town. You acted up that day, too."

Murmurs from the pews.

Hunter narrowed his eyes. "So you know me? So what?" He pushed at the man again.

Jack stepped between them. "That's enough! Mr. Castle's leaving now." He gestured to a line of younger trustees, seated on the second row, for backup, then pulled Hunter's arm from behind.

"Don't do anything stupid, Preacher," Hunter yelled over his shoulder at Jack.

"He won't!" Everybody turned, recognizing the booming voice.

Slater Prince. Chief trustee.

Annalee pressed her mouth, focused her gaze, watching close.

Prince entered the sanctuary from a side door, arriving

from his private office, wearing his fur-trimmed coat, glaring at Hunter.

"Your car take the wrong turn?" Prince asked.

Hunter cocked his head. "That how you treat a church guest, Prince?"

"A guest?" Jack said. "Wouldn't think of it. But an intruder—" He pulled tighter on Hunter's arm, while glaring at Prince.

"You're going to regret this in more ways than you can imagine—" Hunter tried to finish.

"Not nearly as much as you." Jack gave his arm a final twist.

"That's enough!" Slater Prince boomed at Jack. "You'll speak to me later!"

"Time and place!" Jack said, pushing Hunter toward Prince. Prince half caught him and forced him to stand.

Jack nodded toward the organist, gestured to the congregation to stand. "The morning hymn! 'Come, We That Love the Lord.'"

Jack started singing in his brawny baritone. "'And let our joys be known . . . !'"

He climbed to the pulpit, stood at the lectern. Singing loud, confident, leading the melody, assuring the congregation, urging the people to stand. He pumped his arms, pulling the singing from the still-nervous parishioners. He ignored Slater Prince as the chief trustee coerced Hunter Castle up the center aisle—in the midst of the singing and the pipe organ playing—right past Annalee and Bernita and straight out the front door of the historic and defiant building.

Jack's eyes shone, watching the men leave, as he sang the rousing hymn, urging its words to reach the rafters. *Let those re-fuse to sing who ne-ver knew our God; but chil-dren of the heavenly King may speak their joys abroad!"* He seemed to know his sermon on defeating giants, as listed in the church bulletin, would hit home—which it did. So he didn't need to smile at Annalee. Indeed, he didn't. In fact, he wasn't even thinking about her. Annalee could see that.

Instead, his thoughts were someplace grander. Or seemed to be.

Annalee understood. Hunter Castle dealt in mire and muck. Jack was leading his people to higher ground. She smiled to herself, thinking on that, allowing herself to admit: *I adore considering Jack this way. Everything about him, Lord. I adore considering his sermon and his pastoral robe and his brave confidence and even his good enough singing. All of him together. I thank you for him,* she told God. *And I mean that. With all of my heart, mind, soul, and strength.*

As he preached, she considered, indeed, his every word. More than once she said *amen.* Then she and Bernita grinned at each other, soaking in the Sunday church atmosphere.

———◇———

The service drew to an end. *I can talk to Jack,* Annalee thought, *about that shovel. And everything else.*

But the door to the narthex opened.

Everyone turned, looking back. *Castle again?*

Instead, this latecomer was the kind of surprise that takes all the breath straight out of a holy room.

It was a young woman. The most stunning young woman, in fact, that Annalee had ever seen in her life. Surely in a church.

Wispy and wondrous, the splendid beauty stepped with

gorgeous reserve through the sanctuary doors, far too late for service but still all done up in her Sunday best: winter silk and fur and gleaming pearls and perfectly applied brown-girl face powder and *lipstick*.

"Well, I never," Bernita whispered. She elbowed Annalee, appalled at seeing pale-pink lips.

"Hush," Annalee whispered.

But other women in the sanctuary were whispering, too.

The Reverend Jack Blake, delivering his benediction—"'Now unto him that is able to keep you from falling'"—froze mid-sentence, stared at the striking young beauty. This was not some twenty-four-year-old imposter who just got kissed. This young dazzler was the real deal.

Heads swiveled—watching the pastor watching the woman watching the pastor as the woman glided with confidence and purpose into the sanctuary, on a mission. She was followed by a distinguished-looking elderly couple. All three of them appeared united, smiling up at the pulpit.

Still silent, Jack didn't move a muscle.

So the aging hotel janitor—the senior trustee who'd challenged Hunter Castle—stood up slowly, finally breaking into an official smile. He pointed at the doorway, cleared his throat. "Giving honor to God—"

Annalee sat still as a stone, not wanting to think, not trying to hear. She was uncomfortably certain this drop-dead beauty wasn't going to mean good news.

But the janitor just would not let up. He went on. "And on behalf of our pastor, let us give a warm Mount Moriah welcome to our *true* guests this morning: our former pastor and first lady, the Reverend Warren Blake and First Lady Jessie Blake!"

Whose borrowed coat I'm wearing. Annalee looked down. *Not to mention her high-heeled shoes.*

Annalee stifled a moan, shoving the coat under her legs. Crossing her feet, she pushed herself farther back on the pew. But the graying janitor wasn't finished.

"In addition . . . ," he began again, working himself up to deliver words that were honoring and important enough for what he seemed *desperately* eager to say.

Annalee held her silence, determined not to look up at Jack, deciding she feared hearing one more word from the earnest janitor, but the faithful church member pressed on.

". . . let us give a warm 'welcome back' to our young pastor's—" The man paused.

What?

". . . beautiful friend."

Annalee might have sighed.

"But *more than that*—"

Annalee shut her eyes. *Heavenly Father God, when will this be over?* But that wasn't a prayer she expected a holy God would answer. Annalee whispered it anyway, unsure how to reconcile what the hardworking trustee finally and importantly announced, his arms held high in triumph.

"What'd he say?" Bernita whispered to Annalee.

Annalee shook her head. She couldn't speak. Yet, as with all others in Mount Moriah AME Church on that Sunday morning, she couldn't help but hear the last words of the fulsome announcement.

"It's Pastor Blake's new bride-to-be! Our pastor's fiancée!"

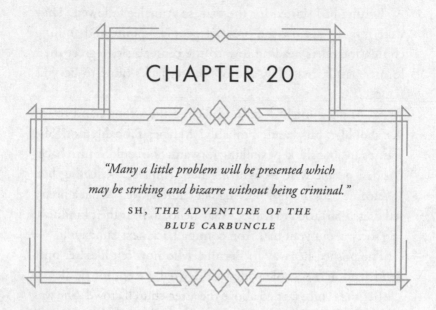

CHAPTER 20

*"Many a little problem will be presented which
may be striking and bizarre without being criminal."*
SH, *THE ADVENTURE OF THE
BLUE CARBUNCLE*

ANNALEE'S BORROWED COAT fell in a lump to the floor. Looking down, she considered leaving it there, stepping out of the shoes *and* Bernita's red dress, standing up tall in her humble slip and borrowed underwear and walking out—letting Jack find it all.

But no. She stopped herself. *Don't even think one thought about Jack Blake. Not ever again in this life.*

Instead, she reached down, picked up the coat respectfully, folded it neatly, precisely, painstakingly, and placed it on the pew—praying somehow for different shoes.

All over the sanctuary, men and women were standing now, looking to Jack to finish the benediction and close the service. He stumbled through to an awkward *amen.*

Bernita had started for the exit, so Annalee followed. They were moving against the press of people—polite and smiling church members heading toward the center aisle to greet their former pastor, first lady, and of course, Jack's bride-to-be. His fiancée.

So Annalee might've missed feeling the strong hand touch her shoulder. His hand? Probably? Maybe? Probably not? She wasn't sure, but she kept walking forward. She couldn't turn back. Besides, people were recognizing her. "Annalee!" Greeting her. "Welcome back, honey!" Giving her church love. "What a pretty red dress." She tried to smile, to say hello, to hear their kindness. "So sorry about your dad. You coming back next Sunday?"

She pushed her way to Bernita, who now felt like her only real friend in the whole wide world. Well, except for Eddie?

Bernita's voice carried above the after-church crowd. She was laughing with friends, standing by the choir room door, pulling on her stylish fur-trimmed chesterfield. Annalee watched her, this time not caring where on earth she'd found enough money to pay for it.

Bernita glanced at Annalee. "Where's your coat? Weather's turning."

"I borrowed it," she managed to say, "and the lady wanted it back."

Bernita shrugged. "Well—hello there, Sister Larson—well, it's too cold to walk home half-dressed. Let's look for something in the lost and found."

But lost and found only yielded three worn sweaters and a man's oversize heavy black jacket, more blanket than coat.

"This or nothing," Bernita said, pushing it at Annalee.

"My favorite color," Annalee said, not caring, shrugging into the jacket, which swallowed her up along with Bernita's pretty red dress.

Bernita laughed. "A dozen folks can fit in that thing with you."

Annalee tried to laugh but didn't feel it.

At the street corner, Annalee pulled back, told Bernita to go ahead. "I'm taking the long way home."

"Today?" Bernita said. "You'll catch your death." She eyed Annalee, then frowned. "You okay?"

Annalee reached over, gave Bernita a quick hug. "Just need to clear my head."

"I understand," Bernita said, but clearly she didn't. "I'll see you later."

"Later."

Always later. As a child, Annalee said that little word every morning to her father when she left for school.

"Later, Daddy."

If he wasn't hungover from the night before, he'd manage to say it back. "Do good work, little bit," he'd mumble, half-waving. But other times, passed out, he couldn't manage even that.

The neighbor ladies developed a second sense about it all.

"Like a hoecake, Annalee?" The woman from next door, Sister Nelson, would wait on the sidewalk, holding wrapped-up food, offering it.

"Thank you, Sister Nelson," Annalee answered. At school, her teachers urged her to be polite, taught her ladylike things. Sister Nelson and the churchwomen did the same. "But I don't want to be late for school," she'd added, gripping her books, hurrying.

Sister Nelson gave her the food anyway. "You'll be fine, honey. Just nibble on the way."

So Annalee didn't starve.

But she was a nibbler. Always just barely getting by.

Now she was just a woman walking, her feet cold and hurting in borrowed high-heeled shoes.

Turning north from the church, she walked deeper into her old neighborhood. Sidewalks were awake now. Church services were letting out. Cordial people said hello, too polite to ask if she needed help but probably thinking, *Are you okay?* Bernita's question, too.

Burrowed inside the man's oversize coat—sleeves too big, jacket way too long—her mouth tight, eyes disappointed, Annalee knew she looked thoroughly not right. Sister Nelson would've noticed, offered a hoecake.

"Just nibble on the way, Annalee."

So is that my destiny? A little nibble of this. Or that. But never the full meal? Annalee shoved her hands in the jacket's big pockets. A folded-up man's handkerchief, clean enough, lay on its side. She dragged it out. Held it to her face, surprised by its scent—a fancy woman's perfume? *Lord, this world.* She wiped her eyes.

Am I crying now?

But that was too dramatic. Then she thought, in fact, crying wasn't too dramatic.

Jack Blake took me into his home.

Fed me a warm meal.

Talked with me half the night.

Invited me to sleep in his bed.

Laid a nightgown out for me to wear.
Dressed me in fine clothes.
Set me up "undercover" to solve a crime.
Fought off bad men to save me.
Taught me to drive his fast car.
Gazed into my stupid eyes.
Then Jack Blake kissed me. She bit her lip. *Yes, me.*

And at that moment, my life forever changed. That's what she'd believed she wanted. A fresh life, grown-up and daring.

Yet before she could let the taste of him fade from her lips—her previously *un*kissed lips—she discovered, on this bright and cold Sunday morning, while sitting in a church, that Jack Blake had a bride-to-be. Indeed, a fiancée.

What a silly word. A trifle. A candy bonbon for distrustful, disloyal people. But the graying janitor seemed to luxuriate in saying it, drawing out each syllable: *fi-an-cée.* As if announcing a royal proclamation.

"Our pastor's fi-an-cée!" Drumroll and coronets.

Jack's fiancée. Who wears pouty pale lipstick.

Pink, doggone it.

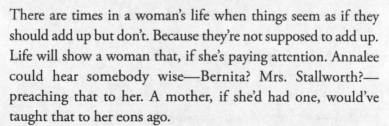

There are times in a woman's life when things seem as if they should add up but don't. Because they're not supposed to add up. Life will show a woman that, if she's paying attention. Annalee could hear somebody wise—Bernita? Mrs. Stallworth?—preaching that to her. A mother, if she'd had one, would've taught that to her eons ago.

But she'd never known a mother. She reflected on that as she watched two elderly Black women, buttoned up in wool coats, both hobbling a bit, coming toward her. They greeted her.

"Afternoon, honey."

"Good afternoon, sugar."

She gave them her soft smile. "Afternoon."

She looked back at the two, unable to calculate how much life both of them had logged between them. But both were still going, still pressing, still headed toward a clear destination.

Annalee suddenly stopped still.

Lord, have mercy.

She crossed a street, looking up at the crossroads sign. *How long have I been walking?* She wasn't miles from the church. She'd been walking in circles. Moving and going.

Aimless.

Distracted.

Letting life happen to her. Never planning it. Or deciding clearly where she was going. That's how she ended up at the Bible college. It was the only one of seven, after learning she was colored, that would take her.

But what did she learn there that mattered now? Finally this: God is visionary. Tactical. A planner. A builder. Laboring with detailed plans.

So here, Noah, construct the ark this *way. Moses, free your people* that *way. Little David, fight the giant* my *way.*

Absolutely nothing random, Annalee reflected, in God's doings. Not just letting things unfold, drifting along, hoping you get to where you're aiming and struggling to go.

Even Jack's fiancée—*whose name I don't even know,* Annalee realized—had stepped into the sanctuary with determination. *I will give her that.*

And me? Solving a murder?

Oh, God. What's my plan? I don't have one.

Looking up at the street sign, Annalee turned west, headed four blocks over, two blocks down—marching herself to the one place she'd avoided since arriving "home."

Her father's house.

Well, call it a cabin.

Well, call it a shack.

Well, call it a lean-to barely still standing up, even on a good day.

Picking her way down a weed-choked, rocky ditch, on the last block of the saddest street in the neighborhood, Annalee stepped in her borrowed high heels around an outcropping of boulders and came to the ramshackle place.

The crumbling brick of one wall actually tilted into the trunk of a peeling cottonwood tree, all of it just a few feet from the South Platte River.

Annalee took in the place. For a moment, she regretted that someone strong and good and honest, as she'd once believed Jack Blake to be, wasn't now with her.

But she shook off the thought.

Then, taking care to watch for rusted nails and splintering wood, she pushed open the half-leaning, unlocked door and stepped inside.

Ignoring the stale odors of a simple man's clutter—the unmade bedroll, rusted coffeepot, stacks of yellowing mining papers, one pair of worn-down cowboy boots—she took in the look of the place. Then she spoke her piece:

"Little bit's home, Daddy. Let's get to work."

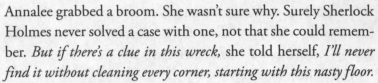

Annalee grabbed a broom. She wasn't sure why. Surely Sherlock Holmes never solved a case with one, not that she could remember. *But if there's a clue in this wreck,* she told herself, *I'll never find it without cleaning every corner, starting with this nasty floor.*

In the half-dark, she tackled the floorboards. Dust engulfed her, making her cough.

Wrong method, she told herself, setting the broom aside, looking instead up at the grimy walls and shelves. The shack's dull light pierced the slats. Boot spurs hung over the rail of a broken chair. A crooked shelf held flour and sugar tins. And more dust. Every surface, including one tiny window, was covered with it.

"Mercy." Why'd her daddy live like this? But she hated her answer. She hadn't stepped foot in the place for years, not since she left town for college. She'd even missed his funeral. Finally free to start her own life in bustling Chicago, she'd left her father to endure on his own, drinking himself further down. So she didn't bother herself when his little money ran even lower. Hardly worried to know if he still owned this place—this sad shack to lay his sorrowing head. It was the only thing he'd clung to and kept. And standing in that place now, she understood it perfectly—a cabin as close to nature in the city as her father could get. It was just like his condition, naturally run-down and still in disrepair, door without a lock, every surface neglected, except for one thing.

A neat shrine of newspaper clippings—with the dates underlined in heavy black pencil—seemed to plaster one entire wall. Each one offered a tribute to an old cowboy's brilliant, curious, clever daughter. The Colored Professor, Annalee Spain.

Annalee squinted. Took one hard look. Felt a rush of . . . *guilt*? Grief. Sorrow. Anger. Frustration. Why this neat-as-a-pin display about her now? And here? She started ripping down the clippings, crumpling the pages, tossing them down on the grimy floor, wishing her father hadn't been so *maddening*.

Lord, when it comes to men, I sure know how to pick them.

Fuming at herself, she grabbed at another clipping, yanking it down in a fury, enraged but woeful. That's how she looked in the grimy, jagged mirror—mouth pouty, eyes sad. So she shook her head and stepped back. She wasn't just fussing at her daddy. *I'm looking for him.* Hoping like heck, if she were honest, to also stumble onto a clue. Physical evidence. Yep, some little signal—left behind by her daddy for her to decipher, as if in a Sherlock. Some clever solution pointing her precisely to why her father had been murdered. Then, same as Holmes, she'd restore order to this upside-down world.

She crumpled the clipping. She'd been left nothing, only her feeble female instincts. *Doing me little good.* But they'd have to get cracking—to jangle her attention, just as a rustling noise was doing now, making her jerk and look up.

Her breath caught. She gasped. *Lemonade Hank?*

"Don't scream," he told her.

She didn't move, looked down at the dusty broom. A weapon? She pursed her lips, her breath fast. If he intended to harm her, she'd never reach it quick enough—let alone wield it. Besides, she wasn't in the mood for it. She'd attack him with what? Cowboy dust?

She let go of the newspaper article. It fell to the floor.

She spoke evenly. "Make this good."

He nodded once, seeming to give her a second to look him

over, to see him dressed for, what, church? Impossible. Yet here he stood, in her dead father's cabin—wearing an ordinary suit and tie. No fancy tuxedo. No stench of whiskey. *And no good reason to be here.* If she hadn't seen him drunk on the train and sloshed at Elizabeth Castle's dinner table, she'd never make him out as the same man.

In fact, he looked plain as day. If she had passed him in the street, she'd never have noticed him. So had that happened?

"You *followed me*?" She shook her head, feeling . . . violated? No, angry. *Really* angry.

"I'm with the government," he said. Flat voice.

Annalee sucked in a breath. "What do you want? Who are you?" She picked up her father's splintered chair. Another useless weapon. She slammed the chair down. One leg cracked, emoting dust, making her cough.

"I don't—" cough—"know—" cough—"who you are, but . . ."

"Bureau of Investigation."

"Bureau—" cough—"of what?"

The man reached into a pocket, pulled out a business card. He took a step toward her.

"Leave it," Annalee said, cutting him off. She pointed to the dusty table.

"Robert Hank Ames. I'm a special agent." The man stood taller. "And I know who you are, Professor Spain."

She pulled to her height too. "State your business!" She'd stopped coughing. "Start talking."

"I'm here to warn you."

She laughed hard once. "You're a little late for that."

The man nodded. "Your father, Joe Spain—"

Annalee winced.

"—was killed on a train."

"Absolutely. 'Regrettable accident.'"

"No," the man said. "Murder."

Annalee sighed. At last. Confirmation.

"You're investigating?" she asked.

"Well . . ." The man shrugged.

She felt her spirit drop, lower than it already was.

"Oh, so you're *not* investigating." She could see where this was going.

The man straightened his collar. "Something bigger—"

"Bigger than a murder? Or whatever my father was involved in."

"A major fraud, Miss Spain. More money than you can imagine is involved."

"You'd be surprised what I can imagine."

"These people are dangerous."

"Why?" She cocked her head. "Because they're your family?"

The man narrowed his eyes. "You're treading deep water now. You need to back off."

"I keep hearing that. And I know it. My father's dead. But you're not investigating his death, are you?"

"Something bigger, like I said—"

Annalee grabbed for the chair again. "Please leave, Mr. . . . Ames. Or whatever your name is."

The man reached for his card but left it on the table. "I didn't have to warn you, but if you don't stay out of this . . . and stop meddling . . ."

"Meddling?"

"Well, yes, you're meddling. So we can't protect you." The man sighed. "You're a smart lady, Miss Spain." He paused, looking her over in her red dress. "You're a good-looker, too. Even if you don't seem to know it—"

"Time's up!" Annalee said. She might've ignored his fresh mouth, picked up from him a clue or key fact. The man must be loaded with information. But Ames, or whoever he was, followed her on the wrong day.

He opened the warped door, headed out.

He shook his head. "Please don't make a mistake."

"Won't be the first time." She turned her back on him, moved to grab more newspaper clippings off her father's cabin wall, turning back only once.

"Take your card." She pointed to the table. "Then shut the door behind you."

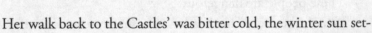

Her walk back to the Castles' was bitter cold, the winter sun setting fast. A snappy breeze cut the air without mercy, chilling her to the bone. *Just keep walking,* Annalee told herself. *You'll get there.*

She blinked in the cold. That sounded sublime. *You'll get there.* But what was *there?* All she had were false starts. A useless key. She blinked again. And a "bureau man" with a deadly warning. *"Stop meddling."* And her so-called female instincts. She pushed her hands deeper into the coat pockets. *And a man named Jack who kissed me. But that's all over.* She heard Mrs. Stallworth. *"Stop your pitying."* But surely she'd never had a more lousy day, spiritually, in her life.

She kicked at a pebble, looked down at her feet. *I don't even own a pair of decent shoes. And Jack has a fancy bride-to-be? But stop pestering on that.* She'd just grieve her soul.

Besides, she had work to do. Get back to her case. Still, she was alert enough, a few blocks up, not to miss seeing Eddie, of all people, on a street corner. In fact, she heard him before she saw him, letting her ears follow the sound from a huddled shape under a flickering light on Sixteenth Street. Eddie clutched his fraying scarf in his hand, waiting on the near-empty street corner for handouts—without any coat. Singing.

"I'm al-ways chas-ing rain-bows . . . ."

The pitch perfect. The sound clean and pure. When everything that she was trying to accomplish *wasn't*.

"Watch-ing clouds drift-ing by . . . ."

She threw back the hood of her lost and found jacket. Racing across the intersection, she called, "Eddie!" Not worrying about her ridiculous borrowed high heels. Or cowboy cabin dust on her ridiculous borrowed coat. *Gracious,* she thought, *I miss my own clothes. Except,* she sighed, *I don't have any clothes.*

Eddie saw her running toward him.

He stopped singing, started explaining.

"Professor, I made *twenty-five cents.*" He stood shivering, his lips half-blue.

Annalee reached for him, wrapped her arms around him, gripping tight. Under a thin shirt, he was cold as ice. She opened her coat, pulling him in, and hugged him tighter, trying to stoke heat. He'd catch his death.

"Thank God!" She wiped her eyes, trying to ignore passersby gawking at them, looking appalled. Making comments and catcalls.

A man yelled, "Hey, kid! You know this gal?"

Eddie glared at him. "She's not a gal. She's a prof—"

"Ignore him, Eddie," she said, not feeling up for even a

minor confrontation. Or for coaching his eleven-year-old soul on the complexities of the infernal color line—the line that couldn't be bothered with solving her dead father's murder. *But what's a color line?* At the Bible college, her students had begged her to explain it, the daily insult of it. Indeed, the holy obscenity of it. *Mercy, Jesus*, the lynching, burning, jailing, raping, degrading sickness of it—by people wearing his cross.

How does your professor feel? About all of that? Her honest truth?

"I feel sad for God."

So when was God going to stop it? But how could she ponder that with her students—or with Eddie? Or profess about the twenty-four-hour-a-day blasted soul killing of it? That was the point, right? To kill off your body and soul. To remind you that, in your own country, you meant *nothing*. You weren't seen as redeemable, a member of humanity. Or worth the effort to make it so. Worse, nothing you achieved ever changed it. Was that her fate? Just keep nibbling?

"Professor, what's wrong?" Eddie held out his hand. His filthy glove cradled a tarnished quarter. "*Look*. I made a whole two bits."

"Goodness, that's fine, Eddie. But why are you out here—and not at the boys' home?"

"I *hate* that place. And besides, I'm making money!"

"Oh, Eddie. Let's please not talk about money." She held his face with her shaking hands. "You're ice-cold. Did you eat?"

He shrugged. "Just a little. A lady from the restaurant over there gave me some soup at lunchtime."

"Well, it's suppertime now."

"Wow! At Reverend Blake's?"

Annalee turned sober. "No, at the Castles'. I work there now, remember?" *If I still have a job.*

"I know. You're an undercover detective, working on crime!" Eddie frowned. "Are you mad at me? About last night?"

"It's okay," she said. "Actually, you helped."

"That's because you're working on a crime!"

Annalee smiled, hugged him tighter as they walked, ignoring the gawkers, whispering to herself the only truth she could muster in reply.

"No, Eddie. Crime is working on me."

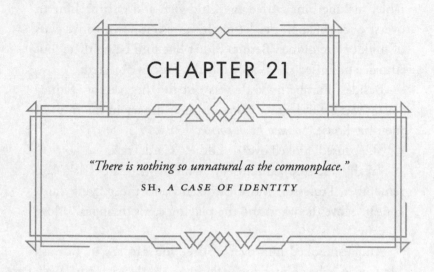

CHAPTER 21

"There is nothing so unnatural as the commonplace."

SH, *A CASE OF IDENTITY*

So SHE LET THE CRIME WORK. Studying the angles as she set the table in the Castles' fancy dining room. She moved through the motions of helping Bernita with dinner, wearing the maid's uniform again, smiling about it, in fact, as if everything were perfectly fine. Then she might trick her emotions into forgetting about Jack and his Sunday setback . . . and her dismay about his Sunday setback . . . and her confusion about it. Instead, she reminded herself what mattered to her most: *Truth and justice for confusing Joe Spain.* And? *Nobody is fighting for him but me and Eddie.* She thought of Lemonade Hank. *And willing to die for him, too?*

"If I clean my plate," Eddie asked, "can I see Card Trick again?"

"What'd you say, honey?" She'd set him up at the kitchen

table, making him a fried egg sandwich and cutting him an oversize slice of apple pie, letting him wash it down with a glass of milk before dinner. Bernita didn't like him being there, but Annalee promised she'd explain if the Castles objected.

Besides, Elizabeth Castle was out for the evening. Sidney Castle was behind closed doors in their library in the front of their big house. *So now I can think.*

She paused, looked over at Eddie. "Card Trick?"

"Yeah!" He stopped himself. "I mean *yes*. Card Trick. You remember, Professor. Move the wand and the playing cards appear. Move the wand and the playing cards disappear. I love that toy!"

Annalee looked him over. "Sure, you can see it. But ask Mr. Castle." She pointed to the darkened butler's pantry. "Walk through there and down the hall. But quiet. No running!"

"Thanks, Professor!" Eddie said.

"Then knock on the library door. Ask Mr. Castle if he'll show Card Trick to you again. Say *please*."

Eddie jumped up.

She gave him a look. "And wipe those pie crumbs off your mouth."

Card Trick. Eddie's mention of the sleight-of-hand toy made Annalee think of her father's ramshackle cabin and her struggle to find something there. *In plain view? Like a card trick?*

Nope, that's just a silly game. But what about Hunter Castle? He wanted both her and Eddie dead. Jack now, too, after their tense encounters. But why? Because one of them probably could tie him to her daddy's murder? But that wasn't enough. Hunter was hiding something else himself.

Annalee peeled another potato, quieting her mind. *Stop trying so hard. Let the answers find their way to you. Let yourself see.* With sharper instincts. She squinted while she peeled.

"What you doing over there?" Bernita interrupted.

"Oh, just thinking about—"

"I already know what you thinking about. Pastor Blake."

Annalee turned away. She grabbed another potato, pretending to be clueless. "What in the world are you talking about?"

Bernita laughed. "I *knew* it. I saw the two of you whispering and huddling before service." She wagged a finger. "And shame on you both. The man's *engaged.*" Bernita gave her a look, headed into the pantry for more dinner things.

Annalee let her go, refusing to let herself think tonight about Jack Blake, forcing her thoughts back to Card Trick. To Hunter Castle. Who wanted her and Eddie dead so they wouldn't discover . . . what?

"Secrets, secrets," Bernita said through the pantry door. "Everybody round here got secrets."

"You making a point?"

"No," Bernita said. "But Pastor Blake is."

"I have no idea what you mean."

"He came by here this afternoon, asking for *you.*"

Annalee blinked. Returned to her potato. She started peeling hard, feeling as if she suddenly couldn't breathe.

"Well," she managed to say, "that was a waste of his time."

Bernita put down her dish, crossed her arms. "Annalee."

The professor kept peeling.

"Professor," Bernita said again. She walked toward her side.

"Is there something you want to tell me? 'Cause if there's one thing I can do, I can keep a secret."

Annalee put the potato in a bowl of cold water, looked evenly at Bernita. "Bernita, how long has Mrs. Castle collected music boxes?"

Bernita gave her a look. "And that's called changing the subject." They both half grinned. "Besides, don't you want to know what Pastor Blake said?"

"Not really. Not tonight. But what about those music boxes?"

"Why you wanna know that?"

"It's nothing wrong. I was just wondering. When'd she start collecting them?"

"On her honeymoon, I guess." She shrugged. "She's always talking about her honeymoon this, honeymoon that. Her fancy china. Her crystal goblets. Her honeymoon music boxes." Bernita frowned. "I don't know, girl. They some funny people, the Castles. And guess who's the rich one?" She lowered her voice. "Miss Elizabeth."

Annalee took that in but moved across the room. Started folding napkins. Turned to Bernita. "Do they ever ask you to do things that you don't, well, understand? Like go someplace or look for something?" Annalee kept her voice steady. "Or hide something?" She made a little stack of the napkins—a perfect tower of linen—waiting for the answer.

"I already told you. You're not gonna make me lose my job."

"I wouldn't dare. Especially if you're saving up for college." Annalee let the words find their mark, her back still turned, *not* regretting she'd maybe gone too far. She wasn't surprised to hear Bernita stomp across the room.

"Listen to me, *Professor*." She spoke close to Annalee's face.

Annalee turned, facing her head-on. "I'm listening."

"I know you're working here for some funny reason. Miss Elizabeth don't even know why you're here. Told me to watch what you do, but *try* to be cordial and all 'cause Mr. Castle say so. Pastor Blake knows him and they both seem to think awfully highly of you." Bernita pursed her lips. "Even though Pastor's *engaged*."

Annalee stayed silent.

"But Miss Elizabeth don't like it one bit. And to tell you the truth, I'm not sure I like it either. *But* if you recall—" Bernita took a deep breath—"I'm the one who kept you out of that nasty, dirty attic." She raised her voice a notch higher. "But that don't give you *no* right to look through my personal, private information."

"You're right. It doesn't." Annalee refolded a napkin, feeling Bernita's righteous anger, appreciating it, thinking how it felt to be disrespected or taken for granted. Or misunderstood. Or rejected.

She thought, indeed, about Jack, drawing in a deep sigh.

"If you want me to say it, then I confess, Bernita. I snooped around." Annalee added, "A little bit."

Bernita huffed.

"But not much. Just while you were sleeping, I looked at your fashion articles and whatnot from Miss Elizabeth's old magazines."

"Oh, those." Bernita shrugged.

"And your photos."

"*What?*"

"I didn't actually pick them up or anything. I just noticed them."

Bernita chuckled. "Oh, you mean while you were just notic-ing my clippings and whatnots?" Mocking. "So what else you notice in my room?"

"Well . . . letters." She looked down. "From the colored colleges."

Bernita got quiet. "That wasn't none of your business."

"But is that your dream? Going to college? Bernita, that is *visionary*. That's strategic. That's thinking ahead, planning for a beautiful future, which you deserve. You're too smart not to have a dream. *Please* say you'll follow it."

Bernita listened, laid down her potato knife. "Tell the truth, I don't know nothing about college. But all the colored girls in town—I mean, the ones doing something with their lives—they're going down South to the colored schools. Well, the rich girls are going." She shrugged. "And the smart ones. Like you, Annalee."

"Well . . ."

"And Mr. Prince's daughter." Bernita turned for a moment.

"Mr. Prince has a daughter?" Annalee tried looking away. "Guess I forgot that."

Bernita nodded. "Ain't seen her in a while. Well, not until today. She was at church. Home for holiday, I guess. They say she went to that high-struttin' girls' school down in Atlanta." She let out a long sigh, grabbed a potato, started peeling. She lifted her gaze a second. "Lord, Atlanta! I would love that, for sure."

Annalee smiled. "What does she look like?"

"Who?"

"Slater Prince's daughter."

"Why you want to know?"

"No reason. I saw some young ladies at church. Thought she might be one of them."

"But you met her."

Annalee frowned.

"In the cry room, Annalee. She was holding Sister Sparks's little baby. Rocking him and, well, singing to him and everything."

Annalee stood stone-still. Trying to *think*. "That wasn't the baby's mama?"

"No. The mother is Sister Sparks, the soprano. She was in the choir this morning. Singing too loud. Calls herself a soprano anyway."

Annalee smiled, but she wasn't thinking about choir members. She was thinking about pretty daughters of rich men, beaming with love and holding sweet babies.

"So Slater Prince's daughter was babysitting?"

"Mercy, you ask so many questions."

"It's nothing really," Annalee said, trying to look indifferent. But she couldn't look indifferent. Because she saw that young girl's eyes—a mother's eyes. She'd bet her life on it.

"What kind of professor are you anyway?" Bernita asked.

"What? Oh . . . theology."

"What the devil?"

They both laughed. "Theology," Annalee said. "The study of God."

"Mercy, Lord," Bernita said.

"That's what I said when they gave me a scholarship—the last scholarship they had."

Bernita looked at her strangely. "Think I can get a scholarship?"

Annalee reached for her. "Bernita, if you want to go to

college, I'll find you a scholarship myself. You pick your subject. Oh, so many choices. Makes your head spin—psychology, sociology, history, English, biology, zoology."

"What is *that*!"

They laughed again.

Then Annalee sighed. "Last night, Bernita, while I was looking at your letters—well, I did read one of them."

Bernita scowled.

"But I wondered why you'd want to leave your hometown— your church, job, friends—and go clear across the country to school?"

Bernita pulled back a kitchen chair, sat herself down, hands in her lap. "If you really want to know the truth," she said, "it's because I'm scared."

Annalee sat down facing Bernita. "Of what?"

"Lot of things, really."

"Like what?" Annalee barely whispered the words.

"Of getting *stuck*," Bernita whispered back.

Annalee didn't interrupt, knowing Bernita was following her own thoughts down an unexpected path. Not a crime-solving path, as Annalee had hoped. Or a love-explaining path, as Annalee needed. Instead, Bernita was talking about her life. Annalee searched her face, knowing she needed to grant her the grace to keep talking it out.

"Mercy, getting stuck," she said.

"That's right. Getting stuck *here*. In this kitchen. In this *job*. Ending up like my mama, at age fifty-five or sixty-five—or seventy-five, God help me—and finding myself still sitting at this table, still peeling potatoes and rolling out biscuits, still washing and drying the blasted dishes."

She tossed a half-peeled potato in the bowl, sloshing milky water all over the table. "My whole life just wasted." She wiped at her eyes. "That's what I'm afraid of. A wasted life."

Annalee sat back in her chair. Thinking. Listening. "Most everybody's afraid of that. Young, old. Poor folks. Rich folks."

"Rich folks," said Bernita. "They more scared than anybody. Scared money won't fill up that big hole in their souls. Scared that even with all their money, they still end up not knowing who they are, end up being nothing!"

Annalee nodded, knowing Bernita was right—trying not to weigh if that same fear might be burning itself into her own soul, but she already knew it was.

She stood up. "What if there were a way to make sure that doesn't happen—to you? A wasted life."

"What you mean now?"

"I mean, what if you could start a new life, like you say, and get out of this kitchen for good? By not fearing life. By not being afraid of it. Standing up for what's right. What if there was a way?"

"I can't do it, girl. I'm just not sure I can do it."

"But what if we helped each other? Helped sort things out? So you could pull yourself together—and leave here, Bernita? To start over?"

Bernita whispered, "Everything's messed up for me here, Annalee."

"Doesn't have to stay that way." Annalee wiped her hands on her apron, untied it, straightened her uniform, headed toward the butler's walk-through.

"Where you going? What about dinner?"

"Dinner can wait," Annalee said. "I've got something more important to do."

"Oh *no*. You gonna do something crazy."

"Goodness, I hope so." Annalee pushed open the door. "Starting with Sidney Castle."

"But don't make me lose my job!"

He was sitting in his wood-paneled library at the front of the house. Waiting in the dark for dinner, sipping at an evening cocktail. The bowl of his lit pipe glowed white, a flash of hot light in the dark room.

Annalee observed him from the doorway. "It's me, Mr. Castle."

He shifted in his chair. "Eddie's in the parlor. Playing with expensive toys."

"You're spoiling him," Annalee said. "He likes talking to you."

"He's a good boy." Castle puffed on his pipe. "Now what about you, Professor? What took you so long to find me and talk?"

"I didn't want to rush you," she said. "Or myself."

Sidney Castle chuckled. A dark, sad laugh. "You're awfully young to be so wise, Miss Spain."

Annalee listened, contemplating Castle's deep presence in the corner. "Wise? I don't know. 'Wisdom uttereth her voice in the streets.' But is anybody listening?"

Castle pulled on his pipe. His bowl glowed, still hot and anxious. "Too much competition to hear Wisdom," he said. "And what a waste. Something so priceless is valued less than all the empty, vapid, ridiculous earthly treasures—like gold."

"Or oil," Annalee said.

Castle set down his pipe on a hard surface. "Or water."

Annalee took a sharp breath. "Or votes."

"Like I said. You're awfully young to be so wise."

"Not really, sir. But is that what this is about? Winning an election? And all the ways to twist it and sell it and invest it into profit and . . . kickbacks?"

"You're dealing with dangerous people, Professor." His voice was cold, vacant.

"Yes, so I've heard." She paused. "Then why did you let me get involved?" She answered her own question. "To keep an eye on me? See what I'd uncover?"

"You make that sound wrong."

"Does that mean I have your permission to continue with my investigation?"

Castle's voice grew harder. "Could I stop you anyway?"

"Probably," she said. "But I'm praying you won't, even though you know my search will lead to a place that could hurt us all."

Castle sat up, tapped his pipe tobacco in an ashtray, let it smolder. "I can already guess where it's going to lead, young lady. I just want to know if somebody smart like you can find it."

"Smart? I don't think so," Annalee said, thinking of Bernita's intelligence but thinking also of her troubles with Jack. And her confusion about her daddy. And about Eddie. But also about Mrs. Stallworth. *Lord, is she doing okay by herself?*

Annalee peered across the dark room, aiming her eyes at Sidney Castle. "A lot of things confuse me, sir. But that's never stopped me before. I just keep working and trying and going until I figure a thing out."

"Not everybody goes that far."

"Not everybody's daddy was thrown off a train and killed."

"Indeed," Castle said. He clicked on a small lamp. The handsome room came into focus, showing his solitary spirit seated there. He pulled a pipe tamper out of his jacket pocket, tamped down the burning tobacco. "I'm not that smart either." He stood up, smoothed down his smoking jacket. His eyes bored into hers. "But it's time I was honest."

He walked past her, heading for the dining room, pressing a key into her hand. "I'll drive Eddie to the boys' home. And you—"

He turned off the lamp. "Go find your killer."

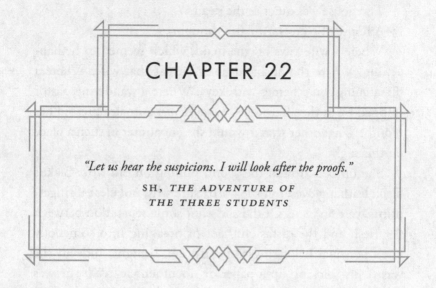

CHAPTER 22

"Let us hear the suspicions. I will look after the proofs."

SH, *THE ADVENTURE OF*
THE THREE STUDENTS

THE KEY UNLOCKED Elizabeth Castle's rolltop desk. A smooth click. One neat turn to the right. The lock sprung.

Annalee let out a tight breath. She glanced at a pearl-faced clock on a nightstand. Half past eight.

She crept to the bedroom door to double-check for sounds but heard only silence, a Sunday night quiet. Bernita had departed in a rush for the evening service at a Baptist church in Five Points. Elizabeth Castle still wasn't back. At her mother's across town—something about preparing for a ladies' bridge luncheon the next day.

Sidney Castle was gone, too—returning Eddie to the children's home, then stopping at Chessman Park for his Sunday night, after-supper walk, probably brooding with every step.

The house was quiet as the dead.

A house of secrets, Annalee thought.

Where a wife pays off the maid, which seemed to be happening. Where the husband doesn't trust that wife. Where a threatening son schemes with keys. Where a wandering pastor stopped by in the afternoon . . . *to see me?* Annalee pressed her mouth. What other secrets would she encounter in such a place on this night?

She tiptoed around the room, pulling on old Mrs. Blake's black leather gloves, but she wasn't sure why, not clear if fingerprints were an issue. Or did she want some separation between her flesh and the distasteful fact of breaking into somebody else's personal belongings on purpose? Tonight, indeed, she wasn't just picking up a paper or document to read; she was breaking and entering.

In the dark.

The room sat in the shadows, the pale glow of a sconce lamp barely lighting the hallway.

Annalee stood in the bedroom at the desk, raised the roll top slowly, heard it creak a bit, thinking for a second she heard a noise downstairs. But that wasn't possible. The household had scattered in different directions for the evening.

She surveyed the desk clutter, knowing it would be harder to search through clutter and make it appear untouched than to search a desk that was neat and ordered.

So she pulled up a chair. This would take a while, requiring she make a mental picture of the desk. She clicked on a tiny desk lamp, a miniature Tiffany. Probably cost a fortune. What did she see in the pale glow? A pile of mail in the front. Store receipts and advertisements in back. Ink bottles. Splatters across various papers. Elizabeth Castle's embossed calling cards spilling out of the printer's box. Postage stamps. A painted glass figurine. Glass paperweight. A tropical butterfly trapped in perpetuity inside the globe. A tangled gold-chained necklace, the clasp broken. Reading glasses falling half out of their needlepoint case.

Then above the desk's main platform, she saw a row of open cubbyholes, each one jammed with papers. Old envelopes. Rubber bands. Pencils. Paper clips.

Annalee let her eyes take in the jumble. *What in the world am I supposed to see here?*

She pulled in a breath, thought about perspective—that was, about sight. So she recalled the blind man waiting alongside the Jericho Road, an important story recorded in three of the four gospels. *"Help me, Jesus, to see."* A precise, perfect prayer. The blind beggar man could've asked for money, a job, a place to live, a new Cadillac, fancy clothes, a white coat, new sandals, something to eat. Instead, the blind man asked for strictly what he needed most. His sight. A simple, vital miracle.

Help me, Jesus, to see. To see this desk.

Because Sidney Castle had slipped her the key for a reason. He suspected his wife of harboring something. Now he hoped Annalee would find it and disclose some vital clue.

Annalee sat back in the chair, closed her eyes, listened to the night sounds. A car passed by the front of the house, tires crunching in freezing slush.

The big house creaked in the chill, pulling itself inward, retreating from the night's spreading cold.

Annalee pulled her thoughts in with it. Thinking, of course, of Jack. Why did he come by? To let her down easy? She felt her heart sink a bit. But also she pondered her daddy. Not at all sure what to make of him now.

She shifted in the chair, forcing herself to get back to her search, rambling through the fresh stack of mail near the front. Lots of decorated envelopes. Fancy handwriting. Calligraphy on heavy, expensive papers. Christmas cards probably. And invitations for holiday parties. All of them still sealed except one.

This same one showed no return address—just Elizabeth Castle's first name printed on the front in black ink, in a heavy hand. A man's handwriting, Annalee thought. The same man's penmanship on, what? Further back in the desk she counted a dozen or more envelopes already opened, too many to be random.

Or too many not to mean what Sidney Castle must have suspected. His wife was straying. Yes, unfaithful.

Annalee pulled open one of the already-unsealed envelopes. She read the letter half through, felt certain that Elizabeth Castle wasn't at her mother's home tonight preparing for a ladies' bridge luncheon.

Instead, on this cold night, Elizabeth Castle was at the Lazy K Ranch, in the snug embrace of a man who wasn't her husband—the money-strapped Lent Montgomery.

Annalee allowed herself a wry smile, thinking about Elizabeth's discomfort when Annalee asked Sidney Castle if he knew of the Lazy K Ranch. In fact, on reflection, Annalee wasn't amazed at all about an illicit tryst between Elizabeth and Montgomery. The woman seemed indulgent, self-centered, maybe even cruel. It was no surprise to Annalee she also was an adulteress. Montgomery, meantime, seemed to need money—and Elizabeth, according to Bernita, had money to spare.

Indeed, standing before Elizabeth's desk filled with her lover's letters, Annalee marveled once again at Elizabeth's only son—her beloved bad boy, Hunter. Switching keys in the coat closet to place his *mother*'s desk key into his *father*'s coat pocket. Knowing exactly what his father would find in his mother's desk—the evidence of his mother's unfaithfulness.

A ruthless son, yes. He was willing to hurt his father that way—just because he could. His mother would probably deny the tryst, not worrying much about his father's accusations or questions or worry—or even the evidence of letters. Or she'd say she ended it, and Sidney should drop it. And Hunter? He'd probably just enjoy causing pain. *Mercy*, what a family. Sidney Castle's poor soul must be crushed.

No wonder he didn't look through his wife's desk himself. He couldn't bear it.

Unlike Elizabeth, he'd hate that his son was nothing more—and nothing less—than a swindler, con man, fancy two-bit schemer. A cheat and a crook. Worse, he was setting his sights on a seat in the US Senate, in a few years anyway, and the purse strings of any number of appropriations committees, according to Bernita. God knows what else a Senate seat would yield him.

So the question for Annalee wasn't what he was doing exactly. Because with Hunter, everything that offered potential for gain or even pain, illegal or not, seemed to capture his attention and his involvement. Annalee let her mind slip into the slippery darkness of possibilities—convinced that, with Hunter Castle, anything was possible.

She counted off options:

Oil fraud.

Liquor running.

Vote fixing.

Dope selling.

Land swindling.

Prostitution.

Hunter could have a finger—heck, both of his slick hands—in some or all of it. Without breaking a sweat. *With* police protection to boot. And his mother's blind approval. And kickbacks. The town was rife with such corruption. Everybody knew that. Just like everybody knew Hunter Castle would never go to jail for any of it.

If anybody flew above the law, it was him.

But did he kill her father? And if so, why?

Annalee rambled through more papers, trying both the desk key and the key on her neck ribbon in the small drawers at the back. None gave way.

She tried to think.

What would Hunter kill to cover up? In Denver, in particular, what unforgivable sin would be going too far? Even for Hunter Castle?

Who aspired to be the state's upcoming US senator—"down the road"? A man hungry, yes, for votes in a state run by self-righteous Klansmen intent on keeping "their" America—as if they alone held claim to it—"all pure" and "all Protestant" and "all white." As their posters said: "Keep white civilization PURE."

Annalee's mouth fell open.

Oh, my goodness.

She let her gaze travel around the room, barely seeing it now, no longer looking at Elizabeth's rumpled, paper-strewn desk.

Because at this point, Annalee believed she finally knew

what bad boy Hunter Castle had done. What he would cover up with murder.

Hunter Castle had crossed the color line.

Of course.

She nodded to herself.

Didn't men do it all the time? Winking at her on the streetcar. Whispering behind their briefcases. But in a town of corruption, run by the KKK, Hunter Castle had broken the one unassailable rule.

Annalee wanted to tell herself no. But she'd heard it firsthand while serving at the Castles' dinner table: the taboo. The Klan had a rigid rule. A rule about sex and "mixing blood" and crossing racial lines.

Never mind that the Klan, in pockets around the country, seemed to sanction all manner of other crime: bribery, graft, vote fixing, and tyrannizing folks off their land so that a white Klan member could buy it cheap—or take it outright—and every other manner of corruption to meet their zealous goals.

But intentional, secret sex between a Klan member and a woman who *wasn't* white? That went beyond the pale, literally, even though it still happened. Let word of that get out and a man could lose everything. His business. His reputation. His banking contacts. His political future. But that wasn't all, not regarding Hunter.

His doting mother would forgive many things, but never this? Not if he tarnished the family name. Ruined the family reputation. Too much for them to lose? No, too much for *her*.

Annalee caught her breath, understanding that because of the one thing he had to hide—his secret sex life?—Hunter Castle wouldn't for one second hesitate to wipe Annalee off the face of the earth if such a thing came to light. But he'd also hire a thug to kill Eddie, Jack, Bernita—all of them—without thinking twice.

Indeed, if he'd target his own father to flaunt his own mother's sins and wickedness—just to twist a knife in his father's weary soul—what worse thing, Annalee thought, *would he do to me?*

She froze.

Or Elizabeth Castle? What wouldn't she do? Didn't she have the most to lose if the truth was unveiled?

Annalee scavenged deeper into the desk pile. Needing to find *something* that would tie a murderer to the night of her father's death. Like a handwritten note outlining his plan. Unlikely.

Or a guilt-ridden confessional letter to his beloved mother. Unlikely.

Or a railroad ticket.

Crumpled. Yellowed.

A Chicago Limited logo visible in its folds.

Annalee stared at the logo for a long moment.

Please, Jesus.

Annalee reached with a gloved hand and, out of a mess of receipts and papers in a back corner of the desk, picked up the ticket. She willed her fingers not to shake.

She thought about Elizabeth Castle's panicked look as Annalee left the upstairs powder room with Hunter's friend Olivia Franklin—Annalee holding a scrap of crumpled, yellowed paper. "What's *this*?" Elizabeth had asked, shaking with her question.

But now Annalee unfolded the crumpled ticket, her heart racing. She settled her breath, let her eyes read the words on the ticket. First, the logo—*Chicago Limited Railroad.*

Then an instruction: *Good for one continuous passage from DENVER to CHICAGO.* Printed in heavy black ink.

Then a mandate: *Good only on date stamped on back.*

Annalee breathed. *Jesus, please.*

She closed her eyes. Turned the ticket over. Held her breath. Opened her eyes in the half-dark to read the stamped words on the underside.

GOOD FOR ONE PASSENGER. FOR THIS DATE ONLY:

The ink was smudged but legible.

November 26, 1922.

For a long minute, Annalee looked at the date, her eyes dry. She set her jaw hard, considered the *gall* it takes to decide somebody has to die. Because they're in the way. Or they know something. *And I'm going to find out that something now.*

She reset the piles of papers, eased down the desk top, locked it—thinking again about the other key hanging around her neck. She tried it in the desk lock. Not a match. Then she hid the real desk key in her apron pocket, considering ways to return it to Sidney Castle, convincing herself that getting it back to him wouldn't be a problem.

So back now to the hallway. She stuffed the railway ticket in her pocket, ready to take the staircase downstairs.

Then she whirled back, realizing the chair in the bedroom was out of place. She set it aright. Checked around the desk.

Heading once again for the stairwell, holding her breath, she took the stairs two at a time—almost losing her balance midway down. Then she righted herself, hit the bottom step, whirled around the banister.

And froze.

Somebody was in the house.

She could feel it. Hear it. A rustling and bump. In the dining room?

She felt certain Bernita wasn't back yet. Or Sidney Castle. Too early for both. Much too early, to be sure, for Elizabeth Castle. She'd surely call later with her Sunday night, telltale lie—probably that it was too late to return home for the night, so she was staying over at her mother's and *blah-blah-blah*. Making the call from Montgomery's bedroom.

Thus, Sidney Castle must hate the Sunday night phone calls from his errant wife. Annalee could imagine him. Stretching out his walks, defying the winter cold, sitting on a park bench and smoking, hating what he knew about his wife and another man—knowing what he could do to stop it but recognizing he didn't have the stomach for it. Instead, he smoldered in the dark.

"He's usually back by ten or eleven," Bernita had said, rushing out herself for her long evening.

But now some intruder had breached the sanctity of the home and waited inside. Waited inside for what? But Annalee knew. Waited for *her*.

She cocked her head.

Then let that somebody come.

CHAPTER 23

"Surely my deductions are simplicity itself."

SH, *THE ADVENTURE OF THE GOLDEN PINCE-NEZ*

ANNALEE TOOK OFF HER SHOES and tiptoed to the long console table in the hallway, thinking she needed a weapon. She grabbed a silver candlestick, slipped down the back hallway and into the kitchen. Listening, not hearing sounds anymore. But she could feel the other presence in the house. She considered two hard things: First, where to hide to secretly see the intruder—so she could confirm her suspicions about who he or she was. Second, where to hide to stay safe.

In Bernita's tiny bathroom? Under the bed in her narrow bedroom?

Instead, she slipped open the door to the basement, smelled a rush of musty air. She stared down at the black emptiness below but knew it was her safest choice.

In a flash, she was on the rickety staircase, half-closing the door silently behind her. A tease. Still, the cellar blackness enveloped her. She felt on the ledge above the stairs for a flashlight she'd just seen, almost knocking it over.

But she grabbed for it with her free hand. Caught it. Clicked it on. Letting the point of light lead her to the bottom of the stairs, she slipped past the concrete landing and into the black, cold emptiness.

Except the dank basement wasn't empty.

Crowded was the right word. A jumble of the Castles' surplus household stuff jammed one whole end. Christmas decorations. Badminton sets. Fishing rods. Camping gear. The stuff of a family that was never a family. Dusty decorations for family holidays that were never festive. Summer games for vacations that were never getaways.

None of that surprised Annalee.

Nor did the boxes and boxes and boxes of illegal booze, stacked in tight, repressed rows. They almost swallowed up the basement.

She aimed the flashlight at a box.

Sacramental—For Church Use Only.

Every box, as far as she could see, bore that label. But this wasn't Sidney Castle's stash. Annalee knew, before she even looked at the labels, that this delivery of illegal liquor was the property of Hunter Castle—securing his boxes in his mother's basement and hardly for church use only.

Who had he bribed in Washington to get his hands on a license to distribute sacramental wine? During Prohibition? The speakeasies in Denver were probably paying him more than generous kickbacks.

Annalee squeezed past the boxes, letting the flashlight lead her to the farthest corner, hoping for a place to stay hidden if the intruder showed face.

To yank off her gloves, she shoved the flashlight and candlestick under an arm, pushed the gloves in her pocket with the railroad ticket. With a click, she turned off the flashlight, listening at the sounds upstairs. The clumping. The confident heavy foot. The sound of a man who knew the house well and assumed permission to walk around inside of it.

And scrape something along the floor. Something heavy. Heavy enough to make Annalee maneuver to a musty corner— pretending the spiderwebs weren't caught in her fancy hairdo— and stand in the dark, but not to cower.

Instead she thought, *I'm right where I should be.* Even if, for now, she was here alone—and not in a safe place with a strong, good, loving, handsome helpmate.

But she didn't dare say *his* name.

She backed further into the musty corner, cringing at the feel of spiderwebs. She shook her leg, knocking something off. Or hoping she knocked it off. Determined to sit it out.

Another spidery-web thing on her other ankle. She shook her leg. Flicked on the flashlight for a quick second. Double-checked her hiding place. Making sure she hadn't landed smack in the middle of a spider's giant nest. She clicked the light off, felt with her hand to test the space.

Something rough, stiff, and dry pressed back.

She yanked back her hand. Dropped the flashlight. Heard it bounce once on a scrap of old carpet, click itself on, then roll onto the hard floor. Hit a box. But still shining its light, still showing what she wasn't supposed to see or know about.

An old bare mattress, pushed up against the farthest corner of the basement, despoiled and rank with its human stain. Dried blood.

The basement door creaked open. Light from the kitchen creased down the stairs.

Annalee drew in a silent breath and pressed her back into the wall, deep in the shadows, easing out each careful breath, straining to remain hidden. To hide undetectable.

But the intruder on the stairs seemed to sense her exact location, pushing past the liquor boxes, aiming for her hiding corner. The heavy foot stopped, the breathing closer. Annalee crouched lower.

The intruder picked up the flashlight. Pointed it every which way. The light careened around the gritty, spidery walls but kept coming back to the corner. And getting closer. So Annalee stopped trying to hide. No point anymore.

She eased out a loud sigh. She stood up, set down the candleholder, pushed at the old mattress, cocked her head, and spoke.

"Stop your searching. I'm right here."

The flashlight swung. Found its mark, right in her face. Just like the intruder's whisper:

"Annalee?"

Annalee jumped. Peered into the light. Heard her own voice whisper, *"What?"*

"Annalee!" The voice louder.

"Mrs. . . . Stallworth?" Annalee gasped a whisper, her voice shaking. Not sure she could believe it.

"Annalee! Didn't you hear me knocking?"

"Mrs. Stallworth?"

"Why didn't you answer the back door?"

"Mrs. Stallworth!"

"Why you keep calling my name? And why you whispering so loud?"

"What in the world . . . ?" Annalee tried to find words. "But you're in *Chicago*."

"*No*. I'm *not*. I'm right *here*. In *Denver*. In this big ridiculous house."

Annalee grabbed the flashlight, shining it on her landlady, then back on herself. Their faces looking ghoulish. So they both tried to laugh.

But nothing was funny here and they both knew it.

"Girl, what in the world are you doing down here?"

"I could ask you the same thing! Besides—"

Annalee tried to say more. But why debate? She dropped the flashlight, ran into Mrs. Stallworth's embrace. Mrs. Stallworth did the same, both of them holding on for dear life.

"It's okay, child," Mrs. Stallworth said, trying to soothe.

Annalee steadied her breathing, pushed back, picked up the flashlight. "No, it's *not* okay. Not yet, Mrs. Stallworth."

"Hush—and wipe your eyes!"

"Am I crying?"

"Maybe a little, but you're *alive*. That's what matters most." Mrs. Stallworth pulled back. She grabbed the flashlight, searched Annalee's eyes. "But what in the world are you doing down in this dirty old basement?" She frowned, looking Annalee up and down. "And look at you. Dressed up like a *maid*."

"Yes, well, 'I'd rather be a doorkeeper—'"

"Don't you start with me."

"Let's just go upstairs. But oh, Mrs. Stallworth, I'm so glad you're here. I'll tell you everything—well, as much as I know."

In the big Castle kitchen, she sat her landlady down at the wide wooden table, helped her wriggle out of her big winter coat, clicked on a small lamp over the sink and told her about everything. The train ride. William Barnett and Eddie. The choking hands. Jumping off the train.

"You jumped off a—"

"Oh, *please*, Mrs. Stallworth, let me finish. And don't interrupt me."

"Well, whoever heard of a proper young woman like you jumping off a moving train? And with a *child*. How old is that boy?"

"Too young to be on his own," Annalee said. "But *please* listen." She picked up her tale. Recounted her escape with Eddie in the train yard, hiding in downtown Denver, the Ku Klux Klan parade.

And Jack. The dinner that first night with him.

"Now that Jack's one good-looking young pastor," Mrs. Stallworth said, allowing a bright smile.

"You talked to Jack?"

"I found the parsonage. He's the one told me where to find you. He wanted to come with me. But of course I declined."

Annalee nodded, determined to not ask more.

Instead, she moved her narrative to Slater Prince. And all of the Castles. The dinner party. The big ranch. Lent Montgomery. Learning to drive.

"A *car*?"

"Please, Mrs. Stallworth. There's more." Annalee kept it short but told it all. Wrecking Hunter's car. Going to church—but not Jack's fiancée. Elizabeth Castle's love tryst. The railroad ticket.

And the bloodstained mattress.

"Blood? Are you sure? Let me see it."

"Yes," Annalee said, thinking a moment. "I want you to—"

"To confirm something about it?"

"Well, to act like a detective."

"I'm just following after you," Mrs. Stallworth said.

"Me?" She let out a sigh. "Oh, Mrs. Stallworth, solving a murder is not about crime. It's about finding fear and greed and, well, about *lust*."

"Oh, I believe you, honey."

"I must've been half-crazy, thinking I could figure out murder and stay alive—all in one piece."

"Oh, you're alive, all right."

"What?"

Mrs. Stallworth looked over her spectacles. "Tell you the truth, Annalee, you look better than you've looked in a year. Your face is bright and glowing. Your hair looks pretty and done up. Your eyes are shining. Glowing and shining and pretty . . . just like that good-looking young pastor—"

Annalee squirmed. "What did Jack say?"

Mrs. Stallworth arched a brow. "That's what I wanted you to tell me."

Annalee sat back in her chair, folded her arms, shook her head. "Not now. It's . . . complicated."

"I bet it is."

"Don't say it like that. But what about you? Why are you in Denver?"

"Oh, honey . . ."

"Oh, honey? That sounds—" Annalee stopped. Swung toward the back door. "Someone's coming," she whispered.

She looked at the clock. Five minutes to nine. Too early for Bernita. Or Sidney Castle. She got an odd feeling.

"Don't panic. But we need to hide."

"Not back in that basement?"

"No place else. I told you this business is inconvenient. Dangerous, too."

"No, *I* told *you*. But who's coming, Annalee? Slater Prince? Hunter Castle?"

"We'll find out soon enough!"

She helped Mrs. Stallworth grab up her coat, pushed her landlady's satchel into the tiny bathroom, swung open the basement door, hustled both of them down the stairs, back into the dirty, dank basement.

Where they couldn't be seen.

But they could hear.

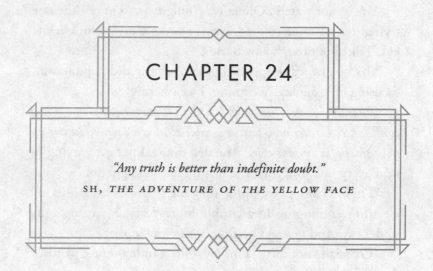

CHAPTER 24

"Any truth is better than indefinite doubt."

SH, *THE ADVENTURE OF THE YELLOW FACE*

"You're a blasted fool."

That was the first thing they heard.

Hunter Castle's voice, hard and irritated. Speaking to another man? Annalee strained to listen.

"I can overlook *that* comment." A woman's voice.

But the voice wasn't the new girlfriend's. The pouty one. Instead this was the other woman. What was her name?

"You better overlook it, Olivia. You're already in hot water yourself, Miss Franklin."

That's right—Olivia. Olivia Franklin. But for some reason, Annalee didn't think that was her real last name. Nothing in Denver was as it seemed. She weighed her doubt, crouching under the basement stairs, letting Mrs. Stallworth grip her hand.

"*Me* in hot water?" Olivia was indignant. "I'm not the one trying to find some colored woman and a scrawny little white kid. Talk about tough adversaries."

Mrs. Stallworth gripped tighter. Annalee didn't pull away, focusing on listening. Weighing. Deciphering.

What are we hearing here? Is Olivia a partner in crime? Or a confidante? Or her own sort of double-dealer? Playing Hunter on both sides of a curious coin? Annalee strained her ears, trying to hear every side. But first, she heard Hunter's agitation.

"I'm *this* close to wrapping up a big financial deal. Plus my election's coming up in a couple more years. My campaign's underway. And *nobody*'s getting in the way of that."

"Especially not dirty laundry." Olivia didn't mince words.

"What do *you* know about dirty laundry?"

Olivia Franklin laughed, sneering. "I know plenty. Isn't that why you brought me here?"

"Give me a break. We're wasting time. And I brought you here because you're the only person I can trust. Now help me get that infernal mattress out of here." He yanked open the basement door.

Mrs. Stallworth pressed closer to Annalee, both of them wedged deep under the basement stairs, in total darkness.

Hunter Castle pressed on a light switch at the top of the stairs. A pale, naked bulb flickered, casting its light in the middle of the cellar space, lighting the stacks of boxes. The corners were still in shadow, Annalee and Mrs. Stallworth still hidden.

"I don't like this, Hunter." Olivia, reluctant. "Every single time I come down to this basement with you—" she put a foot on the rickety top step—"something bad happens." But she made the descent, following Hunter Castle.

"It's not that heavy," he said.

"That's not what I mean!"

"Are you going to argue? Or *help*?"

"It's not fun anymore, Hunter. Your dirty business. Not like when we were kids, just getting into mischief. Now it's one nasty scheme after another. Each one dirtier than the last." She hit the landing, bumped into a box. Groaned. "When is it going to just stop?"

Hunter laughed. "Not till I've got an office in the US Capitol. With benefits for *all* the good folks back home, including you, sweet pal."

"I don't want any part of it. Not elections. Not the *benefits*. Not the . . . *Blast it all.*" Olivia let out a string of curses.

Annalee could feel Mrs. Stallworth tense.

"What in the devil happened down here, Hunter?"

"*You*, acting squeamish? *And* righteous? Just shut up and help me push."

"*No.* There's dried blood all over it. Did somebody *die* on this mattress?"

"Of course nobody died. You think I'd kill somebody in my own mother's basement? You must think I'm an idiot."

Olivia paused. "Who said you *killed*?"

The room grew quiet. Annalee could feel her heart pound, feel Hunter's mind working.

"Nobody said anything. You're hearing things. Besides, it was a year ago."

"Then why didn't you get rid of it then?"

"I got busy. Grab that other end."

"A year ago? That colored girl . . . Not the other one. The *last* one! The rich one!"

"It was nothing. I took her down to Pueblo for a drink."

"Lovely, Hunter. Illegal philandering with some underage, innocent child."

"*Not* underage. She's grown, goes to college. Barely younger than me. And *innocent*? Hardly. She was fast and too big for her britches. Then she jumps up pregnant, trying to shake me down for money. *Me*."

The mattress got bumped along the floor. But stopped.

Hunter snapped, *"Pick up your end."*

But Olivia was balking. "Hunter Castle, I don't believe you." Her voice dropped to an angry whisper. "That girl didn't want your money. And she wasn't fast. You sweet-talked her—and she had your baby. On this mattress."

"Stop theorizing, Olivia. Pick up your end."

"Not until you tell me what happened to that girl."

"Tell you? That she almost hemorrhaged to death?"

"What?"

"Should have been in a hospital or something—"

"And what hospital in Denver will take in a colored girl? Even if her father is rich!"

"Well, showing up here, at my mother's house, on the night of my mother's big birthday ball, threatening to tell the newspapers! If it wasn't for Bernita . . . She had the good sense to pick up the telephone and call me. Helped me get the girl to the basement. That girl bled like a stuck pig!"

"You disgust me."

"Oh, stop being so self-righteous. I got her to the colored doctor."

"And she's okay? She's alive?"

"Who knows? That was a year ago."

"And what about the baby?"

Hunter Castle was silent.

Just as Annalee's stomach twisted, a tight and hard knot.

Olivia Franklin's voice rose. "*The baby.* What happened to the baby?"

Hunter's voice cleared. "The baby's dead."

Annalee's knees went weak. Mrs. Stallworth sagged in the dark.

"*Where?*" Olivia hissed.

Hunter was quiet a moment. "What do you mean *where?*"

"I mean *where?*" Her voice rose. "*Where,* Hunter? Where did you take that baby?"

"What a ludicrous question."

Olivia got quieter. Her voice darker. Finally whispering: "Oh no . . . I know where. That ridiculous ranch. What'd you do out there?"

"You—you're an *idiot,*" Hunter stammered. "Nothing happened at that ranch. And I don't need anybody snooping around out there, asking ridiculous questions. I'm *buying* that ranch."

"You disgust me."

"You told me that already."

"You and your stupid Ku Klux Klan cronies."

"This isn't about them."

"And you disgust your father."

The mattress dropped. Got kicked.

"Get out of my house, Olivia."

"This isn't your house. It's your father's house—and you disgust him. And that's what this is about, isn't it?"

"Shut up, Olivia."

"You're a crook. And a liar. *And* a baby killer!"

"*I said shut up.*"

"And all your underhanded big-money deals, not to mention your pathetic political ambitions, aren't going to change that. He hates the sight of you."

Olivia pushed past him, started for the stairs, turning to say what Annalee now understood.

"Because after years of suspecting you *weren't* his son, he's finally figured out that you *are*. And that makes it worse. Because you're the worst kind of a son—a con man, a braggart, a disappointment, and a lazy failure."

"I should kill you right now myself."

"But you won't," Olivia said. She stepped forward, her feet inches from Annalee's hiding place. "Because there's something else about his son that Sidney Castle understands, and I finally understand it, too."

"You're pushing your luck, Olivia."

"Maybe. But you don't scare me, Hunter." She took to the stairs, spoke from the top step. "The biggest thing about you is simple. You're a coward. You let other people do your dirty work. Just like a coward."

She flicked off the light.

"Hey!" he yelled. "I'll show you who's a coward."

But Olivia slammed the door, stomped through the kitchen and out the back door, slamming it hard, showing she'd turned her back on a friendship she no longer could bear.

In the tense dark, Hunter Castle spat out a curse.

While Annalee and Mrs. Stallworth crouched still as stones, holding their breath, waiting in the dark. They both knew— Annalee especially and maybe Mrs. Stallworth, too—that even if Hunter discovered their hiding place, he never handled his dirty business by himself.

In fact, in a matter of minutes, he was gone, the filthy mattress still lying on the floor where he'd dropped it.

Annalee and Mrs. Stallworth sat still in the dark. Waiting to hear Hunter stomp and bound and growl out of the house and slam the devil out of the poor back door. Gone at last. At least for this night.

Annalee gripped her landlady's hand, guiding her through the dark and up the stairs, urging her to be careful, Mrs. Stallworth holding her bad hip.

"Killed a *little baby*," Mrs. Stallworth said.

"Hired somebody to do it? And somebody found her?" Annalee said in a whisper.

Mrs. Stallworth gripped her hand. "*Her?* You mean a little girl?"

Annalee stopped midway up the stairs, feeling an odd sinking feeling. *A little girl.* "I . . . I don't know," she whispered. "I just feel it." She gripped the stair rail, shuddering, not wanting to be so sure.

Her hand shook on the rail. She felt along the wall for the light switch. Couldn't find it. Stopped.

"*Oh, God,*" she whispered.

"What, Annalee?" Mrs. Stallworth reached out, trying to comfort.

But Annalee had slumped to the stairs.

"*Oh, Daddy.*" She struggled to say it.

"*What*, my child?"

"Daddy . . . found the baby?" Her voice broke. Saying his name over and over. "Oh, Daddy . . . Daddy . . ."

Mrs. Stallworth mumbled under her breath, fumbled for

the light switch, couldn't find it either. "*Gracious*, what are you saying, Annalee?"

"*Oh, God.* Forgive us, God. Forgive us our *trespasses.*"

"Lord, I don't understand!" Mrs. Stallworth groaned, helped Annalee to her feet. Together, in the dark, they took the last step into the kitchen.

"Goodness, what are you saying, honey? Oh, Lord, what a mess."

"I'm saying I think my daddy found that tiny little baby."

"So somebody killed him?"

"To silence him." She shuddered.

"About the baby?"

"Probably about a lot of things. He worked for all of them. He knew too much."

She looked down at her borrowed clothes, wiped dust and dirt off the uniform, looked at her landlady. "Can I confess something to you, Mrs. Stallworth?"

"You? Of course, baby. What is it?"

Annalee sat down, looked up at Mrs. Stallworth. "When I left Chicago to come back home, I thought I could solve my daddy's murder. Me, 'the Colored Professor.' Chasing after bad guys. And catching them. Justice done! End of story."

Mrs. Stallworth listened, nodded, staying quiet.

"And now I learn that solving a murder isn't about redemption or truth or justice. It's about *sin*." She paused. "But what theologian thinks about *that*? I doubt I've ever said the word out loud." She frowned. "Not about my own sin anyway."

Mrs. Stallworth reached for her. "Yes, you did. Remember, you told me? That evil proceeds 'out of the heart of men.'"

Annalee searched her landlady's eyes. "Maybe I said that in theory, Mrs. Stallworth. Or in a stupid paper."

Mrs. Stallworth frowned. "What are you saying, Annalee?"

"I'm saying I finally see. A detective uncovers the rebellion. Isn't that what sin is? Same with murder—the cunning, ugly, ordinary mutiny of it? It's rebellion—against God. Just like any sin—greed, wrath, envy, lust . . . all of them." She got quiet. "Lord, if I'd known that, I would've stayed in Chicago, teaching and grading papers. Just crawled into bed with my Sherlocks or thumbed through my professor friend's book on the little prophet—" She stopped.

"What are you talking about, girl!"

"Mercy, Saint Augustine. He said the company we keep determines our path."

"Oh, I told you that," Mrs. Stallworth said. "You best keep company with God."

"You shine his light. Right." Annalee arched a brow. "But you keep company with the devil, you'll take the dark road to hell." She stood. "Lord, I've been so blind."

"About what?"

"Hunter Castle and Slater Prince . . . they're not rivals or foes. Or strange bedfellows. They're in all this together. Maybe even blackmailing people. Why else would Denver's elite support Hunter Castle for Senate? Or hobnob with Slater Prince? They're charging hush money. For private letters, sensitive documents, evidences of scandals and lusts. Ol' Prince is in and out of prominent homes all week. Or breaking in when they're empty."

She thought of William Barnett sweet-talking Bernita to learn when the Castles would be away. Yep, working for Prince. God only knew what secrets the men could wield.

So it all made sense.

Thank you, instincts.

If her father figured out their scheme and threatened to expose them, he'd pay with his life. And he had.

She ran to Bernita's room, slipped out of the maid's dress, slung on Aunt Jessie's suit and her lost and found coat, turned back to write a note. *Thanks for everything, Bernita. But I found . . .*

She screwed up her face. Her eyes stopped at the newspaper clipping: her father at the church cornerstone laying, standing in the background, looking straight at the camera, telling her *what?*

What did I find, Daddy?

She went back to her note. *I found the light. I'll be in touch. Annalee.* She rushed out. Ran back. *P.S. Please keep my wages from Saturday—for helping me understand. Thank you! A.S.*

In the kitchen, Mrs. Stallworth was already squeezing into her coat. "We're leaving this place, right?"

"And never coming back. But I know one or two places where we can stay—rooming houses over in Five Points. There's several right behind the church."

So they're right behind Jack's, but so be it.

"That's where we're going?"

"For now. It won't be fancy."

"Baby, if I wanted fancy, I wouldn't have married Mr. Worcester Stallworth."

"That was your husband's name?"

"The last person I should've said yes to. But I did. And I'm still not sorry. I'm grateful to God I married him."

Annalee smiled. "I think I need to hear that story."

"Well, you don't have a choice. Because I'm going to tell it."

"We'd better hurry," Annalee said, hustling her out the Castles' back door and past the porch, out to the sidewalk and down to the bottom of the street. They turned left, yanked up their collars, and headed north toward Five Points.

"In fact, we've got plenty to talk about," Annalee said, "like what I'm going to do next."

"Find Jack?" Mrs. Stallworth gave her a look.

"No." Annalee pulled her coat tight. "First, I've got something to do for Eddie. To take him to a meeting. To see his father."

"You're not making sense, Annalee. I thought the child was an orphan. What meeting?"

Annalee hiked a brow. "Tomorrow night's meeting. We're going to the Denver klavern of the Ku Klux Klan."

CHAPTER 25

"We must look for consistency."

SH, *THE PROBLEM OF THOR BRIDGE*

THE MEETING WAS at the old Overland Cotton Mill on the southwest side of town. Big, cold wreck of a place. Mill shut down. Other buildings closed. A good-for-nothing dust trap. Once notorious for child labor. And now? A perfect hideout for an invisible empire. Close to an outdoor rally site. The original public-address system would still be in place and working, just right for tonight's endless speeches and tirades and spitting and spewing.

And the fear. *Lord, so much fear.* Mostly of losing, Annalee thought. One of her teaching colleagues called it a "scarcity model"—believing if somebody else gets a foot up, then my foot gets knocked down. Bad thinking. In truth, bad theology, too.

So thousands would crowd inside. Annalee expected that.

She'd read the newspaper articles and condemning editorials. Seen the flyers announcing tonight's mass meeting. But she'd also heard the whispers: That a good number of the thousands, sitting on folding chairs in their white robes and hoods, hated every minute of it. Thousands joined for the "fellowship," but others joined out of pressure and threats from klavern leaders— and the threat was formidable: No KKK membership, no customers for your store, dry cleaner, restaurant, law office, dairy, pharmacy, movie theater, bank, or whatever business you were struggling to keep going in postwar Denver.

So the thousands joined up, consoled by the so-called "traditional values" of the "pure white" and "America only" fellowship of the Monday night meetings.

But could Eddie sneak into the gathering this Monday night? Sneak out, that was, from a growing bond with a Black woman known as *professor*?

Annalee rode quietly thinking about it, alone on the streetcar, riding to the end of the line. The car was empty save for the indifferent operator. He took her token without a greeting or a goodbye. Only shrugged when she said, "Overland mill."

She got off at the last stop, a block or so from the outlying mill, watched the streetcar turn its curve on the track and head back toward town. She felt her mouth go dry. Should she have stopped first to see Jack? Make amends so he could help her? Ignoring his fiancée? Annalee knew she was being foolish by trying this scheme alone. As if to confirm it, the night sky around her darkened to pitch-black as the lit streetcar pulled away, growing smaller as it turned a corner and disappeared. She was alone.

It was nine o'clock and cold. Annalee pulled on the borrowed gloves. Took in a hard breath, thinking Jack's aunt Jessie would do flips if she even suspected all her gloves had been doing.

But for now, she pushed the hood up on her oversize blanket of a coat and berated herself for not finding plain, flat shoes. She put her head down and headed into a steady cold wind.

On the distant hill ahead she could make out the profile of the old mill. Around it, cars sat parked in endless rows. The meeting probably was just starting. Perfect timing. If only she could find Eddie.

She checked the dark horizon, ignoring the cold, and started whistling—her signal to him. Or at least that's what she'd written in the note she sent to him. With a nickel, borrowed from Mrs. Stallworth, she'd paid a neighborhood kid to deliver the note. *Meet me tonight at 9. Overland mill.* But did he get the note? A fifty-fifty chance.

Annalee couldn't dare to guess. Instead, she whistled.

I'm . . . al-ways chas-ing . . . rainbows . . . .

A raggedy whistle. *Goodness, I sound horrible.* She wasn't too bad at singing. But whistling? Not her gift.

Still, as she forced herself to approach the old mill, heading around toward its dark east side, she whistled for all she was worth. Knowing whistling was odd, especially here, surrounded by the darkened cars of a legion of the hooded, the invisible, the angry, and the frightened: frightened of people like her. So she had to alert Eddie, if he was out there somewhere. *Please let him be here.* But whistling also helped tamp down her worry, her fear, her second-guessing—like the voice revving up in the farthest corner of her brain.

Have you lost your ever-loving mind?

Crashing a Ku Klux Klan meeting?

Oh, Lord, I am crazy. Like a fox? She hoped. Because if she could figure out a way to spirit Eddie inside to meet his long-lost father—and tell the man how klavern member Hunter Castle had tried to kill Eddie in order to cover up a tryst with an impassioned Black girl—a certain justice was sure to be the result.

Well, not a pure justice. But a justice nonetheless.

So she kept whistling the little song, stopping every minute or so to strain her ears, hearing only her feet crunching on gravel and the light night wind carrying sounds from inside the hulking old mill.

A man's deep voice boomed over the public-address system.

"Are we mighty enough? The Denver klavern? *No!* Not ten thousand! Not twenty thousand! Not thirty thousand! No, *fifty thousand* members are needed in Denver—Queen City of the West!"

A roar of applause thundered out of the building.

"Now go out and *make it happen.*"

A larger roar. Angry. Loud. Annalee's mouth went dry. For half a second, she turned, wanting to race back to the streetcar to safety, away from her questioning. *What in the world am I doing here?* But as the applause faded, she heard it:

A boy's whistle.

I'm al-ways chas-ing . . .

Beautiful and sweet. Pitch-perfect.

She sucked in a hard breath. Whistled back. *Watch-ing* . . . *clouds* . . . *drift-ing by.*

Eddie's high, pure sound. *My dreams are just like all* . . . *my* . . . *schemes.*

She whistled the next line. *End-ing* . . . *in the sky.* Gracious, she couldn't whistle to half save her life, but she sure was trying.

Thus, Eddie whistled again, drawing her out of herself and toward the back of the big building, behind the big silos.

She picked up her pace. But a different man at the microphone had picked up his, his thin voice straining. "So flood the highways and the byways! Knock on doors. Go to Klan businesses—and here's our brother to tell us more! Our leader, Dr. Eddie Brown!"

Eddie's whistle cut off midstream.

"Eddie," Annalee whispered as loud as she could. She ducked between automobiles, hoping a security detail wasn't roaming the grounds.

At a rise beyond the parking lot, she called out for Eddie, started running toward the unlit side of the building. Calling out his name. *"Eddie. Eddie."*

She turned the corner of the building, saw something move in the shadows, knew it was Eddie, ran forward to comfort him, to embrace him, to remind him that he might be his father's son, but he wasn't like his father. So he didn't have to cower or cry or second-guess his value or his worth.

But Eddie wasn't cowering. Or crying. Or cold. He was wearing Sidney Castle's expensive big coat. Tan cashmere wool with initials *SC* embroidered on each cuff.

More than that, Eddie was sharpening a long knife. A kitchen knife. Pilfered, for sure, from Elizabeth Castle's kitchen. Except it wasn't a killing knife by any means. Instead, a pie knife. Annalee resisted the urge to roll her eyes. But Eddie was running the long blade across a hefty stone picked up from the ground behind the mill.

He looked up half a second at Annalee, determined not to acknowledge her and still sharpening, breathing hard. Exhaling and sharpening. His hot breath turning white in the night air. He was silently daring Annalee to try to stop him.

So Annalee watched him, measured but tense. Her breath matched his, white vapor clouds churning between them.

"You can't stop me," Eddie finally said.

"I wouldn't even try, Eddie."

He sharpened harder. "Then *why are you here*? Why'd you ask me to come?"

She started to answer, just as a tinny voice crackled over the loudspeaker.

"Fellow Klansmen!"

A gigantic roar erupted.

"Thank you for such a welcome. It does my heart good to see with my own eyes the level of support and commitment and sheer, righteous brawn represented in this humble hall."

Applause thundered out of the mill.

"*Please* put that down, Eddie." Annalee reached for Eddie, but he pulled away.

"Why'd you ask me? *Tell me*." He sharpened harder.

She ignored his sharpening. "Because I figured you'd help me trap the killer. Instead it looks like you'd rather turn into a killer yourself."

Eddie sucked in a breath. "I'm already a killer! What's one more dead, stupid jerk?" He spat on the ground, trying to look tough but looking young and unsure in his oversize coat. "*Stupid jerk*," he hissed again.

"True for sure," Annalee said. "Except last time I checked, being a jerk still isn't a capital offense."

She spoke over the racket of the public-address system, ignoring the tinny voice and the wild applause still spilling out over their heads into the night. She was determined to ignore the applause and the size of the crowd that the applause implied. Instead, she was intent on finding in Eddie some sense of prudence. Or at least downright common sense.

But the whiny voice at the microphone made it worse.

"As we join our energies, putting our collective votes behind the right men, just watch what we can achieve. And so I ask you—*can we take back our beautiful city?*"

A roar greeted the question.

"And our beloved Rocky Mountain state?"

Another roar.

"And this matchless and beleaguered *nation?*"

The applause was deafening.

Annalee shook her head, trying to silence the voice, marveling at how such a tinny, nondescript, *un*manly tone could raise the passions of thousands of taxpaying, churchgoing citizens. Yet the audience seemed rapt as the thin-voiced man read off a "list of klavern members we must vow to support in this upcoming election year—and even beyond. And I mean good *Protestant* men." He added: "*White* men!"

Cheering, stomping, screaming. The place went wild.

So the thin, squeaky voice kept at it. Naming his names. For governor. For justice of the state supreme court. For lieutenant governor of Colorado. For regent of the University of Colorado. And on and on. Then finally:

"For United States senator from Colorado—down the road. We're grooming him. *Hunter Castle!*"

Annalee winced at the name. She turned to Eddie. "You thought your father would be a different man. I understand that, Eddie."

"What do you know about it?"

"I just know about my own daddy—that he wasn't a perfect man."

"Yes, he *was*. He didn't leave you."

She shook her head. "There's many a way to measure that, Eddie. But staying around isn't the only thing that makes a man a good father!"

Eddie shoved the knife in the leather sleeve in his boot. He rose almost to her height. Surprising her by shouting at her. "You wouldn't say that if your daddy left you. And *your mother*, too. When she was *sick*. With you just a *little kid*."

He pushed past her, slipped on the gravel a moment. He righted himself, headed toward the building, Sidney Castle's big gorgeous coat dragging the filthy ground.

Annalee scrambled after him, reached for his coat sleeve. *"Stop."* She yanked hard. "Stop, Eddie. *Now*."

He wriggled away. "Leave me alone. You can't stop me."

"Then stop yourself."

He whirled around. "I don't have to. *Now leave me alone.* And I mean it. Besides—" he flailed at her—"I hate you, too!" Eddie spat on the ground. "You're just a *nig*—"

She reared back.

She could hear the word coming, saw it forming on his trembling eleven-year-old mouth. Hate starts itself early. She searched his eyes, saw his hurt, felt his anger, felt her own.

She faced him square, dead in his face.

"Go ahead, Eddie Brown Junior," she said. "Say it if you have to."

"No!" he yelled at her.

"Say it!" Her voice hardened. "Get it out!"

"No!" He fell to his knees, sobbing harder, his body bent, still gripping Elizabeth Castle's fancy pie knife.

Annalee pressed her lips, shook her head, knelt beside him, let her breathing start to ease. She put her arms around his shoulders, letting him cry, drawing him close to her. "You *don't* hate me," she said. She dropped her voice to a hard whisper. "So stop your crying. And your shouting. You'll raise the dead, not to mention . . ."

"The KKK?"

They both looked up. She stood, grabbing Eddie up, too. The deep voice held them, chilling Annalee's blood, right to the bone, because the voice was one they both knew but hoped they wouldn't hear on this night and at this place.

It was Slater Prince.

In all his glory, his look said *behold me*, showing his pride. Sly, beefy, and sinister-looking in his perfectly cut ermine coat, he was clearly pleased with being himself. Black leather gloves encased his hands. His head was bare—every inch of his barbered, salt-and-pepper fade and his beard and mustache trimmed razor-sharp. His dark eyes were two flints. Blank and hard. Despairing?

Annalee could feel the desperation trapped inside his eyes. She stepped back. Silent. Waiting.

"I should be surprised," he finally spoke, "to see you here." His voice was quiet and dark. "But somehow, Miss Spain, I'm not."

"Then we're one for one," she said, her tone even. "Because I have to admit, I'd be surprised *not* to see you here."

Slater Prince let his face break into a half smile, but not with amusement—with knowing. He arched a brow. "This is my town, young lady. I think I told you that once already."

"Indeed you did, Mr. Prince. But I confess I didn't fully understand how much. Or maybe I didn't believe it. Until—"

"Until tonight?"

"Until a lot of things. Including seeing you in the parking lot at a KKK meeting."

"Yes, well, as I said. This is my town. There isn't a single square inch of Denver, or anywhere around Denver, for that matter, where you won't find me at one time or another—which means it's not unusual to see me here. But . . ." He edged closer to Annalee, crowding her, daring her to object.

"Well?" she pressed him, holding her ground.

"But you don't have a reason to be here." Slater Prince flashed his dark gaze at Eddie. "And certainly he doesn't."

Eddie was silent but looked defiant. Slater Prince ignored him. Instead, he steadied his gaze back at Annalee. "So I suggest you start explaining."

A burst of applause interrupted him. "And quick. The meeting is almost over."

How does he know the meeting is almost over? Annalee asked the question in her mind. Then she stalled.

"But . . . I thought Five Points was your area of influence."

Slater Prince didn't bite. "You're clever, honey. But so am I." He grabbed Annalee's arm. "You shouldn't try to distract me. Now tell me why you're here!"

"I'll handle this, Prince."

Annalee squinted in the dark but suddenly knew exactly who had spoken. The woman stepped out of the shadows, gleaming in the moonlight in an all-white getup—chic two-piece suit, white mink stole, even white dyed-to-match kid leather shoes.

"Mrs. Castle?" Eddie said. Elizabeth Castle ignored him, not bothering to notice her own husband's coat. Instead, she gestured to Annalee. "Come with me." Her voice ice-cold. "You and the boy."

"Leave us alone!" Eddie lurched, aiming for Prince and Elizabeth Castle both.

But with his bulk, Prince shoved Eddie away. "Back off!"

"The *baby*," Annalee shouted.

Elizabeth Castle reacted. Her eyes narrowed.

Prince blinked hard, turned to Elizabeth, then to Annalee. "Excuse me?"

"I'm here about the baby," Annalee said, deciding to just tell the truth.

Eddie looked at Annalee oddly. Elizabeth Castle glared, picked her words. "And I'm supposed to know what that means?"

Annalee searched Elizabeth's eyes, saw only hardness. She looked for some recognition, some awareness that she knew *something*. Was Elizabeth Castle bluffing? And Prince, too? Annalee couldn't tell. She kept fishing. "Well, shouldn't you know? Especially if you and Brother Prince are planning to deliver colored votes to a murderer like Hunter Castle?"

"You have ten seconds to get off this property," Elizabeth Castle said.

"Is that a threat?"

"Only if you care about that pastor friend of yours—and his two-bit church."

"Watch it, please, Elizabeth—" Prince tried to interrupt.

"Jack's not afraid of you." Annalee glared at Elizabeth. "You either, Trustee Prince."

"Spoken just like your worthless daddy," Prince said.

"More than you know," she shot back. "Was he done stealing for you? Done picking up hush money for you? Or—"

"Well, listen to this." He turned to Elizabeth. He sneered. "Accusing *me*."

"As if she knows anything."

"What I know, Miss Spain, is you have *two* seconds to clear off these premises." He nodded to Eddie. "Both of you. The boy, too."

Eddie pulled to his height. "I'm not going anywhere."

Prince ignored him. He just picked Eddie up by the shoulders, hurled him away from his presence, leaving Eddie groveling in the gravel, kicking and spitting and cursing.

"*Watch your mouth . . . ,*" Annalee started to say to Eddie.

But she was stopped. By the singing.

Tortured singing. So awful and tortured it stopped her in her tracks. Eddie, too. It was the worst singing either of them had ever heard.

Slater Prince groaned. "The closing song—with their one and only," he added, glancing at Elizabeth. She narrowed her eyes.

But Eddie was frowning. So Annalee asked his question. "*That's* Eddie Brown Senior?"

"You know so much," Elizabeth snapped. "Why ask me?"

Eddie bounded to his feet. "*No, it's not!*"

Annalee turned to Eddie, wanting to console. She brushed him off, brushed off Sidney Castle's coat. "It's okay, Eddie. C'mon. Let's get out of—"

But she stopped. "What'd you say?"

"That's *not* my father." Eddie pointed toward the public-address sound, to the cawing piercing the night air. "*Professor,*" he shouted at Annalee, "that's not my father."

Annalee took in his smile, watched its brightness, marveling at the transformation on Eddie's face. His anger had melted into a kind of glory. His eyes bright and relieved and smiling. So she started grinning herself. "Lord, you're *right*," she whispered.

Elizabeth Castle turned on her, snapped at Prince, "Get them away from here!"

But the two didn't have to convince Eddie. Because Eddie had already started running—away from the building, between the rows of cars. He didn't seem sure exactly where he was going, but he was running crazy, liberated with glee, Sidney Castle's beautiful coat dragging in the dirt. Annalee whirled and followed, trusting that following was the right thing to do, thankful he wasn't heading *into* the building.

Instead, Eddie darted in and around the Chevys, the Buicks, the Packards, the farm trucks, the police cars. He blazed a zigzag trail for the two of them, letting them revel in the awful singing and what it meant for him—or even for both of them. In fact, the sound suddenly got louder as the doors to the big mill were thrown open, allowing the thousands of Denver Klansmen to pour out of the assembly hall and into the night, eager to find their cars in the crowded lot and head to the sanctity of their obsessively protected neighborhoods.

"*Hey!*" Somebody saw the two of them running and yelled after them.

But Annalee and Eddie had a real head start. Besides, they weren't running. They were flying. Or so it seemed, with Annalee grateful she'd confirmed her guess about Slater Prince. But more than that, Annalee and Eddie were stunned and amazed that the man Eddie Brown Sr. of the Klan *couldn't* be the father of the boy Eddie Brown Jr.

Never mind having the same name. Never mind their assumption that he was Eddie's father. Now they knew he couldn't possibly be.

And for such a good and perfect and irrefutable reason.

He couldn't carry a doggone tune.

That's how Eddie explained it.

To Jack.

With Annalee standing on Jack's porch, watching him through the screen door. Jack stood facing her on the other side of the threshold. Arms crossed. A rigid statue. Not smiling. The sparkle in his dark eyes barely a smolder.

It was late. Almost midnight. She and Eddie had run for blocks before flagging down a streetcar, one of the last still swaying back into town.

But the streetcar was slow as molasses, inching its way along the late-night line. The driver languished for long minutes at each stop, finally pulling into the downtown car barn about eleven. He made a show of turning off all the switches, gathering up his thermos, lunch pail, the day's newspapers, announcing without speaking that, regardless of their need or desire for passenger transport, the streetcar service was shut down for the night.

She pulled Eddie off the silent car, crossed the tracks, and fast-walked through the cold to Five Points, the nearest, safest neighborhood. Thus, they aimed for Jack's house, pretending it wasn't so late and *freezing*. Still, she asked the evening's one *un*asked question: "If that man isn't your father, Eddie, then where is he?"

Eddie's stride broke a second. "Honest, I don't care, Professor. It's not *that* guy."

"But we still have to find out."

Eddie looked at her, gray eyes blinking. He stopped walking, turned to Annalee. "I'm sorry. I called you that bad name. That was wrong. I'm sorry."

She faced him. "I know you're sorry."

"You're not mad at me?"

"Do I look mad? Who's got time to be mad? We've got bigger things to figure out. Like where's your real father? What happened to him?"

Eddie resumed walking. "What difference does a father make anyway?"

"Having a father? And knowing your father? It makes all the difference."

"But what if you find out the truth about him and it's something bad?"

She thought a moment. "Truth can be hard to hear, Eddie. But when you're searching for your father, it's his truth—no matter what—that helps you find him." She thought of Slater Prince. "In fact, I'm sure of it. Truth, if you keep searching, will just show up."

Eddie sighed, acting doubtful, indifferent.

But Annalee could see he seemed glad to find a lone light burning in a window in Jack's parsonage. It was the kitchen light. Even though the hour was way past dinner.

Jack had a napkin thrust over his shirt collar. The leftover from his late and worried meal?

He clicked on the porch light. His face showing stress. Anger, too? But he opened the screen door. He looked at Eddie, watched Sidney Castle's coat dragging behind Eddie across his porch. "You better come inside, son." He gestured to Eddie, showing he didn't mean Annalee.

But she spoke anyway. "I'm . . . I'm just bringing Eddie here. Wanted to make sure he had somewhere to stay the night. We had quite a time. But we're . . . okay—"

Jack's eyes flashed. *"Okay?"* His voice seethed. "You took him to a *Klan* meeting!" He yanked her handwritten note out of his pocket. He crumpled it up, tossing it at the door.

"Excuse me!"

"Both of you! At a *Klan* meeting!"

"How did you know—?"

"Because you asked a church member's boy to contact Eddie!" He glared. "My church members actually talk to me."

She stepped back, shocked at his anger but distracted as much by, once again, just seeing him. Mercy, she *hated that*, especially tonight—especially right now, with him fussing and fuming at her. Clearly he wasn't distracted by her, not anymore. *"Annalee. You're beautiful."* Sure, tell a silly young woman anything.

"But we solved the mystery!" Eddie said, bounding through the door. He grinned at Jack, not worrying one molar about his teeth. "Reverend Blake, we solved the mystery. That man— Eddie Brown Senior. He *can't sing*! So he's not my father."

"What? That's great, son." Jack still held the door. "C'mon inside. Fix yourself a plate." He pointed Eddie to the kitchen, urging him out of earshot. "Turn the radio on if you want. It's on the shelf."

Then Jack whirled on Annalee.

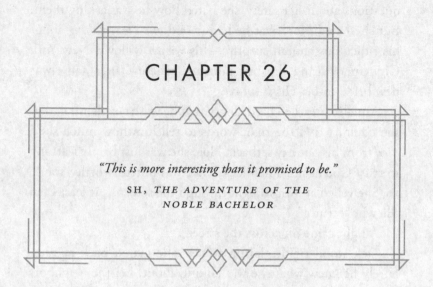

CHAPTER 26

"This is more interesting than it promised to be."

SH, *THE ADVENTURE OF THE
NOBLE BACHELOR*

"YOU COULD BE *DEAD*." Jack glared at her. "Both of you. Just like at the ranch."

Annalee breathed deep. "But I'm not. I'm *alive*." She thought of Mrs. Stallworth's nice compliment, so she didn't hold her tongue. She pushed back a wild curl, still wearing her new hairstyle and still feeling just fine about it. "Besides, what do you care?"

Jack's black eyes flashed, searching hers. "Alive? Do you know what you're saying? Of course not. You're 'alive' with what? Revenge? Your own lust for justice? For control? For finding 'the truth'?" He actually sneered.

Annalee opened her mouth. Shut it. Nothing she'd try to say now would come out right. Even if he had a right to ask his questions about her safety, she hated how he was asking them. But she hated more that he hadn't said *one blessed thing* about his ridiculous church surprise—his wispy, willowy, New York City, fur-wearing, lipstick-pouting, whatever-her-name-was new bride-to-be. His *fi-an-cée*.

Annalee breathed hard, angry that he wasn't explaining, that she couldn't find the right words to tell him how much she'd *died* from his Sunday setback. Here she was just barely learning to trust God again. Then Jack Blake was untrustworthy, too.

She yelled at him straight through the screen. "At least I tell the whole truth!"

A light came on across the street.

Jack stood rigid, glaring at her. She glared back at him. Surely he knew what she was talking about. Let the neighbors hear it, too. There was no way he couldn't understand her confusion about, well, everything. He dared chastise her for her Klan adventure. But what was he hiding? Didn't that count?

Besides, he knew what she meant. She could smell it. She didn't doubt it. But he kept raging at her about the infernal Klan.

He banged open the screen door. Pointed her inside.

She stepped in, eyes flaring. "Forget the Klan—" she hissed at him. The neighbor's light flicked off.

"Those men are the devil. Prowling around—"

"Prowling? Now that's something you know about!" She turned on her heel, grabbed at her stupid oversize coat, trying to make it tighter. She jerked away. "Good night!" She reached for the door handle.

"Annalee!"

She stood firm, not turning—seething at herself for showing her hand, letting him see she actually cared, yes, about the two of them. If there were a *Vogue* "Guide to Arguing with a Man You've Fallen Head Over Heels For," she was failing it.

She could, for sure, give her all to a man like Jack—something she'd never imagined before laying eyes on him and crawling into his big welcoming car—but not at the price of her dignity. *So I will not cry,* she told herself. *Nor will I beg. Not for anybody.* Her unreliable daddy even taught her that. Joe Spain didn't give her all he could've, but he never stopped telling her to walk tall. *"You're as good as anybody, little bit. I can't buy you all the pretty whatnots like the other little girls get, but hold your head up."*

She pulled to her height, not looking back. "Like I said—good night!"

"I'm not getting married," Jack said. "Not to . . . her."

She didn't move. "Who even asked you!"

"Look at me!" Jack stepped closer. "What do you want me to say?"

She whirled. "Say? That you understand my daddy was murdered and you're impressed that I went to a Klan meeting—by myself, not afraid." Well, she'd had those awful nerves. "So you're willing to just listen and let me tell you what I found out—"

"*Listen?* Is that what you're suddenly asking me to do? After going off half-cocked by yourself! With an eleven-year-old kid!"

"Well, why not?" she sputtered. "'Two are better than one.'"

"Oh, so now you're quoting the *Bible*?"

She stepped aside, surprised at him, trying to understand. She searched for another tack, to calm them both down. "If I was wrong to lure Eddie out there, I can admit that. Once I got out there, I knew it was dangerous."

Now his turn.

She waited.

He took a deep, long, deliberate, labored breath.

"I have not led you on," he said.

Not enough. And not true. That kiss led her all over town and back. Ten times around Five Points, then back again the other way. Now she needed to hear more. She waited longer. Refused to beg him to explain.

Finally he offered it.

"My aunt Jessie gets ideas. About her good friend's daughter. Aunt Jessie insists we're an item. Long story, Annalee. You don't want to hear all that mess. Please don't make me talk about it."

"How do you know what I want to hear?"

Jack sighed. "That's what you don't understand, Annalee—that with you, I'm not 'prowling.' That's not me. Why can't you see that?"

"See? I see that I can solve my daddy's murder myself. Because not one person cares about him but me. So I can figure out what happened my way!"

He stepped back. "Is that what you think solving crime is about? *Your* way?" A vein pulsated above his brow. "Never mind that I've got solid leads you haven't even bothered to ask me about. Like about your father and—"

"I already know about my father. He was stealing for Prince, until he got sick and tired of it." Her voice fell. "I think he finally wanted to change."

"Then you understand."

"Understand *what*?"

His voice got quiet. His eyes searched hers. "That once you commit to something good—or to standing with someone—it doesn't matter the climb is hard and the rocks are sharp . . ." He stopped and frowned. "I sound like I'm preaching."

He started over. "In life, you don't run off by yourself, trying to go it alone. The past couple of days I've been all over town looking for you. Leaving messages for you. And you? Solving crime *on your own*, deciding *on your own* to turn tail and stop believing!"

She drew breath. "I'm not sure what you're saying."

"No, you're not. You don't even understand the most important thing about everything to do with fighting a crime—not to mention the most important thing about me—and about us."

She blinked, not knowing how to hear this. "So, *Reverend* Blake—tell me!"

"Tell you? That two *are* better than one? Ecclesiastes 4:9. Remember *learning* that, Professor?"

She held her tongue, not daring to speak—knowing what was on the tip of her tongue. *What's that? An insult? Or in fact, a sermon?*

Oh, let me say that, Lord. But she stayed silent. Breathing hard.

Jack was staring at her. He yanked the napkin off his collar. "Annalee, I wish I just could explain how hard it was for me to learn this—that fighting a battle is about trusting other people, not to mention trusting somebody bigger than all of us. It's not about taking control of the problem, but letting it go." He laughed. "Yep, to God—and that *is* a doggone sermon!"

"Sounds more like prayer," she said, trying to show a little theological muscle. But without even trying hard, Jack threw her a curve.

"Yeah. So it's just like love." His voice had dropped to a whisper.

She stepped back, not sure how to hear that from Jack. Not

tonight. She didn't have the experience to hear it or understand the promise of it or know what it all was supposed to mean. Or could mean. Because she knew what she longed for, and still hoped for, for them.

That they could rediscover the path they had started to walk. Together. Even while trying to solve a crime. She let out a deep breath. *Why can't he understand?*

But he was holding open the screen door, not looking at her now.

She stepped onto the porch. "Well, good night," she said. She closed the screen door.

"It's morning." He pulled out a watch on his vest chain. "One twenty-two a.m. A new day." He pocketed the watch, latched the screen. "But the one thing I wouldn't call it is *good*."

He clenched his jaw, pushed the inside door hard, closing it. Locking it.

Annalee stood for a moment on the porch. Alone again.

"Thanks for taking in Eddie," she whispered. Knowing he didn't hear that.

She wondered if perhaps she should knock again, try to tell him again what she'd discovered about Hunter Castle and Slater Prince and—*good Lord*—about Elizabeth Castle, too. And this time, ask for his help. Because she was starting to understand that the goal of a detective isn't to break down doors to find answers—it's to let them find you, but never alone. Instead, you work side by side. Every detective worth her salt has her trusted sidekick.

"Two are better than one." But if that were true, then so was something else:

She wanted her somebody else to be Jack.

But while she stood there, he seemed to be giving her his answer. By turning off the porch light, leaving her in the dark, forcing her to understand, without a question or a doubt:

He had already decided. His answer was no.

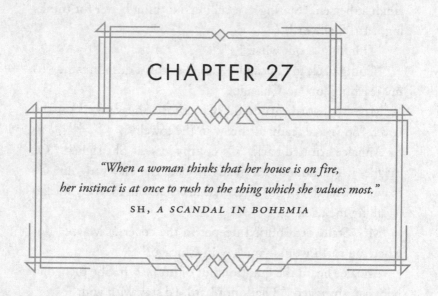

CHAPTER 27

"When a woman thinks that her house is on fire,
her instinct is at once to rush to the thing which she values most."
SH, *A SCANDAL IN BOHEMIA*

"YOU LAYING THERE ALL NIGHT? Staring at the ceiling?"

Mrs. Stallworth yawned, mumbling out her question. With a groan, she yanked a pile of bedcovers up to her chin, settled a kerchief tighter around her head, curled her body onto one corner of the narrow bed, muttering at the cold-water flat they'd rented in Five Points for three dollars a week.

Annalee flopped on the opposite side of the bed, still wearing her borrowed coat. She wasn't ready to wriggle out of it, unscrew the light bulb, and climb under the covers. Instead, she decided to answer Mrs. Stallworth's question with one of her own.

"You mean *that* ceiling?" She looked up at the water stains and jagged holes in the broken-down plaster, managing a wry laugh at herself. "Staring at a ceiling. Nothing better for thinking, Mrs. Stallworth."

"Thinking about what?"

"Going back to Chicago." Annalee took a deep breath. "To my teaching job. To Chicago."

Mrs. Stallworth grunted. "Chicago?" She yanked on the cover. "So you're ready to throw in the towel?"

Annalee grunted back. "Or cut my losses." She sighed. "Or maybe, if I'm honest, I'm ready to take the easy way out. Or maybe the hard. I'm not sure what to call it. But maybe Chicago is calling me back."

Mrs. Stallworth buried deeper in the covers. "Maybe. But where on earth would you stay in Chicago?"

Annalee heard the question but didn't *hear* it. She turned in her coat, shrugged. "That's not hard. I'd stay with you."

Mrs. Stallworth sighed again, burying deeper in the covers. "Oh, dear," she finally said.

"*Oh, dear?*" Annalee frowned, turned, leaned on her elbow. "And what's that supposed to mean?"

"I didn't want to tell you!"

"Tell me? Mrs. Stallworth, tell me what?"

"About the rooming house." Mrs. Stallworth sighed. "It's gone."

Annalee sat up. "Gone where?"

Mrs. Stallworth looked over the covers. Stared at the ceiling. "I lost three tenants this year, honey. Not counting you. And well, the bank—"

"*No,*" Annalee said. Hearing but not believing. Needing to say it out loud. "Your house is gone?"

"The tax sale was last week. The day after you left. And . . ."

"What about your rainy-day money?"

"With *my* bills? That money was gone before I could count it up and spend it."

Annalee got quiet. Watched the cracks in the wall. "So everything's gone."

"There's nothing left, Annalee. After I bought my train ticket and paid for a week in this poor room we're sleeping in, there's nothing left. Well, a nickel or two."

Annalee fell back on the broken-down bed. Then sat up. Then stood up. Paced the floor a minute. Started to laugh.

"What's so funny?" Mrs. Stallworth said.

"Jack is right."

"And what are *you* talking about now?"

"I'm talking about everything."

"Girl, if you don't start making sense, I'm getting up from this bed and walking back to Chicago by myself right now."

Annalee pulled off her borrowed coat. Hung it over a chair. Kicked off her shoes. Rubbed her cold feet. She unscrewed the light bulb. Climbed under the covers. Snuggled in next to Mrs. Stallworth, feeling her warmth.

"Jack told me tonight that I try to do everything myself. Put myself before God. I'm always pushing my way out in front of my every problem. Trying to fix everything. By myself."

Mrs. Stallworth sighed. "If it's okay to mention it, I believe I told you the same thing myself."

Annalee smiled in the dark. "But you know the funny thing?"

"Funny? What's funny about losing a house? Your money? And everything else?" She sighed, sounding deep and sad. "Annalee, I had to sell your books."

Annalee swallowed. "All of them?"

"Everything's gone, honey. Your Sherlocks. Your teaching books. Your bottles of ink." Mrs. Stallworth sighed again. "Even your three-legged desk. Only thing not sold was your daddy's old Stetson hat. I brought it with me." She moaned. "Oh, I'm so sorry, Annalee. If it takes the rest of my life, I'll pay you every dime, get everything back."

Annalee lay on her back, staring up in the dark. "Even if I had all those things, I'm still not in control. None of us is."

"Well, God's in control, honey," Mrs. Stallworth said. "In control of everything."

"So we don't have to try so hard," Annalee said. "To hang on to things—things we never really had. Just like you said."

"*Lord*, it took me a long time to figure that out."

"So folks like us might as well stop worrying."

Mrs. Stallworth laughed. "And get some sleep."

Annalee burrowed under the covers. "That's right, Mrs. Stallworth. Let's get some sleep. There's not a thing either one of us can do tonight about your rooming house. Or Jack. Or Eddie. Or Daddy's murder. Or my books." She yawned. "Or my worn-down three-legged desk. Or anything else." She reached over to squeeze her landlady's warm hand. "So sweet dreams, Mrs. Stallworth."

"You too, honey," Mrs. Stallworth said. She rolled over, her back to Annalee, her breath settling down.

Soon, in fact, Mrs. Stallworth was fast asleep. Her breathing even, a light snore lulling Annalee to her own rest, letting Annalee close her eyes, quiet her soul, pretend she wasn't thinking about Jack. And Eddie. And Hunter Castle. And the precious little baby. Her collection of books. Mrs. Stallworth's lost house.

Annalee opened her eyes.

And Slater Prince.

She drew in a long breath, reflected on the feeling of her body longing to relax. Her eyes felt heavy, so she exhaled, pulling the covers past her nose.

She was determined *not* to think about Slater Prince and his own indictment of himself. That there wasn't a single square inch of Denver—"or anywhere around Denver, for that matter"—where he wouldn't be found. *At one time or another.*

A prideful detail man. Annalee thought about that. Whose beautiful daughter got pregnant. By a white man.

A messy detail, especially for a man whose livelihood depended on decent relations with Denver's elite—well, Denver's *white* elite—because they'd shun him. Except they didn't shun him because he knew their secrets. And he hid them where?

Think, Annalee. What did her father's key open?

She moved away the covers, felt the beribboned key. It opened nothing in the Castles' house. Nothing in her daddy's cabin. Nothing, probably, at Lent Montgomery's ranch. Her breath caught.

The church.

Slater Prince's unofficial headquarters. His second home. He hid his stash of hush money and scandalous secrets and dirty whatnots right there under everybody's nose. In plain view. His own card trick. Mount Moriah.

But is that right?

She thought of the church news clipping taped to Bernita's mirror. Prince holding his pompous fancy shovel. Her daddy's eyes boring into hers. Prince Hall Masons dressed to the nines. Everybody standing around that silent cornerstone. She sighed.

Oh, God, why is the world so blasted complicated? she pondered.

And so murderous? She hiked a brow.

And so afraid to open our eyes and see?

But she didn't want to think about such questions. Not now. Not with sleep coming. So she lay still in the bed, listening to Mrs. Stallworth's breathing. Reflected on her own. Felt her lips move. Needing to speak.

But what do you want me to say? That I'm sorry, Lord?

For all my trespasses? And for every wrong, ridiculous thing I've ever done myself. And for always getting so far ahead of you. Because I thought that's what good soldiers did: stayed ahead of the game.

Or did good soldiers simply wait, as Jack said, for the right help? Believing that two are better than one—because to believe that truth is what matters most. Maybe more than solving a crime. *Oh, is this right, God?*

Annalee wished she had Jack's hard-earned wisdom, even if he was still angry. And Eddie's passion, even if he was impulsive. And Mrs. Stallworth's imperfect love, even if she was ornery and lousy at money. And homeless. Both of them now were quite homeless, in fact.

But thank you, Father God, Annalee sighed, *that I'm not afraid of any of it. Because when I get quiet with you, I find my way back home.*

Usually.

I'm just being honest.

Amen.

Jack would like that prayer, Annalee thought, before pulling up the covers and closing her eyes on her weariness, her excited gratitude, and her relief. *He's not marrying that woman.* Then she slept.

A deep and sound sleep. The kind of sleep that restores a weary body, refreshes an aching soul, reprises a turbulent mind. So she luxuriated in it. Unaware, on any conscious level, she was getting renewed. But more than that, she *was* aware in some deep place in her spirit of answers getting unraveled and untwisted. She could feel herself sighing, sinking into the feeling of being blessed with a rest so deep it could only be a certain kind of holy gift.

Thus, at some point during the cold night, she didn't feel the bed shaking and rustling.

"Annalee. *Annalee.*"

She fought it.

"Hm? *What . . . ?*"

"Annalee!"

"I'm . . . still asleep . . ."

"Annalee!" The bed shaking more.

"Please . . . sleep . . ."

"Annalee. Wake up. Something's *wrong.*"

Annalee groaned, knowing some light in her brain flashed on. "What? *No.* Please . . . no, Mrs. Stallworth."

She groaned again, trying not to open her eyes. She squeezed them tight. Not wanting to see, hear, feel, *know* anything. Trying not to see Mrs. Stallworth pressed against the room's narrow window.

Annalee mumbled at her, "Come back to bed . . ." She dug deeper under the covers.

"No, Annalee. Something's not right. *Look.*"

Annalee moaned dramatically. Mumbling, she threw off

the covers. Her feet hit the cold floor. She groaned again. "Oh, *what*, Mrs. Stallworth?" She stumbled across the floor, banged her toe on *something*, grabbed her foot, fell onto Mrs. Stallworth, grabbed the windowsill, wishing she wasn't appalled by what she was seeing through the half-frozen window.

"*Fire.*" Mrs. Stallworth's whisper cut the dark.

Annalee's knees sank. She could see it, couldn't understand it. But finally did.

"*Jack's house,*" she whispered. She clawed at the window. Her body trembling. She looked across the alley, halfway down the block. "Oh, God. *No!*"

"Annalee! What is it?"

Annalee thrashed across the tiny room. Grabbed for shoes. Coat. Grabbed the door. "Wake up the landlady. Her phone's in the hall. Tell her to call the fire department."

"Is it the Klan?"

"I don't know! *Now*, Mrs. Stallworth."

Annalee stumbled down a narrow staircase at the back of the ramshackle rooming house, thrashed through the back door, through the yard, banged over garbage cans. Set dogs barking. They snapped at her through the fence as she scrambled into the alley. The flames poured from the kitchen of Jack's house— injecting an eerie, angry, blistering glare into the inky sky.

"*Jack.*" Smoke gripped at her throat. But she swallowed a lungful, screaming anyway. "*Jack!*" She ran, the alley a black blur. She slid in dirty snow, crashed to the ground, clawed back up.

"Jack!" She coughed in the choking smoke. Her screams sounded loud—and alone. The night so dark but bright with *fire*. She scrambled through the gate to Jack's backyard. Sliding on ice. Trying to get to the back door of the house. But smoke and flames pushed her back.

"*Jack!*"

She ran to the side of the house. Stopped dead in her tracks, not believing what she was seeing. The church was aflame, too. The spire and roof and tower and one side of the building ablaze, flames snaking out shattered stained-glass windows, the night sky alight with the angry glow.

With both hands, she pounded on windows along the side of Jack's house. "Jack! *Fire!*" Her voice screeching. Begging.

"*Jack!*"

Pleading.

"*Eddie!*"

She scrambled to the front porch, pounded on the door. She heard a massive explosion in the back of the house. Just as the door swung open.

"*Jack!*"

He was carrying Eddie. "Annalee! *Thank God!* Oh, Annalee, I'm so sorry!"

"Jack!" She shook her head. "No! Jack! You're right! But *Eddie!*"

"I found him in the kitchen! Trying to douse the fire. Smoke got him. Gotta get him outside."

He gestured. "Across the street. Hurry. Follow me."

Annalee took a step. But turned. "No, the church."

But Jack was halfway across the street, carrying Eddie. Motioning for Annalee to follow.

She shook her head. "The church."

Jack yelled, "Annalee! *This way.*"

"*No!* The *church*." She turned toward the blazing building.

"No. It's *burning*!"

"But there's *evidence*. In plain view!"

Jack frowned.

"Evidence, Jack! *In the church.*"

But he was pleading. "Annalee! *No, this way!*"

"The cornerstone!" Annalee yelled. She thought of the photo taped to Bernita's dresser mirror. "Slater Prince! He's blackmailing the rich, the prominent, politicians, elected officials, rich wives, *everybody*. And he looked the other way about his *daughter's* baby. Hunter Castle was the father."

Jack struggled to kneel, laid Eddie on the ground just as Mrs. Stallworth panted up the street. "Please watch the boy!" Jack yelled.

Mrs. Stallworth dropped to her knees, scooping Eddie into her arms, hollering at Annalee to come back. But Annalee waved off both of them.

"*No.* The evidence. I think it's in the cornerstone!"

Annalee turned, racing back toward the church, shocked the flames were already engulfing the sanctuary. The roof. The spire. Licking at the delicate metal cross atop the spire. She stopped dead still. *The house is burning.*

"I have the key," she whispered, shielding her face from the heat, coughing at smoke, scowling at the angry blaze, assessing how to get at the contents of the concrete cornerstone, past the flames and thick smoke roiling out of the main church doors.

She ran at the building.

But Jack jerked her back by the arm. Almost knocking her down.

He pulled her toward him, embracing her close, as a hulking black car careened around the corner, the door flying open.

Slater Prince scrambled out. Took one horrified look at the blaze.

He rushed at the building. Drew back at the flames. Whirled around, stumbling.

"You two are *dead*." Slater Prince pointed at them with both hands. "The *two* of you. Snooping around. Stirring up trouble. Getting my church burned down."

He raged, circling, his ermine coat half-off, dragging in smoke-blackened snow. He cursed. Spat out threats. "Hear me? You two are *dead*! *Both of you!*"

"It's not your church," Jack said evenly.

"But it's my city. And you two? Not worth my time."

Annalee stared at Prince, dead in his face. "You left your own grandchild alone in a field to *die*."

"That's not your business," he spat out.

"A little *baby*," Annalee shot back.

"And good riddance to it!"

Annalee's throat tightened. *"Why?"* she yelled. "For *money*? How much did Hunter and Elizabeth Castle pay you?"

Slater Prince laughed darkly. "You know *nothing* about that. Nothing about *me*. Nothing about what I've had done for this town, this church, this *neighborhood*. Water lines. Sewer. Phones. Streetlights. Parks. *Paved streets.*" He waved his arms, gesturing. "*I* did all this."

She shook her head, understanding it all too well. Seeing the weakness in him. In Hunter Castle. In Elizabeth, too. Maybe in everyone who ever lived, including herself. Pride. Except Prince was dripping with it.

"So how much did they pay you? Year after year. For the votes? And your silence?"

He narrowed his eyes, pointed at the burning building, hands shaking. "They? *I* am *God's* inside man. The *chief* church trustee. I built this church from the ground up. *Me.* And *nobody* gets in my way!"

"Especially a little baby," she whispered to herself. But he was pushing past her, rushing at the building, backing away from the heat. Scrambling to his car, he yanked open the trunk, grabbed a heavy shovel. Her daddy's shovel. Fought his way past flames to rush at the cornerstone.

Annalee backed away, watching soberly as Slater Prince swung into a brick over the cornerstone. His secret entry point? His stash of papers must be locked away carefully—but vulnerable now, to the fire raging around him.

He flailed at the bricks, found his entry, wrestled out a box-size metal safe. Blind to fire trucks racing around the corner, bells clanging, the colored captain yelling. "*Hey!* Mister!" The captain looked harder. "Mr. Prince. Get back!" The captain scrambled with the others to hook water hoses to the nearest hydrants, the firemen already cursing. "No water pressure!" one yelled.

The captain noticed Jack. "Reverend Blake. The rest of this block could go up like tinder."

Jack turned to Annalee. But she was already scrambling away. "We've got to warn people."

"What about Prince?" Jack yelled.

"It's over for him." Annalee repeated it to herself as she ran from house to house, knocking on doors. *All over.*

She started warning church neighbors as Jack worked the opposite side of the street.

Neither of them was near the church or near the burned-out parsonage when the walls of Mount Moriah AME Church imploded, leaving the granite tower, the spire, and a tangle of timber and metal to crash with angry force to the ground below.

Annalee shuddered at the noisome sight. She watched as Slater Prince flung away her daddy's shovel. Backing away, he saved his body—and the safe holding his stash of papers or letters or receipts or whatever he'd stashed to blackmail his victims—from the falling bricks and flames. He pounded at the lock with his shovel. A man ran out of the crowd, trying to help him. Annalee squinted, looking, but she wasn't surprised. The train waiter, William Barnett, made a half-hearted try to help Prince. Then Barnett pushed himself away and slunk into the night.

Annalee slipped the key from around her neck. Gripped it tight for a moment. Handed it to the fire captain. "There's criminal evidence in that box."

The fire captain searched her eyes, nodded, took the key from her hand.

Annalee walked away, not put off that Slater Prince hadn't met his death in the fire.

Or as she would say later, when his daughter told police the awful things that her own father had done: in many sad ways, he'd died years ago. *"For what shall it profit a man, if he shall gain the whole world, and lose his own soul?"*

Annalee believed she knew the answer. Such a man gains naught.

CHAPTER 28

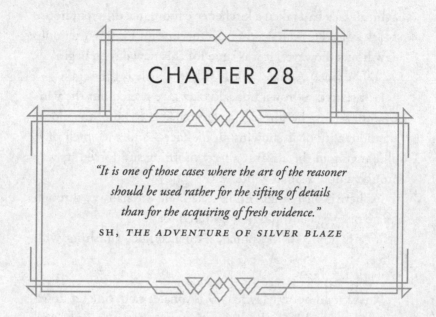

"It is one of those cases where the art of the reasoner should be used rather for the sifting of details than for the acquiring of fresh evidence."

SH, *THE ADVENTURE OF SILVER BLAZE*

"Don't wait for me," Annalee said. "You'll drive out later?"

Jack grabbed his jacket—still wearing his clothes from the night before, all he owned now. But he faced a bigger worry. "The church trustees are waiting," he said to Annalee. "*Loads* of work to do. Lots to figure out. Much to recover."

Annalee nodded, searching his eyes.

For a quick moment, he reached for her, but he pulled back. He grabbed for his coffee instead, held on to it tight. "I need to talk to you, but—" He broke off.

"You better go." She nodded again, telling him it was okay.

They were standing in the kitchen of the rooming house, down the alley from the burned-out parsonage. Around daybreak Jack had taken a kitchenette room in a different house a block away. He rented a room in this one for Eddie. After only a few hours, however, it was time for this new day to begin.

"I'll be fine," Annalee said. "Sidney Castle is driving."

Jack started to frown but said okay. He peered out the window, not seeing the smoldering church at the end of the block, but the reality of it showing in his face—and the smell of it still hanging in the air. But a hazy morning sun forced its way through a door's small window.

"Where is she going?" Eddie asked. He was halfway through a plate of eggs, chomping on buttered toast.

"*She* is going to the ranch," Annalee said, finishing with coffee.

"The Lazy K?"

"Just for an hour. Maybe two," Annalee said. She set down her cup, washed it in the sink, set it on a drain to dry. "And no, you can't go this time. I'm riding out with Sidney—Mr. Castle."

"But I'm *fine*, Professor. That lady doctor said so."

"She ordered a good bed rest. Besides, I'm not making a social call."

"Not social?" Mrs. Stallworth asked. "So why those flowers?" She limped into the kitchen, got busy making her toast, mixing cocoa, stopping to smell a tiny bouquet of a florist's wild roses, borrowed with the rooming house owner's permission from a front hallway table and resting now in Annalee's hands.

Jack eyed the flowers too. "Because she understands," he said, looking at Annalee, searching her eyes across the table, his face thoughtful.

"Understands what, sir?" Eddie asked.

Annalee turned from the sink, slipped into her borrowed coat, pulled on the gloves, and spoke the words Jack seemed to be thinking.

"How to finish well."

But she didn't finish much of anything at the Lazy K. At least not right away. The ranch was deserted. Dead quiet. Just as Rosita's little girl, Dominga, said it would be.

"Nobody up there," Dominga said, watching Annalee climb out of Sidney Castle's somber Cadillac sedan. *"Go away,"* the child insisted. She was standing by the gate of the truck farm where Annalee last saw her.

Annalee held back, trying not to look like a threat. "I rode out with Mr. Castle." She gestured to the car. "He needs to talk to Señor Montgomery. Do you know where he is?"

The little girl shook her head. "Nobody up there."

"Your mama's gone too?" Annalee asked.

"She is working. She not here," the little girl said.

Annalee nodded, backed away. She was making the little girl nervous. "I understand, Dominga. She's not at home."

The child squinted. "She is cooking. For lady in town."

"Of course," Annalee said, acting nonchalant. "I'm just going to the grave. To take some flowers." She offered a wave, turning to go.

"For the little baby?" the girl said, suddenly interested.

"Yes. You know where it is?"

"I go many days, all the time. It's on the hill." She looked excited. "I can show you."

Annalee thought a minute. "Only if we bring you right back. But I'll leave a note for your mama. So she won't worry."

Dominga already was running back to the small farmhouse. "I can write a note. Wait for me."

So eager, Annalee thought, to see the grave of a dead baby? Annalee felt a shiver. Pulled her coat tighter against the raw and bitter day, pulled on her jacket hood.

"Whose infant is in the grave?" Sidney Castle asked, still sitting in the car. He looked uncomfortable. Impatient? "Did you find out?"

Annalee hesitated, knowing the answer was complicated. "I'll just say she's God's child," she finally said.

"I don't argue that," Castle said, "although I'd like to know more. But I can see you're not going to tell me more. At least not now."

"I guess I want to see the gravesite first."

"So do I, actually," Castle said. He held the back door open for Dominga, giving her time to scramble inside and wriggle under a pile of car blankets. "That's the ticket," he said, trying to sound friendly, to make small talk with the child. But the girl could see he wasn't a man fully comfortable with children. So she burrowed into the covers, keeping her silence, closing her eyes—and right away, as they started to drive, to their surprise, Dominga was fast asleep.

Sidney Castle steered the car toward the ranch house—a winter stillness spreading out before them, a long ribbon of road unfolding behind them, and a tense discomfort growing in the car.

Annalee finally turned to Castle. "Is this when you finally tell me?"

"Tell you what, Miss Spain?"

"Who killed my father."

He let out a hard sigh. "I'm sure you already know."

"I know many things, Mr. Castle. But will you *listen*?"

"Do I have a choice?"

"A choice? To hear that your son is a crook? Your wife is an adulteress? Your caterer is a blackmailer? And your maid takes bribes to stay quiet?"

"Not a pretty picture, the Castle household." His voice was dark.

"Especially since one person is missing."

He turned. "When did you find out?"

"About Eddie Brown Senior?"

Sidney Castle gripped the steering wheel. "How did you figure it out, Professor?"

"I didn't. I just couldn't understand the reaction everybody had to seeing Eddie. First, to his appearance, like they'd come face-to-face with a ghost."

"He's the spitting image of his father."

"But especially the reaction to his name—Eddie Brown Junior. I mean, you. Slater Prince. Your wife. Your son, Hunter. It seemed unusual that a boy and a name would evoke such horror in all four of you. At first I thought it was because the Klan chief's name is Eddie Brown Senior. Then last night, I learned that Eddie Brown of the Klan *couldn't* be his father."

"You should stop this—"

"I *can't* stop this. I came to Denver to find the truth. For a lot of reasons, Eddie's truth has become as crucial as my own. So *I* need to know. *Where is his father?*"

"I'm sorry. But Eddie's father is dead."

"*Sorry?* Somebody killed him, too?"

"He was the first," Sidney Castle said. "Such a decent man. Came to town. Worked the mines for a while. But ended up downtown, preaching on street corners, helping drunks like—"

"Like my father?"

"Yes, like your father. The papers did an article about him. 'Chicago Street Preacher Saving Drunken Souls.' Something like that. Then he started organizing ex-alcoholics to fight street crime, fight the speakeasies, fight the Klan."

"A 'troublemaker.'"

"Darn good at it. But I gave him a job. Working odd jobs. Keeping him out of harm's way. The mob, the Klan, the police, all were out for him."

"And somebody killed him anyway."

Sidney Castle breathed hard. "My son." His voice sounded dry. "I never imagined. But Hunter has such ambitions. Eddie's father threatened to report Hunter to federal agents. So Hunter brought him out here and killed him. Or probably had somebody do it. I doubt anybody will find his body." He pressed his mouth. "Later, I learned Hunter had your father killed, too. Took a train trip to Chicago and had him pushed onto the tracks. As if by his *own hands.*"

"How do you know this?"

"Many people tell me things. Sadly, I had no reason to doubt it."

Annalee stared straight ahead, sitting quiet, letting the cold vista spread out before them, seeing the roof of the ranch house appear on a hazy, distant hill.

"Were you going to let your son kill me, too?"

"Not if I could help it."

"*Help it?* Why didn't you just *turn him in?* Mr. Castle, your son is a cold-blooded murderer."

Castle gave her a dark, sad look. "Because he's my *son.*"

Annalee whirled on him. "*No.* Tell the truth, Mr. Castle. *Just tell the truth.*" She breathed hard. Both of them tense, uneasy.

"Meaning what?" Castle said. "That I'm supposed to sit back while my family unravels around me?" He yanked open the top snap on his overcoat. "Professor, what do you want me to say? That I didn't turn in my son for my *wife's* sake? Is that so *wrong?*"

Annalee shifted in her seat, not certain of Castle's tone, deciding to head it off. She settled on a question.

"Families are complicated, aren't they?"

Sidney Castle laughed, dark and dry. "There's a word for a remark like that."

"Right, *understatement.*"

Now Castle didn't laugh. "In fact, I'm certain the word is *theological.*"

"Spoken like a man who believes in God."

"And you don't, Professor?"

Annalee peered at the wintering horizon. "At certain times, I *didn't.* Or maybe I *couldn't.* Some days, there are oh-so-many reasons not to believe. But then other days arise, with all their graces and mercies." She held up the bouquet. "And before you know it, there are too many reasons *not* to yield to belief."

"And now?"

"And now I can live with doubt. I don't need guarantees about God. I just choose to believe, trusting that if I do my part for him, he'll take care of the rest."

"But how can you trust what you can't see?"

Annalee turned to face Sidney Castle. "Because I'm riding in this car with you, and you know whose baby is laying out there in an icy grave. So you know what it would mean to your family if the truth of her identity got out into the world. On top of that, you've just confessed to knowing of horrible crimes—crimes you could've stopped. Yet you haven't opened the car door and pushed me out into a cold, deep ditch. Me and the girl, too."

Sidney Castle sighed. "I despair of being ruthless."

Annalee listened, finally asked, "The man on the train? *You* hired him?"

"Not the dead guy. Not my man. I hired someone else—to keep an eye on you. I thought it better if you stayed out of Denver. For Hunter's sake. For Elizabeth." His voice broke. "I've had people watching you for quite a while. When you bought a train ticket to Denver, I thought I could scare you away. But the man I hired, a good policeman, hasn't been seen for days. I fear for what's happened to him. As for my household, I'm losing it all anyway." He laughed darkly. "Even Bernita is gone."

"*What?*"

"Left a pile of fancy clothes in the kitchen with a note for you. 'Gone to college.' Whatever in the devil that's supposed to mean."

Annalee breathed deep. *What a way to settle all this, Watson.*

"So your son is . . ."

"Not the man I hoped for. But I *tried*. God knows I tried—to steer him, to be a good father to him. Just like I tried to be a good husband. Just like I'm trying to make it right for you. But I failed."

Annalee reached for Sidney Castle's arm, trying to find the

right words. "I don't need you to make things right for me. I'll only find that in one place."

"With young Jack?" he asked.

Annalee shook her head. "With my Father."

In the back seat, Dominga was waking up, wriggling out of the blankets. "We are getting close." She pointed past a curve to a rounded hill. "The baby's grave. It's over there. Past the big house."

Annalee pulled her coat tighter as Sidney Castle steered the car to a stop. She wrapped a blanket around the little girl's shoulders, reached for her hand, gestured for Castle to follow as they crunched through the snowy, rock-strewn path onto a slight rise.

The cemetery, hidden from the road, spread out on a rocky plateau. A family affair—Lent Montgomery's kin from two generations before—all quietly resting. Maybe not quietly. But resting nevertheless. Each grave sat under an elaborately carved granite headstone. For them, the good fight was over.

"Over *there*," the little girl said. She pointed west, pulling Annalee with her to a bump on the landscape.

Annalee felt her throat tighten, seeing the slight rise in the earth. It was bare and barren, devoid of any marker. But she knew for certain, just as this child knew, exactly what this was: a tiny grave.

Dominga loosed her hand, walked with purpose across the rock-strewn field to the small bump in the earth, stood over it for a moment, then knelt to brush away dead twigs and dried leaves.

She spoke in Spanish, her voice a whisper. Then in English: "She lives in heaven now." She looked up at Annalee, searching her face. "She look like you—like a little angel," the child said. "That's what your daddy said. He say you look the same when he found—"

Annalee exhaled. "My father said what . . . ?" she whispered.

Her knees went weak. But something interrupted. A woman's voice.

"Sidney, you shouldn't have come."

Annalee didn't have to turn. Instead, she felt an odd sense of eagerness.

"Elizabeth," Sidney Castle shouted across the landscape. "I thought you were in town."

Elizabeth peered at him. "Oh, for heaven's sake, Sidney. You never were a good liar."

"Not on a par with you, anyway. Actually I drove out here to talk to you. And to Lent."

Elizabeth, dressed in a full-length black mink, turned up her expensive coat's collar. "None of that matters now. Because I see you've brought me your girl."

"What the devil are you talking about? What are you doing here—?"

Annalee cut in, "She's here to dig up the grave. Destroy the baby's remains." She pointed to the mounded dirt. "She's destroying evidence. Her evidence."

"What? Don't make me laugh." Elizabeth flipped her mink closed.

"I thought it was Prince," Annalee pressed on. "But it was *you*. You drove the baby out here, wrapped her in Hunter's fancy shirt, left her in a field to die."

"If you know so much, why are you telling me?" Elizabeth said.

"So I can give her a taste of *this*." Hunter Castle, approaching them from over a rise, sauntered over to his mother. He opened his coat, slid out from his vest the revolver Annalee remembered, pointed it at her. The long barrel shone flat in the dull winter sun.

Sidney Castle moaned. *"Hunter."*

"Stop!" the little girl shouted.

Annalee helped her to stand. She whispered, "Go get in the car, honey." Dominga hesitated, then started running, dropping the blanket right away, stumbling, scrambling up, running past Hunter down the rock-strewn path, beyond the cemetery. "And *stay in the car*," Annalee yelled to her. "Everything's going to be okay!"

"Oh, so maternal. So touching. Picking up stray children. You and your broken-down cowboy daddy."

"You're being ridiculous," Sidney Castle snapped.

"Ridiculous is driving out to this ranch," Elizabeth said. "And for what? For me?"

"No, for our family! To try to save us!" Castle pointed at Hunter. "Why do you stand up for him?"

"Call it fear," Annalee said. "Her son knows too much."

Hunter's eyes narrowed. He waved the gun at Annalee. "Look at her! In fact, I hear you're big on Sherlock Holmes. Is that what this is about? Trying to be a detective? Trying to uncover the *truth*? Unravel little *secrets*?" He sneered, lifting the gun, aimed it at Annalee.

"Hunter, enough!" Sidney Castle yelled.

"He may never be enough," Annalee said.

"Can't help yourself, can you?" Hunter seethed at Annalee.

"No, I just understand you. All my life, I tried to be just like you, trying to prove myself."

"Is that so? Well, what did you learn, Professor? You want me to ask that?"

She thought about her father. "There's nothing from you I want."

"You call a cool hundred million dollars nothing?"

"Your money pot? The sum of all your schemes? So much lucre you just put any number on it, so long as it sounds big." She rolled her eyes. "And what will that buy?" Annalee asked. "Another expensive car? Another fancy white coat? Or maybe a Congress seat? Or Senate? Maybe even the presidency? Is that what you want?" She turned to Elizabeth. "Is that what you're protecting?"

Annalee stepped closer to the grave. "Is that what this innocent baby's life bought?"

She didn't wait for their answer but suddenly saw it, as clear as a bell. "Power? That's what you crave?"

Hunter Castle narrowed his eyes.

"You're a little too smart for your own good," Elizabeth said.

"You let this baby die—alone in the cold. Brought her out here, left her alone to die in an open field. For power? To protect your name and status?"

Sidney Castle bristled. "*God almighty*, Elizabeth. Why didn't I stop this? Our own flesh and blood."

"Don't lecture me, Sidney."

"The baby? It was *nothing*," Hunter said.

His father stiffened. "I *lied* for you." His voice trembled.

"And for your mother. When you broke the law, I turned away and didn't do a thing to block you."

Castle stepped close to Annalee, protective. "I let you live, Hunter. But I can't promise I'll do that now." He opened his waistcoat, pulled out a gleaming, long-necked pistol.

"*Sidney!*" Elizabeth shouted.

Annalee froze. "Please put it away, Mr. Castle. *Please.*"

Hunter sneered. "Don't beg on my behalf, *Professor.*"

"The professor's not begging—not for you," Castle said. "But I refuse to stand here and let you kill her. Not another innocent person."

"And what do you intend to do?" Elizabeth hissed.

"You'll shoot *me?*" Hunter asked, walking toward his father. He waved the .45. "You'd shoot *me*, old man? If I do *this?*"

Hunter Castle pointed the barrel of the gun at his father. Laughed. Then whirled, aiming it at Annalee's temple. He grabbed her around the neck. Pressing the gun hard onto her flesh.

Annalee flinched. But didn't scream. Ignoring the cold steel. Instead, she thought of her daddy, reflecting on the horizon, the snowy, rocky landscape, the low-hanging sky, Mrs. Stallworth's homespun wisdom about letting small things conquer big.

Annalee kept her gaze on the distant skyline, stared at a lone, leafless tree. *Please, Jesus.*

"I'm warning you, Son," Sidney Castle shouted.

"*Stop it, Sidney!*" Elizabeth yelled.

"Warning me? Calling me *Son?*"

Annalee jerked her head. "He's your *father*," she said through tight lips, pulling at his grip.

Hunter gripped her tighter, the odor of his unwashed body apparent. "And what would *you* know about a father?"

Annalee struggled for the right words, came up empty.

Hunter laughed, his breath on her neck. "That's right, smart girl. You know *nothing*."

Her throat tightened. She strained to speak. "My father . . . Joe Spain."

"Joe Spain? That no-count drunk. He's not your father. He never was."

Annalee opened her lips. Her mouth went dry. Her knees sank.

"Just what I thought." He turned to his mother. "I told you she didn't know."

Annalee's breath caught. "But he was . . . my . . ." Her voice was a whisper, pained and wounded, knowing a lying man had just spoken the truth she'd sought her entire life. Her stomach lurched.

"Dumb drunk, finding you . . . half-dead baby."

"*No . . .*" She could barely whisper.

"*Abandoned . . .*"

"No!"

"What the devil are you talking about, Hunter?" Sidney Castle gripped his pistol tighter, aiming it at his son.

"In a filthy mine shaft—"

"*No!*" Annalee couldn't breathe.

"In *Annalee*. Of all places. That little mining ghost town piece of *garbage*."

Annalee looked at Hunter but managed, impossibly, to smile, seeing what Hunter couldn't.

"Thank you, Daddy," she whispered.

"You are *garbage*," Hunter Castle shouted.

"You *saved* me, Daddy."

"Your 'daddy' was a drunk and a loser," Elizabeth said.

"And your 'sweet' mother. Just another Black whore —"

"Stop it!" Sidney Castle's face was a dark, angry scowl.

"And *everybody* knew!" Hunter kept on. "Neighbor ladies. Schoolkids. Your nice schoolteachers. Everybody but you, *Professor*. Couldn't see the truth in front of your face. So Joe Spain wasn't so easy to bribe." He laughed. "But he was real easy to kill."

He turned to Elizabeth. "Tell her, Mother?"

"A drunk? We didn't even have to push hard."

Annalee seethed, jerked away, pulling against Hunter Castle, but he gripped her tighter.

"*Stop it.*" Sidney Castle's face grew angrier. "I don't know how you found this out—or even if what you say is true. But stop *now*."

"Oh, it's true all right—and I'll stop it *right now*." Hunter cocked his pistol.

Just as Sidney Castle cocked his.

The metal clicks snapped in the cold air.

Annalee looked outside of herself at the two warring men, at the woman who should've been their bond, and made her peace. She gazed at the horizon, knowing then what was true about her daddy, about her God, about getting picked out of mud so that we can live, and we can choose to keep on living.

She looked directly at the hazy sun. Listened to her racing heart, nodded at the light. *Jesus, I want to live. But not for myself, Jesus.* She was through with all of that. Still she longed, yes, to live—to survive, indeed, for the God she couldn't see. That God who sits high and looks low saw her in a filthy mine shaft and used a broken drunk to save her. By giving up his own life first? Wasn't that right? She *had* to keep on living, not for herself and not for her daddy. But for him?

Then she could live with someone else, someone strong and capable and passionate. Like Jack?

Striding now over the rise.

And Eddie? Following right behind him, wearing his father's coat again, holding the child Dominga by the hand.

All of them yelling her name.

They wanted her to know, to understand, to accept: *You ain't got time to die.* Unless she gave up.

But Jack was insisting, his eyes demanding it. *Don't you give up. Not now.* So he was running toward her, racing for her, reaching across the barren landscape for her, while Elizabeth Castle sneered and Hunter Castle spat at her feet, ready to fire—and Sidney Castle aimed. But so did Annalee.

She whirled against Hunter's grip, half-breaking his hold, pushing Hunter into his father.

"Hey!" Hunter grasped at her, not expecting resistance. But Annalee pulled back, falling away from him, while he stumbled. *"Hey!"* he yelled louder, his foot caught in the blanket Dominga had left behind. He struggled to regain his balance, not expecting what happened next. In the confusion, a gun fired. A loud, hard pop.

Hunter Castle groaned once. Fell hard. Unmoving.

"Hunter!" Elizabeth Castle let out a sickening scream.

Sidney Castle gasped, glared at his wife, opened his hand, letting his gun fall to the ground.

His only son hit the frozen earth without a word, a thin

ribbon of his blood oozing onto frozen snow—so Hunter would've hated this. He was felled by a stumble, an errant shot from his own stolen military gun—not because his bullet hit a vital spot, but because it did the job.

Sidney Castle saw that too well. Elizabeth Castle knew it more.

Their errant boy was dead.

So Annalee could've turned away, could've stopped her heart from racing, her lungs from burning. She could've turned her eyes from the sight of dead Hunter, stopped hearing the twisted, killing words dead Hunter had said. *He's not your father. He never was.*

She could've started walking, feeling her legs move, walking across the hard, cold earth and falling into the strong arms of someone like Jack. And she could've stayed still while he held her. Assuring her that, no matter what she knew now, he hadn't changed, even if she had.

Instead, she turned back, looked at Sidney Castle, turned her face from Elizabeth, a mother without a son.

As she looked, she knew she could turn from this man and his wife—walking away while the husband bent over their disappointing son, calling his name over and over.

Instead, Annalee dropped to the cold ground, reached for Sidney Castle, held his heaving shoulders while he scooped his son's lifeless body into his arms—calling for him, sobbing his name. But Annalee couldn't help him see. Nobody was there to answer.

CHAPTER 29

"Elementary."

SH, *THE ADVENTURE OF
THE CROOKED MAN*

JACK DIDN'T ASK ANNALEE to talk. Not for a long while, not when the police cars came or when Elizabeth Castle was handcuffed or when a frantic Lent Montgomery scrambled from his car, screaming her name. Or when Elizabeth collapsed, looking back at her dead son. She then started railing at her husband, railing at Annalee, blaming everybody she could but herself, finally falling broken and sickened onto her knees.

Annalee turned from it all, moving away from the cars and people, letting Jack talk to Sidney Castle, while she aimed for a random path and started walking.

She wanted never to stop, not even to ask Jack to stay close. He stayed behind, protective, keeping others back until Annalee turned and looked over her shoulder, showing him her questions.

So he followed, catching up and matching her stride. He reached for her hand, holding it softly in his. Then after a while, he put his arm around her shoulder, pulling her close. She didn't pull away. She just kept walking beside him, following the cold path as it headed west—the massive mountains in the distance but always appearing so close.

"Would you go up there with me?" she finally asked. Her voice was resolved and clear.

Jack pulled her tighter. "To the hills?"

"To the old mine." She didn't say the name.

Jack stopped his stride, turned Annalee to him, pulled her into his arms, sheltering, letting her feel his warmth. "I'm sure you know my answer, Annalee. There's no other way to say it. I'd go to the ends of the earth for you."

"Even if you don't really know who I am? Or what I am?" Her voice broke, but she didn't cry.

He whispered in her ear, "I know exactly who *and* what you are." He stepped back, searching her eyes. "And you know too. You're Joe Spain's beautiful daughter. That's why you came back home—to finally discover *every* part of that truth."

"I just wish he'd told me himself."

"He was still searching for truth himself," Jack said. "Not just about you but about life, God, faith. Those things take a long time to figure out, and too many people never get there. They're trying too hard or looking in the wrong places." His eyes searched the horizon. "Or they're not believing."

"Believing in *what*, Jack?"

"Believing that God doesn't make mistakes."

"So now I have to forgive? Forgive my daddy, of course."

"But not just him." Jack held her tighter.

"You mean myself?"

Jack smiled. "So you can stop trying so hard."

She nodded, thinking about Mrs. Stallworth and their letting go of big things, to make room for small. "Then all the little pieces started falling into place. So then I could see Slater Prince snooping around Denver for years, catering to the rich and famous—and collecting all their dirty, ugly silence."

"Blackmailing them."

"And hiding the evidence in the *church*."

"But a pregnant daughter is hard to hide."

"Not to mention her baby," Annalee said. She looked up at Jack. "How did you find out?"

"The daughter wrote me from Atlanta. She goes to school down there, but she had to tell *somebody*. So she put it all in a letter—how she let her daddy take her baby, promising to find a family for it, but his story never seemed right. Besides, she suspected what really happened all along, knew it in her soul. Poor girl is racked by guilt."

Annalee understood. She took a bend in the path, kept walking, Jack with her, for a long, cold mile. At a high point near a half-frozen stream, they walked to a huge cottonwood tree not far from the path. Together, they leaned back on it, looking up through bare branches at the sky's flat light.

After a while, Jack reached over and pulled Annalee into his arms, comforting, waiting. He let her cry. It felt like a gift, so she opened it.

"My mother," she finally said. "What about *her*?"

He held her tighter. "Hush. Don't, Annalee. It's all over."

"But did she *care*? Or just toss me in the dirt and leave me behind? And who *is* she?"

He held her hands. "You're freezing."

"I want to know, Jack."

"The whole truth?"

"Not some little fairy tale or some lie. Just what happened."

Jack pressed her hands together, sheltering them in his own. For a long time he stayed quiet. But he wanted her to know what she'd asked.

"Truth doesn't stay hidden. Neither do secrets. One day, to a praying heart, they disclose themselves."

"How?"

"God finally answers."

Annalee gave a long statement to the police, telling it all. The train. The bloody mattress. Sidney Castle's involvements. Elizabeth Castle's murders. Everything in between.

Then Annalee showed them the baby's grave. She knelt there a long time, arranging the bright flowers, trying to make it right. She'd do the same soon at her father's grave. *Soon,* she told herself. *I'll go there soon.*

But for now, before she left the ranch, she took Eddie aside, told him about his father.

"I guess I already knew," Eddie said, looking up at her.

"I think we both did."

"When he didn't come home to get us, I knew. Then Mother died. I guess I just wanted it to be different." His gray eyes looked older but settled.

"So did I, Eddie," she said, letting him hold on to her, thinking about everything. "So did I."

She stood then for a long time talking to Sidney Castle, watched him get in his car by himself, seeing him leave Elizabeth Castle to the life she'd chosen but not waiting until they took her away.

This wasn't a matter for Annalee. Not on this day. So Jack organized their drive back to town, dropping off the little girl. Her mother, Rosita, was waiting at the gate. She gave Annalee a pan of home-cooked food, then stood by the gate with her daughter, watching them drive away.

On the way back to the city, Eddie fell asleep, his head on Annalee's lap. But soon her eyes got heavy too. So she slept, letting Jack steer the big car into town, surprised when he jiggled her elbow. *We're back,* she thought, not eager to see the ruined church and the burned-out parsonage.

But she opened her eyes.

"Jack, *look.*"

They were in the mountains. Not the town of Annalee. Just in some ghost town. Mine tailings all over the place. A couple of shacks still standing, but even more shacks fallen down on themselves in the snow.

"Where are we?" She tried to get her bearings. The ground was white, but so was the sky. Trees cut the landscape in tall clumps.

"Just beyond Central," Jack said. "The road ran out." So Jack idled the Buick. They got out of the car. Eddie, too, waking up fast.

They walked around a bit, but the snow was deep, the wind brisk and raw.

"Not much here," Eddie said, clomping around in the drifts, his coat dragging.

"Kind of bleak," Jack added, nodding. "Rugged, too."

"Is this where you were born, Professor?" Eddie asked.

Annalee heard the question, looked at Eddie, shook her head. "Actually, no. It's not." She squinted at the sky, gave them a shivering smile. "And it's cold." She turned toward the car. "Let's go home."

CHAPTER 30

"Give it time. It will clear."

SH, *THE ADVENTURE OF THE GREEK INTERPRETER*

BACK IN DENVER, dusk falling, Mrs. Stallworth met them on the sidewalk in front of the rooming house, gathered up Annalee and Eddie, offered up hot food, steaming baths, clean beds, time alone for quiet. Time, indeed, just to be.

Eddie went back to the boys' home the next day.

Then for three days, Annalee stayed to herself, declining even to see Jack for now—though he came by every day. "Can I retreat?" she asked Mrs. Stallworth. "Unless you need something from me."

"Not a peep," Mrs. Stallworth said. "Take all the time."

But by week's end, Annalee pointed herself down Welton Street, dressed for the sunny cold—Joe Spain's Stetson on her head—heading toward her father's cabin, despite Mrs. Stallworth's complaints.

"You're a marked woman now," she told Annalee. "The newspapers printed you up. Said you solved the crime. Described your dad's old cabin. Even gave the location."

"Yesterday's news, Mrs. Stallworth," Annalee said. "Already forgotten. Like a vapor." She waved a hand.

Mrs. Stallworth gave her a look. "You writing another one of your papers? For that company that hardly half pays you?"

"Yep, I'm writing a paper. Started it last night. Not even worried if it gets published. But right now I'm going to clean a cabin."

"By yourself? Go fetch Reverend Blake. He'll help you." Mrs. Stallworth eyed Annalee over her glasses. She was stirring cake batter, helping the rooming house lady, a dismal cook, to make the meals—and getting a pay envelope at the end of every other day.

"He's likely busy," Annalee said. She reached for her coat, a slim one that actually fit her—lent to her by the rooming house lady, who, with one look at her wearing it, declared, "It's yours, sugar! Fits you like a glove."

She buttoned the coat tight. "Don't bother him today. I'm cleaning out Daddy's place—so I'll have somewhere to live."

"In that old wreck? What about getting a job?" Mrs. Stallworth pressed her mouth, showing her regret for saying it. But "the Colored Professor" without a job? Mrs. Stallworth's face said she couldn't bear thinking about it.

"I could worry over that, too." Annalee cocked her hat. "But to tell you the truth, I'm aiming for what you have—a proper life. Simple, forthright, uncomplicated." She smiled. "Even

Eddie has that. He's the hero now at the boys' home. *Crime solver!*"

Mrs. Stallworth sighed. "If I never hear another word about crime, it won't be too soon."

Annalee gave her a hug, turned toward the door. "Not one word. Not from me. Never again. But now I'm heading to Daddy's place." *To make sense of everything that's there,* she thought. But she couldn't say that out loud or tell Mrs. Stallworth her biggest question:

Who was my mother? Or her tougher question: *Why do I care?*

Instead, after ironing a freshly laundered dress and washing her hair the night before, she'd piled her curls under the Stetson and tied on a kerchief, smoothed on her warm secondhand coat, tightened a leather belt around her waist, and took off walking. In flat, sensible, unfrivolous shoes.

In her arms, she carried a sack of cleaning things, all borrowed from the generous rooming house lady.

Arriving at the little cabin, she pulled off the hat and coat, hung them on a nail, and got to work.

For hours she swept, dusted, pulled down cobwebs with rags, scraped dirt off shelves and floorboards, hauled out trash, washed the one tiny window, letting in light.

The freshly laundered dress was now stained with dust and dirt, her kerchief crumpled on the floor. Her wild curls aimed ten different directions, she thought, glancing at herself with a smile in a cracked mirror hanging on a wall.

So, of course, in time, he came—finding her looking her absolute worst, as she wanted to say, like the first time he'd seen her that night she and Eddie had jumped out of a moving train.

But as with that night, Jack didn't seem put off by how she looked. In fact, entering the cabin, Jack quickly took his measure of her, seeming to approve with a tilt of his head, but didn't say a word.

Instead, he looked at her pile of cleaning rags, grabbed one, rolled up his sleeves, and started attacking grime—not with a vengeance but with curious calm.

So she didn't stop him.

Grabbing her broom, she returned to her final sweeping. Digging into corners. Attacking walls, even attacking the ceiling. *Not one inch in this place,* she told herself, *shall go untouched. This wreck of a cabin gets a fresh . . .*

Hammering?

Jack had conjured up a toolbox. A hammer and nails, too. Now, with nails in teeth, he was pounding rickety shelves back onto walls, the cabin door onto its frame, the leaning windowsill stable and straight. Then crawling under a makeshift bed frame, ignoring his knee, he renailed all four posts.

Annalee stopped now to watch him. He'd somehow managed to find a crisp clean shirt and pants, despite getting burned out of house and home. He'd even had a haircut, his dark hair groomed and fresh. *Does he ever* not *look handsome and wonderful?* Annalee wondered.

But Jack had headed back outside to his car. He came back carrying a cardboard box filled with waxes, putty, two cans of paint. *Paint?*

"Jack." Annalee finally spoke his name.

He didn't turn. Instead, he'd pulled on gloves, grabbed a putty knife, started filling cracks in the cabin's splintering pine walls. His back still turned, he finally spoke to her.

"If you're going to live in this place by yourself," he said, "which I understand you intend to do—" he paused to refill his putty knife, started swiping another crack in a pine board—"if that's your plan, which it is, right?"

She didn't answer, just kept watching him—not sure how he was making her feel right now, but still listening. After all, what else could she do? She stood silently, waiting for him to tell her.

Jack kept working. "If you're going to live here by yourself," he said again, "I'm going to do everything in my power to make this place as tight as a drum. No leaks, drafts, cracks, critters—"

"Thank you," Annalee said, interrupting.

He didn't reply. His back was still turned.

"Thank you," she said again. Still he didn't respond. But she needed him to *stop puttying* or whatever he was doing.

"Jack."

He turned, looked evenly at her, his breathing steady.

"Thank you," Annalee said, "for this." She gestured at the cabin. "You don't have time for this . . . for me. You've got an entire church to rebuild—"

"I've got nothing but time." He refilled his knife, held her gaze. "For you." He puttied another swipe.

She held her grin. "But what about—?"

"Mount Moriah will be just fine. We've got our committees, a building plan, new trustees, volunteers, 'official' helpers." He chuckled. "I'm having to turn away folks. You know how it works. We'll come back stronger."

"And the Klan?"

"We'll never know." He shrugged. "And I'm not worried. Not worrying our church members either. Nobody's been charged with arson or anything. Meantime, a pastor across town invited us to worship at his church while we rebuild."

"Good people." She started sweeping again but stopped. "Eddie! How's he doing? I miss him."

"You'll see him on Sunday. Mrs. Stallworth's frying up a chicken. Eddie said, 'Make it two!'"

She smiled at that.

Jack watched her then, put down his knife, pulled out a chair he'd repaired earlier, took a long, deep breath. Gestured for her to sit down.

Sighing, she shook her head.

"Please, Annalee."

She nodded and sat.

He pulled up the other chair, sat facing her. "You deserve some answers from me. A lot of them."

"You don't owe me anything, Jack."

"Can I just clear the air? The young woman who came to church that Sunday—"

She cut him off. "Not now. You don't have to tell me."

"She's—"

"I don't need to know now. She has a story, I'm sure, but I don't need to know it. Not today." She gave herself a crisp nod.

"But what if . . . ?" He breathed deep. "What if there was somebody who did matter to me?"

"Okay." She felt her stomach tighten. "But you don't have to tell me." Still, she asked, "Is she in New York?"

"No, in France. During the war."

"A Frenchwoman?"

"No. But they were real grateful. That would've been easy." He smiled, reaching for Annalee's hands. She didn't pull away.

"Her name was Katherine."

Annalee sighed but sat still, making her heart open and listen.

"That's such a perfectly lovely name. So beautiful." She repeated it in her mind. *Katherine.*

"She was a volunteer with the YWCA. The US Army wouldn't accept colored women in overseas war jobs. So some went to France with the American Red Cross or the Y." Jack searched Annalee's face. "Can I go on?"

She nodded.

"I met her at a dance."

"That's so lovely," Annalee said but immediately thought, *That's so romantic.* She imagined Jack in his dress uniform, if he'd had one, cleaned up in the way he loved to be, looking remarkable and shaved and smelling his wonderful aftershave way and meeting a pretty girl at a dance.

"Are you a good dancer?"

"I love to dance," he said, searching her eyes. "I'm going to take you dancing as soon as I can—if you'll go with me."

"I'd love to go!"

"At the Rossonian—"

"The nightclub?" She gave him a look. "The hotel night-club?"

"They get the best acts. They play in the lounge till all hours."

"Lord, have mercy."

"It's not what you think. I wear my collar. Carry a little Bible. Soon as I walk in the door, folks start coming around. 'Pastor, you got a minute?' I go for the music, but every time, I end up having church."

She looked at him, hearing, not judging, but feeling her

stomach do its flips, as it did whenever she was with him. Still, she had a question:

"Are you teasing me?"

"Not about this. It's the Lord's work, Annalee. I've sent husbands home to their wives, wives home to their husbands, wayward girls back to the church."

"And wayward boys?"

"I take them to the King."

"Mercy, I feel a paper coming on."

"'The Theology of Nightclub Ministry.' I want you to write it."

"My dean would throw himself out a window."

"You don't work for him anymore. Although I hear he wants you back."

"Have you been reading my mail?"

"No, but if he calls, tell him half the folks volunteering to rebuild the church are people I met in the club."

"But what in the world would I wear?"

"Your red dress!" He laughed. "I'm teasing you now."

"That dress has history."

"Whatever you wear, just let me take you to . . . everywhere, Annalee. To the theater, the movie show, bicycle riding, wherever. Would you like that?"

"In fact—" she tilted her head—"I'd love to learn to ride a bike." She laughed to herself. *Did I just say that?*

"Then, afterward, I'll take you out to eat—at a French restaurant."

"French?" She laughed again. "In Denver?"

"No, in France!" His eyes brightened. "Their food! I'm

taking you there. That's a promise—to a French café. *C'est magnifique!*"

She smiled at him. *"C'est magnifique!"*

"Hey, you're good with languages?"

"Just a little. Greek, Hebrew—"

"Show-off."

He sat back but held her gaze. Then he pulled her chair closer, moved a wild curl from her forehead. He opened his mouth, searching her eyes. "May I kiss you again?"

"Never in life! Not unless you wear a Danger sign."

He chuckled. "Then may I have this dance?"

"Do I know you, soldier?" she teased back.

"I'm doing all I can so that you will."

She smiled, waiting.

"Katherine," she said.

He nodded.

"Tell me, Jack."

"We met in Paris. At a little club. Having a great time. Nobody dying for once. A bunch of us—Negro soldiers and the girls from home. Dancing, having fun. So I asked her out. 'Let's grab something to eat sometime.'"

Annalee listened, hearing, knowing?

"It wasn't serious or anything."

"Maybe not."

"We went out just once, had a nice time. I took her back to her place. 'Thanks a lot. See you around.' I went back to my unit." He paused. "And that was the last time I saw her. The next day she was dead."

"Katherine?"

"Killed in a bombing raid near a battle hospital." He

blinked. "Dead. Just like that. Nice young girl, in her early twenties. I was a couple of years older. My unit had seen action, so I already knew death. *God in heaven*, so much killing over there. Our division saw death like it was nothing." He took a breath. "War death. It's butchery. A curse. No mercy in it whatsoever."

He went on. "I didn't love Katherine. I didn't know her—not really. But she taught me war's hardest lesson: Life *is* short. So do whatever it takes to survive your blasted combat and get back home."

"Mercy, your Katherine. *Lord, have mercy.* I'm so sorry."

"So when I met you—and you caught me off guard so fast—from that first night, and I wasn't looking for anyone because I was afraid to risk it. Still, I realized right then that I don't ever want to lose you, especially like that."

"Because of Katherine?"

"Because of *you*, Annalee."

"With all the ridiculous arguing we've done?"

"I know we got off to a crazy start. I did everything wrong. First, I moved too fast—"

"You led me on."

"That was my heart!"

She rolled her eyes at him.

"I mean it. I could barely keep up."

"With your *heart*? Now, that's a first."

"Well, so were you. From the second you climbed into the car, everything changed. I wanted *right then* for you to be safe. I don't know what I was thinking, asking you to come to Denver to help *solve a crime*. But here you were—bright eyes sparkling, hair flying, jumping off a moving train." He hiked a brow. "Wearing that red dress."

She laughed. "Don't expect to ever see that dress again."

"Doesn't matter, as long as I can see you. You're everything I was looking for and I didn't even know it."

"And now you don't know what to do with me."

He gave her a look. "Oh, I know what to do with you. Believe me, I know."

She felt herself blush. Still she smiled, needing to hear every word he was saying—and accept it. First, for herself. "But what happens next? What *are* you saying?"

"I'm saying that after the church is rebuilt, and my house and all—when it's ready for me—I pray to God you're ready for me, too."

She sat back in her chair, not sure how to react. "But what if I don't know yet? I'm so new at this." She gestured to both of them. "Besides, I'm just . . . Joe Spain's daughter."

"Oh, that's all? Joe Spain gets my thanks for the rest of my life for what he did for you."

She looked away, not ready to hear again of her awful beginnings. But Jack wouldn't let up.

"I know your daddy drank too much. He stole corn and hogs or a couple of scrawny chickens from time to time to put food on this table—*for you*—and to make ends meet. Even took a turn with Prince. You think I don't know what happens in life? Your daddy and some of his old buddies up in the mountains—working the mines, pulling fast ones on suckers and greenhorns. Stealing folks' gold, selling fake. Then one day, stomping around in the mud, he found you."

Annalee grabbed her broom and stood. She tried attacking

the floor, but Jack wouldn't let up. "Annalee, if a preacher knows anything, he knows that sometimes people fall down. All God asks is that we make the effort to get back up."

"You're preaching again."

"That's because we can't pin people to the ground for the worst thing they ever did. Or maybe it was the best thing they ever did, but it doesn't feel like it."

Annalee sat down again. The cabin had grown half-dark, the late-afternoon sky turning gray.

"But throwing a little baby away in the mud. My *mother* did that. Or my father? Whoever the devil he is."

"You're not an orphan," Jack said. "You know the Bible better than that. You're not motherless or fatherless."

"I know that in my head. But my heart keeps calling me here, telling me to rip away all this trash—and find underneath it my treasure."

"What, gold? Silver? Ore?"

"No, my mother's name. On a document, in a letter, on a ticket stub. On *something*."

"A clue."

"A clue." She nodded. "Is that too much for a rookie crime fighter to ask?"

Jack reached for her, to assure her. But he suddenly stopped. A rustling at the door.

He stood, moving to listen.

Annalee slipped across the floor to face him, squinting at the sound. Someone nearby?

He leaned not to the door but closer to her. He brushed a smudge of dust off her temple, pulled her closer, then closer even more to him, then whispered, "Will you—?"

But Annalee put a finger to his lips, quieting both of them.

He sighed then, grabbing at her hand, feeling her finger on his mouth, pressing it against his lips. Then before she could move away, he kissed the tip of her finger. Then the bend of her finger. Then the dip of her palm, pressing her hand to his mouth. "Oh . . . Annalee—"

She let his mouth linger. Jack bent closer then, moved a wild curl behind her ear, leaning as if to whisper again. Annalee pulled back her hand. Jack didn't fight her, but his sigh was endless.

He searched her eyes. "Can I kiss you again?"

"Maybe."

"Soon?"

"Probably?"

But now she peered through a sliver of space in the splintered door, already feeling she knew who was on the other side. It was someone like her, praying for what she'd prayed every day of her natural-born life. *Take me to the water, Jesus. To find what?*

All I should see.

Walking away from the cabin, in fact, was someone she wasn't surprised to discover.

"It's Olivia Franklin," she whispered to Jack. "Hunter Castle's friend."

Jack let out a low whistle. "You're in demand."

"What are you saying?"

"Rosita Montez came by earlier, looking for you. The past few days, other folks have come knocking, too. Mrs. Stallworth didn't bother you, but she has the names."

"But *why?*"

"People need help, Annalee. With their confusions and problems and mysteries. They saw the write-up about you in the newspapers, 'Praying Detective Solves Crimes,' and they want your help solving theirs."

"*Praying Detective.* That's what they wrote?"

"They showed you praying at the baby's grave."

She grew quiet. "Did they write where my daddy also found me?"

He drew her gently to him. "That doesn't matter now."

"Jack, did they write that?"

"Yes." He nodded. "They wrote that. Sidney Castle told them. He said you're a survivor. A *real* hero. That's why people want to talk to you. They know you won't judge them, that you'll help them."

"Go to the *real* police!"

He laughed, shaking his head, telling her *no.*

"Then go to God!"

"That's what they did. God sent them to you."

"Impossible. I can barely figure out my own life. Besides, after working on Daddy's murder, if I tell the truth, *I'm* downright scared. Take on another *one?*"

"You should be scared. It's like the war. If you're not scared, you're just marking time, waiting for your number. You better open your eyes and pay attention."

"Sounds like a sermon," she said, looking up at him.

"Not a long one," he said. "Just this: when you help folks solve their problems, don't be surprised if you solve your own."

"*Preach, Pastor.*"

———◇———

They cleaned a while longer, Annalee listening to Jack reflecting on life and its dangers. "I don't want you worrying, but there's the Invisible Empire," he said. "And the police. The chief's a member."

"I'm already praying for him. For all of them."

"But also—this blasted cabin. You need indoor plumbing, Annalee. And electricity. You can't live here in the dark, solving people's problems and crimes, with just a kerosene lamp."

"I'll find somebody in the morning," she said.

"No, I will. Plumber, electrician." He shrugged. "And you need a car."

"Which I can't drive. Not really."

"You can use mine. I'll teach you." He grinned. "The right way this time."

"Or I can ride."

"Ride what?"

"A horse."

"*What?*"

"A horse. This is Colorado. I can ride a horse. I can shoot a rifle, too. Actually, pretty good, not that I'd ever want to try again. I guess I never told you."

He gave her a look.

"Daddy taught me," she said, looking away. Her voice caught. "Because I was his girl." She searched Jack's eyes, looking for confirmation, her voice a whisper. "Wasn't I, Jack?"

Jack reached for her. "Don't you ever doubt it."

———◇———

Annalee packed up the cleaning supplies, admiring the results of their labor. On the inside, the cabin actually shone. Outside would come next, then the little yard and other touches. They locked the place up. Jack's toolbox had produced a padlock and two keys. Annalee gave Jack the extra one.

As they secured the door, Annalee found a tiny brown envelope stuck in the wood frame, note inside, Annalee's name written on the front, the handwriting plain but solid. She fingered the envelope, placed it in her sleeve.

"Olivia Franklin must've left this."

"Or it might be a love letter." He pulled her to him, teasing.

"Think so?" She snuggled closer. "Either way, I'm getting excited." Annalee's eyes sparkled.

"That's the spirit." He grinned. "But *a horse*?"

She gave him a look, clicked her tongue. "Just watch me ride."

A NOTE FROM
THE AUTHOR

THANK YOU SO MUCH for reading Annalee Spain's first mystery. I grew up in Colorado, so I'm sharing some historical notes that grounded her fictional story.

Denver's Rossonian Hotel, a Five Points landmark, is listed on the National Register of Historic Places. At the time of this novel, it was known by its original name, the Baxter Hotel. I used the Rossonian name to honor what the hotel became—"one of the most important jazz clubs between St. Louis and Los Angeles," according to the Denver Public Library's Western History Collection.

Jazz greats such as Louis Armstrong and Duke Ellington stayed there because they were refused lodging by downtown Denver hotels, even after performing there. At the Rossonian, however, Black musicians were welcomed, often staying up "till all hours" playing in the Rossonian lounge.

The Ku Klux Klan's 1920s revival, meantime, was legendary in Colorado, where membership was the second largest per capita in the United States (after Indiana)—claiming between

55,000 and 75,000 members, including women. The Grand Dragon of Colorado's Klan was not Eddie Brown Sr. (my fictional name), but a homeopathic physician named Dr. John Galen Locke, who engineered a hate campaign against Jews, Blacks, Catholics, and immigrants, declaring that only native-born, English-speaking, white Protestants were 100 percent American. Cross burnings, bombings, threats, and economic boycotts of "non-Klan" businesses drove home this philosophy. Sowing such seeds of discord pitted "neighbor against neighbor, friend against friend," as one dismayed opponent described it.

Locke's "hood and the cross" comprised a powerful voting bloc that came to include Colorado's governor, the entire lower chamber of the Colorado state legislature and almost half of the upper, Denver's mayor and police chief, as well as judges, sheriffs, police departments, jury commissioners, and other elected officials across the state.

Locke's influence began to wane when he was charged in the kidnapping of a white nineteen-year-old high school student, forcing the boy to marry a younger girl whose honor, Locke claimed, the male student had offended. Many white Coloradans already were actively opposing Klan discord, including Sidney Whipple, managing editor of the *Denver Express*, and Denver's district attorney, Philip Van Cise, whose campaign against Colorado's Klan made him their political target. (In my novel, the character Sidney Castle, described as a former DA, isn't meant to represent Van Cise. But some of Van Cise's well-known traits of fairness and integrity are seen in Castle's better actions, including his kindness to Annalee Spain and Eddie Brown Jr.)

Colorado's Black community, meanwhile, was resolute in

fighting Klan hostility through its network of business owners, church leaders, educators, medical professionals, and Negro women's clubs. Earlier during World War I, some 350,000 African American men had joined the US Army to fight for democracy but were assigned to menial tasks, labeled unqualified for combat. The French, however, had fought with Senegalese sharpshooters in other wars and welcomed American Blacks into their ranks, including the famed 369th Infantry Regiment from New York City—known as the Harlem Hellfighters—whom the French awarded their Croix de Guerre for their gallantry on the front line.

Sadly, after the war, Black soldiers returned home to the sting of mounting discrimination. Lynching of Black citizens increased from fifty-eight in 1918 to seventy-seven in 1919. At least ten of those victims were war veterans, and according to the Army Historical Foundation, some were lynched while in uniform.

Black women, meantime, were barred by the US Army from serving overseas in World War I. Yet thousands volunteered to serve in Europe in various relief organizations, including the American Red Cross and the war council of the YMCA, but were restricted to segregated units.

Amid this hostility, my character Annalee Spain found respite in stories of Sherlock Holmes, the iconic fictional detective created by Sir Arthur Conan Doyle. All of the Holmes epigraphs featured in *All That Is Secret* are from stories first published in *The Strand*, a popular British periodical, including the first Holmes story, "A Scandal in Bohemia."

Annalee doesn't solve crimes like Holmes, famous for creative solutions using deductive reasoning. She affirms his belief, however, that a woman's instincts are valuable crime-fighting skills. So I enjoyed letting Annalee deploy her instincts to unravel the mystery in this novel. How will she grow as a detective? Her next mystery, coming soon, offers intriguing answers.

ACKNOWLEDGMENTS

MANY PEOPLE, ALL PHENOMENAL, supported me in the publication of *All That Is Secret*. They include my invaluable agent, Greg Johnson of WordServe Literary; Rachelle Gardner (another Colorado-based agent and the first champion of Annalee's story); and encouraging author heroes Rhys Bowen, Julie Cantrell, Jerry Jenkins, Manuel Ramos, Dr. Brenda Salter McNeil, and Sophfronia Scott. My warmest thanks also to my supportive publishing team at Tyndale: Karen Watson (my fearless publisher), Stephanie Broene (my visionary acquisitions editor), Sarah Rische (my eagle-eyed line editor), Lindsey Bergsma (talented designer of the gorgeous book cover for *All That Is Secret*), Andrea Martin (author representative), Isabella Graunke (amazing publicist), and the enthusiastic sales and marketing teams, including Kody Alexander and Rebecca Wirth, for their early and great support.

Kind thanks also to these friends and supporters: author friend Jennifer Grant, fiction coach and author Ginny Yttrup, author friend Susy Flory, Tyndale publisher Jan Long Harris, author Mary Taylor Young, Brian Allain (tireless author advocate), Beth Justino (author and marketing visionary), Dr. David Buschart (professor of theology and historical studies at Denver Seminary), Stephen L. Harris (author of *Harlem's Hell Fighters: The African-American 369th Infantry in World War I*), JC Bravo (of the 369th), author Francelia Belton of Sisters in Crime-Colorado, author Kellye Garrett of Crime Writers of Color, author Robert Justice (podcast master of Crime Writers of Color), the INK Creative Collective, the writing teams at DaySpring's *(in)courage* blog and *Our Daily Bread*, and the remarkable community of independent bookstores, bookstagrammers, and booktubers who root for authors.

Special mention also to Denver Public Library's Western History Digital Collection, the Colorado Historical Newspapers collection, and Rocky Mountain PBS's award-winning series *Colorado Experience*—each a priceless resource.

Finally, of course, my warmest and special thanks for supportive family who cheered me on in the writing, rewriting, editing, and praying over *All That Is Secret*. I love you all so much: my husband, Dan Raybon; sister Dr. Lauretta Lyle; sister-in-law Diana Rochon; faithful friends Nancy Charbonneau and Ruth Shepard; daughters, Alana Raybon and Joi Afzal; son-in-law Paul Galloway; grandchildren, Anthony, Nia, Laila, Noah, and Serene; brothers-in-law Dr. Richard Lyle and Sylvester "Mac" Rochon; and countless other readers and friends. You're simply the best.

For each of you, and for the joy Annalee's story is giving me, I thank my God.

DISCUSSION QUESTIONS

1. Annalee starts her story uncertain about both herself and her relationship to God. How might those two interwoven challenges impact a young Black woman of her time? Do those two challenges in any way impact you in this season of life?

2. Both Annalee and Eddie have to deal with the legacy of imperfect fathers. How are their experiences similar? How do they differ?

3. Mrs. Stallworth advises, "When it comes to unraveling life's big mysteries, you don't aim at the big parts of the problem. You work on the *small*. . . . You don't grab a hammer and beat down the door. You work on the hinges." Do you think she's right? How does Annalee "work on the hinges" as she solves the mystery of her father's murder?

4. Annalee develops a tense but close friendship with the Castles' maid, Bernita Jamison. What was your initial reaction to Bernita's character? How did your feelings

about Bernita change or deepen during the course of the story?

5. In the midst of searching for her father's murderer, Annalee finds herself falling for the young pastor Jack Blake. Is it unwise for her to attempt both things at the same time—pursuing a murderer and a man? In what ways does Jack affirm her? In what ways does he confuse her? In future stories, what do you expect or hope for their relationship?

6. What does Annalee's knowledge of Sherlock Holmes teach her about what it takes to conduct a crime investigation? Where do her instincts help her along the way? Do they ever steer her down the wrong path?

7. What theories did you develop throughout the story about Joe Spain's murder? Who seemed most fearful of secrets being exposed? What twists did you see coming? Which surprised you?

8. As he and Annalee talk about the Klan, Jack says, "They're afraid of being afraid. Losing control of a world they never controlled in the first place." Do you agree with his assessment? How do you see the same fears playing out in the world today?

9. Annalee begins to wonder if what she has really longed for is to be loved and treasured. What does she learn about self-worth, about giving proper value to herself, through the events of the story? What does she learn about her worth to others? To God?

10. Annalee thinks about the difficulty of explaining the "color line" to her students: *"Mercy, Jesus*, the lynching, burning, jailing, raping, degrading sickness of it—by people wearing his cross." What do you think she means by her answer: *"I feel sad for God"*? When asked to explain racial prejudice to a young person, what do you say?

11. Eddie believes his father is the Denver Klan leader and hates him for it, yet in a moment of strong feelings, he almost hurls the same ugliness at Annalee. Why do you think that is? Have you ever been shocked by what came out of your mind, heart, or mouth in a moment of anger? How did you deal with what you learned about yourself?

12. Annalee solves her father's murder but uncovers new secrets in the process and finds herself suddenly visible in a way she wasn't before. What do you think is next for her? In what ways does she inspire you?

ABOUT THE AUTHOR

PATRICIA RAYBON is an award-winning author and essayist whose published books include *My First White Friend*, a Christopher Award–winning memoir about racial forgiveness, and *I Told the Mountain to Move*, a prayer memoir that was a *Christianity Today* Book of the Year finalist. Patricia's other books include *The One Year God's Great Blessings Devotional* and *Undivided: A Muslim Daughter, Her Christian Mother, Their Path to Peace*, coauthored with her younger daughter, Alana Raybon.

Patricia's essays on faith, race, and grace have been published in the *New York Times, Newsweek, USA Today, USA Weekend, Country Living, Chicago Tribune, Denver Post, Guideposts, Our Daily Bread, In Touch* magazine (In Touch Ministries), *Christianity Today, HomeLife* magazine; posted on popular blogs including the *Washington Post's Acts of Faith* and DaySpring's *(in)courage*; and aired on National Public Radio.

A journalist by training, Patricia earned a BA in journalism from the Ohio State University, an MA in journalism from the University of Colorado Boulder, and formerly was editor of the

Denver Post's Sunday Contemporary Magazine and a feature writer at the *Rocky Mountain News*, Colorado's oldest newspaper, which published for 150 years. Midcareer, she joined the journalism faculty at the University of Colorado Boulder, teaching print journalism for fifteen years. She now writes full-time on matters of faith, also teaching at writing conferences and workshops nationwide.

Patricia lives with her husband, Dan, a retired educator, in her beloved home state of Colorado, where they enjoy movies, popcorn, soapy costume dramas, and Masterpiece mysteries.

They have two amazing daughters, an attentive and smart son-in-law, and five glorious grandchildren. *All That Is Secret* is her first novel. Visit her online at patriciaraybon.com.

Connect with Patricia online at
PATRICIARAYBON.COM

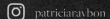

TYNDALE HOUSE PUBLISHERS
IS CRAZY4FICTION!

Fiction that entertains and inspires

Get to know us! Become a member of the Crazy4Fiction
community. Whether you read our blog, like us on
Facebook, follow us on Twitter, or receive our e-newsletter,
you're sure to get the latest news on the best in Christian
fiction. You might even win something along the way!

JOIN IN THE FUN TODAY.

 crazy4fiction.com

 Crazy4Fiction

 crazy4fiction

 @Crazy4Fiction

CP0021

By purchasing this book from Tyndale, you have
helped us meet the spiritual and physical needs of
people all around the world.

Tyndale | Trusted. For Life.